DUE DILIGENCE

THE TAKEOVER SERIES BOOK THREE

ANNA ZABO

To Lynne, Pam, Dave, Ray, Shawn, Tracy, and Renee.

CONTENT NOTES

This novel contains descriptive on-page kinky consensual sex, including use of toys, light D/s, bondage, sex where they could be caught, and roll playing.

Characters consume alcohol socially, including at bars.

There are instances where Fazil doesn't eat due to stress, and gets close to passing out.

Todd discusses mental trauma from some anonymous sexual encounters he had while cruising.

Class issues are mentioned.

There are on-page instances of homophobia and racism (Islamophobia and antisemitism), including the use of homophobic and Islamophobic slurs.

CHAPTER ONE

Fazil Kurt craned his neck to look out the window as the hired car drove along a highway from the hotel to the company Sam Anderson's team was trying to save. There was an actual mountain out there. Snowcapped and everything.

"That's Mount Rainier," his coworker Eli Ovadia said.

The peak sat out in the middle of nothing, imposing. Fazil rubbed his neck and turned to Eli. "It's huge—is it a volcano?"

"Yup." Eli shifted on the seat, toying with the handle of his cane. "They say it could go off any second."

Fazil snorted. Typical Eli, sounding too pleased at the thought of sudden catastrophe.

But the mountain was beautiful and awe-inspiring. The whole place was gorgeous. Hills and water and green and freaking mountains everywhere. God, wait until he told Kris. She would love this.

Then reality hit him like a wash of ice water. She wouldn't care. He wasn't dating Kris. Hadn't been for a month.

That was part of the reason he was here in Seattle on business with Eli—to get away from that mess. Sure, the split had been mutual, but he hadn't expected her to dive right into another relationship, least of all with his friend Lance. Had it been someone else, someone he hadn't known, that would have been easier. Watching them drape themselves all over each other at pinball league had been a bit much.

Hell, watching them drape all over each other at every single event their social circle held had been way too much, too soon. Sure, he and Kris had been going down the tubes for a while, but it still hurt to see.

So when his boss, Sam, had asked for a volunteer to travel to Seattle with Eli to do some due diligence at Singularity Storage, Fazil had jumped at the chance to get the hell out of Pittsburgh and away from old history, especially if S. R. Anderson Consulting was footing the bill to fly him across the country. Even if it meant spending today in a suit and two weeks stuck in the corporate hell he hated. He was, after all, a blessed *consultant*. Thank God. The work seemed interesting. Singularity was a start-up that had developed a new way of storing and accessing big data—twice as fast as its competitors.

Plus, he'd never been to the Pacific Northwest. Visiting a new place seemed like the best way to mark a change in his life to never dating another soul again.

He sighed and leaned back into the seat.

Eli lifted an inquisitive brow, but Fazil shook his head. Even if he'd liked Eli better than he did, he wasn't going to talk about his personal life with a coworker. Especially not a recently happily married one. Time to change the subject.

"Are you ready for this?"

Eli's smile was bright and devilish. "More than. But are

they ready for us?"

"Are they ever?" He'd yet to see a company truly understand what they were getting themselves into when they hired Sam Anderson's team. The fact that Eli, Anderson's CFO, was here spoke volumes. That Eli was downright gleeful meant Singularity was very screwed in the finance department.

Eli chuckled and the car pulled up to a typical boxy office building, one of the types that held several small companies. After getting their laptops from the car, they were escorted into the office by Dr. Sandra Jackson.

Sandra was one sharp woman, from her suit—which almost outdid Eli's for style—to her technical knowledge. Hired on recently to set the company back on track, she was the reason they were here. "The agenda is fairly open today. Sam said you both like to hit the ground running. We'll get you into an office, introduce you to the senior staff, and then to engineering, and after lunch, you can dig in."

"Perfect," Eli said.

After a whirlwind tour of the office, they settled into a large conference room that overlooked a parking lot. Not a spectacular view, but off in the distance were yet more mountains that put the ones near Pittsburgh to shame. Though he'd been introduced to them, Fazil forgot half the names of the upper management by the time they'd all entered the conference room.

Thank goodness for nameplates on cubes and offices. That and the list Sandra presented would save his ass, though he would only interact with the head of engineering —Stephen Davidson. It was the technical staff he'd work with and need to convince he wasn't here to get them fired, but to improve what they were doing.

Fazil made his way to a side table that held bagels,

pastries, and enough different forms of caffeine to power an entire IT department. He grabbed a cup of coffee for himself and one for Eli, who was in an intense but quiet discussion with Singularity's CFO.

Neither looked to be enjoying the talk. Fazil sat the coffee down near Eli, breaking up the awkward conversation.

"Thanks, Fazil." Eli took the cup, drank, and turned back to the other man. "You might not like it, but that's the law."

Singularity's CFO rose and towered over the sitting Eli. "You keep saying that, but I have yet to see proof." He glanced at his watch. "I have another meeting to attend to. We can discuss this more after lunch."

Eli smiled. "It will be my pleasure." Soft words, but they held the sharpness of a knife. The other CFO faltered for a moment, then walked away, and the expression on Eli's face shifted—not to a frown, but something more intense and calculated. He sipped his coffee.

That was why Eli had flown out here, to bring the financials into proper alignment, but the strains of an awkward silence descended around the table, and that wasn't good. Fazil cleared his throat. "The technical teams are first up, yes?"

Sandra glanced at the clock. "They'll be here in a few minutes." She rose and stepped over to the table of coffee and bagels, and that was all it took to break the tension.

Stephen slid a piece of paper across the table to him. "Here's a list of the engineers you'll be working with."

He picked it up and scanned the sheet until his brain rammed up against a single familiar name: Todd Douglas.

Todd. Broad, tall, blue-eyed. Memories of his old leather jacket and cologne and that beat-up junker he'd driven to high school all those years ago, the one they'd made out in a million times. He'd given his first blow job in Todd's car. Received his first, too.

He set the page down on the table because it was shaking too much in his hand. "Thanks." No way it could be the same guy. Todd hadn't gone to college. He'd planned to take over his old man's garage in Warminster, PA. *Seattle* and *computer engineer* didn't jive with the Todd Douglas he'd known all those years ago. A common enough name, but the memories set his skin on fire and for a moment he hoped it was his Todd.

"Here's the team now," Stephen said.

Men and women filed into the conference room, eyeing both him and Eli warily, except for the last man. He locked gazes with Fazil and stopped.

Holy shit. Same blue eyes, same dark hair, but the roundness of seventeen had given way to the angles, lines, and hardness of a man in his prime. Todd still looked like he belonged in a mechanic's shop, except for the decidedly geeky t-shirt that read *There's no place like 127.0.0.1* and clung to his chest in sinful ways. God, to run his hands down the length of *that* body.

Eli's chair squeaked as it rotated and Fazil peered at his laptop. The presentation he had to give in a few seconds might as well have been in a language he didn't read. *Shit. Get it together.*

Thankfully, Todd sat as far from Fazil as he could in the suddenly way-too-small conference room. Todd was an engineer? No way in hell. He'd barely passed math class until Fazil had tutored him. Then again, after that, he'd gotten straight As. He met Todd's stare a second time and he couldn't tell if Todd wanted to fuck him or kill him.

Guess some things never changed. He shivered.

"You're up." Eli spoke quietly and with a hint of concern.

Fazil stood and nodded. "I'm fine." He was. He had to be, despite Todd glaring at him from the back of the room. No other option.

Not like they could step outside and undo the past fifteen years.

"Good morning." He clicked the laptop into presentation mode and picked up the remote. "I'm Fazil Kurt. I know you think we're here to take your jobs, but we're not. We're here to save them."

And he was off and running as if his first lover hadn't walked back into his life.

MEETING CONCLUDED, FAZIL FOLLOWED ELI AND Sandra from the conference room. Next up was lunch, and if they hurried, he'd avoid having to speak to Todd. Too many years, too many unresolved conversations, and too much temptation packed into a body that wasn't at all seventeen anymore. Those arms. That jaw. He'd tripped over his words whenever his glance at the technical team had fallen on Todd.

He'd had to stop looking just to get through the damn talk. Luckily the presentation seemed to have gone over well. The Q and A had been intense but friendly, and the staff seemed to have good heads on their shoulders.

Todd had sat there, nodding sometimes, chewing on his lips at other points, but hadn't asked any questions. Fazil's heart thudded in his chest. Usually presentations didn't faze him. But he'd never tried giving one when he actually knew what someone sitting in the room looked like naked.

Or at least he had known. His brain was rapidly trying to fill in the blanks as to what Todd's naked body might look like now.

You could find out. Nope. Fazil exhaled. Not even going there. Their past was the past for a *reason.*

Sandra paused in the hall near an office that bore her name. "There's a nice pho restaurant nearby. Katiya from human resources will be joining us as well," Sandra said.

"Excellent." That from Eli.

"Fazil?" Todd had a deeper voice now, but utterly recognizable. It slid into Fazil's brain and down his body, tightening his heart and heating his blood exactly as it had in high school, back when he never said no to that temptation.

So you like boys, too? Good, 'cause I like you, Z.

As he had then, Fazil turned and there Todd was, hopeful, surprised, and far sexier than he had any right to be after all these years. "Hi, Todd. Long time."

"I'll say." He ran a hand through his hair. Same nervous tic. Fazil knew that look, too. No, Todd certainly didn't want to *kill* him.

Damn.

Fazil stuffed his hands into his pockets, partly to keep himself from reaching out and pulling Todd into the embrace he wanted, and partly to hide what that stare did to his dick.

"You two know each other?" A hint of surprise colored Eli's voice.

"We went to high school together." That was a much shorter explanation than *He was my best friend and lover and broke my heart so many times it's a wonder it still beats.*

"A long time ago," Todd said.

Not long enough. He'd thought he'd gotten over Todd,

that the years had removed the need to touch that skin and taste those lips. Maybe they had, but somewhere along the line, those same traitorous years had transformed Todd from a cute guy into a smoking-hot man, and Fazil wanted to know all those little details all over again. Right now. "Fifteen years."

He'd flown all this way to escape Kris and run headfirst into the biggest regret of his past.

Life was so unfair.

"Anyway." Todd fiddled with his watch, but never stopped looking at Fazil. A hint of scruff dusted his jaw. "You're probably busy today, but let's grab lunch sometime and catch up?"

Of course. Todd always had a plan for Fazil. Saying yes to it was such a bad idea, even if he did want to see what was under Todd's shirt and taste the skin there. "Sure."

"Great!" And there was the smile that always melted Fazil's heart and kick-started his lust. Same effect, too. "Send me mail when you know your schedule." Todd nodded to Eli and Sandra before vanishing down the hall.

"Sorry about that," Fazil said.

"Not a problem," Sandra said. "Always interesting to catch up with old friends." She gestured and they headed toward the entrance.

Fazil felt Eli's silence and a glance confirmed his perplexed expression. Well, at least he had that. Throwing Eli off his footing was *the* office pastime, even more so than Ping-Pong. He'd take victory anywhere he could find it.

Especially when what he wanted was Todd Douglas naked and in his bed—the hell with all the years and the anger and the fucking *guilt*. Fazil rubbed the bridge of his nose. *Shit*. This trip was going to be a lot harder than he'd thought.

CHAPTER TWO

Someone had turned the surreal dial up to eleven in Todd Douglas's life. That was the only explanation for Fazil Kurt standing in a conference room, in a suit, and giving that presentation. He couldn't even touch the guy to make sure he was real. Wanted to. Though he wasn't sure whether to hug Fazil and never let go or punch him in the head for nonchalantly walking back into his life after all those years.

Todd flexed his fingers against the counter of the unisex bathroom he'd ducked into. Actually he knew exactly what he wanted to do to Fazil, but that involved a bed, a lot less clothing, and a couple of uninterrupted hours. Jesus, that body. Last time he'd seen Z in a suit was at their high school graduation, and that had been *nothing* like this. Fazil had filled out from the gangly kid he'd been. Same slim hips that begged to be grabbed, now topped by a powerful torso and arms that seemed acquainted with the inside of a gym. The jet-black hair that had been long and wandered every which way back then had been tamed into a short cut that highlighted how dark his eyes were.

Beautiful. Even more so now. But given fifteen years of silence, he doubted Fazil had any desire to jump into Todd's bed. He'd made his point quite clear the autumn after they graduated.

Hey, I'll give you a call or drop you an e-mail once I'm settled on campus.

Days had passed. Then weeks. Then years.

He couldn't ignore Fazil, not when he was here from Sam Anderson's company. Nor could he pretend they didn't know each other. His only option had been to ask for lunch. Maybe they could clear the air enough to get through the next two weeks without too much awkwardness.

Todd scrubbed a hand over his face and stared at himself in the mirror. He'd needed to catch his breath and remind his dick that Fazil didn't want anything to do with him.

He wasn't ready to face his coworkers' questions yet. Too many had overheard his brief conversation with Fazil. They'd want to know what he knew about him. Which was absolutely *nothing*. Well, not anything he was willing to share.

This was going to be interesting. He straightened, washed his hands for the hell of it, and left the room. He almost made it back to his cube before someone stopped him, and in seconds, half of engineering was piled into the hall.

"You *know* that guy?"

He wasn't sure who asked. The voice had been male. Maybe Ganesh.

"Out with the intel, Douglas." That was Nathan, who pushed his way to the front of the crowd.

Todd held up both hands and backed into his cube. "I went to high school with him. I have no idea what he's like now." *Other than completely fuckable.* Pretty sure Nathan was the last person who wanted to hear that. "This is the first time I've seen him since we graduated."

"Oh come on." Erin leaned against the cube wall, arms crossed. "Give us something."

Todd flopped into his chair and peered at his coworkers. He was only a project lead, but he'd been Stephen's right hand man recently, documenting as many procedures as possible before the Anderson team arrived. Every person in the hall had worked with and for him at one point. He owed them *something.*

"He was smart and dedicated. Graduated fifth in the class." Todd ran a finger under his watchband. "He's the reason I went to college. Tutored me in math. I thought I was hopeless. Turned out I just needed some help."

So many of those nights had turned into make-out sessions on Fazil's bed, kissing and grinding and sucking until they'd both come.

"Good kid. Sarcastic around the edges, but we were teenagers. We lost track of each other after graduation." He shrugged to cover the pain in his chest. He'd *tried* to keep in touch with Fazil, but that effort had been one-sided.

"Where's he from?" Nathan again.

"Outside Philly, same as me." He'd seen Fazil before high school—they'd gone to the same middle school—but he'd been so far above Todd in everything, he'd never spoken to him.

"No, I mean where's he *from?*"

Todd stared at Nathan. "He's—I told you. We were born in the same hospital." All true, and he certainly wasn't about to give Nathan what he wanted. "That's all I know, honest."

There was some grumbling, but eventually they trickled

away. A few out to lunch and others to eat at their desks. His stomach was in too much turmoil for him to think about shoving anything into it, so he grabbed some water, brought up his tasks for the development sprint they were in, and tried to lose himself in code. Didn't work. He could trace a line of history from his current job back to the first time he'd kissed Fazil.

Todd rubbed his eyes. He didn't remember how *I can't believe I got an A on that test! I so could kiss you right now, man* had turned into kissing, then touching, then humping so hard they'd both come in their jeans.

But he could remember the taste of his lips and mouth, the blinding orgasm, and Fazil's whispered *holy shit* before he'd kissed Todd again. God. He wanted to know how Fazil kissed now, if he tasted the same, if he moaned like he used to.

There went any illusion he'd ever gotten over Fazil. It fucking hurt, too. There should have been a phone call. An e-mail. A damned Facebook or LinkedIn request. Something. Not... walking back into Todd's life as if he hadn't run away all those years ago.

None of the code on his screen made sense. "Fuck it." He grabbed his water bottle and headed for the exit. Maybe a walk and some fresh air would clear his head and he'd have a better reason for his pounding heart other than Fazil fucking Kurt.

THE WALK WORKED WELL ENOUGH. TODD SNAGGED A sandwich before arriving back at his desk and descended into the bliss of problem hunting and solving. An hour and a half later, a gentle rap on the cube frame and the low murmur of his name startled Todd away from the code he'd been fixing.

"Yeah?" He glanced over and his heart stopped.

Fazil stood there, balancing his open laptop in one hand and holding a Starbucks coffee in the other. He'd lost the suit jacket, but not the tie. "Is now a good time? Stephen said you were the procedure guy."

Yes. No. Never would be the best time. *God, why is he still so beautiful?* Todd cleared his throat. "Yeah. Pull up a chair."

Fazil set down his coffee and laptop before dragging the guest chair over. Next thing he knew, Fazil was sitting there, close enough their shoulders nearly touched. Yes, he was real. The heat, the scent, and the sound of Fazil's breathing all proved that. "What do you want to know?"

Fazil brushed the keys of his laptop with his fingers before answering in a voice that was too deep to be entirely professional. "Everything."

God, those eyes. Dark and full of the emotions Todd didn't want to contemplate. *You're the one who left.* "I'm not *The Hitchhiker's Guide to the Galaxy.*"

Fazil's smile was worse. Sharp and sweet, highlighted with a bit of a blush. Thankfully he looked away. "Well, how 'bout we start with the procedures you've written, then I'll figure out what's missing?"

"That I can do." He brought up the procedure folder and walked Fazil through it all, from development to testing to bug fixes to releases. Everything he'd been able to collect and write down when he'd heard Anderson's team had been hired. Didn't matter if this was a mission to save them or sell them—something had to be done or they were all out of jobs.

The process of creating all the procedures had helped.

They'd known how they did things was dysfunctional—the right hand never knew what the left was up to—but codifying what they did had pointed a spotlight on the deficits.

He hadn't scraped the surface of what he expected Fazil —and Sam Anderson—might want. Two jobs back, the company he'd worked for had undergone ISO certification. The amount of paperwork had been madness. He put all the files on a thumb drive and handed it to Fazil. "It's all yours."

Their fingers brushed and he nearly dropped the damn thing. A flash of heat and a cascade of memories. Those lips, those eyes, that skin.

Fazil's breath caught. "Thanks." He stuck the drive into his laptop. "Do you mind if I sit here while I look at these? In case I have any questions?"

Yeah, he did. There was that desire again, to grab that dark tie and either throttle or kiss Fazil. He couldn't decide which one he wanted more. "Sure. My cube is your cube." He opened the window he'd been working in before Fazil had arrived.

Surprisingly he slipped back into the groove. Oh, he knew Fazil was there less than an arm's reach away, but rather than distracting, his presence soothed, like a cool breeze on a hot day. Just as it had so many years ago.

"Hey, Todd?"

Like that, he snapped back into a world not made of Python syntax and statements. Fazil's voice tickled through his limbs and down into his balls. He glanced at the clock. At least forty-five minutes had passed in his trance. "Yeah?"

"Do you have any documentation on the open source code you guys have used?"

His expression probably answered that question, since Fazil sighed and typed something on his laptop.

"It's one of the things I've hounded people about, but..."

"Never enough time?"

His chuckle was ever so slightly bitter. "Been there, done that, huh?"

"Oh yeah." Fazil sipped his coffee, though it had to be cold by now. "Many times. But that was before Sam hired me."

So many things Todd didn't know. Words slipped from his head, vanishing completely with the need to draw close to the man who had once been his best friend. He gripped the armrests of his chair. *What happened, Z?*

Before the pause grew more awkward, Fazil set his coffee down. "Anyway, nice job with this. It's all well-organized." He gestured at the screen.

A barb lay in the little turn in Fazil's voice. "You sound surprised."

There was that lovely flush again, this time accompanied by a swallow that bobbed Fazil's Adam's apple. "I guess I am. I don't remember you being... so neat about things."

Todd snorted. "The mechanic's son thing made everyone think I was a slob. Greasy rag and all." His amusement fell into pain. "I thought you knew better, Z." Had Fazil changed *that* much?

Fazil's blush deepened, and he looked at his hands. "I... You weren't a slob. I didn't mean that."

He bit back the *Then what the hell did you mean?* Because the cube had ears. So many ears. "Do you remember my dad's garage?"

Fazil got that faraway look. "Yeah."

So did he. The sounds, the smell of oil, concrete, and grease. "You know the back wall, with all those bins?"

A nod.

"Every single one was organized alphabetically by make, model, and part type. Dad was so cool he was OCD before hipsters were."

Fazil laughed but sobered quickly, his smile smoothing into seriousness. "Your book collection. I forgot."

Organized by genre, author name, and publication year. "Yup. Didn't fall too far from the tree in that respect."

Fazil tapped his fingers lightly on the keys again. Touching, not typing. Nerves, probably. He'd never been able to sit still when anxious.

A sense of grim delight slithered up Todd's spine. He was making Fazil uncomfortable and he had to stop himself from pulling Fazil into a kiss.

Fifteen years ago, that was the usual outcome when Fazil had gotten that lost look after being beaten at his own game. One of them ended up with the other's dick in their mouth. Or they both would, in an enjoyable contest to see who could make the other come first. Todd shivered, the memory of Fazil's tongue a little too close to the surface. Thank God the keyboard tray hid his lap, because his jeans were tighter than they should have been.

Fazil's voice was soft. "I just wanted to tell you that this is really good work. There's still a lot to be done, but this is far more than I expected Singularity to have." He closed his laptop and stood.

Well, how about that. Given the not-so-subtle rumple in Fazil's pants, someone else was remembering their past, too. "Thanks. I've heard good things about Sam Anderson."

"All true." He tossed the cup into the trash and headed for the hall. "See you tomorrow."

Not so fast. "Fazil?"

He spun on his heel, eyebrows up.

"Lunch tomorrow?" The sooner they aired out the past, the better, because another afternoon like today would be hellish.

Fazil fidgeted in the hall and his shoulders dropped. "Yeah, tomorrow's pretty flexible."

Apprehension in that response. Todd ignored the pain in his chest. "Good. Tomorrow it is."

Fazil's smile was genuine, if small. "See you later, Todd." Then he was gone.

Hearing his name spoken by that voice was like honey and lemon. So sweet, if you ignored the bitter sting.

CHAPTER THREE

Dinner with Singularity's management happened much like all the corporate wine-and-dines Fazil had attended since he'd started working for Sam: a fancy restaurant, too much alcohol consumed by the clients, and far too many people trying to impress them. When Sam was at one of these things, he was always graceful and poised in a way that neither Fazil nor Eli could manage.

The suit was getting to Fazil. He never understood how Sam and Eli managed to wear them day in and out. He had dressed this way every day before, but that job—working for a corporate bank—had been sheer hell, from the quips about his ethnicity to his off-the-rack clothes.

Eli wore a suit like he'd been born in it, but was out of his element when faced with small talk and pleasantries. Not that he wasn't the consummate professional, he just never relaxed on these trips, and this one seemed to be eating away at him. His smile was too sharp, as if it wanted to turn into a snarl or worse—a frown—and he couldn't stop fiddling with his watchband.

Eli met Fazil's gaze. He was stuck in a conversation

with Ryan Kendall, Singularity's mouthy CFO, who was bragging about how much money he'd saved the company. There was a hint of desperation in Eli's lifting of an eyebrow. *Please help me out here*, he seemed to say.

Fazil cleared his throat. "So, the Seahawks have become quite the team." It was as if the whole table sighed in relief, and boy, did everyone have an opinion.

"You a Steelers fan?" That from Stephen.

Fazil shook his head. "Eagles. Born and raised near Philly. Can't quite escape my youth."

Someone laughed and Stephen grinned. "We have a guy like that. Todd."

A cool numbness followed by heat trickled up into Fazil's skull. How many times had watching the game in Todd's basement turned into making out on the couch until they both couldn't breathe?

Before he could say anything, Sandra cut in. "Fazil knows Todd, don't you?"

He caught the edge of Eli's look. Curiosity. That was on the faces of everyone else, too. He tried to shrug and hoped to hell it didn't look like the wince it felt like. "We went to the same high school. He was a pretty serious fan back then." But not so much that he hadn't sucked Fazil off a few times while the sports announcers droned on in the background.

Those memories superimposed with the stunning man Todd had become didn't do anything to keep his dick down. Yeah, he wouldn't mind replaying those old times.

Fazil shifted in his seat and reached for his water. "I have to admit, I'm pretty surprised I don't get flack when I wear my jersey in Pittsburgh."

"Really?" Stephen said. "I thought people there were rabid about their team?"

"Oh we are." Eli toyed with his glass. "But it's not like he's a Ravens fan."

The conversation devolved into stats, predictions, and how the refs had screwed both teams over.

Fazil leaned back and sipped his water. Deed done, though he hadn't expected Eli to be into football. Or hockey, for that matter, when talk slid into that for a moment.

For the rest of dinner, the conversation remained light and thankfully devoid of Todd's name. Still, he couldn't keep the more adult version of Todd's smile from slipping into his brain. He'd put on muscle and scruff and stopped Fazil's heart.

So very unfair. If they hadn't known each other, if Todd hadn't broken his heart repeatedly, he'd have been tempted to flirt *hard* with the man. That was one of the better ways to get over a breakup—a nice, hot one-night stand. Would certainly put Kris from his mind.

But Todd *was* a breakup. Many, many, *many* breakups. And there weren't enough men *or* women in the world to get Todd out of Fazil's head.

His swirling thoughts of Todd weren't helped by a silent and twitchy Eli during the ride back to the hotel. Eli fiddled with his watch again.

Okay, something *really* was bothering him.

Sure enough, those proud shoulders dropped the moment they stepped into the hotel. Eli gestured at the bar. "Care for a few? On me?"

After sitting next to Todd all afternoon and nothing but water for dinner? He fucking *needed* a beer. "Don't you mean on Sam?" He followed Eli into the hotel bar.

"No, this is on my dime. I'm not charging Sam for my sins."

"*Your* sins?"

Eli signaled the server and took a seat at one of the booths. With his leg, bar stools were probably not the most comfortable. "I've been expressly forbidden from beating the finance department into submission. Doesn't keep me from wanting to, especially given the state of their records. The fools are just *asking* for an audit." He flicked open the bar menu. "And after that stint of bragging by their CFO? I'm going to get a bit drunk."

Eli the control freak, tipsy? This ought to be interesting. "Engineering isn't bad. Lots of stuff not written down, but the procedures are coming along."

Thanks to Todd. Who knew someone so lackadaisical could also be so organized? Then again, thinking back, his room had always been neat. "There's some undocumented open source code I noticed, so speaking of audits, I'll need to do one."

Eli twisted his lips into a bitter expression. "Let Sam know."

Fazil nodded. The server finally appeared and took their drink orders. A large gin martini for Eli and a Pike Stout for him.

Eli leaned back. "The people in finance aren't bad. Most of them are doing what they've been told. Ryan needs to be canned, with prejudice." Eli worked his jaw and shook his head. "How that man got into that position— Fucking idiot's schemes are barely legal. If that."

Fazil winced in sympathy. No wonder Eli wanted a drink. He might not understand the financial end of things, but he trusted Eli's knowledge. He was tough, could be an ass sometimes, but the man was fair to a fault.

The server returned with their drinks. Fazil waved

away the glass. It was, after all, a drink-from-the-bottle kind of night.

Eli took a sip of his martini and slumped against the booth. Like that, he looked younger and far less intimidating. "I'm glad things are better for you."

"I haven't met all of engineering yet. Stephen is frazzled, but he knows his tech. Main problem is that they need to not have all the important shit stored in someone's head. And get them following their own processes."

"So, no problems with Todd?"

Goose bumps rose all over. Fazil took a pull of beer from the bottle and hoped that covered the shudder. "No."

"Good. I can't quite tell if he's an old friend or an old enemy." Eli took a large mouthful of his martini. "I almost guessed enemy."

"Not a bad guess." Fazil toyed with the neck of his beer. "He's my ex-boyfriend."

Eli's exhale was nearly a squeak. "But you're..." He didn't say the rest. Didn't need to.

Fazil ripped the label off the neck of the beer bottle, then took a swig. "Actually no, I'm not straight." He tried to keep the anger from his words, but they fell like daggers. "There're a couple more letters in *LGBTQ* than just *G*, Eli."

Eli shrank, his face pale but for very red cheeks. He reached for his drink with an unsteady hand. "I... Shit." He stared into his glass. "I'm sorry. I should know better than to assume."

Now, that was a tone of voice he'd never heard from Eli. Absolute and contrite sincerity.

"Yeah, well, you know what they say about assumptions."

Eli flinched. After a sip, he looked up. "I guess I'm quite the ass tonight." Color now touched his face and neck.

Fazil shrugged. "It's not like I haven't heard it before. Being bisexual means you're just faking it one way or the other and you should make up your mind."

Eli rotated the stem of the glass between his fingers. "I didn't mean... I don't think..." He took another swallow. "I should just keep my mouth shut, lest I jam my foot even further inside."

"Well, that's a first. Leaving you speechless." Probably the beer talking, but what the heck.

Eli choked on his drink and lifted a single brow, and Fazil *finally* understood why Justin had fallen for this guy. Under all the posturing, there was a real person with quite a bit of heart.

"No, come on. Tell me. Why'd you think I was straight?"

Eli shrugged. "Well, aside from the whole girlfriend thing, I never noticed you checking out men."

He'd never risen to Eli's off-color banter. "Just because I don't check *you* out doesn't mean I don't look."

Eli's blush grew deeper and Fazil smiled before he drank more beer. "Besides, you're not my type. If I want tall, dark, and cranky, I can look in my mirror."

"Wait, I'm cranky?"

His turn to raise a brow and stare.

Eli studied his empty glass. "Okay, I'll give you that." A smile played around his lips.

"Not as much lately. Justin's been good for you."

He rubbed his thumb against his wedding band. "You have no idea." Soft, dreamy, distant look.

That was how love should be. Fazil had never found that, never felt that with anyone he'd dated, except once.

But Todd had broken his heart again and again and again, then had mapped out their lives after graduation without even considering what Fazil had wanted. Now the bastard was *here* and had grown into everything that turned Fazil inside out. He drained the beer. "So, what are we going to tell Sam?"

Eli slid his glass to the edge of the table. "Well, let's figure that out."

Over another round, they outlined their plan for the first week, Eli typing it in on his phone. "I'll look at it in the morning and edit out most of the *fuck*s, then send it off to Sam."

True to his word, Eli paid.

By the time they returned to their room, they were both yawning and Eli was practically asleep in his bed before Fazil crawled into the other and turned out the light. Despite his exhaustion, Fazil couldn't sleep. His brain replayed every image of Todd from the day and contrasted them with the memories Fazil had. The way he kissed, the quiver of his abs when Fazil touched his stomach on his way down to his dick, the hope in his smile when Fazil had said yes to lunch, the pride when he'd shown Fazil his work.

He rubbed his face. What would those lips feel like now with more experience behind them? Those hands had known Fazil's body so well.

Beneath the t-shirt and jeans, Todd had hardened into quite a man. If any other guy that hot had asked him out to lunch, Fazil would have pushed him against a wall and let his mouth answer in an entirely different way than saying yes.

And speaking of hardening... *Fuck.* Fazil rolled onto his side and ignored the throbbing in his dick and the ache in his balls. He was not about to jack off with Eli in the other bed. Enough was enough.

Todd was part of his past for a *reason*, no matter what

fifteen years had done to sweeten his body. The core of a person didn't change that much, and Fazil had promised himself he'd never go back to Todd. Too much *drama*.

Even if his dick felt differently.

Fazil closed his eyes and started coding in his head. It was one of two things that ever removed him from the world entirely.

The other was a good, hard fuck, and he would not even think of that in conjunction with Todd Douglas.

CHAPTER FOUR

THE NEXT MORNING WAS A WHIRLWIND OF MEETINGS for Fazil, mostly with members of the engineering staff. Thank goodness he could ditch the suit from the first day. It was jeans for the rest of the time. Much better to meet engineering on their terms, dressed to blend in, not stand out. They went over the timeline and what Fazil needed. Todd had collected quite a lot, but there were still significant gaps in the information. For the most part, the staff was helpful, though as they closed in on lunch, and everyone got their *hangry* on, things got contentious.

"There's a release coming up," one of the engineers said. "We don't have time to sit around and write up procedures all day." He threw a poisoned glance at Todd.

Todd shrugged. "I managed, Nathan. So did other people." His tone was mild, but his muscles flexed underneath the t-shirt that clung to his frame. Another geeky offering, this one of a caffeine molecule.

Had he worn it for Fazil? Because, damn, did it wake him up. *Oh get over yourself.* He tossed *that* idea from his mind. Or tried. His brain lingered over those shoulders and the cut of Todd's arms. He'd always looked good. Now he looked spectacular.

"There's no need to assign blame," Fazil said. "I'm not here to do that. I can work with you to get what I need, fill in those missing procedures, or develop better ones."

"Do you ever miss real engineering?" Nathan said.

Todd tensed, but Fazil laughed. "Sam encourages us to have side projects to keep our skills sharp. I've filed two patents while working for him." The best way to cut off snottiness was honesty. "Look, every procedure can be improved. We learn new ways—better ways—at every company. I'm sure there are things Singularity does better than anyone else. After all, your tech is superlative."

Praise always helped as well. Todd looked worried, but Nathan nodded. "That's why you're here, right?"

"Pretty much." Fazil straightened out the stack of paper in front of him. Something in the way Nathan eyed him that told him there were more questions behind those closed lips, but Nathan didn't ask anything else. The ruffled feathers must have been smoothed down enough.

They made it through the rest of the meeting and Fazil managed to tease out the information he needed. For the most part. When the clock clicked to eleven forty-five, he leaned back in his chair. "That's it for now. I'll leave you alone this afternoon so I can go over this... and likely send you mail you'll hate tomorrow."

Nathan grunted. Both he and Todd closed their laptops.

"Ready for lunch?" Todd asked.

Nathan raised an eyebrow. "Oh, you're fraternizing with the enemy now?"

Enemy? Ouch. He'd need to share that with Eli and Sam. If they saw them as interlopers, this job wouldn't go well.

Todd smiled, but it was tight. "I'm catching up with someone I haven't seen in a very long time. You got a problem with that? Because we can take it to Stephen."

Nathan shook his head. "Whatever, dude." His gaze fell on Fazil. "Todd never said where you're from."

Oh, *this*. Fazil's heart sunk. He rubbed his brow. "Born and bred in the wilds of suburban Philadelphia." When Nathan opened his mouth again, he held up his hand. "I know what you're asking. My parents are from Turkey." Next was usually about his religion, but he crossed his arms. "If you want any more *personal* information from me, buy me a beer after work."

Nathan flushed and picked up his laptop. "So you're like *him*. Good to know." He stalked out of the conference room.

What was that supposed to mean? Fazil peered through the doorway. "He's... touchy."

Todd ran a hand through his hair. "It's not you, it's me. He's never been happy that I got this job." He rolled his chair away from the table and rose.

Fazil ran a hand over his laptop and stood. "It's normal, the pushback. Everyone's still figuring out why I'm here and how I'm going to change their world." He paused. "I figured someone would ask about my name eventually. It being spectacularly *American* and all."

Todd cringed. "Nathan is... well... I'll tell you in a bit."

They walked to Todd's office to drop off their computers before heading out. The day was overcast, clouds hanging high in the sky, but humid and warm. Almost felt like a typical June day in Pittsburgh. "Umbrella?"

"Eh, no one carries those but tourists." Todd peered at the sky. "Besides, it won't rain."

"You know, say that in Pittsburgh even on a sunny day, and you're begging for a thunderstorm to roll in."

"Generally, what we have in the morning is what we'll have all day." He waved at the sky. "So, this."

Fazil's gaze lighted on the barely discernible peaks in the distance. "And mountains."

Todd's brilliant smile lit up his face the way it used to. "Yes, those, too." He unlocked the car and they climbed in. "Takes some getting used to."

"They're beautiful."

"Maybe over the weekend, we can take a trip to see them closer up?"

Fazil's heart skipped a beat. "Maybe." Spend part of the weekend with Todd? *Yes*, the irrational side of his brain said. His common sense wasn't so enthused. "What's the deal with Nathan?"

"Oh." Todd eased the car out of the parking lot and onto the road. "He's never gotten used to working with a gay man."

So *that's* what that quip meant. Close to the mark, too. Fazil scowled at his reflection in the window. "I thought Seattle was liberal and open."

"It is. And it isn't. There're a lot of conservative religious folks in the area, especially Mormons." An ever-so-slight tremor shook Todd's voice. "And large amounts of money tend to bring out the family values set."

Fazil watched the storefronts zip by. But for the mountains, this looked pretty much like any suburban area. "Pittsburgh's a little like that. But it's weird. Lot of live and let live. Old blue-collar values. Working with Sam, I've become sheltered from the shitty side of corporate culture."

They drove a little farther, then pulled into a strip mall. It had a dry cleaner, a salon, some insurance place, and a restaurant called the Karadeniz Café, complete with a blue eyelike emblem Fazil recognized instantly.

Of all the... "You're taking me to a Turkish place?" His voice pitched higher. "Really?" Especially after Nathan had prodded after his ethnicity?

Todd looked sheepish. "Well, I have no idea how you feel about pho or Thai or any of that. But I do know you like Turkish."

Well, yes. So did Todd. Or he had, back in the day. In so *many* ways. Heat rose to his cheeks. "You know, I have pretty high standards."

Despite all the spots in the front, Todd pulled around to the back of the buildings and parked. "I know. This place's food is almost as good as your mom's."

It had been fifteen years since Todd had tasted his mom's fare. "It had better be."

Todd undid his belt and laid his hand on Fazil's arm, gluing him to his seat with those lovely blue eyes. "Hey, have I ever led you astray?"

Yes. Many, many times. And Fazil had loved it. He swallowed. The turn of Todd's lips was too knowing, but he let Fazil go and got out of the car.

Fazil followed, his heart in his throat. There was friendship and there was flirting and Todd had crossed over to the latter sometime during the drive.

Man, his jeans had become too tight in the front. Todd's warm hand on his arm only led to his wanting that hand elsewhere. Or everywhere. He wasn't sure he should be flirting with Todd, given the work situation and their past.

Or the fact that they were walking into what appeared to be a typical Turkish place. Blue evil-eye beads, rugs, tulips, photos of Istanbul, the whole nine yards. The murmur of Turkish from the music fell against Fazil's ears and took him straight back to his parents' house. The language's familiar rhythm and the itch to speak it. "Wow."

Todd smiled knowingly. "Thought you might like it here."

He did. It was a bit cheesy, but he understood that need, that desire. Like he'd told Nathan, he'd been born in the US. His parents loved it here, but there'd always been that pull, the need to surround themselves with the trappings of the culture they'd left behind.

So yeah, this place felt like home.

"Todd! Good to see you again!" A man about their age came to the host podium. "Two?"

Todd nodded. "Hi, Ozan. This is my friend Fazil."

Ozan paused. "Not *the* Fazil."

Oh God. He gave Todd a sharp look.

"Yep. That Fazil." So much teeth in his smile. "Weirdest thing. I told you about the company that was coming? Turns out he works for 'em."

Ozan shrugged. "God works miracles." He led them to a table in the back, under a large photograph of the Black Sea.

"This is quite nice," Fazil said, chancing Turkish to see if the host understood.

Ozan answered in kind. "I know it's a bit much, but my parents..." He gave another shrug.

"Oh, I understand completely."

Todd chuckled and sat. "I love it when I'm right."

Fazil's cheeks heated, even more than before, and lo and behold, Ozan turned red, too. Interesting.

Ozan coughed and switched back to English. "Do you guys want to see a menu or should I tell my folks to surprise you?"

They opted for no menu. Another server brought water and bread and when she'd left, the most inappropriate question lodged in Fazil's throat. Had Todd fucked Ozan? And if he had, had it been because of Fazil? "You *really* like Turkish, huh?"

Todd sipped his water and rolled his eyes. "You haven't changed."

"What's that supposed to mean?"

Todd set down his glass. "The only thing I've taken out from here is the *food*."

"I didn't..." The look Todd gave him stole his breath. Part anger and part... something else. Pain? Resignation? He might have well have punched Fazil in the gut.

Todd fingered his glass. "I met Ozan at a bar on Capitol Hill. Yes, we're friends, but no, I haven't slept with him."

"I didn't..." But he had. Fazil dropped his gaze to his hands. Over the too-small table, Todd reached out and clasped one. Fazil sucked in a breath. Damn, those fingers and those warm palms. He looked up into older, wiser blue eyes.

"I don't sleep with everyone I talk to. I never have."

He had no answer to that. Only a weird feeling of vertigo and the knowledge that Todd was touching him in public. He was utterly lost in this strange new world. What Todd said didn't line up with the past Fazil knew, but he stared into Todd's eyes and kept holding his hand anyway.

What had happened back then? What was happening *now*?

It was the meze that rescued him, a whole tray's worth of little appetizers, hot and cold. When Ozan brought them, Todd released Fazil's hand.

It was a loss tempered by the joy of what had been placed before him. They started with the İmam bayıldı, little stuffed eggplants, and after a bite Fazil groaned. "Damn, this *is* like Mom's."

"Told you." Todd smirked.

Fazil's heart fluttered and his pulse jacked up. Todd was nearly always right. That had been his trait in high school and why he'd taken charge and planned *everything* back then, even their lives, which had turned out nothing like Todd's plans.

When Todd wasn't right, he was spectacularly wrong. "I thought..." No, that wasn't the way to ask why Todd wasn't working in his old man's shop. "How'd you end up becoming an engineer?"

Todd consumed a stuffed grape leaf, raised an eyebrow, and answered. "Same way as you. Went to college. Got a degree."

He... actually had three. But he wasn't about to tell Todd he had a masters *and* a PhD. Not when his face was so damn hot and probably very red. "I know that. I mean..." So now he had to say it. "I thought you were going to take over your dad's garage." Fazil, meanwhile, was supposed to have gone to a local university and then taken up teaching to remain in the area for Todd—when Todd had wanted him and not someone else.

He'd opted for another course.

"Yeah. Plans changed." Todd leaned back in his chair and looked out the front window. "The year after you left wasn't good." A hollowness in those words. Deep sadness.

Regret cut into Fazil, clenching at his heart. "I'm sorry."

Todd snorted. "I'm sure."

It was Fazil's blood that heated this time, but he kept the barb inside. *I wasn't going to sit around and watch you with other people.*

"The year after that," Todd said, grit in his voice, "I decided to stop being the person everyone thought I was and be who I wanted to be. I went to community college in the evenings. Decided I liked school, I *missed* school, and I actually had a brain." He shrugged and turned back to his food. "Then it was just a matter of transferring and finishing."

"I never thought you were stupid." Fazil finished up the eggplant.

That teased out a small smile. "You were the only one who didn't. You're the reason I went to college. I figured I had nothing to lose, everything to gain, and if we ever met again, maybe you'd—" Todd's voice broke and the cool exterior crumpled for a moment. He coughed and reached for his water.

Fazil couldn't feel his toes. Or his fingers. His heart thumped hard against his ribs, aching his chest and he didn't want to hear the end of that sentence.

Todd cleared his throat. "I wanted you to be proud of me. If we ever met again." He shook his head. "I don't know why. But it carried me through."

And here they were. "I..." He felt like a pile of shit for leaving his friend. Yeah, he had needed to go, but maybe he should have kept in touch. "I don't really know what to say."

Todd shrugged. "You don't have to say anything."

Fazil finally met Todd's gaze. No anger there. Not even any judgment. But there was sadness, and that hurt worst of all.

They were interrupted by Ozan and the main course, which was three dishes: eggplant mousakka, İskender kebap, and several lahmacun. "Afiyet olsun," he said, then was gone.

"This... is a lot of food!" More than they could ever eat. It smelled like heaven, and Fazil didn't know where to begin, so he took some of everything. So did Todd, and for a while they both savored the meal.

It was certainly authentic, especially the İskandar. So hard to get the lamb and the sauce right. It *did* remind him of his mom's cooking. That took him straight back in time, especially since Todd sat across the table from him as if they hadn't been apart at all.

"So what about you, Z? What have you been up to all these years?"

Hearing Todd call him Z used to warm his heart. Now it punched a hole through him. He didn't *understand* this Todd, the one that programmed code and hid his pain.

There'd been plenty of other, better people for Todd to date—he'd had his pick back then—and when Todd had grown tired of Fazil, he usually chose someone else without even a thought.

But *this* Todd hurt, and Fazil had caused that pain by leaving him all those years ago. *Except you left first, Todd. Every time. Left me for someone else.*

Fazil took a sip of water. "Well, you know I went to Stanford. After that, I went to Boston for grad school. Worked there for a while, then ended up back on the West Coast. Job-hopped a lot." He pushed pita through his hummus. "That's basically it. School. Work."

"How'd you end up in Pittsburgh, of all places?"

"Hey, it's a nice city!" He poked the pita at him. "Getting better every year."

Todd held up his palms in mock surrender, but the smile was back, thank God. "Just asking."

He chuckled. "Sam called. I'd worked with him at one of my past jobs when he came in and saved our asses. When he asked me to join his company, I said yes. It's my dream job. Good engineering. Solving problems. Making a difference."

"Closer to home, too."

A five-and-a-half-hour drive to his parents' place. "Yeah, I get back now and then."

Todd cocked his head and looked poised to ask a question. That vanished into a small, pained smile, and Fazil's heart sank into his feet.

He still knew Todd well enough to guess the question. *Did you look for me?*

And Todd still knew him well enough to know the answer. He hadn't. After all, he'd run for a reason. Hunting down and finding Todd would've ignited everything that had been between them all over again.

Just like now.

Ozan reappeared. "I hope you saved some room for dessert." He deposited a small tray of various sorts of baklava on the table, including Fazil's favorite: pecan in the shape of birds' nests.

"We've hardly finished our plates," Fazil said. Still, he took a piece of baklava.

"I'll box up the rest," Ozan said. He cleared all but the dessert tray off the table.

"There's a fridge at work." Todd picked up one of the pieces of rolled walnut baklava. "Lunch for tomorrow."

Work. The reason he was here with Todd had entirely slipped Fazil's mind. They'd go back, the day would end, and Todd would be lodged in his thoughts all night, no matter what Singularity had in store for Eli and him in the evening. "Are you seeing anyone?" The question fell out of his mouth, almost without thought. A stupid thing to ask.

But he really wanted to know. *Please say yes.*

Todd leaned back and his smile was like the sunlight in winter. It made Fazil ache in ways he hadn't in *years*, and he longed for Todd and the warmth of his arms around him.

The quiet sound of summer nights together. *Please, please say you have someone.*

His answer was soft but undeniable. "No."

Damn. Because that tempting door opened a crack. The one he'd nailed shut and labeled DO NOT ENTER when he'd left for California. Inside were all the feelings, the hurt, the frustration—but all the joy, too.

The smile dimmed a bit. "You?"

"I broke up with my girlfriend a month ago." He tried not to sound bitter.

"Bad breakup?"

"No." Fazil balled up his napkin. "Mutual. We liked each other. Got along fine. But..." He shouldn't tell Todd this. Should shrug and shut up. "When I thought about the future, like ten years down the line, she wasn't part of that."

"You didn't love her."

God, that sounded cold. "We cared for each other, but it wasn't that heart-stopping love. It wasn't like with..." He met Todd's gaze, those clear blue eyes, and his throat closed. *It wasn't like it was with you.*

Todd shifted in his seat, his smile fading just enough that Fazil saw the concern and the wonder.

"Anyway, like I said. It was mutual. Turned out she didn't see a future with me either. She moved on." Faster than he had. "Dating another guy."

Todd nodded, but Fazil would have laid odds that he wasn't thinking about the present. Again, words left his mouth that shouldn't have. "We should talk. About what happened."

Todd barely moved, but the intensity in his stare, the line of his mouth and jaw, made breathing hard. "Yeah, we should. Because I'm betting what you think happened and what I think happened are very different things."

Fazil tingled to his toes. No hostility, but the way Todd spoke—with finality—played with his nerves in ways that required a darker room and a whole lot more privacy. "Maybe over the weekend?"

"Yes." Same voice, but with a very sly grin.

Same effect. Fazil's balls tightened. *We're going to do this, aren't we?* Such a bad idea. God, he wanted Todd, wanted to know everything about him now. If they had to rake over the past to get there? Sure. After all, he was only here for two weeks. How bad could it be? He swallowed.

Todd looked at his watch. "We should get going."

As if on cue, Ozan arrived with their packed leftovers and another little box for the remaining baklava. "It's on the house."

Todd huffed. "Don't be silly." He pulled out his wallet and dropped two twenties onto the table.

"Wait, I can…" Fazil reached for his own wallet.

"Nope. I've got this. Some other time." Todd collected the bag of leftovers and stood.

Ozan looked amused. "I hope you enjoyed everything."

It was all he could do to stammer out the traditional Turkish reply as he rose. "Elenize sağlık." Health to your hands.

"Have a good one, Ozan," Todd said.

"You too." He grinned at Fazil. "İyi şanslar."

Good luck. Fazil could only swallow and nod.

He was going to need it.

Todd didn't know what to make of Fazil. He did, however, know what he wanted to do to him, but it was Tuesday, and three days lay in between him and that possibility. Taking him to lunch today to start airing out their past hadn't been the brightest idea.

That little glimpse of a contrite Fazil had sent his body temperature skyward with every maddening blush. He knew what else used to make Fazil that red. Probably still did, too. How deep would Fazil's groans be now when he came?

Fazil strolled next to him as they headed behind the little strip mall, but his eyes were focused on the ground, brows furrowed and his lips turned into that pout he used to get when his mind whirled too fast.

Same old Z, but also a different one. He was far more interested in the grown-up Fazil, though. He'd had it up to his eyeballs with the high school version. This Fazil had better not try to pull any of *that* crap now.

"Is there a reason you parked back here and not out front?" Fazil surveyed the mostly empty lot.

A quick press of the car fob unlocked the doors, and Todd put the leftovers in the backseat. "Yup. Plenty of coworkers drive this way to lunch."

"Don't want to be seen with me?" And there was the other pout, the one that spoke of insecurities and worry and never quite being good enough. He'd never understood it back then.

But now? Todd chuckled. "I don't mind being seen with you. But I didn't know how lunch would go."

"How do you think lunch went?" Fazil lifted his chin.

"I don't know." Todd stepped too close. Fazil inhaled sharply, but didn't step back. "How'd lunch go, Z?"

Standing like this, inches apart, Fazil had to look up. Not much, but enough to lengthen that beautiful neck of his. "It brought back a lot of memories." His voice was soft but full of depth.

"Yeah." It had. So many. Like those soft lips against his. Breathless whispers in the middle of the night. "I really want to kiss you, Fazil."

He swallowed and his Adam's apple bobbled. His brown eyes couldn't get much wider. "I... won't say no."

"But will you say yes?" A long moment passed, and a pit of disappointment opened in Todd. He stepped back. "If it's not a yes, then it's a no. I don't play games, and I don't read minds."

Fazil's stiffened, his jaw setting. "This whole thing has been a game! A Turkish place. A sexy gay waiter." He waved at the strip mall, the wind catching the curls in his hair. "And yes. Yes, okay? I want you to kiss me."

Well, someone got angry when pressed. Todd stepped in, cupped a hand behind Fazil's neck, and kissed him hard. He opened to Todd's tongue, tentatively at first, then groaned and relaxed his whole body into Todd's.

Todd tangled one hand into Fazil's curls and cupped his ass with the other and pulled him even closer, rocking into him, letting him know exactly what he wanted and how badly he wanted it. They were both hard, grinding against each other.

Fazil tasted of pecans and honey and all the wasted years between them and kissed back, exploring and sparring with a ferocity he'd never managed in high school. He fisted the fabric of Todd's shirt in his hands.

A half day's-worth of scruff covered Fazil's jaw and chin, and Todd indulged in the taste of that skin and the rough scrape against his lips before he pulled back. Not far, but enough to look Fazil in the face.

His breathing was shallow and his eyes bright and dancing with something that might have been hope, but could've been fear. "Good idea to park in back."

Todd stole another kiss, this one slower and sweeter. He let his hands drift down Fazil's back, even as Fazil found Todd's ass and pulled him closer.

As if they could manage that without removing clothing.

Fazil had been Todd's first kiss. He'd kissed a lot of guys since then—too many to even count and quite a few to chase away the memory of Fazil. None ever had the sweet mix of compliance and desire that Fazil seemed to put in every move of his lips. *Yes, I want more. Yes, I'm yours.*

Todd broke the kiss. "We should go back to work."

"Killjoy," Fazil whispered. "But you're right."

They untangled from each other, both still hard, and in the awkward moment that followed, they climbed into their respective sides of the car.

Todd tried not to cringe, tried not to have his heart drop when Fazil stared out the passenger-side window and worked his jaw while Todd drove them back to Singularity. But then Fazil settled into his seat and laid his hand on Todd's thigh. "Thank you. For lunch. For—"

Todd entwined his fingers into Fazil's. "That's what friends are for. And you're welcome."

Fazil stroked his thumb along Todd's fingers. "I thought you might hate me."

Todd shook his head. "I've never hated you. I hated what you did."

Fazil flinched but didn't pull his hand away. "I hated what you did, too."

"What is it that you think I did?" He could only snatch a quick glance, given the busy road.

Confusion and sadness marred Fazil's face. "This isn't the place to talk. But we really should." He squeezed Todd's hand.

More than talk. Much more. "Let me show you around this weekend. We can catch up then."

Silence. Fazil rubbed his thumb over Todd's knuckles again. "Yeah, okay. Though..." He turned his head and Todd looked over to meet those stunning dark eyes. "This probably isn't the best idea." He lifted their hands.

Todd swallowed a laugh. Best idea he'd had in years. Fazil in his arms. Maybe in his bed. "You going to get in trouble with your boss?"

He was startled by Fazil's laughter. It was joyful and almost too loud. "Oh, fuck no. Only if it causes me to screw up my work. Sam's the last person who'd yell at me. That's why he's in Pittsburgh."

Todd tried to remember what he'd read about Sam Anderson. He knew Sam was a superstar—that's why his team was here to fix Singularity—but why had he stayed in Pittsburgh? "I always thought it was because of the whole start-up boom there. And the universities."

"Well, there's some of that," Fazil said. "But no. He fell for one of his employees. Hard enough to come out of the closet *and* stay in the city."

"So no rule about dating."

"Nope. Just one about not fucking up the job too much because you're dating. Or fucking."

That... was interesting. "Must be a fascinating place to work."

"Well, it makes things eventful."

They pulled back into the Singularity parking lot, and Fazil slipped his hand free of Todd's. "But I bet you guys have rules about dating. And fucking."

They did, and Todd squirmed as guilt tickled the back of his mind. "Though, technically, you're not a coworker."

His smile was wicked. "Just the enemy."

Oh, goddamned Nathan. "You're not my enemy." He pulled into a spot, parked, and killed the ignition.

Fazil opened the door. "You might feel differently once I've finished looking over everything."

Todd climbed out and grabbed the leftovers. "You're here to help. Even if it hurts a bit."

They walked into the building and took the elevator up. On the way to his cube, he threw the leftovers into the fridge. "Yeah." Fazil ran a hand through his hair. "You've done a good job on the procedures you have."

Todd was heartened by that, except the dangling end of that sentence flipped his stomach. "But..."

Fazil's smile was tight. "But there's still a lot of work left." He paused when another Singularity employee walked by and eyed them. Once the woman was out of earshot, he spoke, his voice softer. "It's probably going to hurt everyone's pride. And change things."

Oh. "As long as it gets us moving in the right direction." Todd glanced down the hall. "I'd better get back to it."

"Me too," Fazil said.

They headed to Todd's cube, and Fazil grabbed his laptop. "Catch you later."

Then he was gone. Todd sank into his desk chair, the taste of pecans, honey, and Fazil still on his lips. That hard body against his was delectable, as was the promise of the weekend to come.

But Nathan was right—if they knew, everyone would see it as Todd sleeping with their enemy. Especially if the warning Fazil had uttered was true.

Todd docked his laptop and got back to work. Regardless of everything, bugs didn't fix themselves.

CHAPTER FIVE

For Fazil, the rest of the day moved both quickly and achingly slow. More meetings, some of them utterly pointless. Like a second meeting in the afternoon to discuss what the team had accomplished that day. The process they claimed to use should have one meeting, in the morning, not two. That killed the productivity the process was supposed to foster.

Plus, boring meetings didn't keep Todd out of Fazil's head.

Kissing him had been idiotic. But so very hot. He'd forgotten how Todd felt and tasted and—he shifted and was grateful there was a chair in front of him as they stood around the conference room table.

Nathan droned on and Fazil made a mental note that this had to change. The whole point of the agile style of development was to work on small bites, with fewer meetings, and foster cooperation with team members. Not waste time with endless reports. But every job he'd ever worked at, save at Sam's, there'd been this need for management to control all parts, regardless of the development style.

He'd chafed under that for *years*.

There's a process, Fazil, for management approval. You must work within it.

The process is shit. Let me do what I need to do to fix this!

That was one of the ways his jobs had ended. The other had to do with too many allusions to deserts, towels, and camels. Even if he wasn't a practicing Muslim, the digs sank in after a while.

Right now, though, the only person who needed more control in this room was him—over himself. Everything Todd had done, down to dangling the cute Turkish guy in front of him, turned him on. It was like Todd knew his buttons.

Todd did. Maybe better than anyone, since he knew their foundation and pressed them all. Then dumped him for other people. Then mapped out their futures. Then dumped him *again*.

Todd seemed certain they had a different view of that past, though.

Fazil knew what had happened. He'd *been* there.

The meeting finally broke up, five minutes after it should have, and with no more information passed around than before they'd entered. Yup, this was on Fazil's cutting board.

He returned to the conference room he and Eli shared. Inside, Eli stared at his laptop, a look of distaste curling his lips.

"That bad?" Fazil flopped into a chair and started typing up the notes he couldn't take during the meeting.

Eli leaned his head back. "There are problems. Issues Ryan hid from me."

Fazil's heart sank. "Are we done here, then?" If Eli pulled the plug, there'd be no weekend with Todd.

His expression smoothed out. "No, not yet. It's not *that* bad." He leaned back and stretched out his legs. "It's fixable. But I do need to talk to Sam. You?"

Fazil rested his elbow on the armrest of the chair. "What's been written up is good. But there's a lot that hasn't been, and they don't follow their procedures. Lots of wasted time due to micromanagement."

Eli grunted. "Too much chaos on the financial side—not enough in engineering."

Something like that. There needed to be freedom and creativity in development and testing. "Wrong kind of chaos."

Eli folded his arms. "Speaking of issues, how'd lunch go?"

He'd managed to get Todd out of his mind. All of it came flooding back, including how hard Todd had been while rocking against Fazil's erection. Heat flooded his body and he focused on his laptop. "It was interesting."

Eli chuckled.

"How about I tell you over a beer tonight?" He needed to talk to someone and Eli was all he had at the moment. "I may be making a colossal mistake."

"Oh, I doubt it," Eli murmured. "But yes. Your treat."

"Done."

First they had to finish the workday and then endure another dinner with the executive staff, this time in downtown Seattle. By the time they returned to the hotel, it was nearing nine.

"Still up for that drink?" Fazil asked. The hotel doors slid open.

"Yes, please." Grit in Eli's voice. Though Eli had managed to sit far from the other CFO at dinner, it was apparent Eli wanted to throat-punch the man halfway through the meal. He wasn't the only one. Even Dr. Sandra had looked annoyed at the braggart.

They ended up at the same booth. This time, Eli ordered a Moscow mule and Fazil chose a different regional beer. If this kept up, he'd go through their entire list before they left.

"So," Eli said. "Lunch?"

"He took me to a Turkish place. With an obnoxiously cute waiter."

Eli raised a brow. "And?"

"We talked around everything. But..." Fazil eyed his bottle and took a drink. "I think our pasts aren't the same. I mean, how he sees things."

"Well, of course not." Eli's copper mug glinted with condensation. "Every event is different for everyone." He drank.

How different? He had the weirdest creeping sensation that perhaps Todd had been hurt more back then, and he didn't *understand* that. Todd had cheated on *him*. "He's going to show me around Seattle over the weekend. Then we'll talk."

"I'll have the room to myself?" He nodded in the direction of the elevators.

Fazil rotated his beer. "Yeah. Probably." He looked up. "Is that going to be a problem? I know Sam's lenient, but this *is* work."

"Sam won't mind." Eli looked down at his hand—at his wedding ring, Fazil realized. "But I'm the last person you should ask for this kind of relationship advice." He met Fazil's stare. "I'll just tell you to go fuck him. Literally."

Fire rose from the soles of Fazil's feet to the top of his head. "You think I should—"

Eli cocked his head. "You want to. Why not? Not like he's a stranger. I'm assuming *ex-boyfriend* means you did a lot more than just *talk*." He paused and sipped his drink. "I was a teenager once, too."

Oh yes. They hadn't done *everything*, but they'd done a lot. "I'm not sure how smart of an idea it is hooking up with him, considering..." He waved at the hotel bar. "I mean, we're here for a reason."

"Fazil, I married my boss's assistant because we couldn't keep our hands off each other."

Maybe he *was* asking the wrong guy. Fazil hiccupped a laugh and drank more of his beer. "I don't want to screw up this assignment."

"You won't." Eli contemplated his drink. "Just be discreet while on the job?"

"You mean like you and Justin were?"

This time, Eli blushed. "No. Not *at all* like we were." He gulped part of his drink.

"So, what's the issue with the finances?"

"Don't get me started." But he pushed aside his drink and told Fazil anyway. Most of it went over his head, but not the part where they were out of compliance on a lot of things related to compensation, stocks, and taxes. Things that probably kept Eli up at night.

"You think you can fix it?"

Eli nodded slowly. "If that fucking ass of a CFO lets me. I'm very much regretting the promise I made Sam."

"What promise?"

Eli took a good, long, hard look at him and shrugged. "I promised him I'd leave my crops and floggers at home."

Oh. *Oh.* "That might have been too much information." He already tried very hard not to wonder about Eli and Justin. The image now? He shook it out of his mind. "Yeah. Too much."

"Sorry." But he wasn't, because his smile said the opposite.

"Liar." Fazil drank the last of his beer.

Eli shrugged. "So now you know. I hate hiding it." He paused. "I hate hiding in general."

Fazil had been dreading working with Eli on this trip because he knew so little of the man other than he had a habit of being exacting about everything. Now? He *really* understood what Justin saw in the guy, and why Sam put up with him. "Did you do that a lot? Hide?"

Eli swirled the last of his drink. He made no move to finish it off. "May I ask you a personal question, Fazil?" A softness in his voice that underwrote his hesitation.

As if this trip couldn't get weirder. "Sure."

"Both your parents are Turkish, right? From Turkey?"

Not the question Fazil had expected. And not the way Nathan had probed for the information. "Yeah. They emigrated after the coup in 1980."

"How'd they..." Eli paused, then started again. "Do they know you're bisexual? That you've dated men?"

Fazil watched Eli, the rising blush, the way he rubbed his thumb over his wedding band, and his chest hurt for the man across the table. "Yeah, they know. Told them before I left for college. They were dismayed at first, but now?" He shrugged. "I took a boyfriend home to visit once. They treated him like family. Still ask after him, even though it's been years." They'd probably ask after Kris, too. He'd dated her the longest—if you didn't count Todd.

Todd, who, in all likelihood, he was about to start dating again. Or at least fucking.

Eli still stared into the last bits of his drink. "Mine... well, it's a long story, but they immigrated to the US, too. It's hard to grow up with that, sometimes."

Bits and pieces clicked into place. He'd seen Eli's folks at his wedding, how awkward they'd been, how conservatively they'd dressed—and guessed at the direction Eli was going. "My parents were never that religious. We fasted during Ramadan and went to a mosque sometimes, but they also drank and developed a taste for pork." He pushed his empty beer off to the side. "I was raised secular Muslim. Like an Easter-and-Christmas Christian."

Eli looked up. "I was raised religiously."

Fazil winced. "So, the whole being-gay thing..."

"Didn't go over well."

That explained a lot. "But your folks came to your wedding."

"They did, and things between us are changing for the better." A small smile. "Look, I don't know what happened between you and Todd. It's not my place to know." He cupped his hands around the copper mug. "But the one thing I've learned, the one thing I *know* from my life, is that people change. The past can be overcome. While there's life, there's hope."

Pinpricks from his toes to his skull. "Eli..."

"If I had a chance to talk to my high school boyfriend..." Eli blinked a few times, his eyes far too watery, and he tossed back his drink. "I'm going to head upstairs. See you in a few." He slipped out of the booth and collected his cane.

Fazil's heart lodged in his throat as he watched Eli head out of the bar. Eli could never see his first boyfriend again. He'd died in the same accident that had damaged Eli's leg beyond repair. Everyone at work knew that story.

Todd was *alive*. They both were. There was hope. Fazil leaned back and studied the spot Eli had occupied. Pretty obvious from the comments at lunch that Todd had a different view of their shared past—and he did want to know more about that. And more about the Todd of now.

The waiter came with the bill, and Fazil paid but lingered in the booth for a while. He suspected Eli needed some time, and he wasn't quite ready to go to sleep yet. Todd would be there in his thoughts when the lights went out. The engineer and the mechanic's son. The cheater and the man who said he didn't sleep with everyone.

He almost ordered another beer. Instead, he rose and made his way back to the room.

Three days until he discovered who Todd had become.

CHAPTER SIX

Todd rarely saw Fazil for the rest of the week. A few meetings, some work-related conversations, and Fazil had been at the engineering group lunch on Thursday at Stephen's invitation. There were some moments alone at the coffeepot, but those were few and far between. Fazil kept his distance.

But those unguarded looks and the way he licked his lips. The smiles. Todd hoped he wasn't reading too much into it now that it was Friday.

Would Fazil run? Tell him he'd made plans with his coworker or something? Only one way to find out. After he finished plugging another hole in their code, he walked down to the conference room Fazil and the finance guy had been given, knocked, and pushed the door open.

Fazil sat inside, his hands hovering over the keyboard. "Hey."

No sign of the other Anderson guy. Todd slipped inside and leaned against the closed door. "Hey. Wanted to see how things were going."

"They're going." Fazil leaned back in his chair. "There's a lot that still needs to be done."

"Well, you have another week."

He nodded. "You didn't come by for that, though." His smile was a sly thing.

Todd curled his toes. "I wanted to see if we were still on for this weekend." *Please say yes.*

Worry flickered across Fazil's face. "Yeah, but if something's come up..."

"No, no. I..." He pushed himself off the door and crossed the room. "It has to be yes, Fazil. Like I said. I won't play the guessing game with you." Not again. Not anymore.

Fazil looked at his computer for a moment, then rose and rounded the table until he stood close.

Not close enough. Too many inches still lay between them. Too many years.

"How much of a yes do you want?" Fazil's lips swept up into his little smile. "We're still on the clock."

There was that.

"I have no idea if there's a camera or something in this room." Fazil furrowed his brow. "I hope not, because Eli and I spend a lot of time flipping each other off. People might think we have an antagonistic relationship."

This was a side of Fazil he hadn't seen. "I can't imagine that guy flipping anything off. He seems like the proper type who can't wait to get home to his wife."

"I used to think that. But our office is tiny, his *husband* is Sam's assistant, and... go on enough of these trips, you learn things about your coworkers."

Todd slotted that information away. "Sounds like a great place to work. Like family."

"A rowdy, dysfunctional family. But yes. It's the best job

I've ever had." His smile was golden, and he took a step closer. "Any cameras?"

Todd warmed all over. "None that I know of."

"So if I were to kiss you, that be fine?"

"More than." He reached for Fazil.

Fazil pulled Todd's head down and took his mouth like he owned it. Which was fine with Todd, because it left him free to cup Fazil's ass and pull Fazil against him. He'd never get tired of the way Fazil melted when their dicks ground against each other. The way he arched his back, that little catch of breath.

Fazil broke the kiss. "Yes. We're still on."

More than. If they weren't at work, he'd be tempted to use the office furniture in this room to enact some scene out of a porno. *Bad Business Boyz Seven* or some such thing, even if they were more geek than executive.

The conference room door handle rattled.

They jumped apart. Fazil looked down at his feet and Todd backed up against the table. The door swung open and the finance guy walked in, his jaw set hard and his knuckles white about the handle of his cane, but everything about his demeanor changed when he saw Todd and Fazil.

"It's... Um." Todd stumbled over every word. *Shit.*

Eli focused on Fazil, his grin a little too deep. "I thought I told you to hang a tie on the door."

What? Todd glanced at Fazil, who looked like he might have swallowed his tongue.

"Eli!" Fazil choked with laughter, but there was also horror written on his face.

Kind of like the terror in Todd's gut. The finance guy knew about them?

Eli shrugged. "Oh come on. You've seen me banter with Sam. And with Justin."

"Too many times," Fazil said. "And you're the one with the damn ties."

"You can borrow one, if you'd like." He folded both hands over the top of his cane. "They have *lots* of uses."

"Stop." Fazil turned an interesting shade of red and met Todd's gaze. "Um, have you two met?"

"Not officially." He eyed Eli, who looked every bit the businessman in his three-piece suit.

"Eli, this is Todd Douglas. Todd, Eli Ovadia, Sam's CFO."

They shook hands, and Eli's was both warm and strong. Todd cleared his throat. "You, uh, know." He gestured between Fazil and him.

"It's a small company," Eli said.

"There's not going to be a problem?" Either the AC didn't work in this room, or he was really red. He hoped it was the lack of cooling.

"Not from me." Eli chuckled. "I'm sure Fazil will explain. But if you'll both excuse me, I should go over my notes and call my boss before he leaves for the day."

Todd glanced at his watch. Nearly two. Almost five on the East Coast. "Right." Man, this was weird and awkward. "Stop by when you're done, Z?"

"Sure. Won't be until five, since you guys are paying us for a full day's work."

Yeah, really weird. "You know where to find me." With that, Todd fled the conference room.

Back in his cube, he stared at his darkened screen. Fazil definitely wanted him, wanted this weekend, which was good. Eli walking in had been odd. Anyone else and he would have had kittens, but Eli had taken it in stride.

Anderson's married, gay finance guy. Shit, that was some company Fazil worked for.

He nudged his screen awake and got back to work.

Fazil slumped back into the chair in front of his computer. "Really?" He didn't know whether to choke Eli or give in to the laughter that threatened to burst out of him.

Eli leaned his cane up against a chair and slid into another. "I didn't want you two to be embarrassed. I take it things are going well?"

He tasted Todd on his tongue. Felt the softness of his hair at his fingertips. "Yeah. They are."

"Good." Eli's hands hovered over his laptop. "'Z'?"

"His nickname for me. No one else uses it." He didn't want anyone else to, either.

Maybe that was apparent when Eli studied him. "I won't, then."

"Thanks." He touched the track pad to wake up his computer. "We ought to call Sam."

That drove the smile from Eli. "I'm not exactly looking forward to this." He reached over to the Polycom and punched in Sam's number.

Two rings and Sam answered.

"Hey. It's us."

"E. I'd been wondering when you guys would call. How are things?"

Eli sighed and rubbed his forehead, and it was as if Sam could see him.

"That bad, huh?"

"How much of the truth do you want?" Eli opened his own computer.

A pause. "All of it."

Fazil winced. That was most definitely an annoyed Sam.

Eli shook his head and launched into his report. Like before, a lot went over Fazil's head, but it was obvious Eli thought there were major problems. "They need an audit. Badly. But it won't go well for them."

Silence for a while. "Can you fix it?"

There was the heart of it. Eli put both elbows on the table. "Yes. It'll be somewhat irregular and might ping against another company's due diligence, but I can fix it. Legally. If their fucking CFO is fired."

"That's... asking a lot, E."

"I'm serious, Sam. He's hindering everything I do. His staff want to work with me, but he has them under his thumb. He let go one of the guys who was helping me go through the tax paperwork because he... was *friendly* to me."

"He what?" Sam's voice cracked over the speaker. That had been Fazil's thought, too. Holy shit.

"You heard me." Eli sounded grim. "I don't demand things that often, Sam. Not like this."

Fazil studied Eli's face, the long lines, the tightness of his shoulders. He stared at the speaker, as if he could reach Sam that way.

A sigh from the other end. "I'll see what I can do. I know one of the board members. I'll talk to their CEO, too."

"Thanks Sam."

"Not a problem. Well, it is. But you know what I mean." He huffed. "Is Fazil there?"

"I am."

"Please give me some good news."

He hesitated, glancing at his laptop. "Well, it's better than Eli's."

"Oh God," Sam groaned.

"It's only work," Fazil said. "There's a lot of it. The team's okay, just managed too heavily because they're understaffed and haven't been hitting their deadlines."

"I'm guessing there's a boatload of inefficiencies and not enough actual streamlining."

"Pretty much. The general vibe I get is that they ignore the management because the management doesn't listen. It's a horrible cycle of distrust."

"So, can *you* fix it?"

Good question. He glanced at his laptop again. "I think so. But..."

"But?"

"Not in a week."

Sam was silent. He looked up at Eli, who nodded in encouragement.

"How long?" Sam said at last.

"I'm still figuring that out. I also need to do that open-source audit and make sure everything's documented."

"Do you have a guess?"

This wasn't a situation he'd encountered before. Fazil chewed on his lip, and once more Eli nodded.

"Another two weeks, maybe? In addition."

There was a rhythmic thumping of some kind on the other end, then a clattering. "Right. I'll see about that, too. We're into it now, so let's make it work." Sam sighed. "I owe you dinner, E."

"You know, this time, I don't want to collect. Let's cancel the bet." Eli leaned back and looked grim.

"Well, shit," Sam said. "Okay. Point taken."

"I hate to be the bearer of bad news," Eli said.

"I need to know, E." Another thud of something.

"Anyway, try to have a nice weekend. Seattle's a great town. Go see the sites and relax."

"We will." Eli reached over and hovered a finger over the disconnect button. "Have fun, too. We'll make this work."

"I have no doubt. Night, guys."

"Good night." Eli hit the button and leaned back. "You heard the man. Have fun. Relax."

Fazil snorted. "I'm not sure he meant the way I have planned."

"You might be surprised." Eli played with the end of his cane.

Fazil held up his hands. "I *don't* want to know. Truly."

Eli's grin was wicked.

"What about you?" He was leaving Eli to fend for himself, though the man was very capable. Still—couldn't be easy being away from your new husband.

Eli gave a small shrug. "Justin and I came here on our honeymoon and met some folks. I've been invited to head up north and try my hand at horseback riding."

"Never been on a horse?"

Eli shook his head. "I don't like not being in control." Something shifted in Eli's face. He looked up and looked *young*. "But horses can *run*."

Oh. *Wow*. He'd never thought about Eli's leg much, or his cane. It was such a *part* of him. "You should try it."

Eli took a deep breath. "I usually don't get like this."

Fazil waved the words away. "Look, you've put up with me so far this week."

Eli chuckled. "True. Let's finish this day so we can get off on our respective adventures, yes?"

That sounded like the perfect way to end a Friday.

CHAPTER SEVEN

A LITTLE AFTER FIVE, FAZIL APPEARED IN TODD'S CUBE, his laptop case hanging from his shoulder. "Hey."

"All done?"

He nodded and stepped close. "How are we going to do this?" He kept his voice soft. "If I leave with you..."

That would look out of place. "No executive stuff tonight?"

"No." Fazil's brow furrowed. "Apparently it's the weekend."

No shit. "So you and Eli need a ride back to your hotel?"

"Yeah. Eli canceled the car service in the evenings because of all the wining and dining." Fazil backed out and called down the hallway. "Hey, Eli?"

"Turns out, I live in that direction." Todd grinned.

Eli peeked around the corner of the cube. "Yes?"

"Need a ride to the hotel?"

Eli leveled a *look* at Fazil.

"He offered. Lives that way."

The devilish chuckle was nearly inaudible and right

then, Todd decided the man was okay even if he was an executive. "It wouldn't be a problem."

"That would be nice. Saves waiting for a cab." Eli smiled at Fazil, who blushed.

Mr. Finance certainly knew what was going on. "Give me a sec to wrap up. I'll meet you in the lobby downstairs?"

They both nodded. Todd's fingers flew across the keyboard, finishing up his daily report to Stephen. He clicked send, locked his computer, and was down the hall, car keys in hand. Stairs were faster than the elevator. He came to a halt, though, when he saw Eli and Fazil talking to Sandra. It was a fairly benign conversation, from the looks of Eli's placid face and Sandra's smile.

"Todd," Sandra said. "Eli tells me you're playing chauffeur."

He tried to keep his face neutral, despite the hooded look Eli gave him. "Well, they need a lift, and home *is* that way." He shrugged. "Also, gives me and Fazil some time to catch up, you know?"

She nodded, and a car honked outside. "Speaking of rides, there's my husband. Have a good weekend."

Once Sandra left, Todd exhaled. "Shall we go, too?"

They followed him out and got into his car, Eli in the back and Fazil next to him, where he belonged. He patted Fazil's knee.

"Do remember I'm in the backseat," Eli said.

Fazil snorted. "Somehow, I doubt you'd care if we did anything."

"Oh good, you're learning."

Todd's pulse hit the roof, because he knew that banter and that tone. From the gleam he spied in Eli as he backed out, Fazil wasn't off the mark. "Are all of you like this in Pittsburgh?"

"Well, Fazil isn't," Eli said. "Which is a shame."

"I'm not. And it's *not* a shame. Eli's worse there, especially with Justin."

"I'm allowed," Eli said. "Even have the paperwork to prove it."

Todd glanced in the rearview mirror, and Eli wiggled his ring finger at him. Right. Husband. Anderson's assistant. How the hell did that work? "Sounds like a fun place."

"It is." There was a hint of longing and homesickness in Fazil's voice.

Todd's stomach lurched. He never thought about home anymore, partly because home was *here*, and reminiscing about Warminster meant remembering Fazil. Now Fazil was here and longing for somewhere else.

Old pain crept up his chest. Maybe this weekend wasn't the best idea, but with Eli in the backseat, there was no way to talk about it.

They pulled into the hotel parking lot. He studied Fazil. "Should I wait in the lobby?"

"Yeah. I need to throw some stuff into a bag."

"The offer of a tie still stands," Eli said, his voice dry.

Fazil's blush was exquisite. Man, he needed to learn how to make Fazil do that. "I think we'll manage," Todd said. "Besides, I do own a suit or two."

Fazil rolled his eyes. "Stop. Both of you."

They all got out of the car and headed into the hotel. Todd settled in one of the chairs while Eli and Fazil headed upstairs.

Every worry parked its ass next to Todd. Fazil had run before, pushed Todd away at the barest hint of an attraction to someone else, even when they'd made plans. Teen Fazil had been noncommittal about everything, yet expected total commitment on Todd's part. That had been maddening as a teen, and had done a number on his self-esteem. He hadn't thought himself good enough for Fazil. Now? He knew better.

But old patterns and habits were hard not to fall back into, including the sexual ones. His heart skipped when Fazil stepped out of the elevator with a gym bag swung over his shoulder.

He'd never stopped wanting Fazil. Physically or emotionally. Todd stood.

"Hey."

"Hi." That was all he could push out of his mouth. All the old fears, all the years. *Don't walk away now,* Z. Might as well tell himself that. One of them was going to wind up broken, like before. Almost as inevitable as a sunset.

Fazil studied him. "What's wrong?"

Todd looked everywhere but into those eyes. "Do you really want to do this?"

His shoulders dropped. "Do you?"

Yes. No. God yes. Todd met Fazil's gaze. "There's a lot of water under the bridge."

Fazil shifted from foot to foot, and his voice was quiet and contrite. "I know. But how do we get over it if we can't talk about it?"

Good point. "Yes, I want this. I've wanted this for *years.*" His voice cracked.

Fazil deflated more, and his jaw set. "Then let's go." He turned to the door and headed outside.

Todd followed, his stomach in knots, and unlocked the trunk so Fazil could toss his bag back there. Neither spoke as they climbed in. The steering wheel felt hot against his palms—from the summer sun, or maybe that was him. "What now?"

Fazil shrugged. "Dinner? We can start with that." He

placed a tentative hand on Todd's thigh. "Hey, I know you've changed. Maybe I have, too?"

Maybe he had. Todd hoped to God he had, because if he hadn't... "What are you in the mood for?"

A hint of a wicked smile and another shrug. "I'm easy to please food-wise. But you did say something about showing me the sites?"

That might be a good start. Something touristy. Take the pressure off. "It'll be crowded as hell and take forever to get to this time of night, but how about Pike Place Market?"

Fazil's touch became far less tentative and Todd's pulse notched up. "Sounds great."

He backed the car out and headed into Seattle proper. Fazil never removed his hand. When traffic turned into a slow-moving nightmare, Todd rested his own on top, just like old times. His heart had settled into his throat nicely, too.

He still loved that fucked-up kid from his past. He hoped that kid and the man next to him were different, or he'd waste more of his life undoing the hell Fazil roiled in him.

Todd hadn't been kidding about Pike Place Market being a madhouse, but here he was, staring at that iconic sign. Like every other tourist in the place, Fazil snapped a photo with his phone, then tucked it away. He'd taken a bunch of photos on the walk over, including one of the Starbucks mother ship. "I don't know why I bother with pictures. I never share them with anyone."

That seemed to surprise Todd. "No Facebook? Instagram? Twitter?"

Fazil shook his head. "I should get accounts to reconnect with people, but I haven't."

Todd seemed to chew on that. "I thought... Never mind." He looked out into the throng of people. "There's a bar and grille just up from here. It'll be slammed, but..."

"That's fine." Fazil's blood had gone cold. "You *thought*?" There was more to that. He felt it in his bones.

Sadness twisted Todd's face. "I thought you had them locked down to keep me from finding you." He ran a hand through his hair. "Which sounds stalkerish, thinking about it."

Yes, but he'd Googled Todd's name trying to find him, too. But there were a billion Todd Douglases. "That's how people find one another now."

Todd nodded. They stopped near an entryway into what looked to be another section of shops. "Let me see how long the wait is." He ducked into the building.

Whatever was cooking smelled great, except for the nausea in Fazil's stomach. Too many thoughts, feelings, and their damn *past*. Of course Todd had searched for him on the Internet. He'd also called and e-mailed and even written letters for *years* before giving up. Fazil had ignored them all.

He chewed on his thumbnail. People swirled around him on the sidewalk and street. At the time, ignoring Todd made sense. He'd wanted a clean break, and replying, letting Todd in, would have kept Fazil from forging his own way. He'd have only ended up with more of a broken heart and in a job he hated... all to appease Todd.

But maybe he should have read the e-mails and the letters. E-mails and voice mails were easy to delete, so he had. The physical ones with stamps he still had. He'd never had been able to throw those away. He'd never opened them. Never read them. He'd carried them from place to place. They were in a shoe box on top of a shelf in the closet of his home office.

Todd walked out. "Twenty minutes. Not bad." He stopped and the smile fell away. People flowed between them.

What did Fazil look like to get *that* reaction? In an instant, he wanted to walk away. Put as much distance between him and the pain in Todd's eyes, the ache in his own heart. "Twenty minutes is good," he croaked.

Todd winced and crossed the space between them. "We can walk a little, then come back."

Fazil fell into step beside Todd and headed up a hill, back toward where they'd parked. Though their hands brushed, a million miles lay between him and Todd. "I didn't want to be found. That's most of the reason." His throat was so tight. "With social media, everyone knows where you are."

Todd slowed and the look on his face was dark and miserable. "Did you hate me that much, Z?"

They turned a corner and walked down toward the sound. "I didn't hate you at all."

"You have an odd way of showing friendship." His gaze was focused ahead, off past the water.

"What the hell was I supposed to do?" He stopped. "I needed space and time." Not to be held down by a relationship that broke him to pieces every other week.

Todd turned, his hands stuffed into the pockets of his jeans. "You certainly got it, didn't you?" A huge helping of scorn there.

He had. And he'd been lonely, especially that first year, but he'd met other people. Dated men and women. Found his footing. All without Todd there to trip him up. "I did."

He watched Todd's expression. "But I don't want that now."

Todd closed his eyes, pain skewing his face. When he opened them, there was heat and anger radiating from every part of his body. "Good. Because I swear, Fazil, if you leave me again..." His shoulders dropped in defeat. "Not that the threat has any meaning. If you go, you won't *care* if I ever talk to you again."

Might have hurt less if Todd had punched him in the face, but that was something Todd would *never* do. Those words, though, stung and scraped and cut into Fazil. He'd cared back then. Hadn't been able to *stop* caring. "I'm not the one who fucking *cheated* every chance he got."

Todd straightened as if slapped. "I didn't..." He looked around them, then at his watch. "Let's see if the table's ready, because this is *not* the place I want to have this conversation." Todd headed back up the hill.

Fazil almost didn't follow him. He hadn't *what?* Cheated? Fazil had a fucking *list* of Todd's conquests. Heard all about them through the rumor mill, in stunning detail, and usually from the lips of the other person. How Todd's hands had felt. His lips. All that shit.

Curiosity got the better of him, and he stalked after Todd.

Maybe he should have spent the weekend with Eli, learning to ride horses.

Eli's words and pain flooded back to Fazil. Todd was *alive* and here. Second chances didn't always happen. For Eli there were lifetimes that never would.

People change. Had Todd? Had he? Didn't know anymore.

He caught up to Todd and they shuffled their way inside

the restaurant. A few more minutes to wait, but their table was almost ready. Todd was a rope of tension and stared over other people's heads. He didn't glance Fazil's way at all.

None of Todd's reactions spoke of guilt—and as long as they'd known each other, Todd had always owned up when he was at fault, without thought, without any anger. Todd loved being right, but he was also fine with being wrong.

Finally the waitress took them back to their table, and thank God it was near the end of a long row of windows that overlooked part of the market. He slid into the closest chair and Todd took the other. The waitress placed the menus and cheerfully mentioned the specials. Fazil didn't comprehend one word because of the way Todd stared at him.

Oh yeah, Todd was *mad*. Really fucking mad. Well, *shit*.

When their waitress left after a promise to bring them water, Todd took a breath. "You're going to fucking listen to what I tell you. Actually listen. Because it's the truth and I wouldn't lie to you about this. I *never* lied to you about anything."

"Okay." Every inch of Fazil's body stung.

"I never, ever cheated on you," Todd said. "Not once."

"But..." Todd lifted his chin and the words died in Fazil's throat.

"Never."

That couldn't be true. He had a list! He'd heard the stories! "But I—"

"Not once," Todd ground out. "You can't say the same."

Oh God. Todd knew about that? Fazil thumped back against his chair.

A nod and a grimly satisfied look. "Yeah, I saw you sucking Debbie's tonsils down your throat behind the gym."

Oh fuck. Yeah, he knew. He'd been mad at Todd at the time. Rumor had it he'd spent the weekend with Susan Finnegan and, well, Debbie had been on him for ages to go out, so why not? They'd kissed, and he'd gone back to her house and knocked one out of the park, so to speak. His first time with a girl.

She hadn't been the only one, either, in retribution for the times Todd had cheated.

I never cheated on you.

Todd's anger, hurt, and righteousness sucked the air from Fazil. "Not once?" He'd never felt so cold in a crowded restaurant.

Todd put his elbows on the table and dropped his head into his hands. "Oh God, Z. You believed them? You fucking believed all those stories?"

He had. Every last one. Fazil couldn't breathe. The whole world shifted into some horrible reality where he was the villain.

The waitress dropped off their waters and paused, her cheeks paling. "I'll, uh, give you two more time to look over the menu."

They hadn't even touched the menus. Fazil's hand shook as he reached for his water. He drank a little to wash the bile back down his throat.

Todd hadn't cheated. Ever. Fazil had, though. Several times. He couldn't feel his heart—probably because he didn't have one anymore.

"I don't know whether to laugh or cry." Todd looked like he might do either. "Fifteen years," he muttered. "You fucking *asshole*."

Fazil stared down at his menu and flipped it open, tears in his eyes. He *never* cried over Todd, not since he'd arrived at Stanford that August day so long ago. He'd been alone

then, and he'd cried for everything Todd had put him
through just to get it out of his system. Put it behind him.

It hadn't been Todd who'd put him through all that
pain. It had been *him*. *Oh my God.* "I can't..." His voice
caught and then a tear fell, and another. He wiped at his
eyes when they kept falling. "I don't think I'm hungry." Yep.
Asshole. Todd had gotten that right.

Silence from the other side of the table, then a sigh.
"They make good burgers here."

Fazil looked up. There was moisture in Todd's eyes, too.
"Yeah?"

"Yeah. You should try one." The sweetness in Todd's
voice, that hint of forgiveness.

Shit. He wasn't going to lose it anymore than he had, not
here. Maybe when he was back in the hotel room. "Bacon
cheeseburger, then."

Last thing he wanted was forgiveness. He didn't deserve
that, not if what Todd said was true.

Todd took the menu from him. Fazil clung to his water
glass and combed his brain to find any memory that pointed
to Todd lying. His heart flayed itself in his chest and burned
his lungs.

The waitress came and Todd ordered for both of them.
Fazil still couldn't get his mouth to work right. The only
memories there were the times he'd cheated on Todd in
retribution for infidelity that had apparently never
happened. "I..." Words were meaningless. *I'm sorry* had no
weight, no reality. It couldn't change the time that had
passed, nor any of the actions he'd taken. "But you hung out
with them! I saw you!" The guys. The girls. Everyone who
turned Todd's eyes, everyone who would have been better
than the awkward Fazil, with his weird name, odd food, and

way too geeky interests. "You'd go out with them. Drive them home. Do more, from what I heard."

Todd tilted his head. "Oh, Z." Sorrow lay there, but the anger was gone, and that was something amazing, because forgiveness was also out of the realm of possibility.

Todd reached across and touched one of the hands Fazil had wrapped around his ice water. "Come on, you'll freeze your fingers off."

He let Todd pry one of his hands free, let him hold it to warm it up. Eventually Fazil let go of the glass entirely. "It's not cold enough to do that."

"Mmm-hmm." Todd's smile was small and sad. "Just go with it, Z."

Todd was holding his hand. Why, he wasn't sure.

A gentle squeeze. "Yeah, I hung out with other people. Especially when you got snappish and weird. Most of the time you *told* me to go off with them, so I did. Figured you didn't want me around. And yeah, if someone asked me to go out with the group, I did. It was better than sitting at home alone. Yes, a couple of the girls flirted with me and sat on my lap, and I kissed a few on the cheek—as a *friend*."

That did match up with Fazil's memories. Todd fluctuated between social circles. Guys and some of the girls liked him because he knew cars—really knew them—and Todd had always been stunning to look at. Working at the garage kept him in shape. He'd gotten shit for being a grease monkey, but also appreciative looks. Both had driven Fazil crazy, but the later made him jealous and... small. "I guess I did do that."

"I never understood why."

Oh, now, that was easy. "Any one of them would have been a better choice than me."

Todd looked like Fazil had hit him with a brick made from confusion. "You—what?"

Their meals arrived and Todd let go of his hand. That only served to remind him exactly how far apart they were.

When the server slid a burger and fries in front of Fazil, his stomach rumbled. He hadn't been hungry—he still felt more than a little queasy—but he could eat. Probably help his shaking hands.

Nothing was going to put his mind back together any time soon. After half the burger, he steeled himself and studied Todd. Those blue eyes watched him in return. Gone was the hurt that had been there, but God only knew why.

Fazil took a sip of his water. "Thank you for ordering. I wasn't—I couldn't..." The right words were still out of reach. Everything ached, including his head.

"I know," Todd said. "But you needed to eat. We both did."

Fazil poked as his fries. "I was this ugly, scrawny kid with a weird name and parents who talked strangely. I never understood why you liked me." Or why Todd had kissed him. Sucked him off. Made him come. *Any* of it.

Todd's brow furrowed. "You weren't ugly. Or scrawny." He inspected his burger. "And I liked you because you were fun. Clever. You didn't think I was an idiot, and we liked a lot of the same things. Music. Books."

They had gotten along well. Shared comics and paperbacks. Played games on the PlayStation. Peas in a pod, Todd's mother had said. The best of friends. It's why Todd wanted them to stay together after graduation.

Fazil ate until he couldn't stuff any more into his gut, then looked up. "I had the roundest moon face. I tripped over my own feet, and there was my name."

"There's nothing wrong with your name. And don't listen to that fuckface Nathan, either." Todd dunked a fry into some ketchup. "You really never saw yourself back then, did you? So many of the girls wanted you. I saw it, Z. Hot. Smart. Well-off parents. Teachers liked you, so you got away with the shit other kids couldn't."

"Hey, so did you."

Todd's eyebrows lifted. "I held the record for detentions that year. I was the bad influence, the troublemaker. The kid from the wrong side of the tracks."

He had lived on the other side of the tracks from Fazil, but many kids had. Fazil rolled his eyes.

"You had a lot less reason to like me than the other way around." Todd picked up another fry. "You were—and still are—stunning."

"I'm..." He laughed, but it was a bitter thing. "Apparently I was a grade-A fuckup and a righteous asshole."

Todd shrugged. "You were seventeen. We both were."

"It wasn't just with Debbie." He'd kept a list of his own exploits, too. Like a damn fool.

"I know," Todd said. "You were never good at being stealthy or coy."

Fazil rubbed his forehead and fought the urge to tear up again. *God.* If he could go back in time. "You never? Not with anyone? What about Susan?"

"Nope. Only you, until you left." He paused. "I know what was said about Susan and me. There was a night I crashed at her place—on the couch—because we'd been up talking too late. She was gay, too. Well... lesbian, but we had something in common, and it was worse for her, so we let those rumors fly. It protected her. From her family. From the jackasses."

Well, didn't that just make him feel lower than the dirt. His chest felt like shredded glass. "I'm sorry seems so trite."

"That's because it is."

Fazil flinched. "I don't know what else to say. What do you want me to do?" He paused. "You were always so good at deciding things for me."

"I don't want you to say *anything*," Todd said. "Just understand the *truth*, Z. Accept it."

Fine. Fazil rubbed his temples, which hurt like hell. He had no choice, because it *was* the truth. "Where does that leave us now?"

"Sitting in a restaurant in Seattle," Todd said. "Where do you want to go now?"

Home. Or back to the hotel. Away from this—except the pain and his past were part of his skin and bones now. He couldn't trust his memories, couldn't trust what he'd remembered of Todd.

I never lied to you about anything. But Fazil had lied to Todd. Lied to himself, too.

If he couldn't trust himself, maybe he could trust Todd for a change. He'd always had their best interests at heart, even when his plans stretched out years into the future. "I could use a beer."

Todd flagged down the waitress, but rather than order a drink, he asked for the check. "Change of scenery. You want to see some of Seattle? I'll take you to my part of town, then you can figure out what you want to do from there."

Once more, Todd paid, but rather than go directly back to the car, he took Fazil's hand. "Let's walk a little. It'd be good for both of us."

Warm fingers and a soft grip. Fazil's heart somersaulted, and his chest ached. "Okay." It came out as a whisper. He'd follow where he was led, like old times. Todd's fingers entwined with his, and Fazil's muscles unwound as they explored the market. Bright colors, interesting scents, and plenty of cool things to look at. Sometimes Todd pulled him to a stop—other times Fazil did and they chatted about whatever was in front of them. Food. Knickknacks. Carvings.

Their tastes overlapped, as before. Todd tended toward more colorful items that bordered on garish, while Fazil enjoyed more sedate things. The funny, the whimsical, and the stunning? They both enjoyed those.

If Fazil had met Todd in a bar or a coffee shop, he'd have been taken immediately by his charm and smile.

But they had this past that choked and tightened and threatened to drown Fazil. *I have it all worked out, Z. You go to college nearby, and go into teaching. I'll take over my father's garage. We can be like this forever.*

Some plans were wrong from the start.

They wandered into a comic shop, and for a moment, Fazil was back in high school, buying books for Todd. The memory was like an ice pick to his spine, because everything was *wrong* now. He'd been a horrible, awful, cheating person. Fazil had broken his own heart. So easy to run from Todd, but how could he get away from himself?

He couldn't find the breath he needed.

Todd gripped his shoulder. "How about that beer?"

"Sure," Fazil whispered.

"It's going to be okay."

Fazil followed Todd from the shop. No, it wasn't. It would never, ever be okay. Everything was broken.

CHAPTER EIGHT

Todd could have chosen another bar, but a part of him was fucking furious at the quivering contradiction that was Fazil. So here they were, at the hottest club on Capitol Hill, packed in with beautiful men dancing and flirting and kissing. It was staffed by even more gorgeous men wearing outfits that were a jacket shy of a full tux.

This place would have had him salivating and hard when he'd been nineteen. Fazil? He looked positively dazed.

Todd had never scored here, but only because he'd overdone the whole hookup thing after Fazil had left. While the sex had been okay—and occasionally mind-numbingly good—that whole time had left him hollow and jittery, as if he'd been on something. In a way, he had. Not alcohol or drugs. Todd had drowned his sorrow in fucking and being fucked by men. Lots and lots of men.

Not all of the trips had been good. He'd only pulled out of that life thanks to a chance encounter with a doctor named Martin. Bless his soul, wherever he was now.

"Wow." Fazil's eyes were wide—but at least they

weren't moist. Somewhere along the line, he'd put himself back together.

"Wait until you try the drinks." They made their way to the bar and Todd ordered. The cocktails were served with a smile and a wink, and then they were back into the crowd, brushing past leather, silk, linen, business clothes, casual clothes—and them.

Todd hurt, the pain as deep as the marrow of his bones. All those wasted years!

Maybe this *was* revenge against the guy with self-esteem issues who'd fucked his way through their high school friends and had the audacity to be mad at Todd for doing the same thing, *when he hadn't at all.*

"Todd," Fazil said. "This isn't a beer."

"It's still a fucking drink." Fazil had believed every lie the little shits had spread about him. His "conquests." All the stories of the *women* he'd had, because of course, a brainless idiot brute like him was only good for one thing. He took a swallow of his drink and didn't taste it at all.

"Why are we here?" Fazil sniffed his drink and sipped. "I mean..." He waved his hand. "This isn't quite what I had in mind."

"You rarely ever say what you have in mind."

Fazil looked at the floor, his brow furrowed and his knuckles white around his drink. "You rarely ever let me."

Oh bullshit. "This is part of Seattle. Part of my life."

Fazil took a longer drink and looked around the club.

"You left me, Z."

That made him jump. Not much, but enough. He focused everywhere but on Todd. "I went to college. I didn't leave you on purpose." Fazil's cheeks flushed, as they always did when he lied.

"In California." Todd stepped closer and lowered his

voice. "You had offers from MIT, Cornell, and Carnegie Mellon, plus the University of Pennsylvania... but you chose the school in *California*."

"Stanford's a great place." Fazil swallowed and looked into his drink. "One of the best."

"So were the others."

"I didn't *leave* you, Todd. I—"

Todd gripped Fazil's chin, tilted it up, and stepped in so Fazil had no choice but to look him in the eyes. "Why Stanford, Z?" A whisper of words.

The mask cracked, just as it had at dinner and the truth, the painful, *ugly* truth poured out between gritted teeth. "Because you couldn't drive there."

"And I was too poor to fly." They managed okay with the shop, but it didn't leave much for luxuries like new *anything*, let alone a ticket to California. He'd thought about driving across the country, but that would have cost too much, between the gas and keeping his beater on the road.

Later, after he'd gotten a job out there, he'd made that trip.

Fazil tried to nod, but couldn't manage much movement against Todd's hand. "I *ran*. I didn't leave, I ran from you." The last word was rougher than sand.

Todd tightened his grip. "Why?" Anguish in his heart. He knew the answer. Everything Fazil believed had been built on a trash pile of lies. That's where kids like Todd belonged. Not in college. Not in engineering, and certainly not in Fazil's bed.

"I was sick of having my heart broken every time you left!" A couple near them started and looked their way.

"When *I* left?" Todd's grip was iron strong.

Fazil exhaled and spoke without yelling this time. "*Fine.*

When I pushed you away. But you had our whole lives planned out, and I knew the moment you saw someone better, cuter, or prettier, you'd be gone. So I left. Ran from you before you could break me again."

Todd let go. "I never broke you in the first place." Fazil had done that to himself. Beautiful Fazil, who thought he wasn't anything at all.

Fazil shook. Maybe from rage, maybe from the tears that lurked in those moist eyes. "There were so many *better* people in high school." Fazil took a sip of his drink. "You hung out with them all."

"You *slept* with all of them. Is that why? Because they were better than me?"

Fazil paled. "No! I thought you were sleeping around. So I did, too."

He'd never *thought* to ask Todd the truth. Todd shook his head, more at himself than at Fazil. They'd been such dumb teens.

They weren't now, and this had to *end*.

He set his drink down on a table and pulled two twenties out of his wallet. He folded the bills and shoved them into the pocket of Fazil's shirt. "That should be enough for a cab back to your hotel. You can go live your perfect life without me in it. I won't stop you, and once you're gone, I won't bother trying to find you. A clean break."

Fazil worked his jaw, his whole body as tense as a steel cable. "See someone else you like?"

Oh, of *course*. "This act is *old*, Fazil. You haven't listened to *anything* I've said, have you?" He gestured around the bar without looking away. "You see all the men here?"

"Yeah."

"What do you think of them?"

Fazil twisted his face in anger. "They're all hotter than sin."

"They are. You know what? The only man I want right now, the only man I want in my life is the fucking *ass* with forty dollars in his shirt pocket."

Fazil opened and closed his mouth a few times. "I'm an ass?" His cheeks were bright red, but the rest of him was so pale. He might have been trembling, but it was hard to tell over the rhythmic thudding of the dance music.

"You've always been an ass, Fazil. And I..." Todd's voice cracked, like his heart had. Like it always would. He blinked a few times. "Z, I've missed you every day for fifteen *fucking* years."

Fazil set down his drink on the table and, yes, his hands were shaking. "Then take me home." He stepped close to Todd. "Take me home, Todd."

He slid his fingers into Fazil's hair and took his lips and kissed him like he used to, back when they couldn't get enough of each other. They might as well have been hiding in the woods near his parent's house rather than in the middle of a club in Seattle. Fazil opened to his tongue and pressed into his body. His ass of a friend, his beautiful Fazil.

They say you can't go home again. Yet here they both were. He'd missed it so much.

It took Todd too long to get his apartment door unlocked, which meant Fazil wasn't in his arms, their bodies twined together, hands exploring each other like this was all new.

Thirty-three was so different from seventeen and

eighteen. No awkward fumbling. They both knew what they wanted and how to get it. As soon as they made it into the apartment, Todd threw the lock and pulled Fazil against him. Their lips met and Fazil slid his hands under Todd's shirt.

That move was familiar, though. Fazil grazed his fingers over Todd's abs and up his sides. More demanding, but still classic Fazil. All of the places that had made Fazil gasp and twist in Todd's arms—they were still there. He nibbled at Fazil's collarbone, and Fazil bit out a long, breathy moan. In return, Fazil found the small of Todd's back, slipped his hand past the waistband of his jeans and briefs, and ran his finger lightly down to the top of his crack.

He shuddered. No guy had ever touched him so lightly or so easily.

"I don't even know if you're a top or a bottom." He spoke against Fazil's neck.

They'd never fucked anally. Too scared to try back then. But the year after Fazil had left—oh, had Todd tried. So many times. Enough that he knew what he liked.

"Both. Either." Fazil's reply vibrated through him.

A switch? "Good." He sucked Fazil's earlobe. "So you won't mind if I fuck you down into the mattress tonight?"

He didn't give Fazil a chance to answer, devouring his hot mouth and swallowing his moans. Given the way Fazil rocked his erection against Todd's, the answer was obvious. He rammed Fazil up against the nearest wall and ground into him until those moans became throaty whimpers.

Teen Fazil wouldn't have had both hands down the back of Todd's pants, wouldn't have been practically rutting himself against Todd at the thought of being fucked up the ass.

When they came up for air, Fazil's voice was breathy

and soft and so *very* sexy. "God, please. Bed now." His pupils were large in the dim light. "I want you so bad."

With shaking fingers, Todd worked Fazil's button-down shirt open. "Good. 'Cause you're going to have me. Deep and hard." He'd only been fantasizing about this particular moment how long?

Fazil tugged Todd's t-shirt upward. "Too many clothes. Not enough mattress." Up and off that came, and landed somewhere in the room behind Todd.

Good idea. He pushed Fazil's shirt off his shoulders and yanked down until Fazil's hands were trapped in the sleeves behind his back. Oh, the gasp when he pushed Fazil back against the wall, his knee pressing against Fazil's cock. "You going to behave tonight?" He sucked on Fazil's neck, then bit down.

"Fuck." Fazil twisted and moaned. "Really depends." His words came in gasps. "Want me good or want me bad?"

"Bad. Want you bad, Z." Somehow, Fazil freed his hands and cupped Todd's face, devouring his lips and tongue. He rolled himself against Todd's thigh.

Todd found the button and the zipper of Fazil's jeans and had those open and that thick cock in his hand before Fazil even came up for air.

A few strokes later, Fazil threw back his head. "Close. Too close."

"Tough." Todd had him up against the wall, and kept jacking him off. He wanted to see that abandonment, the moment when he made Fazil come, wanted to feel his seed on his hand, see it on their jeans. Needed that control—and Fazil's mouthwatering groans.

He got it all: the hot rush of semen, Fazil's uncontrolled quaking, and that perfect moment of ecstasy etched on his face when he cried out.

Fazil rocked into Todd's hand, even after he'd come. When he opened his eyes, they were practically all pupil.

"Now, there's my Fazil."

Fazil coughed a laugh and his breath was deep as sin. "That sure as shit better not be all tonight."

"Just the appetizer." He took that mouth for a moment and then picked Fazil up in a fireman's carry.

That pushed the breath from Fazil. "Oh my God, you're not going to—"

"Carry you into my bedroom, throw you down, and fuck you? Damn straight I am."

He didn't even care that Fazil's jizz got all over his chest. He'd make him lick it off later.

"You were never like this before."

Todd marched into his bedroom. "Well, you missed a lot." He tossed Fazil onto his bed. And wasn't that a perfect sight? Hair mussed, chest flushed, and his softening cock hanging out of semen-stained jeans.

"I'm going to pay for that, aren't I?"

Todd could only smile. He pulled Fazil's shoes off and stripped the jeans and briefs, too, and that was even better— Fazil naked on his bedspread. He'd filled out in all the good ways over the years. Lean and strong. Gorgeous.

His.

At least for tonight. They'd have to take every day one at a time. But right now? "There's lube in the nightstand," he said. "Why don't you get it out and get yourself ready?"

Fazil's lips parted and his breath hitched, and wouldn't you know it, his cock stirred.

"Ever done that before? Finger fuck yourself?"

Despite the flush that had risen up his neck, Fazil laughed. "Plenty of times. With more than my fingers, too."

The image of Fazil fucking himself with a toy—any toy
—pulled a groan from Todd. "Love to see that."

"I bet you would." Fazil flipped over and crawled up far
enough to reach the nightstand, his ass in the air the entire
time. He slid open the drawer. "Condoms, too? Or are you
just going to watch?"

"Yes condoms. The box, Z. I intend to go through them
before morning."

Fazil's turn to moan. He looked over his shoulder, a
picture of need and desire and longing. "Promise?"

"*Now*, Z." Todd kicked off his shoes, undid his pants,
and pushed everything down. Naked, he stepped close to
the bed. Fazil handed him the box but kept the bottle.

"Knees or back?" There was that wicked grin Todd
remembered.

"Knees," Todd whispered, and stroked himself. This
was going to be interesting.

Fazil lubed up his fingers, knelt, then settled down onto
one elbow, his legs spread wide. Without any hesitation, he
stroked his crack and hole, spreading the slick around his
ring, and teasing it—teasing Todd, too, with tiny moans.
After a second application of lube, Fazil stroked his
entrance and pressed a finger in. Very... slowly.

Todd stopped moving, stopped fisting his cock, and
watched Fazil's finger slide inside as far as he could manage.
The guttural groan of pleasure from Fazil almost undid
Todd. Fazil slid his finger out as slowly, then pushed it in
with more force. The third time, he twisted two fingers in
and started fucking himself in earnest, his grunts and moans
filling the room.

Todd stroked himself to the same rhythm. If he kept it
up, he'd shoot his load at the foot of the bed, not while
buried in Fazil.

He wanted Z, to be on him and inside him.

Maybe he made a sound, because Fazil chuckled. "Like what you see?"

"Yeah. It's fucking dirty." He got a condom out, rolled it over his dick, and knelt on the bed behind Fazil. He ran a hand over one of his ass cheeks. Fazil hadn't stopped finger-fucking himself, and this close, it was even hotter. "Keep going," Todd said, and took Fazil's balls in his hand.

The rhythm slipped, as did Fazil's breathing. "Oh... God. Todd."

"Trouble?"

"N-no." He pumped faster.

Todd slid up higher and gripped Fazil's shaft. "You're nice and hard again." A few strokes and Fazil collapsed, his fingers slipping free. "Can't— Please, just—" He buried his face into the pillow.

Oh yeah, Fazil was ready. Todd found the lube half under Fazil's chest and prepped his cock, then pressed the head against Fazil's hole. "Why don't you fuck yourself on me?"

There was a dark shake of laughter—and Fazil pushed back, taking the tip of Todd's cock inside.

Fuck. Hot and tight. He was about to thrust in, when Fazil grunted and bucked back farther. Enough of that. Todd gripped Fazil's hips and slammed the rest of the way in. They both groaned.

"Oh, fuck yes." Breathless words—and not his.

Well, if that wasn't an invitation for more... Todd pulled out and plunged back in deep. He pressed hard against Fazil, planting a hand on either side of his chest. "All the way down."

A hitch of a moan, and Fazil slid to his stomach.

Todd let his full weight rest on top of Fazil and

stretched Fazil's arms out above his head, flesh to flesh. He curled his fingers between Fazil's and rocked slowly, moving only a fraction inside Fazil's tight heat. Beneath him, Fazil shook and squirmed, his gasps absolutely delicious.

All his at last. Every inch. "Like the way I feel inside you?"

"God, yeah." Fazil rocked and clenched around Todd's dick, obviously wanting far more than the tiny movement Todd was giving him. "Why didn't we do this before?"

Oh, Z, you little shit. Todd lifted his hips and drove into Fazil, grinding in as deep as he could go. "Because you left me before we could." Todd rose and slammed into Fazil again.

Fazil's long groan was halfway to a sob.

He hovered above Fazil. "Do you want me to stop?"

"No." As if to punctuate that, Fazil rocked back against Todd, his body feverishly hot.

"Good." He let go of Fazil's hands and pushed up to gain leverage and power. "Fifteen years, Fazil. You're going to take every bit of that, too. Until I come."

He shuddered. "Todd?"

"Yeah?"

"Shut up and fuck me."

With pleasure.

He did just that, slow at first, then picking up the tempo and force until he was pounding into Fazil, the bed beneath them creaking protests in counterpoint to Fazil's hiccupped moans.

Fazil curled his hands into white-knuckled fists full of comforter when Todd slipped from hard fucking into brutal. Through it all, Fazil moved with him, rocking back, again and again, answering Todd with acceptance and a demand for more.

So he gave in and let his anger and frustration fuel that fire, used it to grind deep and hard into the man he'd wanted for so long. All the missed birthdays. The unanswered e-mails. The ringing phone clicking over to voice mail. Every minute and moment of loss and longing, he pounded into Fazil until the moans became sobs and Fazil's fists uncurled and flattened against the mattress.

"Oh, God." Despite the tears in his voice, Fazil pushed himself up. "Don't stop, I'm gonna..." Fazil shuddered and came, tightening so hard around Todd's cock that he could barely move.

Didn't stop Todd from trying. He slammed against Fazil, blood pounding in his ears and Fazil's tears making his head swirl. He chased the oblivion Fazil had found. In a blinding moment of light, there it was, and his whole body felt like fire. Painful. Perfect. He collapsed onto Fazil, burying himself inside his long, trembling body.

Minutes passed as both their breathing returned to something close to normal. He should have felt horrible—but all that he found was relief. Fazil was in his bed and well fucked as he damn well should have been after all this time.

"I need to..." He pulled himself out of Fazil before he softened too much, and stumbled off to the bathroom to get rid of the condom. He grabbed a towel and returned. Fazil hadn't moved much, only enough to pillow his head on his arms.

His face was wet with tears, but there wasn't any anger there, nor any sadness. Todd couldn't quite make out exactly what emotion hid behind those very dark eyes.

"Hey." Todd sat gently on the bed, twisting his hands in the towel, the way his insides were twisting. "You okay?"

"No." Fazil's voice dripped with pain. "No, I'm not okay."

Shit. Todd's heart lodged itself into his throat. He shouldn't have been so rough, not like that. "I didn't mean to hurt you, Z."

If there hadn't been tears in Fazil's eyes and on his cheeks, maybe his expression would have been a smile. Instead, the upward curve of Fazil's lips stabbed at and broke Todd's heart. "You didn't. Not tonight," Fazil whispered. "I did. Fuck, Todd. I cheated. Lied. Left." He rubbed at his eyes and the remorse in his voice was almost unbearable. "I was so wrapped up in myself, in what everyone else thought and said... I didn't see the truth. Blamed you and... Shit." He rolled away. "God, I'm sorry. I'm really... Shit. I should go."

Fazil scrambled off the bed, and Todd's world crumbled. *No. Not again.* "Fazil. *Stop.*"

This time, he did. He stood breathing as if he'd run a marathon, his jeans clutched vaguely in his hand.

Fazil *was* sorry. It was in his every breath, in the wild beat of his pulse, and in the tears on his skin and in his eyes. It was the apology Todd should have heard *years* ago.

It wasn't too little, and it certainly wasn't too late. They were both older now and they could handle this. Todd strode to Fazil, turned him around, and pulled him into his arms.

Fazil trembled, his breath little bursts of heat against Todd's shoulder. So much pain and anguish, all from a past they both shared. They'd been *kids.*

Yeah, he hurt, too. But they both needed to get over that. He kissed Fazil's shoulder. "It's okay."

"It's not okay." Fazil pulled away, but only a little. "How can any of this be okay?" He gestured around the room.

"You're here. I'm here." That's all he'd wanted back then. The two of them together. He'd told Fazil that over and over. "This isn't high school. Everything's behind us."

"High school. God." Fazil's laugh was heartbreaking. "Even then, you deserved someone better than a self-absorbed prick like me."

Todd brushed moisture from Fazil's cheek. "Z, we were all self-absorbed pricks back then."

Fazil met Todd's gaze, his eyes still wet. "I never grew out of it."

He cupped Fazil's face with one hand. "I don't know. Maybe you did."

Something shifted in those deep brown eyes. His lips parted, and his breathing slowed to a more normal rate. "I screwed you over. Why are you so nice to me?"

He kissed Fazil. A sweet sip of his lips. "You really don't know?"

A shake of his head.

Todd took Fazil into his arms and held him close, pressing his mouth against Fazil's shoulder. He raised his head enough to speak, his lips skimming over skin. "Because I love you. I always have."

Fazil broke. No sound, but he trembled and shook. Hot tears dripped onto Todd's skin. Fazil held on to Todd as if there wasn't anything else keeping him upright.

There might not have been. His Fazil, whom he'd loved and hated and loved again. He scooped him up and carried him back to bed. The bedspread was a mess, but the sheets underneath were dry, and with the two of them, that was enough. He turned off the light and held Fazil tight.

"Can we start over?" A broken whisper in the dark.

The past wouldn't ever leave them. "No." But it didn't have to trap them. He kissed Fazil's forehead. "But we *can* start again."

They could. Tomorrow they would. Rebuild from the ground up. They were older and stronger and now—at last—they both were on the same page.

Please.

CHAPTER NINE

FAZIL WOKE TO SUNLIGHT SLIPPING PAST A CURTAIN and shining on his face. The curtains weren't his, nor were they the hotel's. This room contained personal things that didn't belong to him but felt so familiar.

His body ached all over, but in that delightful way after a night spent being fucked into oblivion. Too bad his head and heart felt like he'd been scraped over a cheese grater.

He was in Todd's room. In his bed. The memories came back in a rush. What he'd learned about himself. The shit he'd done. If he could scoop the sheer horror of his past from his soul with a melon baller, he would have. A lovely little garnish for some fancy dinner party: the horrible sins of Fazil Kurt, who abandoned his best friend and his first love. Cheated on him, then ran away. The consummate and complete asshole.

He buried his face into a pillow that smelled of Todd. He'd wanted to go to Stanford more than any other school, but he could have stayed in touch. Should have. Or tried talking rather than vanishing. He groaned into the pillow.

That's probably what woke Todd, or maybe he'd been awake before that. Fazil felt a warm caress against his back. "Hey."

Couldn't put this off, so he rolled onto his side. Even mussed with sleep, Todd glowed. His eyes, the tousled hair, the scruff, everything. "Hi."

A sleepy smile. Todd brushed his fingers over Fazil's jaw. "How do you feel?"

"Okay? I guess?"

The smile faded. "You guess?" Todd shifted closer and motioned for Fazil to come nearer.

He did. More than anything right now, he wanted to be held. The day wanted to shred, like tattered threads. If he moved too fast, he might rip open the fabric of the universe. "Last night—it was..." He couldn't wrap his brain around it.

Todd pulled him close and kissed his forehead.

So much had been good. The joy of kissing Todd, the way he'd made Fazil's body sing with need. He hadn't managed to come twice that quickly in some time, though he'd certainly tried without much success.

The delicious depravity of finger-fucking his ass while Todd watched—they'd both been pretty shy about anal as teens, not even venturing close to it. He'd liked Todd watching. So had Todd. The sex had been glorious and hard, exactly the way he enjoyed it, especially when guilt gnawed at his head.

Now he knew he'd torn Todd apart all those years ago. Part of the heat and fierceness of that sex had been anger and pain and too many years stretched thin.

Fazil's fault. All of it.

His best night was wrapped around one of his worst. Fazil pressed lips against Todd's chest. "I don't know how to make up for what I did."

"You don't have to." Todd brushed the hair from Fazil's eyes. "Or rather, you did already."

"Huh." He found Todd's hip, and let his hand rest on his warm flesh. "Does that mean I have to make you that angry if I want you to fuck me like that again?" Tears ached at the back of his throat. "Because I really don't want..." His voice cracked.

Todd kissed him, and that kept the moisture in Fazil's eyes. "I'll fuck you like that any time you want."

"Good. I'm gonna want that again."

Todd chuckled and rolled them both over so that he lay on top of Fazil, and given the thickness of his dick against Fazil's thigh, Fazil wasn't the only one with morning wood.

"I thought you said you were a switch? Or at least implied?"

"Depends on the person. With women, it's almost a given that I'm going to be fucking them."

"Almost?" Todd's grin was lecherous, and Fazil coughed a laugh.

"Yeah. Well, I do like being fucked in the ass."

Todd shifted, then rocked into Fazil, their cocks sliding against each other. "Hadn't noticed."

Damn, that felt good. He moaned. They'd gotten each other off so many times like this.

"And you like toys?"

"Mmm-hmm." Hard to think with Todd grinding down on him. Fazil bucked in rhythm with Todd.

"Being fucked by women?"

"Oh, God, yeah. There's something pretty hot about that." He tangled his hands into Todd's hair. "This—is hotter, though." He pulled Todd down for a kiss, though his breath caught when Todd wrapped a hand around their dicks. He groaned, and came up for air.

"Familiar, huh?" Todd kissed his neck.

"Yeah." Just like old times. The pit in his stomach opened, despite the tumble of heat in his blood, the tightness in his balls. "Todd..." he whispered.

"Shh. It wasn't all bad between us back then, was it?"

"N-no." Fuck, he was getting close. How did Todd do that? Pull orgasms from him so well?

The only consolation was that Todd was breathless, too, and sweat beaded his forehead. He nipped the skin on Fazil's chest. "Could do this forever."

"Please." He kissed Todd again. On the lips, on the neck —anywhere he could get his mouth—while they slid and thrust and tangled against each other until they were both full of moans and whimpers and curses and long kisses.

It was heaven to have Todd like this. It always had been, from the first time they'd made love to now. And yeah, it hadn't been all bad. They'd always done well in bed. When they were in each other's arms and minds and the world was gone but for heat and light and desire.

How long they both hovered on that edge, he had no idea, just that bliss remained a moment away. This time, it was Todd who got there first. "Oh Fuck, Z." He fisted both their cocks, thrusting frantically.

Fazil found his shoulder and bit down into the muscle. Todd shouted and came—and the sight pushed Fazil completely over the edge into his own orgasm.

When they both could breathe again, Todd laughed. "Guess I didn't need all those condoms after all."

"Guess not." He couldn't help the grin. The soul-crushing ache of his past had faded into something he could ignore for now—especially when Todd smiled at him like that. "Don't mind. This is fine, too."

"Yeah." Todd's hand was wet with their combined jizz. "Bit messy, though." He ran a finger over Fazil's lips, and Fazil sucked the digit in without thought. Musky and salty. He groaned in the back of his throat and let Todd feed him another slick finger, then another. Todd finger-fucking his mouth until they all were licked clean.

"Jesus, Z. When did you get so dirty?"

"First time I swallowed your come." He pulled Todd into a long, deep kiss full of biting and tongue, until they both came up for air.

"When you fucked yourself last night, I thought I might blow my load right there." Todd stroked his cheek. "You didn't learn that from me."

"No." It was weird talking about a past lover with the taste of the current one in his mouth. But it was Todd. His first. "I had a boyfriend who really liked using dildos on me. I liked it, too—but part of what got me was seeing how hard *he* got off, you know?"

"Yeah. The pleasure of your partner's pleasure."

"Exactly. So I figured if he got off that hard from fucking me with toys, how much better would it be for him if I fucked myself while he watched?"

"I'm guessing that worked?"

"Oh, yeah. Turned out, it got me off really hard, too."

"Well," Todd said, sitting up. "I do own an extra cock."

If he hadn't just come, Fazil might have gotten hard at that. As it was, his blood heated and his mouth dried. "You do?"

Todd nodded. "And if you're lucky, maybe I'll take it out tonight." He paused. "Or Sunday. We'll see." His grin was devilish and perfect.

"So you're not going to throw me out on the street?"

His expression softened. "No, Z." Sad words.

Guilt surfaced in a sudden rush, chilling him from the inside and turning his stomach. "Oh God." He pressed a hand over his mouth. No use apologizing again.

Todd held out his hand, and when Fazil took it, Todd pulled him up and straight into his arms. "I told you. It's going to be all right. Promise."

Right. "Start again."

"Yeah." He kissed Fazil's neck and whispered into his ear. "It's a green-and-purple dragon dildo."

For a second Fazil couldn't breathe. Then the giggles came. "You—have one of *those*?"

Todd blushed but nodded. "I've never used it. It was a gag gift from former coworkers when I left. Something to embarrass the snot out of me."

"Did it?"

"Not as much as it did them when I chased them around the office with it hanging out of my pants."

"You didn't!" He could almost picture that, though.

Todd put his hand over his heart and held up two fingers. "Scout's honor!"

Fazil smacked his shoulder. "You were never a Boy Scout."

Todd chuckled. "I was! For a year after I turned eleven." His smile wilted. "But even then, I think people knew I was gay." He looked away. "That's why I worked so hard at the shop. No one would think a gearhead was a fag, right?"

The word thudded across Fazil's chest and lodged in his heart. "Did you get shit for that? I mean in high school?" He didn't remember that. There were rumors about both of them, but no one ever said anything—least of all called him a fag.

Todd sat back on his heels. "A couple of times. That's why I hung out with the girls. Took the heat off if people thought I was *experimenting*." He air-quoted the last word.

Because liking more than one gender was *always* an experiment. Fazil twisted his lips. "You know, bisexuality exists."

"I know. You're not the first bi guy I've dated." He paused. "Actually, you *were* the first bi guy I dated. You know what I mean."

Fazil scooted over until he sat on the edge of the bed. "It's a sore point." He scratched his head. "I thought you were bi, though."

"Nope," Todd said. "Totally gay. Gold star and everything."

Another piece of his past shifted around... and reinforced what Todd had said. Of course he wouldn't have slept with any of the girls. "I wish I had known." Wish they'd talked, except that was his fault, too. He scrubbed his face.

Todd climbed off the bed. "I should have said something. I mean, I *did* let the rumors circulate. I never thought you'd believe them, though." He shook his head. "When you did, I was too hurt to smack you upside the head."

Fazil looked up. "We were really fucked up, weren't we?"

"We were walking bags of hormones attached to brain stems. We were completely fucked up. It's actually a wonder anyone makes it into their twenties."

There was the Todd he'd fallen in love with all those years ago. Older and a hell of a lot wiser than Fazil would ever be. "I missed you."

Todd blinked a few times and swallowed. "Come on." His voice was gravel. "Let's grab a shower, then do something ridiculously touristy, like have brunch in the Space Needle."

"Sounds perfect." He rose and followed Todd to the bathroom.

CHAPTER TEN

Todd took hold of Fazil's hand and savored the warmth. "You're not afraid of heights, are you?"

"Not really." That little tremble in his voice always gave him away.

He gave Fazil's hand a squeeze. "We don't have to eat here."

"It's not heights," Fazil said. "It's falling. As long as I can't fall, I'm fine. So yes to the restaurant."

They headed past the fountain in front of the Space Needle and through the glass doors that led into the gift shop—and to the restaurant reservation desk. After they picked up their passes, they were directed to an elevator.

"What about the observation deck?"

He looked sheepish. "Maybe. I'll need to see. Probably won't go to the edge."

"The outside deck isn't large, but you don't have to go out if you don't want to. Most of it is on the inside."

Fazil exhaled. "I'll know when I get there."

The elevator arrived, and they headed up. Fazil was perfectly fine on the ride up. Still holding Todd's hand and not nervous at all. They were in a box with nice, thick glass windows—not like anyone could slip and fall in the forty-odd seconds it took to get them to the top.

One of the other passengers gave them a side-eye, but Fazil didn't notice—too intent on watching the scenery. Todd straightened to his full height and casually stared back until the guy looked away. *That's right, mister. Mind your own business.* He might not sling tires in a garage, but he still kept in shape enough to be intimidating when he wanted to be.

He wasn't about to put up with bullshit from anyone but Fazil this weekend.

Despite the bumps along the way, the weekend was shaping up. They hadn't lost any of their chemistry in the bedroom. Gained a *bunch.*

The crap from their youth? They were working that out now that Fazil accepted the truth of what happened.

The elevator reached the restaurant and they got out. They strode to the host stand, Todd gave his name, and they were shown in to a window table. So glad he'd remembered you could make reservations online.

"This is nice," Fazil said.

He nodded. "Food's supposed to be good now, too."

"Now?" Fazil cocked his head.

"Yeah, everyone says it used to suck, but that was before I moved here."

Fazil tore himself away from the slowly rotating view. "How long have you lived here?" He studied the table and spoke softly. "I don't know anything about you."

Todd reached across the table and opened his hand. Fazil hesitated a moment, then took it. "There's so much about me that only you know. Things no one else does."

"But there's so much I don't." That lost sadness was back. "My fault, too."

Yeah, it was. He wouldn't let Fazil off for it. "True."

Fazil loosened his grip, but Todd didn't. He stroked his thumb over Fazil's knuckles. "A date, then. We learn about each other—who we are now. What happened in between. All the stuff everyone else who dates has to do."

"Do you *really* want to date me again? After all that?"

He leaned in. "Who else am I going to fuck with a dragon dildo?"

Fazil's breath caught and his eyes widened. If Todd had to guess, Fazil's pants were tighter, too. "Well, there is that," Fazil said, his voice rough.

Todd leaned back. That would be something to see, indeed.

A waiter brought orange juice and coffee, and they both spent time looking over the menu. They had to give up each other's hands. When the waiter took their order and left, and they'd downed about half their coffee, Fazil reached for him again.

To be wanted and needed by Fazil was perfect. The on-again-off-again thing had been killer. He'd spent so much time in high school wondering if Z really wanted him or if—yeah—he'd been an experiment.

"How'd you end up in Seattle?"

Long story. He glanced out the window at the buildings of his new hometown slowly sliding past them. "After I graduated college, I got a job at a company in Philly. Entry-level programming. Didn't pay much, but enough. More than I brought in at the garage. After a year, they were bought by a larger company." He took a sip of coffee and the dark taste matched his memory. "They said we could either move to Los Angeles or lose our jobs."

Fazil gave his hand a squeeze. "That's pretty shitty. I'm not sure I would have moved for a company that did that."

Todd's stomach flipped. Up until this moment, he'd blanked out the reason he'd gone. He'd never told *anyone* why, other than the money had been good. He freed himself from Fazil's grip and wrapped both hands around his coffee mug. "I almost didn't," he said. "Business at the garage wasn't great. Dad was having a harder time with it, and we'd all realized that I wasn't going to be taking the shop over."

Fazil had flattened his hand against the table. The other was balled into a fist.

There were parts of this that would hurt Z, but that was life. *Their* life. "Luckily, they started building out that part of Warminster. Big-box stores. People buying the older ranch houses, knocking them down, and sticking larger houses on the properties."

An absent nod. "Yeah, last time I went back, some parts were hardly recognizable. They even tore down most of the high school and built a new one."

"Right? Doesn't feel like home anymore." Hadn't since Fazil had left. Todd looked out over the sound. "My parents sold the garage and their house and moved to South Carolina. I went to LA." He slid his gaze back to Fazil and he studied his furrowing brow. "I could have gone somewhere else or gotten another job in Philly. But I had this *hope* that I'd find you. Stanford isn't that far from LA."

Fazil swallowed and paled.

"Obviously I didn't. But on weekends, I'd look. Bars and the like." Whole thing sounded foolish now. "That area's so big."

"Yeah," Fazil said. "It is."

"I sound like a stalker again." He had been, in a way. A

little too obsessed with the friend who'd run. "I don't even know what I'd have done had I found you."

Fazil inspected his coffee. "I wasn't there. I'd moved to Massachusetts for grad school."

Right. Boston. Heat crept up his neck. All those weekends pining over Fazil, who *hadn't even been there*. He'd still been in his fuck-or-be-fucked-by-anyone-who-asked-nicely phase, too. He'd drowned many of those weekends in anonymous sex. That had been one of the things that had driven Martin away.

"God, you must think I'm a fool."

Fazil met his gaze.

And the food arrived. Bad timing. Or good. Todd wanted to crawl under the table.

Neither of them made any move to eat. "I don't think you're a fool," Fazil said. "You were my best friend, and I vanished. Don't..." He gave out a strangled laugh. "Don't blame yourself for *my* shit."

He didn't anymore, but he also had for so long. That was a conversation for another time, because the food smelled fantastic, and there were some parts of his past that required hard liquor to explain.

"Massachusetts? For your masters?"

Fazil nodded and picked up his fork. "Yeah." That reply was soft.

The demure response made no sense. Had to be more, given Fazil's blush. Fazil had either done poorly, or excelled beyond what he thought he deserved. Todd took a bite of his French toast.

The Fazil he'd known would never have failed at academics. Sports? Sure. Remembering to tie his own shoes? Yup. But school? Never. Todd bit his lip to keep from smiling. "Dr. Fazil Kurt?"

Fazil met Todd's gaze with a tiny, pained smile, then went back to eating.

Oh, fucking bingo. "Holy shit, that's awesome! Computer science?"

Fazil cleared his throat. "Yeah."

"Boston University?"

Oh, didn't that darken his cheeks. God, for someone who strived so hard, who'd been pissed off at being *fifth* in his class, Fazil got so damned shy about success. "Out with it!"

"Harvard." It was almost a squeak.

"Dude!" He couldn't help laughing now. "You are so weird. That's fantastic! It's a good thing!"

Fazil exhaled. "I know. I'm really proud of my work, but *please* don't tell anyone. People get really odd around me about the PhD, especially on these jobs. I'm just a guy who wants to help them turn things around. Normal. Ordinary."

Nothing about Fazil was *ordinary*, but he hadn't considered that aspect of Fazil's job, the need to be one of the crew. If he'd come in as Dr. Kurt, guns blazing, no one at Singularity would have listened to him at all. Some people, like that asshole Nathan, were skeptical simply because *Fazil* wasn't Joe or Jack or whatever, but he'd made inroads with other members of the team.

"Do people at your work know?" He poked at the hazelnuts that had fallen off his French toast.

"Sam knows. Eli, too, since they both saw my CV. I don't know about anyone else. We don't use titles at work." He scratched the back of his head.

"And you're not on LinkedIn."

"God, those fucking e-mails. No. Never." Fazil stabbed at his ham-and-cheese omelet.

Todd chuckled at that.

"So?" Fazil waved at the window. "This isn't LA... How'd you end up here?"

"I hated LA. Loathed it. Too dry. Too hot. I wanted somewhere green like home, so I was haunting every site I could find for a job anywhere else. Saw a listing for Singularity Storage, thought Seattle had to be less dry than LA, being rainy most of the time. They liked me, so here I am. Came here three years ago."

Another sip of coffee, then a smile. "It's nice."

"Yeah, Seattle's a great town. Accepting, for the most part. Interesting. Lots of stuff to do..."

"Mountains." Fazil stared off at the horizon.

Todd's heart flipped and he picked up his coffee. *You could stay, Z. Stay with me.* They could finally be together. "Let's try to see as much as we can today and tomorrow. I'm guessing you leave Friday? Or Saturday?"

Fazil touched his juice glass, then hefted it. "Saturday, though..." He shrugged, and sipped.

Wait, what? "Though?"

"I may be here longer. Depends on what Sam works out with your CEO."

The leap in his soul at the prospect of Fazil staying clashed with the *reason* behind it. "Things aren't going as planned."

He blew out a breath. "No."

Shit. "Do you— How can I help?"

"Short of strangling your CFO or making procedures appear out of thin air?"

Oh. He winced.

"It's not horrible. Just means I might be here longer."

"I can live with that part."

That grin again. "I bet you can."

How to juggle Fazil and work, he'd figure out. If it came

to it, there were plenty of other jobs in Seattle. "I have this feeling Mr. Dragon's going to get some use in the near future." The way Fazil squirmed in his seat had Todd hardening in his. He smiled across the table and finished off the rest of his breakfast.

"I should have answered." Fazil's voice was so soft, Todd thought he'd imagined it.

All those lost years. If Fazil had managed a PhD, he hadn't spiraled nearly as badly as Todd had. "Let's let up on that." He didn't want to think about that part of his past. "How many people work for Anderson, anyway?"

Fazil's mood lightened almost instantly. "Seven, including Sam."

Seven? "That's it?"

"Three up front, and four in the back."

"That's..." He'd read about some of the jobs Sam Anderson's team had pulled off. "Seven?"

"Yeah." This grin was shit-eating, which meant Fazil was proud of his work. "We're an odd crew. Mouthy, bratty, really serious when we need to be."

"Like your finance guy?"

"We're all a bit less formal than Eli. Even Sam." Fazil leaned back in his chair. "But everyone's hardworking. We've pulled some long-ass days in that office and had some stellar disappointments. But I wouldn't give it up for the world. Sam is..." Fazil seemed to hunt for words. "He's brilliant."

Todd's breath caught. Fazil glowed. Amazing smile, clear eyes, animated, and none of the weight of their past pressing him down into his chair. Beautiful.

Todd got to take him home tonight. "You're lucky."

"I know." He gestured at the remnants of his ham-and-cheese omelet. "You know I'm not religious, but I wake up almost every morning and thank God Sam called me. I was *dying* at my last job. I hated being a cog in the corporate world, plunking along, not rocking the boat when I saw how things could be improved or fixed or..." Fazil waved. "You know."

He did know. "Pretty well, yeah."

Fazil eyed him, but not as a lover. This was calculated. "You developed most of those procedures you gave me, didn't you?"

"Yup."

"How hard were they to implement?"

Todd's breath caught from the memory of the fights with Stephen, with Nathan, with everyone. Because change was *scary*. Procedures meant they couldn't throw code into the repository and hope it worked. He didn't need to answer. Fazil's lips had set into one hell of a frown.

He knew.

Todd scrubbed his chin. "We didn't have any testing procedures for the longest time. We put out the fires when we noticed them. Easy enough with one customer."

"But when you have two and they want different things..." Fazil's shook his head. "We should *not* be talking about work!"

He had a point. Todd shifted his leg until it touched Fazil's beneath the table and Fazil jumped.

"Yeah, forget work." He ran his calf up Fazil's. "What do you want to do next?"

"You." Fazil breathed the word out. "If we weren't in a restaurant however many fucking feet in the air."

His turn to shiver. An image of Fazil on his knees before him, going to town on his dick, flashed through Todd's mind. Before he could get that picture out of his head or get his cock down to a reasonable size, the waiter brought their desserts and more coffee.

"Enjoy!" Dude winked before he sauntered away, hips moving a bit too jauntily.

Fazil coughed. "I think we might have gotten carried away." He pointed his chin at the table.

Their coffee and two wonderful-looking pastries sat on a very short tablecloth. "Oh." Heat ran through Todd, touching his cheeks, lungs, and—shit—dick, too. He moved his leg back and wrapped it around his chair leg. "Oops."

Fazil picked up his fork. "We're like two horny teens."

His smile was infectious. "We're better than two horny teens."

"How so?"

"We both understand the utter pleasure of delayed gratification."

"Do we now?" Fazil's lips quirked and he slipped a bite of his chocolate what-ever-the-hell-it-was between those full lips of his.

"Oh, I think so," Todd said. "Plus, I'd rather you spend the whole day imagining what I'm going to do to you tonight."

There was that distant look again, but this time coupled with a distinctive flush. "I have a very good imagination."

"So do I." When Fazil met his gaze, Todd grinned. "I guess we'll see how close we come to each other's fantasies."

Fazil reached for his coffee. "Can't wait."

"Ah, but you're going to." Todd started in on his cake. "I promise, you'll love every minute."

He never made promises he couldn't keep.

When Fazil reached for the bill folder, Todd lifted it away.

"At least tell me my share." He had plenty of funds, and could get reimbursed for part of the weekend.

"Nope. My treat." Todd fished out a credit card—a gold one—and stuffed it into the folder. "Don't worry about today." He handed it to the waiter.

He wanted to argue, but Todd gave a small shake of his head and the reasons for splitting the bill—the normal ones —were gone. "You've already paid enough." Fazil wasn't talking about money.

A glimpse of frustration swept across Todd and was gone. "Not all of it was your fault."

But most of it was. "Todd…"

"Z, it's okay."

Yeah, it was. And no, it wasn't. Laughing and turned on one minute because he was with Todd—hot, sexy, funny Todd—then horrified the next because he'd abandoned the friendship for so many years. He still didn't know what had happened to Todd the year after he'd left. Fazil had the feeling it was bad. "I can expense a few things."

"Think Eli's expensing the weekend?"

Not if he was taking horse-riding lessons. "No. But I bet he's paying his way."

The waiter brought back the bill and Todd added a tip and signed. Fazil craned his neck to see the total, but Todd blocked him. "Nope!" The rejection was musical and lighthearted.

"Oh, come on!"

Todd put the pen down and closed the folder. "Look. You paid for everything when we were kids. Most of my comics and books. Movies. Trips to the shore. Our times out, even when we went in a group."

He had. Todd scraped and saved and skimped and barely had enough to put gas in his car—the one he used to drive everyone around in. "But I could. I did it because I could." His mother had once given him fifty bucks to buy Todd a winter jacket that wasn't threadbare. *I worry about him. It's rough for your friend.*

Then he'd left, leaving Todd high and dry. *Shit.*

"Fazil." Todd rose. "I'm paying *because I can.*" He held out his hand. "Come on. Let's see how close you can get to the edge of the outside observation deck."

He scooted out of his chair and took Todd's hand. Why the hell not? Anyone close probably guessed they were a couple.

A couple. His fingers tingled. And followed Todd down a stairwell to the observation deck. The past crashed into the present and mixed with a glimpse of the future Todd had hinted at.

Did he want that? Could he even have it? Todd was here in Seattle and he wasn't. Not for the long run.

They had tonight to play out all of his fantasies, at least. He must have made a noise, because Todd squeezed his hand. "If it's too much we don't have to go outside."

"No." Fazil breathed the word out. "I was thinking about later."

"Oh." Todd shifted his fingers and ran one against Fazil's palm. "How about this—if tonight is not as hot as you imagined, you can pay for everything tomorrow."

Warmth settled in Fazil's core. "Fair." He couldn't imagine anything hotter than what was going through his mind, especially when it came to the mysterious dragon dong and that look Todd had given him during brunch, the one that said, *Knees. Now.*

"But you have to shut up and let me pay for everything

today." An edge to that. Money had always been a sore point.

"Fair as well."

The observation deck was much like the restaurant, except ringed with an outdoor portion. From the inside, it didn't look *too* bad.

Another short set of stairs led to the outside door. Todd paused and pinpricks rose on the back of Fazil's thighs.

"Ready?"

"Yeah." It came out breathless, but Fazil stepped out onto the deck anyway. The needles rose into his ass and up the small of his back. It was *windy*. He eyed the edge— and relaxed. There wasn't any fucking way he could fall off this thing. Sure, it was open to the elements, but entirely enclosed by Plexiglas, safety nets, and wire. "This is fine."

Todd loosened his grip. "Good. The view's fantastic."

Just like in the restaurant, only now he could look down. It should have been terrifying, but it wasn't. They walked around to get away from other tourists and to enjoy the panorama of the city. More walking let them stare out at the sound. Todd let go of Fazil as they gazed out over the water, but only to wrap an arm around Fazil's waist. His warm palm settled against the junction between Fazil's jeans and his t-shirt. Perfect.

Fazil leaned into Todd's chest. They'd never done this in high school— *been* together in public. Todd brushed a kiss against Fazil's temple. "I'm so glad you're here."

"Me too." If only for another week, maybe more. Then he'd be back in Pittsburgh. He tamped down the rising panic at the thought of leaving Todd and wrapped himself in his warmth, the moment, and the beauty of the city, the water, and the mountains.

He couldn't stay in Seattle. But Todd held him. Loved him. Missed him.

You're not good enough for this man. "What's next?"

"I was thinking one of the underground tours," Todd murmured. "I've never done one, but I hear they're fascinating."

"Underground?"

"Part of the city was rebuilt a story or so higher after a fire to prevent flooding and for plumbing reasons. The original street level is still under there."

Holy shit. "That sounds fantastic."

Todd opened space between them. "Like a little history?"

"Oh yeah. Especially that kind of stuff. Bet that was ripe for a different type of underworld." He adored the history of anything subversive. The Whiskey Rebellion. Bootlegging. Speakeasies. Smuggling. Plenty of other cities had underground locations that supported... well, an underground.

They headed back inside to the holding area for the elevator. "That's what I've heard. Opium dens, brothels. All of that." Todd's gaze got distant. "You weren't into history in high school."

"That's because they made it as boring as they could. This stuff is actually *interesting*."

Todd chuckled but didn't say a word.

"What?" Something in the play of his lips made Fazil want to back Todd up against a wall and kiss him until they were both breathless.

"You. I love it when you're passionate. Never saw it with *history* before, that's all. You once told me that moldy old stories were the biggest turnoff *ever*."

Yeah, that did sound like something his younger self would have said. "I may have been wrong."

"May have been?" Todd's cupped the back of Fazil's neck.

Didn't that send a shower of desire cascading over every part of his skin? There were more than a few people watching them. A few weren't—very poignantly. The hell with it. "I was wrong about a lot of things." So many.

Todd grazed Fazil's skin with his fingers. "Good that you changed your mind, isn't it?"

Fazil couldn't breathe. Todd drew close, and they weren't alone. His body met Fazil's, and their lips touched. A gentle kiss, longer than a peck. Not deep, but Fazil melted to his toes and swayed in Todd's arms when they broke it.

Todd took his sweet time letting him go, which was fine. He was having issues getting his pulse under control. Todd had kissed him in public.

There was his quizzical look. "Later." He'd explain later. Especially since the elevator arrived and people were exiting it.

Todd nodded, and Fazil was grateful that their shorthand—the way they read each other—had come back. Or reawakened.

When they got to the bottom and were away from the crowds near the Space Needle, he slowed their walk. "That's the first time I've kissed a guy in public."

Todd's brow furrowed. "You kissed me in the bar last night and in the parking lot at lunch."

"I kissed you in a *gay bar* last night." He'd done that with other guys, too, in places he knew were safe. "And there was no one in that parking lot." There'd been a ton of people by the elevator.

Todd stopped. "You *have* dated other guys, right?"

"Yes," Fazil said. "More women, but I've dated men, too."

"You've never been affectionate in public?"

"I have." He'd held hands. Touched a knee. Hugged. "I've just never *kissed* a guy. In public."

Todd took a breath. "Is Pittsburgh that repressed?"

"No. No more than anywhere else in the northeast." He shook his head. "It's my weirdness." His fear.

"Did you like kissing in public?"

"Oh fuck, yes."

Todd stepped in and kissed him again. Deeper this time, and with his tongue, erasing any thought that doing this wasn't absolutely fine. Todd pulled back and whispered, "Good." After a moment they were walking again.

"Don't get me wrong," Todd said. "There are places we'd get serious side-eye for holding hands. But I don't tend to go to those locations if I can help it."

"So not *entirely* an LGBTQ utopia?"

Todd laughed. "Is anywhere?"

Not yet. "It's getting better every year." Fazil shrugged. "I've gotten the stink-eye for PDAs with girlfriends, so who the hell knows?"

"People," Todd said. "So weird."

Wasn't that the truth? He twined his fingers in Todd's. But this was wonderful.

BENEATH THE STREETS OF SEATTLE, FAZIL PAUSED ON A wooden walkway when the couple in front of him stopped to take a better look at the arched brickwork above them. Those arches held up the sidewalks and had survived earthquakes. If the guide was to be believed, where they stood was one of the safer places to be in an earthquake. The lingering of the couple gave Fazil time to catch his breath. Todd stole it away with a casual press of his hand into the small of Fazil's back.

"Enjoying yourself?" Todd spoke close to his ear and kissed his neck.

The couple moved and they continued down the path to the room where the tour guide waited. "Yup." Fazil glanced back and caught a glimpse of Todd's grin.

The little touches, the quick kisses—they were doing nothing to drop Fazil's desire or temperature. Nor was the tour. They'd been climbing up and down stairs and over wooden walkways and uneven floors for a half hour, and the history was absolutely fascinating. The reasons the city was raised, the corruption that built the place, the Yukon gold rush, and all the shady dealings that took place in the underground spaces where they now walked. Glass blocks were set in the sidewalks above so light could filter down into the old streets below. Dim though that sunlight was, ferns grew from the brickwork nearby. Life still found a way.

The skylights were a reminder that the "ground" above wasn't solid. Neither was the earth beneath them. Seattle was built on a tidal beach. Not the smartest move, but what did pioneers from the Midwest know?

They listened to their guide talk about the history of the "seamstresses" of old Seattle—more women than needed to mend twice as much clothing as worn by the city's men—and then the guide let them wander for a time. Fazil took Todd's hand. "This is a little like a live D&D session, except without the monsters."

Todd touched the brick wall of a building facade. "Do you still play?"

He was going to have to admit that, wasn't he? "Yeah. There's a group I game with. Sometimes D&D, or when we can't spend weeks on a campaign, board games."

"Sounds like fun." Todd looked almost wistful.

"You still game?" Bet Todd wanted to, if he didn't.

"Sometimes." They wandered to an old bank teller cage the guide had pointed out. "Not for a while, though. My group imploded when two of our friends—who were married to each other—ended up divorcing."

Fazil twisted his face. "That sucks." Hit close to home, given his breakup with Kris.

Todd dragged a hand through his hair. "Happens. Especially when you're the guy who discovers the husband lip-locked with a dude at a bar."

Wow. "Ouch."

"To say the least. His wife wasn't pleased."

Shit. "Was he bi?"

Todd shook his head. "Might have been easier. He was closeted. Religious family."

The guide gathered them back together and led them up a set of stairs to an alleyway and down the street—aboveground—to another section of the tour. Fazil used the single-file climb up the stairs to school his expression. He didn't know what to feel.

Todd must have seen *something* when they hit open air. "You get it. Are you supposed to be angry about the cheating? Or happy the dude had the strength to be himself? I... tried to remain friends with both, but it was ugly. In the end, the whole group fell apart."

At least the guy hadn't played into the cheating-bisexual

stereotype. Fazil stopped and his blood turned stone-cold. No, *he* was a walking example of *that*.

Todd tugged him forward, his brow creased. "Z?"

"It's nothing." He drew a breath and hustled to catch up with the group. His innards twisted into pretzels.

Another set of stairs led back into the underground. Todd still had that quizzical look, and he clasped Fazil on the shoulder briefly.

Fazil pushed the count of how many times he cheated on Todd out of his head. "What else do you do for fun?"

This stretch of the tour had been a main street of some sort. Some of the building façades were preserved. Large mechanical pieces littered the floor. Todd took Fazil's hand while they listened to the guide—the equipment had been part of an old elevator tossed out of a building that had crashed through the new sidewalks into the underground. When the guide finished, they moved in to inspect the debris and Todd answered.

"There's a smaller group that goes hiking, but we haven't met in a while. I hang out at some of the bars, but that scene gets old." He shrugged. "I miss the gang. Haven't gone out of my way to meet a new group, then work became hell."

"That'll do it." He studied Todd in the dim lighting. Tall, handsome, with a mechanic's body and the mind of an engineer. "I'm surprised you're not dating anyone."

Todd lifted a brow and squeezed Fazil's hand.

"I meant before I showed up unexpectedly on your doorstep."

Another shrug. "I'd been seeing a guy for a while, but we broke up a couple of months ago." Todd paused. "When I found him lip-locked with my married friend."

Oh shit. "Dude..."

Todd gave a bitter chuckle. "Right? I still don't know whether to be pissed. Last I heard, they've moved in together and are doing just fine."

That would turn anyone off of social circles for a while. "Gotta be rough." At least Kris hadn't cheated. She'd come to him and explained what was going on in her head. In retrospect, that had been a blessing, especially since it had matched what had been going on in his. He stroked the back of Todd's hand with his thumb.

"It was. His ex was super mad at me for the longest time. She was sure I'd known, except I hadn't. Not at all." He ran his hand over the front of an old building. "What about you? Hobbies other than playing in paper dungeons?"

He snorted. "Would you believe pinball?"

"Pinball? As in the game with flippers?" He mimicked pressing a button with his free hand.

"Yup. There's a league in Pittsburgh."

"Pinball... league." Todd furrowed his brow. "Not words I expected to hear together."

"It's less exciting than it sounds."

Todd tugged Fazil's hand. "Come on. They'll leave us behind. Don't want to be eaten by a Grue."

He mock-punched Todd in the arm. "Grue was from Zork."

Todd smiled, pressed his index finger to his lips, and nodded to the tour guide.

Fazil rolled his eyes, but for the rest of the tour, they listened and learned and held hands. He fell back into the comfort, the ease of being with Todd. When they emerged back above ground after a quick perusal of the gift shop, he didn't even care that they walked close—moved like a couple. Touched like a couple.

That was new. Maybe it was Seattle. Didn't care. He

loved it. "What's next on the agenda?" Still a few hours to kill before dinner.

"There's another underground tour."

Another hour in gloom and damp wasn't appealing, even if the history was interesting. "Not enthused."

Todd pursed his lips and got a funny gleam in his eye. "Did you know there's a science fiction and fantasy museum here?"

"Really?"

"Yeah—except it's back over by the Space Needle."

"You dork!" Fazil punched him in the arm again. "Why didn't you say so when we were there?"

"I honestly forgot! Besides, the building it's in is ugly as sin."

To complete the set, Fazil mock-punched him a third time. Never would he forget Todd's grin at that or his laughter, nor the lingering way Todd kissed him. When they moved apart, Todd's eyes were alive with light and joy. "You say *dork* like it's a bad thing."

Fazil's pulse thudded in his ears. "Or maybe we could go back to your place."

That lovely smile turned wicked. "Or I can make you wait and show you something you love, so you can't complain."

Sometimes waiting was its own pleasure.

CHAPTER ELEVEN

Todd unlocked the door to his apartment. It was early, but after overdosing on people at the Science Fiction and Fantasy Hall of Fame and an amazing dinner at a Vietnamese restaurant near Todd's apartment, both he and Fazil were done with playing tourist.

Fazil closed the door and threw the dead bolt.

Todd pulled him close. "Want to watch a movie?"

"Are you asking if I want to watch a movie or if I want to make out on the couch for a while?" The huff of laughter brightened his face.

"Either. Both." He grinned.

"Yes." Fazil's kiss tasted of wine and spice.

He deepened it until Fazil moaned. "Or we could just go to bed," he whispered into his ear.

"As appealing as that sounds, I need to digest dinner first."

There was that. Sex on a full stomach wasn't much fun. "Movie it is." He let go.

When Fazil stooped to inspect Todd's movie collection, Todd was treated to a view of his ass in tight denim. The things he wanted to do to Fazil—or watch Fazil do to himself.

"*Galaxy Quest*? I haven't watched that in *ages*."

Any movie was fine, but that one brought back interesting memories. "Sure." He settled on the couch. "I seem to remember you spent half the time in the theater laughing your heart out, and the other jerking me off." He turned on the TV and switched to the DVD/Blu-ray input.

A touch of color crept up Fazil's neck, and he dropped the movie into the player. "If you're lucky, I'll replay those events." He sank down onto the couch next to Todd and curled up into his arms.

"Or you can put that mouth of yours to work."

Fazil raised an eyebrow. "And miss the movie? I don't think so."

They'd see. Todd was just happy to have Fazil in his arms. Everything else was a bonus.

In the end, they watched the movie snickering and cuddling. No pressure, no sexual one-upmanship—just enjoying each other's presence. Fazil was relaxed against him, fingers laced with Todd's. No tension, not like there'd been hours before, nor years ago. Todd was afraid to move and break the spell, but it was Fazil who shifted when the movie switched back to the menu screen. "Let me put that away."

"I can just turn it off."

But Fazil had slipped from the couch, and his absence was almost a physical shock. Todd winced against the leather.

Fazil returned the movie to its case and shelf. "I know you're particular about your books and things."

He was. "It could have waited."

Fazil waved away the words. "I've also been staring at

your bookshelf. When did you get first-edition AD&D manuals? These are older than we are!" He eased the player's manual off the shelf and carried it reverently to the couch.

"Half Price Books." Todd pulled Fazil back into his arms. "They're not *that* rare." Hadn't even been expensive.

"Still." Fazil flipped open the book. "Ever think of gaming at work? There's got to be enough people interested and less chance of implosions."

"We did have a group that met in a conference room after work."

"But?"

He tasted the bitter in his chuckle. "Our release schedule got fucked up. People didn't want to stay even longer at the office for fun."

"You guys were putting in long hours?" He sounded surprised.

Todd should have expected that. While they'd been asked to cooperate with Anderson's team, they'd also been told not to highlight how hard they'd been struggling. "Yeah. Lots of mandatory evenings and weekends." He scratched his neck. "Not now, of course."

There was Fazil's thoughtful, calculating look. "Makes sense, given..." He focused on Todd. "We're going to try to fix things. Working sixty hours a week isn't sustainable."

"Don't I know it." He tried to keep the bitterness out of the reply. Time to change the subject. "When did you play last?" He gestured to the book in Fazil's hands.

"Last fall. Pinball kind of took over." He turned a page. "One guy in the league has a ton of machines. I ended up helping repair them."

"Sounds like fun." Old-school engineering.

"Oh, it is. But I miss rolling dice, you know? There's something about all those charts."

Todd laughed. Fazil's adorable geeky side was endearing, but he felt the same way. A wicked thought flashed through his mind and tightened his balls. He peered at the bookshelf, eyeing his bag of dice.

Fazil narrowed his eyes. "That's a look I remember. What's up?"

"Nothing." There *was* such a thing as being too much of a geek. Maybe. He glanced at his dice bag again.

Fazil poked him in the side. "Out with it."

Arousal chased embarrassment. "Well, if you miss rolling dice, we could do something about that."

Understanding and curiosity in Fazil. "I'm guessing you don't mean playing with this." He tapped the cover of the Dungeons and Dragons book.

"No." Todd couldn't keep the smile from pulling at his lips. "Well, maybe dragon, but not dungeon."

Fazil squirmed. "What happens if I roll a one?"

Todd stroked his cheek, then gripped his chin. "Guess we'll have to figure that out, won't we?"

Fazil swallowed, something close to fear in his eyes.

Shit. "I'm not going to ask you to do anything you don't want to do. We'll have to make a list or a chart or—"

"Wait, you're actually suggesting we make a *chart* for sex?" Fazil leaned forward, all signs of apprehension gone. "And roll a die?"

Someone liked the thought of that kind of role-play. "Yes." He ran his thumb over Fazil's stubble, relishing the scrape of the bristle. "I think it's also time to bring out Mr. Dragon."

In the silence that settled between them, he couldn't read Fazil's expression or the beat of his pulse. About the time when Todd went into worry mode, Fazil grinned. "Better get a pen and some paper, then."

Oh God, this was going to be fun. He pulled Fazil in for a quick kiss and rose. "Dice are on the shelf in the Crown Royal bag." He headed into his office to collect a pad of paper and a pen and made a quick stop in his bedroom to collect the toy box that contained the dragon dildo. By the time he returned to the living room, Fazil had placed the AD&D manual back. Dice clattered against the surface of the coffee table, a familiar sound that brought back a tumble of memories.

Fazil focused on the box and his breath hitched. "Should I even ask?"

"Take a look. Tell me if there's anything in there you like or don't like. Especially *don't* like." Because he'd take those off the table—or list.

A small nod. "You kinky?" Fazil opened the box and peered inside.

"Not exactly?" Todd settled on the couch. "I'm not part of the BDSM scene, but I like toys and I like a little tying up and shit like that."

"Tying up or being tied up?"

"Prefer tying, but I'm open to both." The thought of Z spread-eagle on his bed made his balls ache.

Fazil frowned, fished out a pair of nipple clamps, and dropped them on the table. "These are a big nope."

"For wearing or using?"

He let out a huff of air. "You'd let me..." Both eyebrows rose.

"Maybe. If I rolled a one."

Fazil licked his lips. "Okay. But not on me. I'm not into pain."

"Says the guy who loves a good, rough fuck."

Fazil blushed beautifully. "That's different." He drew out a few scarves and sashes, then hovered his hand over the box. "Holy shit, you really do have one of these." He pulled out the clear sleeve that housed the sizable purple-and-green dragon dildo and turned it over in his hands. "This is something else."

Not the thickest toy Todd owned, but it was impressive, with its flared head, scale-covered shaft, and vibrant colors. He'd never used it, but the hunger in Fazil only whetted Todd's appetite to put it to use. "You want that inside you, Z?"

A visible shudder took Fazil. Didn't take guesswork to figure out the answer to that question. Still, Todd's dick thickened at Fazil's breathy reply. "Yeah."

No doubt Fazil was hard as a rod. "You know, the sooner we get this chart created, the sooner you'll get what's coming to you."

"Assuming the dice agree." Fazil set Mr. Dragon down on the table. "How are we going to do this?"

"Let's start with a simple list."

"A table might be more fun..." Fazil tapped his fingers on his knee.

That was true. All the lovely combinations they could develop, but in the end, they made a single list. Creating a full-blown table with charts would have taken all night. "Maybe later," Fazil muttered, "when I don't want you so bad."

Definitely something to work on later, especially if that meant pulling out the *other* boxes. "You ready for this?"

Fazil read the list once more, and set the pad down. His grin had a familiar nervous and horny edge to it. "This has got to be the weirdest thing I've ever done. But yes, roll to see how you're going to fuck me." He paused. "Or what I'm doing to you."

As per normal, the low roll results on the list were more penalty than pleasure. What Todd had suggested didn't involve him bottoming. Although Fazil's brows had pinched together, he didn't ask. Which was good, because explaining why would've put a damper on everything.

Instead the penalties ranged from being tied up and tickled to some very clever uses of the nipple clamps Fazil had eschewed for himself. Every so often, Todd found pain fun.

The whole purpose of this was to have a good time, after all.

Most of the list involved Todd fucking Fazil—or Fazil fucking himself. Watching him last night had been a huge turn-on. Whatever number came up, they'd both end up in a sweaty, satisfied heap by the end of the night. How they'd get there was the only thing up to chance.

Todd scooped up his red twenty-sided die and rolled it between his hands. "Here we go." He spun the die down onto their list of sexual exploits.

They both leaned forward and watched it settle on one side, white number facing up.

Eighteen. A damn fine roll. He read the line on the list and his blood warmed. *Yes.*

Fazil melted. "Fuck." There was excitement and gravel in that curse.

"Mr. Dragon's inaugural run."

Fazil wiggled on the couch, his focus completely on the dragon cock. Todd wouldn't be sliding that thick purple-and-green shaft into Fazil. No, he'd watch while Fazil fucked himself on it. As an added bonus, Todd would receive a nice blow job, too, for old times' sake.

He picked up the sleeve. "Should give it a good cleaning first."

Fazil's eyes were wide with need. "No condom?"

"Up to you. Like I said, it's never been used." Either way, he'd clean it before and after. He liked his toys spotless. He eyed Fazil. "Shouldn't you be getting your ass into my bedroom and stripping off all those clothes?"

"Yeah." His soft, lust-filled voice made Todd groan. Fazil rose and the bulge in his jeans was impressive. Todd couldn't wait to get his hands on that. Or his mouth. Whatever.

He tossed Mr. Dragon up, caught him, and followed Fazil into the bedroom. This was going to be hotter than hell.

It was a bit of a miracle Fazil could walk given the buzzing in his head and how turned on he was. God, his dick hurt. Getting out of those jeans would be heaven.

Eighteen. Those two little white numerals seemed to hover in the air, though the die still lay on the list in the living room. That meant taking an impressive, scaly toy up his ass.

Exactly what he'd wanted. He *knew* he should be careful what he wished for—but damn. Being fucked by the dildo was hot and wonderfully weird, and if he had a kink, it was that he loved being stretched wide. Even some of his girlfriends had gotten into that with him.

Something really hot about being drilled by a woman. A giant dragon cock and Todd? Even better.

When he stopped at the foot of Todd's bed, warm fingers closed on the back of his neck. "Didn't I say

something about stripping?" Todd spoke low and his words
slid down Fazil.

"You're not the boss." He kicked off his shoes and
worked his belt and jeans open.

"True." Todd patted Fazil's ass. "Mr. Dragon is."

Yeah, Mr. Dragon was. A pretty little red D20 had
decided Fazil's fate.

Todd chuckled, crossed the room, and rooted around in
a dresser for a second. He tossed a bottle on the bed. Lube.
Suitable for use with toys, the label said. Then he vanished
into the bathroom with another bottle.

Fazil pushed his pants and underwear off and kicked
them toward the nearest wall. His shirt and socks followed,
landing on top of the pile. A few strokes sent lightning up
his veins. He pressed his other hand against his belly. This
was going to be good.

"Hey, now." Todd sauntered back into the room. "No
getting started without me. Besides, you're missing this." He
held out the dildo.

That thing was a strange work of art. The head was
thick and smooth and slitted, while the bulbous shaft was
covered in molded scales. A thick ridge traced down the top
—or what must have been the top if this were an
anatomically correct dragon cock. Desperate to feel the
texture on his tongue, Fazil stepped in, gripped Todd's arm,
and sucked the tip of the cock into his mouth.

It was colder against his tongue than he'd anticipated,
probably from the cleaning Todd had given it, and it felt
nothing like a human cock. The girth forced his lips apart
and he sucked down as much as he could. A bolt of heat
sank into Fazil's balls.

This would be inside him soon. He'd put it there.

Todd's breath hitched. "Fuck, that's hot."

Fazil eased off the toy. "Wait until you see it in my ass."

Todd closed every inch of distance and kissed him, his tongue forcing past Fazil's lips. He groaned when Todd's jean-covered bulge pressed against his naked, hard cock.

Todd released him. "Get on the bed. Now."

Somehow, he managed the short distance on legs made of jelly. He knelt, sending the bottle of lube rolling against his hands.

"Condom?" Todd slid his hand over Fazil's ass, the touch lighting fire in Fazil's blood.

"No." He fought the desire to plant his shoulders on the mattress and beg Todd to fuck him, with or without the dildo. "I think au naturel."

Todd held Mr. Dragon out. "Well, as natural as a rubber dragon dick gets."

"Silicone." He took the toy from Todd. Pretty thick, even at the head. Easy enough to mouth, but taking it in the ass was different. "I need to be on my back." And that meant he could watch Todd's reaction. "I'd prefer you naked, too, if you don't mind."

"Never with you." Todd stripped off his shirt. All those years in the shop had helped build out that frame. Fazil grabbed the bottle of lube and enjoyed Todd pushing his pants and underwear down to reveal a trail of hair straight to his hard dick and impressive balls.

Once Todd kicked away his clothes, he stroked himself and raised an eyebrow. "Sure you know how to use that thing?"

Fazil set Mr. Dragon aside. "Prep first." He slicked his fingers, laid back, spread himself, and slipped a finger into his hole. Fuck, did that feel good. He'd been squeamish about his ass as a teen. Now? Not at all.

Color rose up Todd's chest. "Love watching you do that."

"So I see." Fazil added a finger and fucked himself with slow, even thrusts.

Todd bit his lip and fisted his cock to the same rhythm.

Fazil slid his fingers out. "Better not come, or you won't be getting sucked off."

"Hey, who's the DM of this game?"

Fazil chuckled and grabbed Mr. Dragon. "Your happy little red die." He lubed up the shaft. Slick with lube, the scales and bumps rubbed hard against his hand. Inside him? He could only imagine—but not for long. He lined up Mr. Dragon and pressed the head against his hole.

He'd wanted to watch Todd when he slid the toy in, but the pleasure of being spread open by that blunt head and thick shaft took his breath and vision. He arched against the mattress and groaned. "Oh fuck."

"God, Z. You can say that again." Todd's words were thick with lust.

If he could speak through the energy and agony zipping through him. Fazil eased the toy out, then pushed farther inside. The scales or the ridge or something raked against his prostate and breath left his lungs.

So damn good. He plunged the cock in again and again, until he writhed on the bed against the invading toy.

Wrapping his free hand around his dick, he found a rhythm that filled his vision with light and his nerves with fire. He didn't try to stop his moans and gasps.

Not all the groans were his. "Shit Z. You— God."

Fazil peeled his eyes open. Todd was gloriously hard and whacking himself off in time to Fazil's thrusts. His mouth was parted, breath heavy, and his thighs trembled. "Want you so bad."

"Too bad Mr. Dragon has me." Fazil slowed down, drew the dildo out, then thrust in hard.

Todd's eyes darkened. "So he does." He stepped closer. "Can I... fuck you with it?"

That had been nineteen on the list, but he wasn't going to say no. "Please."

Todd's weight rocked the mattress when he knelt down. "You really like this?" He gripped Mr. Dragon, and slid him out until the head caught against Fazil's ring, then thrust the toy in, hard and deep.

Spots of light formed in Fazil's vision. He clawed at the sheets. "God. That, please! Again!"

Todd's laughter was dark, and he obliged, sending another shower of light and fire raking through Fazil. "You're amazing, you know that?"

Couldn't answer, not when Todd worked the toy faster. Everything was deeper, stronger, and more intense than when the toy had been in his own hand. Fazil had just about caught his breath when Todd leaned in and sucked Fazil's dick into his hot mouth.

Everything went white, and he raked his hands through Todd's hair. His limbs, his fingers, every part of him, spasmed with electricity and fire. His balls were so tight, and he tumbled headlong toward that cliff of pleasure with Todd's every thrust and suck.

The velvet caress of Todd's tongue pressed against his glands.

"Please, don't... don't stop." *God, I love you.* Tears pricked Fazil's eyes. "...gonna come."

Todd drew his mouth off Fazil's dick and replaced it with his hand. "Then come." Todd fucked him harder with Mr. Dragon. "Come all over me."

Those blue eyes and that wicked grin hovered just

above Fazil's cock, and Fazil shot ribbons of semen onto Todd's face.

Maybe it was Todd's jizz-covered grin or the fact the bastard kept pounding him with Mr. Dragon, but Fazil's orgasm went on and on, longer than it had ever before, until he had to close his eyes against the intensity. He groaned with each plunge of the dragon cock into him, then fell back against the bedspread into a loose heap of bones and flesh.

Even after Todd eased Mr. Dragon out and cleaned the head of Fazil's cock with his mouth, the room hadn't stopped spinning. "Holy hell," he whispered.

"Good for you?" Todd absently wiped at his face and licked his fingers. "Tastes pretty good."

"Fucking amazing." Fazil propped himself up on to his arms. "Since when did you like come on your face?"

"Probably about the time you got off being fucked with toys." Laughter in that, but also heat. Which was fair.

"I missed so much."

Todd sobered. "Yeah, you did. So did I." That wicked smile returned. "Means we get to have a whole shitload of firsts with each other again."

There was that pricking at the corner of his eyes again. "Come here." He reached for Todd—and he crawled up into his arms, warm and heavy. Fazil kissed him.

He was so damn grateful for a chance to put things right with Todd, to make up for all his mistakes. He rolled them over until he was on top. "I think I owe you something." Many somethings.

Todd combed his hand through Fazil's hair and closed his fist, pulling at the roots. "Damn straight you do."

The pressure against his scalp was almost painful. "There's nothing straight at all about what I want to do to you."

Todd chuckled. "Good. Get to it."

Fazil nipped Todd's neck, hard enough to gain him a hiss, then worked lower. He'd get to it. Eventually.

THE DELIGHT AT MAKING FAZIL COME SO HARD ON THE dragon dildo was eclipsed only by Fazil working his mouth down the length of Todd's body. Seemed like Fazil had no qualms about all the things they'd hesitated to do in high school.

Who'd been the first man to fuck Fazil? How'd he convinced him? He arched and moaned when Fazil licked over his pecs and up into his armpit.

Damn! Teen Fazil would never, ever have done that.

He liked this Fazil a lot better, and not just for the wicked things he did with his mouth. Teeth scraped along the skin above his ribs. "Fuck, Z!"

"Too much?" Breathless amusement there. "Or are you ticklish?"

Todd tightened his hold on Fazil's hair. "Not ticklish."

"Really? You used to be."

Before he could stop him, Fazil found the one spot on Todd's side that made every nerve in his body spasm. "No! Stop!" He'd been here too many times before with guys he didn't want to think about.

Thankfully Fazil did. "You okay?" Concern erased the lust in his voice.

"Yeah." He took a breath. "Why?"

"The way you said *stop...*" Fazil's eyes were dark, and his lips pulled down.

The way I said... Todd shivered. "I don't mind being tickled. Not by you. It... caught me by surprise."

Fazil laid his head on Todd's stomach. "I don't want to hurt you, not again."

"Oh, Z," he murmured and stroked his hair. "You won't. Not here. Not now." Fazil would never be some older man bending him over in a bathroom stall. Todd focused on the silky strands flowing through his fingers. Fazil was *here* and *now*. "If you move down a little farther, you'll find out how much all of that bothered me." He nudged his hips and cock against Fazil.

A chuckle vibrated Todd's stomach and Fazil pushed himself up. "Where was I?" He nipped his way down to Todd's stomach, licking, biting and kissing the flesh there. The head of Todd's dick brushed against Fazil's chin.

"Lower."

Another laugh. "Nothing said I had to suck you off *fast*."

"You haven't even wrapped your lips—"

Fazil took him deep into his hot, slick mouth and Todd couldn't breathe.

Between Fazil's hand and his mouth and tongue, he had Todd gaping at the ceiling and gasping for air. "God, Z..." Fazil had always been good at giving head, but he'd stepped up his game and lost his gag reflex, too. He swallowed all of Todd and moaned around him.

That view and those vibrations almost had Todd shooting right there. He tightened his grip on Fazil's hair.

Fazil pulled off and stroked him. "Like that?"

He could only groan and nod, and Z went down on him again, taking his dick all the way to the balls.

He tried to set the rhythm, but Fazil resisted the hand on his head and Todd's attempts to thrust up into his mouth. He cupped Todd's balls and rolled them until the only thing Todd could do was grip the bedsheets and curse. "You're fucking killing me."

Another laugh that made his balls ache in Fazil's hands. He was so damn close he could taste the edge of heaven. The heat and the depth of Fazil's exquisite mouth turned his brain inside out. When Fazil wasn't swallowing Todd whole, his tongue pressed in every perfect place and sparks danced in Todd's vision. "Oh, God, Z. That. Keep doing that."

Fazil's grunt vibrated Todd's bones and something made a *click*, then Fazil's slick finger circled his hole and he nearly lost his mind and load down Fazil's throat.

He didn't bottom—too many bad memories—but *Fazil* playing with his ass? So fucking *good*.

Fazil pushed his finger inside and when he skimmed over, then pressed into his sweet spot, Todd shouted, grabbed Fazil's head, and pumped every last bit of his seed into Fazil's willing mouth, lightning blinding his vision.

Fazil licked and sucked Todd until he fell limp against the bed.

Payback. But so so worth it.

Fazil wiped his mouth with the back of his hand, a picture of joy. Tousled hair, huge grin, and a little bit of semen on his cheek.

"That was..." Todd leaned his head back and let his vision return to normal. Fantastic. Wonderful. Awesome. None of those words quite worked, because holy shit, that had been one hell of a trip. "Best I've ever had."

"Good. I'll try even harder next time." Fazil flopped down next to Todd and curled up in his arms. "I *really* enjoy giving head."

"Might kill me next time." Todd pulled Fazil close and kissed him, savoring his taste on those lips. Fazil had been an enthusiastic cocksucker back in high school, but now? "Spent a lot of time practicing, huh?"

That earned him an embarrassed expression that was utterly alluring. "I spent some time playing the field."

"It *shows*." He pressed his lips to Fazil's mouth and he melted against Todd. When the tension eased, Todd broke the kiss. "Nothing wrong with that. I did, too."

As often as he could that first year. Anonymous hard sex. "Wasn't always the best time, but I learned what I like and what I'm good at."

"Everything," Fazil whispered against Todd's chest. "You're good at everything."

If that were true, he never would have lost Fazil in the first place. "How 'bout hiking in the mountains tomorrow?"

A sleepy, happy grunt. "Sounds great."

Todd pulled up the covers and turned off the lights. Cleaning up could wait until tomorrow. All he wanted was right here in his arms. For now.

CHAPTER TWELVE

Sunday morning came too early for Fazil's tastes. He groaned against the sunlight. Todd was already out of bed.

He poked Fazil in the side through the covers. "Come on, you're the one who wanted to see mountains."

Still too much light in the room. Wasn't Seattle supposed to be gray? "I can see them fine from the window."

That earned him a pillow to the face. "Get up, or there'll be no coffee for you."

No coffee? "Those are fighting words!" Fazil hauled himself upright, blinking sleep out of his eyes. He slipped out of bed, wonderfully achy in his hips and thighs from the previous night. He shook his legs out. "God, I'm getting old."

"Rough sex too much for your ancient bones?"

His turn to throw a pillow. Todd dodged out of the way. "Our bones are the same age." He rolled his neck. "Haven't been on the receiving end in a while. Bit different."

Todd nodded and turned. Something in that glimpse of

expression Fazil didn't like, but before coffee was no time for probing conversations. "Am I going to need more than sneakers for this trip?" He rummaged around in his bag for his toiletry kit. He needed to shave, or he'd have a good start to a beard by Monday.

Todd slipped on gray sweatpants. "Yeah, it wouldn't hurt to have a pair of boots, especially if you're staying longer. There are plenty of places to hike. We can hit a store on the way out."

"They going to be open this early?" He didn't know the time, but given that he was still vaguely on East Coast time...

Todd picked up his watch. "No, but by the time you get your ass clean and we get something to eat, they ought to be."

"Speaking of clean..." He hoisted his travel kit. "Mind if I catch a shower?"

"Not at all. I'll get the coffee started."

"Not joining me?" Fazil was on the edge of being disappointed until Todd took Fazil's chin, tilted it up, and devoured his mouth.

The toiletry bag nearly slipped from Fazil's hands. He couldn't even groan through his sudden need.

Todd broke the kiss and caressed Fazil's balls and hard cock. "I'd love to join you, but if I do, we're never going to leave the apartment."

There was that. He felt like a teen again, minor joint pain aside. "We could stay."

A deep laugh. "Always so eager." Todd ran his thumb over Fazil's chin, sending a shiver through him. "That's why I like making you wait." He gave Fazil's dick a squeeze, then stepped away. "Go shower. The trip will be worth it." As he headed to the kitchen, he called back. "There are fresh towels in the linen closet."

He borrowed Todd's shower gel and shampoo, rather than using the hotel stuff he'd brought with him. He had to resist the urge to jack himself off under the pelting stream of water.

If Todd wanted him to wait, he might as well wait. Didn't take *that* long to get his lust under control, especially when he turned the hot water back to chilly. He did want to see the scenery that had tantalized him from a distance.

He'd seen mountains in California, but those hadn't been the green, lush snowcapped things that beckoned here.

When he'd finished, he wrapped a towel around his waist, opened the door to let some steam out, and cleaned off the mirror so he could shave.

He was halfway done when he noticed Todd in the doorway. Fazil straightened.

"No, don't stop." His whole face seemed to echo his smile. "It's hot."

That sent a little tingle up his legs. It was so utilitarian, this action. "Really?"

Todd looked him up and down. "Mmm-hmm."

"Why?"

A huff of laughter. "You don't know?"

Fazil eyed himself in the mirror, but any reason behind *hot* eluded him. "Kris used to say that. I figured it was because it was something she didn't do."

Todd shook his head and pushed himself off the door. "You can be such a butthead." Affection in that tone.

He frowned at his reflection and finished. He still couldn't put his finger on what Todd meant.

"All done," he said.

Todd had laid out clothing on the bed. "I won't be long.

Coffee's in the kitchen." And with that, he vanished into the bathroom.

Fazil chewed on his lip, and got dressed. Jeans and a t-shirt. Typical June fare, but it might not be enough up into the mountains. He mentally added a jacket or hoodie to the list of things he might need, then ventured out into the kitchen.

Why was shaving hot? He couldn't *shake* that question. "Shit." Just like Todd to plant something in his head that made no sense. No answer in the coffee, either, though that was good enough that he closed his eyes and grunted appreciatively.

"I'll take that as a compliment," Todd said. He was toweling off his hair, and had on only a pair of low-slung blue jeans.

For a moment, Fazil couldn't catch his breath. Such an unconscious act, so beautiful a man. Heat touched his body. "Oh."

Todd laughed as if he could read his mind.

"I get it." Fazil leaned against the counter. "But, you're stunning. I'm..."

"Stunning, too," Todd said. "You just hate that you are."

He *wasn't*. It was hubris to think he *was*. "I don't know why it bothers me so much."

"What, being loved?"

Fazil turned away and drank more coffee. Kris hadn't loved him. That had never bothered him, since he'd never spanned the gap between *like a lot* and *love* either. He'd made that leap with Todd years ago, but now? He still loved Todd, but what did that mean now that he wasn't a teen? He was afraid to find out.

This weekend was wonderful. The sex was great. Being

with Todd felt right and like home... but he'd fucked up so badly before.

Todd caressed his shoulders from behind. "Hey, I didn't mean to upset you."

"You didn't. I'm..." He'd always held back his feelings in high school, and that had been a mistake. He turned around. "I'm scared." He waved his free hand. "It's a lot. Seeing you again. Finding out I was such a shit. There's the whole job thing." His heart pounded in his throat. "I don't want to hurt you. I don't want to hurt me."

Todd rubbed Fazil's shoulders. "You know you're not alone in that, right?"

He looked into his mug, rather than at Todd.

"I'm scared, too. It's a chance. A long shot. But you're *here* and I'd rather try to work something out then spend my life regretting the past *and* the present."

"You have nothing to regret." Most of the shit in their past had been his, not Todd's.

A sad, distant look. "Yeah, I do." Then Todd was back and so was his smile, even if it was slight. "Finish that mug, I'll get a shirt, and we can go."

Fazil nodded, and studied Todd's back. What had happened after he'd left for college?

After he'd drained his coffee, he placed the mug into the sink. A moment later, Todd was back. "Ready?"

No. Not for how tangled up his mind and heart had become on a simple business trip. But he could at least eat breakfast. "Yeah. Let's go."

———

FAZIL WAS STILL A BIT OFF-KILTER—THAT GUARDED expression, the way he folded into himself—but Todd let him be. He'd had been open about his emotions. That was new and good, even if it made things awkward.

Seemed like every time Todd opened his mouth, there was a seismic shift. Sometimes he drew Fazil in; other times, he pushed him away. Yes, he was afraid, but more for Fazil. He'd already survived hell. If this fell apart, he'd be fine.

Sad. Lonely, heartbroken—but fine.

Despite the shit Fazil had done, Todd only wanted him to be happy. He wasn't sure Fazil ever was, outside of orgasms and the few moments Fazil stopped thinking so damn hard. Like when he shaved.

There were times when he wanted to shake Fazil. *You're brilliant. Smart. Beautiful. Stop thinking you're a fuckup.* If there was anyone in the car that deserved that label, it was Todd.

He cleared his throat. "How do you feel about hot chocolate?"

That shook Fazil out of his funk. "I'm generally in favor of it. Why?"

"Deciding on breakfast options." They were heading north and could use a big breakfast. "There's this place with hot chocolate smothered in whipped cream and M&M's." He got off the freeway and onto the local roads.

Fazil let out a laugh. "Never pegged you as a hot cocoa man. Especially with M&M's."

"You've never had this. Their breakfasts are good, too." He paused. "Just what the hell's a hot cocoa man, anyway?"

A flush and a shrug, but no more.

"Too girly?"

"No!" The blush deepened and Fazil sank into the seat. "I'm not *that* much of a shit."

"You're the guy who moans over peanut butter cups."

He gave Fazil a grin. "Cocoa seems a bit weird for you to question me about."

He coughed. "I always thought of you more as black coffee and cigarettes. Which I *know* is wrong, since you've never smoked."

But it made sense. "James Dean?"

Fazil glanced his way, still ruddy-cheeked. "Something like that."

Except he was still alive at thirty-three. "The greaser again." He'd never escape the garage.

"The rebel," Fazil said. "The cool kid."

"The misfit." He pulled into the lot of a strip mall and found a spot to park.

"No," Fazil said. "That was *me*. The nerd. The geek."

"Mr. Glamour." He turned off the car.

Fazil stared at him. "You've *got* to be kidding me."

"Come on. You dressed well. You had…"

Fazil's expression turned ugly. "Money?" The word was half snarl.

Shit. That was not the reaction he'd wanted. "A sense of style."

Fazil rubbed a hand over his face. "Style and me so do not belong together." A sour note to go with his bitter face.

Someone was grumpy. Coffee must not have taken. "Bet you look fantastic with whipped cream on your nose."

Fazil opened his mouth—then shut it and stared at him. "Is that on the menu? Nose cream?" A smile peeked out.

Todd laughed. "I hope not!" He opened the car door. "Coming?"

Fazil climbed out and followed him into the Woodinville Cafe.

The hostess saw them to a tiny table for two and took their drink orders. Of course the answer to that was M&M's

hot chocolate. Todd ordered his with half the whip. Fazil gave him a quizzical look and got his with the normal amount.

Well, now, maybe someone would end up with cream on his nose after all. Todd held back the smile and flipped open the menu. Pancakes or eggs Benedict?

Fazil pulled the menu toward him. "Truth is, I never understood why you picked me all those years ago."

Todd laid his menu down. "Oh hush. That's not your problem."

Fazil stared at Todd, his brow crinkling.

"I've told you why a million times. Hot. Sexy. Into the same stuff."

"But—"

"Z... were you like this with all your partners?"

That stopped him in his tracks, and he got *that* look. The one he got when he realized he was being a dork. "Maybe..." A snort and he shook his head. "How is it that you put up with me?"

Love. Lots and lots of love. He leaned across the table and spoke low. "Because you have the most incredible mouth."

Fazil turned a wondrous shade of red and snickered. A moment later, the waitress came and took their order.

Todd ordered the eggs Benedict *and* pancakes, because why not both? Fazil ordered corned beef hash and eggs.

"So, what was that all about, Z?" He waved his hand at the parking lot.

Fazil sighed and leaned back in his chair. "I'm a worrywart?"

"Hadn't noticed." Couldn't keep the grin off that time.

A huff of a laugh, but Fazil sobered quickly. "It's just...

what if this works? I live in Pittsburgh. You're here. I have to leave. It's the nature of the job."

Todd's chest tightened. He hadn't wanted to think that far ahead. "How about we figure that out when we get there?" He didn't *want* Fazil to leave. Every vision of the future had Z in it.

"I'm not good with open ends," Fazil said, his words soft. "I tried a long-distance thing once. It didn't end well."

The answer was *obvious*, but Todd kept it back. Fazil seemed to love his job with Anderson. Luring him away from that wouldn't be easy. "We have time."

The waitress brought their food and their hot chocolates. Fazil's had *all* the whipped cream.

"Holy hell." Fazil stared at the mug... what he could see of it under the pile of cream.

"And *that's* why I asked for half the normal whipped cream."

"You could have warned me!" No anger there, just wonderment at the sheer amount of cream piled on the mug. "Thing looks like one of your fucking mountains!"

Todd laughed and they both relaxed. Good. There was only so much of moody Z he could take.

Fazil picked up a spoon and tried to tame his hot chocolate. Failed. It gushed out all over the mug until Fazil sipped—and there it was. Todd picked up his phone and had the camera on in no time.

"Don't you dare!"

Too late. He smiled and turned the screen around. "I was right. You do look fantastic." Laughing and bright eyed. The man he loved.

Fazil wiped cream from his nose and chin. "All right. You win." A grin there.

"I usually do."

Fazil snorted. "Nose cream."

They both laughed and settled into eating their meals. Food was a good balm against worry, though Fazil wasn't wrong to think about the future.

Maybe he was moving too fast. He wanted Fazil so much, but there was one thing he needed more than sex or a relationship.

"Even if this doesn't work..."

Fazil looked up, his fork hanging above his hash.

"Look, I spent so many years hoping you were okay, and I had no way to find out. Even if this ends... don't shut me out. We were friends, Z. More than anything else, I missed my *friend*."

Fazil's eyes moistened and his face was pale against his black hair. "I... can do that."

If nothing else, he wouldn't lose Fazil. "We can figure out the other stuff."

They finished their meals and Todd paid. This time, Fazil didn't even try for the check, which was an improvement.

As they walked out into the parking lot, Todd watched his best friend shove his hands into his pocket and bite at his lip.

Don't shut me out, Z. I know the future's hard. The best things in life never came easily.

CHAPTER THIRTEEN

Fazil inhaled wet pine–scented air and trod up the path toward what Todd said was a ridgeline. The woods were dense, damp, cool, and green. Ferns everywhere and moss growing on trees like out of some documentary about the primordial era. Beautiful. So different from the forests in Pennsylvania.

He touched the bark of a tree as they passed. They hadn't talked much after breakfast, and apprehension bit into Fazil like the teeth of a trap. He tried to shake it off. Maybe he needed to let go of the fear and just enjoy being here. Todd was right—they could figure it all out. If nothing else, he had his best friend back.

"Can we take a break?"

"Sure." Todd slowed his pace and they stopped near a fallen tree.

Todd shrugged off his backpack, opened it, and offered Fazil a water. "Old bones?" The foliage swallowed his quiet voice, but there had been a touch of humor there.

Fazil cracked the bottle open. "Not yet. This place is amazing. I wanted to take it in." Mist settled near the forest floor despite the brightness of the day. They were working up a sweat even in the cooler temperatures. "Never been in a forest like this."

"Yeah, it's different from home." Todd stood and stretched. "And from California."

"Is this the rainforest people talk about?"

"Not this part. That's on the Olympic Peninsula. We should try to see it while you're here."

He nodded. "I'd like that. Though I don't know if we'll have time..."

Todd finished his water, crushed his bottle, and threw it into his backpack. "Incentive to come back." A gentle smile, soft like the woods around them.

The thought of leaving Todd was sharp and painful. Fazil handed Todd his empty bottle, then touched some moss on one of the trees, and it wasn't as soft as he thought it should be, nor crunchy. Squishy? He breathed in the dark, loamy air. "I want to come back. The best times of my life have been with you."

A whisper of boots on leaves and bark, and Todd wrapped him in his arms. "Same. Despite everything. When we're good... we're damn good."

And when they were horrible, they were really fucking horrible. He hiccupped a laugh. "I'm so afraid I'm going to fuck this up. Sometimes I think a part of me wants to skip ahead and save both of us the heartache." He shook his head. "Stupid, huh?"

"Oh, God. You." Warm breath against his neck. "Okay. Let's pretend." Todd brushed his lips against Fazil's skin with each word. "We've had some big fight, and we've broken up, like we always do." He slid his hands down to Fazil's hips and pulled him back. "We move on, right?

Either to make-up sex when we realize breaking up was stupid, or to a nice round of revenge fucking."

Every nerve tingled and he shuddered in Todd's arms. "That's not exactly what I had in mind." But damn, did that sound good.

"It's us." He snaked his hand under Fazil's t-shirt, hot fingers pressing against his abs. "Never could keep our hands off each other."

This whole trip had been proof of that. "Point."

"We could just be friends with benefits while you're here." He slid his hand out and turned Fazil around. They were both very hard. "No harm in that, is there?"

A calm, as thick as the forest air, settled into Fazil. "No." Not at all. His shoulders loosened.

"I want you in my life. Lover or friend, as long as I can *find* you, Z. Talk to you. Here or across the world, doesn't matter." His brow crinkled. "Don't leave me alone. That's all I ask."

Fazil gripped Todd's shirt and pressed his face against his chest, savoring the warm comfort he found there. "Okay."

Todd held him. Smoothed his hair—and something splattered on Fazil's shoulder. Then the back of his neck. On the ground all around them. The whole forest came alive with patters of rainfall. "Look what you've done," Todd murmured.

Fazil choked on laughter. "See? I'm a fuckup."

"Yes, but you're my best fuckup." Todd lifted Fazil's chin. "Can I kiss you, Z?"

"Please." Todd's best fuckup. When those lips pressed against his, he opened himself to Todd.

He'd be happy with that, as long as he was *Todd's*.

Todd kissed Fazil while cool rain splattered against them, and for a moment, he considered peeling off Fazil's clothes and fucking him right where they stood.

But the trail was horribly public. He broke the kiss. "Keep going or head back?" His pulse was a little too fast and his cock way too hard.

Fazil blinked rain from his eyes. "Didn't you say there was a vista view up ahead somewhere?"

He nodded. "The rest of the trail runs along a ridge. Not too much farther. I'd get out the map and check, but..." He gestured upward. "And the view probably isn't all that great now."

"We're already wet and it's not cold. Might as well keep going."

"Maybe it'll stop." He strapped his backpack on—thank goodness he'd taken the waterproof one—and they worked their way up the trail.

The rain let up and the air cleared when they reached the ridgeline and the view beyond.

"Well, damn," Fazil said. He put his hands on his hips, face full of wonder.

Though misty, the mountains were coming out. He pointed to the north. "Glacier Peak." Others, too, but he doubted the names would mean anything to Fazil. If things went well, they would come back. If not? Then not. He wanted Fazil *here*, but he'd take what he could get.

In the valley, mist rose from the rain. Fazil took in the view while Todd dug Fazil's cell phone out of the backpack. When he offered it, Fazil furrowed his brow.

Todd snorted. "Pictures?"

"Oh God, yeah." He took the phone and snapped several. "Still not sure who I'm going to share these with."

"Friends back home? Why not them?" From the sound of it, he had quite a social life.

"It's complicated."

"More than mine was?" He couldn't imagine Fazil's social circle being *quite* as convoluted.

"Nothing like that." Fazil turned around, taking in more of the view. "Can we keep going? It's stopped raining..."

"Sure. But there's a price."

Fazil huffed out a breath. "I tell you about it."

"You tell me about it." Maybe the key to understanding *this* Fazil was learning about who he was now. That was the *point* of this weekend.

They continued along the ridge, picking their way along the path at a slower pace to take in the stunning views and the hillsides of wildflowers. "I told you about Kris."

"Your ex-girlfriend? Yeah."

"She went from me to another guy. Same circle. Pinball, gaming, parties." He kicked a stone down the path and looked out at the valley. "The breakup was mutual. I have no room to complain..."

"But it still hurts to see her with him?"

"Yeah. Lance. He's a reasonable dude. Cute, too."

Todd couldn't help rolling his eyes.

"What? I can look! Even at the straight guys. Same as you."

"At the girls, too."

Fazil pursed his lips. "Yeah, and I get told I'm..." He croaked and paled. "Well, I *am* a cheater."

"Stop. We were kids and dumb and didn't talk to each other. You said you didn't fool around on anyone else."

"I didn't." Fazil scratched the back of his neck. "Yeah, it

hurts to see Kris with Lance. She's so much happier with him than she was with me."

Todd slowed to a stop as a few things clicked together in his mind. What was really eating at Fazil. "It's not you."

"It *is* me." A huff. Fazil climbed up on a rock outcropping and sat. "Every single one of my exes is married. I expect Kris will be soon, too. I'm like the unlucky coin—get rid of me and you'll find true love."

"Don't be ridiculous." Todd climbed up and sat next to him. "I'm not married."

"You don't *want* to be rid of me."

"Never did."

Fazil's blush was a thing of beauty, especially with his damp hair and the Cascades behind him. If it wouldn't get him into a world of trouble, he'd put that on his desk at work. Still... He shrugged his backpack off again and dug his own phone out. "My turn for a photo."

"Not of me!"

"Why not?"

Fazil looked out into the valley below. "So much more beauty in the world."

He took the picture anyway. "You're part of the world, Z. And you *are* beautiful."

A smile. "And... we're back to the question from this morning."

Why Fazil? "Because I love you. Back then and now. Some things change, but not that."

Todd saw the truth in Fazil's flush, in the way he rubbed his arms. Had seen it last night in his moans and tasted it today in the kiss in the rain. He doubted Fazil would say it and wasn't disappointed when he didn't.

They sat in silence, taking in the beauty. When Todd's stomach grumbled, Fazil snorted, his smile pouring out like sunshine through clouds. "Someone has an opinion."

"Eh, stomachs. You know how they are." He pulled out two trail bars from the backpack and handed one over along with another bottle of water. "Still have to go back down."

That cast a shadow over Fazil's smile. "I could stay up here forever."

Todd doubted it was a desire to become some kind of wild mountain man. "Why?"

"I'm not ready for Monday. Or giving this"—he gestured between the two of them—"up. At least during working hours."

Yeah, work would be hard after this weekend, knowing how Fazil tasted and smelled and felt. Who knew what the higher-ups at Singularity had in store for Fazil and Eli during the next week? "When will you find out if you're staying?"

"I'm not sure. I'm guessing midweek." Fazil crushed the trail bar wrapper and handed it back, his fingers brushing Todd's palm.

Warmth, desire, and need flooded Todd. "I wish I could make it all disappear. The stress. The job."

A huff of a laugh. "Oh, but you do." When Fazil met his gaze, every bit of Todd lit. The moment they stepped back into his apartment, he'd take Fazil away from the world once more. "We should head back."

Fazil didn't move. "In a minute. Can I have my phone again?"

He fished it out, and Fazil motioned for Todd to come closer and turn around. "This is dumb, but I want a selfie of us. Up here. So I can *remember*."

There was an odd emphasis on that last word. He knelt next to Fazil, their heads touching, both smiling into the camera with the mountains in the back. Disheveled, damp, and full of emotions. Fazil snapped the shot.

When he was done their lips met, then mouths and tongues.

Laughter drifted up on the breeze and Fazil pulled back. "No sex in the wilderness, I guess."

Todd snatched another kiss before packing up their trash. "Not on the trail." He stood and clambered down from the rock. "Nature kink?"

Fazil joined him. "Bucket list."

Well, then. Something to add to his list, too. Work or no —he'd find a way to spend time as much time as he could with the man he thought he'd lost forever.

CHAPTER FOURTEEN

No matter how hard Fazil pushed it away, worry slithered in the back of his mind as they headed back to Seattle. The knowledge that his time with Todd had to end because his life—the one he'd created and loved—was back in Pittsburgh. He didn't mind the job at Singularity, but only because he knew it was finite.

He and Todd? Old patterns threatened to surface. *His* patterns. Except Todd had circumvented those. Fazil rubbed his eyes. How ridiculous was it to pretend they'd fought and skip to the end?

It worked, though. He felt better than he had in years. And he desperately wanted to make up for a fight they hadn't had—the way they *always* made up. Fazil snorted and shook his head.

Todd looked over. "What's up?"

"Thinking about make-up sex."

Todd gripped the steering wheel and grinned. "Don't take this the wrong way, but that was the best part of breaking up with you. The mind-numbing orgasms later."

He couldn't help the laugh. "God, we were something

back then."

"We're better now." Todd slid his hand over the wheel and shifted in his seat. "If the past two nights are anything to go by."

"At sex?" Fazil shivered, the anticipation catching his breath and heating his blood. "Well, practice makes perfect."

Todd barked out a laugh. "You've practiced a lot of things you'd never have done in high school."

That went for both of them.

Closer memories surfaced, snatches of conversations. "Can I ask you something"—the question came out tight— "more personal?"

Todd sat up straighter. "Sure."

"What happened? After I left?"

Todd exhaled.

"You said it wasn't a good year." He dreaded asking. Steeled himself against finding out.

Todd focused on the road, his jaw working. Finally he spoke. "I need you to understand that none of what I did was your fault." He gripped Fazil's knee. "*None* of it. Everything I did, I did to myself."

Fazil's stomach dropped out of his body. "I... Okay."

"I mean it, Z."

Not good at all. "It wasn't my fault," he said.

Todd put both hands back on the wheel. "When I realized you were gone for good, I fell off the deep end. Since I hadn't been with anyone else, I figured I should gain some experience—you had more than me, after all. And I wanted to figure out the whole *gay* thing."

Fazil bit his lip. "I'm—"

"Shh." Todd flexed his fingers on the wheel. "My story. I know you're sorry. Still not your fault."

It sure as hell sounded like it was.

"When I wasn't working at my dad's shop, I'd hop in my car and drive into Philly to whatever gay bar I could find. Different one each time. Moved on to Jersey later, but same thing. Never the same place twice."

"They let you in bars at eighteen?"

Todd shrugged. "I had a good fake ID, and I never ordered a drink." His voice became hard. "No one had issues with an eighteen-year-old who wanted a nice, hard fuck in the men's room, so yeah, they let me in."

"You..." Fazil sank into his seat. "The first time you had anal was in a men's room at a bar?"

"Yep." Sharpness surrounded that word. "First night, I sucked some older dude off, then let his friend turn me around and bend me right over." Todd twisted his face. "I was really, *really* dumb."

Fazil couldn't breathe. "I'm guessing it wasn't *anything* like in porn."

Todd barked a strangled laugh. "No. Not at all." He slid his gaze over and there was curiosity there. "You *like* those kinds of videos?"

He flinched and pressed against the seat. "Well, I did." But now his gut twisted. The pain that must have led Todd to that place and time. *Wasn't my fault, bullshit.*

Todd grunted. "Anyway, that year I spent working in the shop, then getting as much anonymous sex as I could, as often as I could, pretty much any way they wanted it."

Fazil wanted to sink through the floor of the car. "That..." He took a breath. "Did you... get hurt?" *Raped? Beaten?*

"By some miracle, no. The sex was really rough, and I figured out pretty fast I didn't like bottoming, especially to older guys who saw me as a piece of meat to pass around."

God. Fazil pulled his legs up and hugged his knees.

"But each time, I said yes. When I said no, I was big enough no one argued. But that was also partly luck." He shook his head again. "It was such a foolish thing to do."

The apology tasted of iron and dust and all the things Fazil couldn't change. He kept it behind his lips, as promised.

Todd reached over and squeezed his knee. "It's over. I'm fine."

Fazil could only croak.

"That's why I didn't want to tell you. You'd take it badly."

"How am I supposed to take it?" Words made of ash.

"I don't know. I mean, it was bad. But I did it to myself, Z."

Because of me. Fazil bit his tongue.

"Anyway, one night I was out cruising, and this guy sidled up next to me. He was dressed nice. Button-down. Slacks. Fancy watch. You could tell the jacket and tie were out in his car. He looked at me and said, 'What the hell are you doing here, kid?'

"And I, the not-so-suave guy that I was, said, 'Wanna find out?' And I nodded at the bathroom.

"Guy downs half his drink and laughs. 'I don't fuck in bathrooms. And I don't fuck people I don't know.' Then he pulls out his wallet and hands me a business card. 'Call me,' he says, 'when you've had enough of this shit and we can have a beer.' Then he paid for the drink he didn't finish and walked out of the place."

Holy shit. Fazil unfolded. "What did you do?"

"I stared at the card for a while. Guy was a fucking *doctor*. Worked over at the University of Pennsylvania. I looked around the bar and I was *done*. Like this switch flipped inside me. I left. Went home. Didn't go to another bar until I came looking for you. Got to use my real ID for that."

When Todd had gone to California. Fazil stared at his hands. "Did you call him?" The doctor who'd changed Todd's path.

"About a week later, after I figured out I wanted to do more than work for my dad in his dying auto shop and be a man-whore in my spare time."

He couldn't help the flinch. "Todd—"

"Don't!" The word came out painfully sharp. Fazil twisted away from it. Todd sighed. "I don't want you turning this into more pain. You've had enough. *We've* had enough."

That was true. His bones ached with memories and regret. He straightened out in the seat. "If I'd stayed in the Philly area..."

"You wouldn't be who you are. I wouldn't be who I am." Todd tapped the steering wheel. "I'm gonna have to stop and get gas soon."

He could use a break from staring into their past. One more thing he wanted to know. "The doctor?"

"Martin Peters. He was a cardiologist. I called and asked if he was serious about that beer—though I couldn't actually drink it. We ended up at a nice restaurant in Philly and we talked. I'd turned nineteen. He was thirty-seven and hot as sin." Todd merged and took an exit off the highway. "We dated for a year and a half until he got too busy and I was ready to move on. Shouldn't have worked, but it did."

"You... he..." Fazil struggled to organize his thoughts. "What do you mean, ready to move on?"

Todd pulled into a gas station, up to a pump, and turned the car off. "He helped put me back together after I'd taken myself apart, but we both knew from the start that anything between us wouldn't be long-term."

"You didn't love him."

"I did, but more like a mentor. He taught me so much about myself." Todd unbelted and turned to face him. "But I still liked casual sex back then and he... Well, it's hard to explain—like this, anyway." He gestured around the car.

Fazil didn't understand, but nodded.

"Give me time." He got out of the car.

Time. Even if Fazil stayed an extra week or two, he'd still go back to Pittsburgh. If he was honest with himself, he *missed* that city. It had grown on him.

He released the seat belt and pushed the door open. "Hey," he called to Todd. "I'm going to grab a drink."

Todd saluted him and Fazil headed inside. He grabbed a bottle of water—anything with sugar or caffeine would keep him awake, and they *did* have to work tomorrow. Then he wandered the aisles—past the Band-Aids and aspirin... and condoms. He'd expected Todd to have gained experience in fifteen years, but not in the way he did.

Disgust crept up his throat, not from Todd's story, but from the images that wanted to play out in his head. Ones that had Todd ramming into him in a cramped stall over and over. *What the hell is wrong with me?* He stomped to the front, paid for his water, and slinked back to the car.

Todd gave him a curious, then calculated look, but finished paying for the gas at the pump. "I'm gonna grab a snack. I'll be right back."

It didn't take Todd that long. He returned with a bottle of water and a large bag of chips.

"That's more than a snack."

"We can catch dinner when we get back, but I *really* need something to tide me over."

Fazil's stomach grumbled and Todd laughed. He handed him the chips. "That's why I got enough for two."

Like old times. He smiled at the bag. "Yeah."

When they got back onto the highway, Fazil opened the chips and let Todd reach in. At this point, if either of them had a cold, they both had it.

Shit. "Um."

"Yeah?"

How to ask? "You had a lot of sex..."

"Yup. With men I didn't know." Todd glanced over. "First thing Martin insisted was that I get tested for everything under the sun. Wasn't about to have sex with me until we both knew the results. I always insisted on condoms, but..."

"They're not perfect." Didn't he know that from watching some of his friends get pregnant, despite the guys wearing condoms?

Todd took a few more chips. "Like I said, I was lucky." He paused. "I still get myself checked periodically. Side effect of Martin."

"Sounds like he was a good guy." Fazil fought against the voice in the back that whispered, *a better man than you.*

"He was," Todd said. "I wish you could've met him."

Fazil took a few chips to cover his flinch.

"How 'bout you?" Todd changed lanes. "Probably should have asked before I fucked you into my mattress, but you've always been fastidious."

Those two things, being tested and the memory of Todd drilling into him so deep and rough, bent Fazil's brain sideways and he choked on a potato chip. "Um." God, he was hard again, the image from the gas station filling his head. "I get tested. Nothing's come up."

"Not a dad?"

He laughed. "No. At least not that anyone has told me, and I think they would have. I'm on good terms with most of my exes."

"Well, that's good."

The conversation dried up. Not uncomfortably. Todd reached over and grabbed chips, and a few times slid a hand over Fazil's knee.

Which didn't help get his dick back under control.

Todd broke the silence. "You *really* like that type of porn? Fucking strangers in a bathroom?"

He nearly spilled the chips onto the car floor. "Kinda?" More like a lot.

"Glory holes?"

Fazil bit his lip to keep from groaning. "Yeah."

"Ever done anything like that?"

They were nearer to Seattle, he guessed—given the exits and the lights and the appearance of long bridges. "No. It's a fantasy, you know? Hard, anonymous sex. I figured the reality was probably not the same."

A harsh chuckle. "See, there's where you were smarter than me."

"If I were smarter than you, I wouldn't have been such a dipshit."

This time his snort was light. "I'll give you that."

"Hey!"

"You said it!"

He had. Fazil chuckled. Despite everything in his head —everything he'd learned—he felt *good*. "I like a bit of role-play. Did some with my girlfriends. The guys I dated weren't into it."

Todd had furrowed his brow and glanced over. "You know, for someone who says he's not kinky, you do have quite a kinky side."

Really? Fazil squirmed in his seat. "I mean I just... like rough sex. Sometimes."

Silence, but Todd was smiling.

"What?"

"Nothing at all." The smile never left his lips.

Heat rose in Fazil. "No... what?"

Still that damn grin. "I'm betting you were the one on the receiving end of that rough sex. It's an interesting picture, you folded over the arm of a couch and being drilled by a woman."

Fazil sucked in a breath of air... Yeah. He'd been there. His face felt like fire. "Armchair, actually."

Todd shifted in his seat and coughed. "Duly noted."

Well, now. Someone else was getting turned on. "I thought you weren't into women."

"I'm not," he said. "Still wouldn't mind watching, though. Love it when you're out of your mind in pleasure." He took an exit from the highway and they entered an area that looked vaguely familiar.

"You want to watch me have sex with someone else?" As long as he'd known Todd, which admittedly had a fifteen-year gap, dating had been an exclusive thing.

Todd's shrugged. "Yes and no? Like you said, it's a fantasy." His lip quirked up and he turned down a street and they were in Capitol Hill. Fazil recognized the rainbow crosswalks. "I'd rather be the one turning inside out. But I like the idea of a woman fucking the shit out of you." He glanced over. "Because I bet that got you off *hard*."

God, this conversation. Embarrassment covered him like bright red wrapping paper. All he needed was a freaking bow around his cock. Gift-wrapped for Todd.

That image didn't help at all. "Um. It did, yeah."

Todd grinned like the fucking Cheshire cat. "Hey, so where do you want to eat?"

And wasn't that an abrupt shift in direction? But Todd was pulling into his apartment building's lot and into a spot. "You know this place better than me."

"I should have asked *what* you want to eat." Todd put the car in park and killed the ignition.

Todd. He wanted to go down on him right here, because he was turned on like *fuck*. But his stomach was rumbling and they were in public. "Isn't this a foodie town? There's got to be some wacky organic German–Thai fusion sandwich and sushi shop, right?"

That earned him a snort. "Are you making fun of my town?"

Fazil smiled sweetly. "I have no idea what you're talking about."

"Out." Todd pointed at the door, his voice full of laughter.

He did as told, aware that he'd probably pay for that later. He shivered, despite the warm summer night. Todd joined him at the back of the car. "Let's unload, then find you something *interesting* to eat." He pulled Fazil close and stole a kiss. "And no, it's not going to be my dick. Not yet, anyway."

"Pity." He nipped Todd's chin.

"I told you. I love making you wait." Todd brushed a hand over Fazil's ass and stepped away to open the trunk.

God. He was so damn turned on and confused and happy and worried. Work tomorrow. Pittsburgh in a week or two. Todd *now*.

That's who he needed to focus on. Todd. "As long as you don't make me wait forever."

A chuckle. "Have I ever disappointed you?" He hefted his backpack.

"No." If anything, he'd been the disappointing one.

"You know, you never told me if last night was hotter than you'd imagined."

Their bet. As if he could get more turned on. "You won that fair and square."

"Thought so." Todd shut the trunk. "And now I have a baseline."

Shit. That only meant Todd would aim to top it. And him. Fazil's pulse picked up. "Bring it."

Todd's laugh was dark and sensuous, and it rang in Fazil's ears all the way up the apartment steps.

Todd took Fazil to a café with great food and good drinks, despite his quip against foodies. Not fusion, but the fare was good enough to make Fazil close his eyes after the first bite. "Okay, the food in this town is awesome."

Good. A happy, satisfied Fazil would be fun later. "Better than Pittsburgh?"

He didn't expect the hesitation. "Actually... there're some amazing places there and more opening every day." Fazil eyed the pasta on his fork. "Probably more here, but the quality is there, too."

Even though Todd fought against it, disappointment welled up. "You really like that town."

Fazil nodded. "I didn't think I would, but it turned out to be a great place. And you can't beat the cost of living."

That didn't sound like someone who wanted to move. Not that he wanted Fazil, too, except he did. *You've been together for a week.* "Sounds nice."

"It is. You should come visit." Fazil's smile was large and made the corners of his eyes crinkle in a way that never failed to turn Todd on.

He'd meant what he'd said on the mountain. Friend, lover, across the country—it didn't matter, so long as he had contact. Still, he couldn't keep the fantasy of them living together out of his head.

"Maybe I will." For now, Fazil was here. Now that he knew Fazil liked it rough *and* dirty, he had plans. He'd managed to slip a condom and a small tube of lube into his back pocket, and it was only a matter of time before he put them to their intended use.

The anticipation kept his dick hard, but his quips made Fazil laugh and grin and look beautiful sitting across the table from him. Thankfully this place served smaller meals, so clearing their plates didn't take that much time. Todd ran the side of his foot up Fazil's calf and enjoyed his intake of breath.

Fazil didn't order dessert. Seemed someone had gotten the hint.

Good. Todd felt like a live wire. All of his other partners had tiptoed around his past, treated it like shattered glass. But none of them had a kink like Fazil's.

They strode back to the apartment. As soon as Todd threw the lock, he turned and forced Fazil up against the wall, hard enough to knock some breath from him.

"I was thinking," he said, taking each of Fazil's arms by the wrist and trapping them above his head, "that we can play another game tonight."

"Oh?" Fazil's eyes were huge, and his breathing nearly as hard as his body.

Todd trapped both wrists in one hand and wrapped the other hand lightly around Fazil's throat. "You want that, Z?

A little fun?" He pressed his bulge against Fazil's and enjoyed the squirming.

"I—could. Yeah."

"I'm not going to be gentle with you." *At all.*

"Good." Fazil rocked his erection against Todd's. "Let me guess—red to stop, yellow to slow down?"

He laughed. "Thought you didn't like kink?" He shifted so his knee was between Fazil's legs and pressed up, forcing Fazil onto his toes.

"Oh my God." Fazil panted and looked up at the ceiling. "Shit." All moan.

He tightened the hand around Fazil's throat, not constricting anything, but enough to make Fazil look at him. "I think what you want is my dick in your nice, tight hole."

Fazil's throat bobbed under Todd's hand. "Yeah."

He pressed his body against Fazil and growled into his ear. "Well, you better get to begging, boy."

Against him, Fazil trembled. Todd pushed his knee up higher. "I know you heard me."

"I..." Breathless and shaking. "Please."

He slid his hand down Fazil's neck down past his chest and cupped him. "Please *what*, boy?" Fazil moaned when Todd massaged his hard cock through the denim.

"Please fuck me." Fazil's shaky voice gained confidence. "Bend me over and fuck me. I want your fat dick in my tight hole."

"That's the spirit." He bit Fazil on the neck, hard enough to leave a mark. Fazil cursed and thrashed, but he didn't say red. Or yellow.

Someone likes a little pain. "You're going to do exactly what I tell you."

"Okay." Practically a whimper.

Todd opened space between them and let Fazil go.

"Turn around."

Fazil did and Todd shoved him against the wall with one hand between Fazil's shoulders. He kicked Fazil's legs apart and felt him up from his taint to his crack. Fazil melted and humped at the wall.

"Horny little things like you want one thing, huh?"

"Yeah." No tremble in his voice now. "I want your cock, man. Gonna use it or just your fingers?"

He flicked a hand against one of Fazil's ass cheeks, drawing a yelp. "You keep running your mouth and I'll stuff something good and thick into it."

"There's only one of you and I don't care what hole you use."

Oh God Damn, Z. This was going to be more fun than he thought. "Maybe next time I'll bring a friend." He wasn't the type to share, but Mr. Dragon would make an awesome gag. He grabbed Fazil by the collar of his t-shirt and by a belt loop and pulled him off the wall. He was light enough Todd could've carried him across the room, but dragging him while he stumbled and moaned was much more satisfying. So was dropping him on the wide arm of his couch. "You like leather, boy?"

A grunt and a wiggle as Fazil tried to lever himself up.

Todd clasped the back of Fazil's neck and pushed him down. "I didn't hear your answer."

"I fucking love leather." Fazil slid his hips in a sensuous dance.

"Good, 'cause I want your face against the seat and your ass in the air." He yanked up on the belt loop and shoved Fazil down until his forehead touched the leather seat. And yeah, his ass was at the perfect height.

"Bet you enjoy that sight," Fazil said. "Old man like you."

He gave Fazil a swat on his other ass cheek. "I can stop up that mouth of yours with more than just my cock." Though listening to Fazil's back talk made this all the better.

"I'll take whatever you give me."

"You'd better." Knowing Fazil, he would.

He found the buckle of Fazil's belt and undid that, along with the button and enough of the zipper to slide Fazil's jeans and underwear down to his ankles, where they were trapped by his hiking boots. Even better to have those legs tangled up. He freed Fazil's belt, though.

"Seeing as you can't keep that mouth shut, you'd better make lots of noise." He pulled each of Fazil's hands to the small of his back and looped the belt around his wrists, securing them.

Fazil's breath hitched. "You want me to scream, you'd better give me something to scream about. Right now all you've got are words." He shook his ass. "Come on, old man. You gonna fuck me? Or tuck me in for the night?"

Dude, Z. Todd's cock strained against his jeans. He slid a finger down Fazil's crack and found his hole. "You ain't gonna sleep through this." He gripped Fazil's hair and yanked. "At all."

There was the whimper. "Oh God." Fazil twisted and rocked on the leather.

Shit, he hadn't even put on a condom, and Z was already close to coming. "That make you want to shoot your load? Me touching your hole? Wait until I'm fucking you so deep you can't breathe." He let go of Fazil, dug out the condom and lube, and shucked his own jeans and underwear.

"You keep promising, but not delivering." Breathless and snarky.

Todd ripped the package open with his teeth and rolled the condom down over his dick. "You keep talking, I'll fuck you dry."

"You wouldn't be the first," Fazil murmured.

Well, *shit*. That was interesting. "Aren't you the dirty boy?" He wasn't about to do that to Fazil, though. He lubed up his dick and Fazil's crack and pressed a finger in deep.

Fazil squirmed against the couch and moaned when Todd found and teased his prostate. "Oh God... Please," he panted.

That was better. "You want more of this?" Todd drilled his finger in as deep and as hard as he could.

"Or you want my cock in your hole?"

"Your cock." Fazil gasped and shuddered. "I want you inside me. Fuck me hard. Make me come."

With pleasure. Todd lined himself up and pressed forward, opening Fazil and pushing past the ring of muscle.

Beneath him, Fazil groaned.

Jesus, Fazil was tight like this. Todd grunted and slid into Fazil's heat slowly. Delicious curses spilled from Fazil, and he twisted beneath Todd, sending lightning through his veins.

"You like that? Being a little cock whore?"

Fazil whimpered and bucked. "Cock slut," Fazil said. "I'm a fucking little cock *slut*."

Todd pulled back and drove in deep. "I think *whore* works, too." He pounded in hard. "'Cause you're sure as hell gonna pay." He gripped Fazil's hips and pounded into him. He'd never fucked anyone this hard, fast, or deep. He slammed in until Fazil gasped and fought under him.

"Fuck!" Pain and pleasure wrapped his voice. "God, please, just—"

Todd shifted his stance and drove in deeper, chasing his

own heaven.

You wanted to know what it felt like, Z? Like this, except the guy ramming into me didn't love me. When Todd pressed in, he held himself there and Fazil sobbed out a cry.

"Told you you'd pay." He pulled out and rocked in with all his force. Beneath him, Fazil gasped against the leather. Todd grabbed his hair. "Tell me you love it."

There were tears in Fazil's voice. "Oh fuck, it's so good. Your cock in me—I want—please!"

He tightened his grip in those soft locks and rammed in as far as he could go. "Please *what*?"

Fazil shuddered. "Fuck me," he whispered. "Fuck me like you care."

His blood burned even as his heart split open. Words stuck in Todd's throat. *I do care! I've always cared!* Instead he gave Fazil what he'd asked for—the roughest sex he could offer. Fast strokes that stole Fazil's breath, then hard, deep ones that made Fazil cry. He pushed Fazil against the couch and drove into him as deeply as he could, savoring Fazil's sobs and tears. It was all he could do, because all those *I love you*s had never made it from Fazil's ears into Fazil's heart. Not then, nor now.

Tears spilled from Todd. *I've loved you since the day we met!*

"Good enough for you?" He couldn't keep the pain from his voice. He hoped to hell Fazil was too far gone to notice.

Maybe he was. Fazil bucked against the armrest, his hands clenched tight behind his back, and uttered an unintelligible cry. He shuddered and gasped and became so tight Todd could barely move inside him.

Didn't stop him from gripping Fazil's hips and plowing into him through Fazil's moans and cries of ecstasy. Todd chased his own release until those gasps turned to shudders and the moans didn't stop and he knew he'd pushed Fazil right to his limit.

"Please..." It was all breath and pain and pleasure. "Please..."

That sound, the timbre in Fazil's voice, pushed him over the edge. He buried himself in Fazil and came, his shout long and loud.

It took Todd too much time to come back to his senses. *Shit.* Fazil trembled beneath him. "Z?" He pulled out and leaned against the couch until his legs supported him again. "You okay?"

"Uh..." Fazil sniffled. "Uh-huh." A pause. "Think so." Crackly, breathless voice.

He didn't sound fine. "Let me free your hands." He loosened the belt and Fazil slipped his wrists out.

"Damn." Fazil propped himself up and rubbed his wrists. "Shoulda borrowed Eli's tie."

So maybe Fazil *was* okay. Todd hiccupped a laugh and wiped his face. Tears and sweat. He needed to ditch the condom, but his legs were trapped by his jeans and boots. "God."

Fazil looked back over his shoulder, his face damp, hair every which way, and his brow furrowed. "Are *you* all right?"

"Yeah." Never mind that his hands were shaking, he'd had the best orgasm of his life, and he wanted to tell Fazil that he'd always love him. "Just—that was pretty wild."

"It was fucking hot." Fazil flopped down on the couch. "Could you..." He wiggled his legs. "Help me out here?"

Pants, underwear, and boots still had Fazil's legs all nice and tied up. "I don't know. It's a pretty view." He patted Fazil's ass.

Fazil squirmed against the couch, then mimicked picking up a phone with his hand. "Hey, Eli? Can't come to work today. I'm trapped in my pants at Todd's and he likes my naked ass too much to help me."

Todd laughed. "I'm in the same predicament. Give me a minute." He unlaced his boots and managed to kick those and his pants off. Then he set to work on Fazil's boots. When he finished, he helped Fazil into his arms. "Better?" He brushed a thumb over stubble and jaw.

"Much." Fazil was all smile, lethargy, and glow. "Except I may have ruined your couch."

Todd glanced over. Drying semen all over the arm. On Fazil, too. He ran his fingers over Fazil's stomach, delighting in the quiver there. "Well, I did use one of those leather-guard polishes on the couch. Guess I'll find out if it worked." He leaned in for a quick kiss. "Don't think there's anything that can clean up how filthy you are."

"You're one to talk." Fazil pulled him down for a much longer, hotter, deeper kiss... and if he kept biting and thrusting his tongue like that, Todd would bend him back over the couch. He broke the kiss. "Let's move to the bed."

"Excellent plan."

They lost their shirts on the way and fell in a tangle of arms and legs onto Todd's bed. Eventually the kissing, nipping, touching quieted down into holding. Todd pulled Fazil close, pressing his lips to his shoulder. Quite a bruise was forming where he'd bitten Fazil on the neck.

Todd didn't have a religious bone in his body, but he sent up a silent thanks to the universe for bringing Fazil back into his life. "Should do that again sometime."

A sleepy reply. "Please."

Yes.

CHAPTER FIFTEEN

Fazil stirred against Todd and squinted at the window. A streetlight blazed in the dark outside. They'd fallen asleep and who knew what time it was, except too damn late. Sun didn't go down until nine.

He couldn't see Todd's clock, and his phone was still in his pants. Those were in a heap by Todd's couch, right where they'd been stripped off his ass.

Hadn't that been exquisite? Todd forcing him over the couch. The dirty talk. Fucking him. Punishing him. Keeping him there until he was good and done with him. Fazil rolled closer and kissed Todd's shoulder. Perfect man. Perfect lover. He'd needed that as much as he'd needed Friday. He hadn't realized how much.

Todd shifted and blinked his eyes open. "Hey." He looked at the window. "Well, shit."

"Yeah. Don't know the time, but I bet I should go."

"You could stay the night."

Todd ran his fingers through Fazil's hair and the gentle pull reminded Fazil of the much harsher ones earlier. "I know. I want to." He pushed himself up on one arm. "But riding in with you and not Eli will cause us a world of trouble."

Todd scrubbed his face. "God." He groaned, sat up, and peered at the clock.

"What's the damage?"

"Ten thirty."

Fazil grabbed a pillow, put it over his face, and moaned into it. A moment later, he tossed it aside and clambered out of bed. "I'm not going to hear the end of it from Eli, getting back this late."

"I'm sure he'll understand." Todd rose and fished around until he found a pair of pants. "He did offer the use of his tie."

They would have used it like Eli intended, too, given Todd's little stunt with the belt. "Oh, I'm sure he'll understand. That's why he'll give me hell." Fazil located his shirt by the bedroom door and headed into the living room. "He's like a snarky older brother. Except he's also kind of my boss."

"Your company is weird," Todd said from somewhere in the bedroom.

True. "Wouldn't give it up for the world."

A few minutes later, they were both dressed, and Fazil shoved the last of his belongings into his overnight bag. "I guess that's it."

Todd rolled his keys around his finger. "Back to the real world."

The pit of fear he'd ignored all weekend opened up again. Fazil glanced around Todd's place. "This is real, too." It had to be.

A flicker of concern in Todd, then he was pulling Fazil into his arms. "You better believe it's real."

Warm lips opening his and Todd's hands holding his

head. Fazil kissed him back, hard as he could manage. When they broke apart, he whispered, "Good."

Todd brushed his thumb over Fazil's lips. "I want you to remember where you were earlier tonight and how it felt to have me inside you." He grinned. "Those chairs in that conference room they gave you are black leather, aren't they?"

They were. His whole body tingled. "Yeah."

"Imagine having your face pressed into one of those tomorrow."

That image, the smell, the way Todd had moved inside him. Fazil closed his eyes.

"The real world." Todd's lips were against his, but only briefly. "Come on. Let's get you back."

Everything seemed a lot brighter when Fazil opened his eyes. Todd was beside him, with him. And that *mattered*.

FAZIL'S WORRIES ABOUT ELI WERE LAID TO REST WHEN they pulled up behind a sleek black BMW at the hotel. There was Eli, in a pair of jeans and a plain green t-shirt chatting with the man who must have owned the car, since he was leaning on it. Spiky blond hair and not someone Fazil thought might own horses.

"I guess teacher stayed out late on a school night, too," Todd said.

So it seemed. "Maybe I should have stayed overnight."

Todd chuckled. "Would've meant more leather for you." He put the car in park but didn't turn it off.

He unbelted and open the door.

Fazil could've gone for that. And those office chairs were going to look so different tomorrow. He got out of

Todd's car and retrieved his bag from the backseat. When he shut the door, Todd was by his side.

"I'm going to be thinking about that all day tomorrow." Todd stepped close and pulled him in for a kiss. Hot, demanding, sensual. It curled Fazil's toes, and he responded without thought, nearly dropping his bag.

When Todd let him go, he was breathless and hard, which was unfair since Eli wasn't far away.

"You did that on purpose."

"Mmm-hmm." Todd had that grin again. "Say hi to Eli for me." Another quick kiss coupled with a hug. "I'll see you tomorrow."

Fazil didn't want to let go, but he did. "Tomorrow."

Todd nodded and got back into his car. A moment later, he was gone and his absence ran through Fazil like a cold breeze. Life had changed. Everything remained the same. He didn't know which.

He looked up to find Eli and the blond man watching him. Both had curious and calculating expressions. His own must be a mess, like it was the end of the world, having your boyfriend drop you off after a weekend together.

Boyfriend.

Some things didn't change, it seemed. Fazil headed to the hotel entrance. The blond pushed himself off the car and gave Eli a friendly hug before making his way to the driver's side of the car. "Give Justin all my regards."

Eli huffed a laugh. "I certainly will."

A moment later, the blond and his expensive car were gone and there was only Eli and the hotel. Eli nodded at the glass doors. "Shall we?"

"I guess so." Not that he wanted to, but that was life. The curse of Sunday nights.

They didn't speak on the elevator ride up, nor when

they got to the room. Fazil set down his bag on his bed and stared at the crisp, impersonal bedding. A glance at the clock told him it was eleven thirty.

Way too late for a drink. "Care for a beer?"

A quiet chuckle. "Please."

On the ride down, Fazil studied Eli. "Did you have fun?"

Eli's look became distant and his expression hard to read. But he nodded. "You?"

That was a damn hard question to answer. "Yeah. Mostly."

Eli tilted his head, inviting more, but the elevator door opened. When they ordered beers and sat down at the booth that was rapidly becoming theirs—Fazil answered. "I had a good time. The best." He stared at the top of his beer bottle. "Except for the part where I learned that I was an utter asshole as a teenager. The villain of my own story."

Eli leaned back, beer in hand. "So you two had very different memories of the past."

"Same memories. I'd... embellished them, I guess."

"Are you sure?" Concern in Eli's voice and in his frown.

Fazil nodded. "All the times I thought Todd was pushing me away, he was giving me space because I was being a *dick*. I also believed every rumor of him fucking around, without *asking*." He snorted. "Some best friend. Turns out, none of it was true."

Eli took a drag on his bottle in a very un-Eli-like fashion, as if he weren't some rich finance guy. Fazil's gaze landed on his own bottle. Then again, he was an overeducated, well-paid software engineer.

Eli put his bottle down on the table. "Fuck the work stuff for a moment—I'm going to ask this as a friend. Are you okay, Fazil?"

He met Eli's gaze, understanding dawning. "Yes. He's not brainwashing me or anything. I had this history built up. It was a fixed thing, but it was built on lies." He shook his head. "Todd's a lot more forgiving than I am."

"Ah, I see. It's self-admonishment." Eli grabbed his beer. "You look a little beat-up around the edges." He took a swig.

"Well, *that's* probably from all the mind-numbingly rough sex we had."

Eli choked on his beer and wiped the back of his hand over his mouth. "That would do it, too."

Gotcha again. "It was a great weekend, once I got over the past. Saw Seattle. Went hiking."

"Fucked like rabbits?"

"That, too." He took a better look at Eli. Someone else looked worn-out. Except there was no Justin here, so he bet it wasn't for the same reason. "How was the horse riding?"

Eli's whole being changed in an instant. "Astounding. I never thought..." He shook himself. "I'm a bit of a control freak."

"Hadn't noticed."

He raised an eyebrow. "I still have a hand in your yearly evaluations, Mr. Kurt."

"That's *Dr.* Kurt, Mr. Ovadia," Fazil said. "And you did say fuck the job for the moment."

That earned him a laugh. "So I did." Eli took another swallow of beer. "I didn't think I'd like riding at all. But my friend convinced me to try. More of a partnership, he said." There was a wistfulness to his voice. "He was right." Eli gripped his bottle. "We ran. Flew, really, because a human could never run like that, and I forgot about my leg, my past. It was... freeing." He blinked a few times. "And painful the next day. Apparently there are muscles used for riding that I didn't know existed."

"Was that the trainer? The guy with the car?"

A huff of laughter. "Oh, no. Another of my friends, caught between the solitude of the ranch and the bustle of the city. He offered to drive me back."

That made sense, given the guy's look and his car. Fazil finished off his beer. "I have no idea what's going to happen next between me and Todd."

A sly smile from Eli. "That's the definition of life."

True. "Well, if nothing else. It'll make tomorrow interesting."

Eli glanced at his watch and twisted his face. "Today, actually." With that he downed the last of his beer. "I suspect we're both in for a world of hurt."

Probably. But he felt more centered now, and tired, as they headed back up to the room.

He'd need one hell of a pot of coffee tomorrow morning.

CHAPTER SIXTEEN

Fazil glanced in the hotel mirror after his shower. There was something decidedly *purple* on his neck.

Shit. He grabbed a towel and wiped part of the mirror clear and stared at the sizable bruise on the side of his neck, right where Todd had bitten him.

Heat flowed to his face... and lower. That whole episode had been amazing, but this? He turned his neck. Not even a dress shirt would cover it.

Damn it, Todd! Though he doubted Todd had been thinking much when he'd chosen that spot.

He shaved, because going in with scruff and a hicky screamed *I got laid this weekend, how 'bout you?* Thank God they hadn't talked about their plans. The only one who knew was Eli.

Eli. That mark had likely been there last night, too. He pulled on his jeans and exited the hotel bathroom.

In the mirror on the other side of the room, Eli was straightening his tie. "Legs less stiff now?"

"Did I stumble that badly into the bathroom?"

A flash of teeth. He tapped his one leg. "I have a reason to limp. You don't."

Fazil coughed. "Am I allowed to laugh at that?"

Eli turned. "Yes. If I'm deprecating myself, feel free."

"Has anyone ever told you that you're damned odd?"

That got him a full laugh. "Justin. All the time."

Fazil snorted and dug around in his suitcase. "Shit." Nope. Every shirt had a normal-height collar. No turtlenecks had appeared in his suitcase while he'd been showering. It was, after all, June.

"Something wrong?"

He let out a sigh and gestured at his neck. "We got carried away last night."

"So I noticed. It's quite pretty." Deadpanned words as Eli slipped on a vest and buttoned his cuffs.

Dude. "Eli..." He shook his head. "I don't want to know."

A very small smile.

Fazil could only laugh. In any other company, everything he was doing with Todd would have him on the street without a job. He sobered. "What am I supposed to do? It's not like I brought a turtleneck."

"Did you enjoy getting it?"

Oh fuck yes. But those words weren't getting past his throat. He nodded.

"Then own it, Fazil." Eli buttoned his other cuff, then started on his vest. "It's an honor, not an embarrassment."

An honor. "It could get Todd into a lot of trouble."

Eli's fingers stilled. He looked up. "Did you tell anyone you were spending the weekend together?"

"Only you."

Eli shrugged and smoothed out his vest before grabbing his jacket. "Then don't worry about it. Over the years, I've discovered that sex is something that makes people uncomfortable. Most people won't see that"—he waved at Fazil's neck—"for what it is, and those who do will be too embarrassed to ask."

"*You* didn't ask."

Eli raised an eyebrow. "Do you intend to wear a shirt to the office?"

Heat straight to his face. Fazil grabbed a polo from his suitcase and threw it on. Score one for Eli flustering *him*.

"No, I didn't ask. I knew exactly what it was, and I know how it got there."

"I appreciate you not pointing it out last night." Fazil checked himself out in the mirror to make sure he did, in fact, have all his clothing on. He grabbed his laptop.

Eli gathered his cane and his bag. "I figured you might."

They headed down to the lobby, but had a few minutes before the car service would pick them up, so they both ended up with complimentary coffee in their hands. "I suppose I should tell Sam about Todd."

Eli sipped, then spoke. "At this point, yes. He needs to know, in case it comes up."

"I'm guessing we should make sure it doesn't."

"That's the wisest thing," Eli said. "But I'm the last person who can complain about that."

The whole office had known when Eli and Justin had paired up. And broken up. And gotten back together. Fazil savored his coffee. That was one thing Seattle had going for it—even the shitty hotel coffee was good.

When their car came, he noticed the driver eyeing his neck, but true to Eli's words, the man didn't say a thing.

"Ready for round two?" Eli said.

"Question is, are they?"

Eli sank against the seat. "They better be."

THERE WASN'T ENOUGH COFFEE IN THE WORLD TO prepare Todd for the Monday-morning engineering meeting, especially today. He was in Hangover City, despite barely drinking anything all weekend. Only Fazil and more Fazil. He couldn't think of his name without a mental glimpse of him in the throes of orgasm, or fucking himself on that dragon dildo, or bent over Todd's couch.

Todd rubbed his temples.

"The little shit is trying to change the way we do things." Nathan's voice cut through Todd's haze.

He gripped his coffee mug. He'd missed something.

"Not *change* things," Stephen said. "Document how we do stuff and offer suggestions."

Nathan snorted and leaned back in his chair. "Whatever. They also took the best conference room and we're stuck with this." He gestured around the smaller, windowless room.

"They were given that room," Todd said. "And we have meetings in here every other week."

Nathan cocked his head. "You're the one helping him."

"I..." *Doing more to Fazil than helping.* Heat rushed to his cheeks. "Isn't that what I'm supposed to do?"

Everyone else in the room except Nathan and Stephen was staring at their cell phones or coffee cups.

Nathan furrowed his brow. "Aren't Muslims supposed to hate your type?"

His *type*? He almost stood. "Dude—"

Stephen cut in. "You're out of line, Nathan."

"Just saying." Nathan folded his arms.

"Well, don't." Stephen sighed. "Look, Anderson's

people are here to help. Don't fight them and they won't be here any longer than necessary."

"Then what?" That from Ganesh. "We get sold? What about our jobs? Are we doing this to work ourselves into unemployment?"

That wasn't a bad question. If Singularity was sold, whoever bought it might not keep them around. Maybe it was the coffee kicking in, but the *reason* Fazil was here hit like lightning. "They *want* to make sure the buyer keeps the people. Anderson's team. If we have all our ducks lined up and look professional, why wouldn't they?"

"That's the idea," Stephen said. "And *your* job. Line up our ducks, Todd."

He was trying. Nathan didn't help, but Todd kept his thoughts behind his lips. "Will do, boss." He sipped his cup.

"Ryan and their CFO aren't getting along. That can't be good." Erin turned her cell phone over in her hand. "If the money's screwed up..."

"Ryan says the guy's an idiot." Nathan again. Todd should have expected that. Thick as thieves, those two. "But what do you expect from a—"

"Enough." Stephen slapped his hand on the table. "This is an engineering meeting, not the rumor mill. I want to hear your statuses." He pointed at Nathan. "You first."

Nathan stammered, then settled in and gave his report. They all did in turn. When Todd spoke of working with Fazil, there were a few people more than just Nathan scowling.

Not good.

Stephen gave his little rah-rah for the week, then let them go. Todd's coffee had gone as cold as his blood. Nathan had his issues with him, sure, but something about that meeting churned Todd's stomach. He headed to the kitchenette to top his mug off.

Erin caught up with him, her cup in hand. "You knew the Anderson guy in college, right?"

"High school." He looked into his near-empty mug before picking up the coffeepot. "His name's Fazil."

She blushed. "I know. I..." She looked down the hall and dropped her voice. "Nathan *hates* him. Thinks he's an idiot. But he seems fine to me."

He grabbed two creamers. "Nathan hates everyone who doesn't toe his line."

She lifted the coffeepot and poured. "Don't I know that." She turned back. "I think what you guys are doing is good. Making sure we have standards and procedures and something other than throwing code at the wall until it sticks."

At least there were other people who felt that way. "If you have any suggestions or want to help..."

She grabbed a pack of sugar. "I'll send mail." A flash of a smile and she was gone.

Todd cradled his cup and looked out the window of the kitchen. The mountains were out today, that view Fazil loved.

He should tell Fazil and Eli that friction was brewing, but not now, lest Nathan notice. He took a sip, soaked in sunshine for a moment, and headed back to his cube.

FAZIL TAPPED HIS FINGERS AGAINST THE CONFERENCE table and ran down his checklist. How Singularity said they did things and how they actually did things were very different. The company-wide e-mail about someone jacking up the code repository was evident of that. Where was the version control? The unit tests?

He rubbed his eyes.

"Problems?" Eli looked up from his laptop. If Fazil hadn't known Eli better, he might have thought Eli was chewing on his thumbnail. Except Eli *was* chewing on his nail. *Shit.*

Fazil gestured at his screen. "I'm sure you saw the mail. It's like they don't *want* our help."

"I saw." Eli leaned back. "Change is hard. You know this."

He did. They'd done this before—not him and Eli, but this was far from Fazil's first rodeo. "I don't know what it is about this job, Eli. It seems—"

There was a knock on the door and they both froze. When the door swung open, it was Dr. Jackson. Fazil glanced at his clock. Right on time. He straightened in his chair.

"Gentlemen."

Eli also looked the consummate professional again. "Dr. Jackson."

She waved away the title and took a seat. "Please. Sandra." Once settled she took a deep breath. "I have news, but I'm afraid you won't like it."

There was Eli's thin smile, right on cue. "Ryan stays."

"Ryan stays," she confirmed, a tired note in her voice. "I argued your points, but the board has faith in him."

"I'm sure." Eli's expression didn't change. "Or he has something on the board."

She flinched. "I did press that your work is vital if they wish to sell the company. He's been instructed to *help*, not hinder."

"That's better than nothing," Eli said. The smile fell away. "I'll do what I can with Ryan around."

She nodded and rotated to address Fazil. "How are you finding engineering?" Her gaze seemed to flick to his neck for a moment, but then met his eyes.

Eli leaned back in his chair and tented his hands. A subtle sign.

Probably not the best policy to lie. "They're of two minds. The procedures are coming together, but there's a reluctance to implement. It's one thing to say you'll unit test your code before checking it in, but another to do it." He pushed his laptop to the side. "I know developers think testing takes away time they could be coding, but it saves them time in the long run. If they'd do what they said, your QA department wouldn't be slammed filing bugs against easy-to-fix mistakes."

She folded her hands into her lap. "What do you suggest to get them to change?"

"Someone from Singularity to make a hard case for it. I can't. I'm an outsider."

Sandra pursed her lips and nodded. "Good suggestion. I'll talk to Stephen." She rose. "There's been more interest in Singularity since you arrived, and not just for the tech."

Eli tapped a foot against the bottom of the table. "Then help us do our jobs so your people can keep theirs."

A smile from her, thin as Eli's. "I'll do my best."

When the door clicked closed, Eli looked up at the ceiling.

"Did you actually expect them to fire Ryan?"

"No." He rubbed the bridge of his nose. "Just hoped. If he stays out of my way, that's good enough."

"Well, if they can get someone to push for change, that will make my life easier." He hoped the person they picked *wasn't* Todd. They didn't need any more complications in their lives.

Speaking of which... He checked the time. Almost noon. "Should we call Sam?" His heart ticked up several notches. No idea how to explain that he was dating one of Singularity's engineers. It had happened so fast. Or too slow, given the years wasted.

Eli leaned forward and pulled the Polycom over. "Yeah. He should be in."

A quick punch of numbers and two rings later, Sam was on the line. "Hello, E."

"Good afternoon," Eli said. "Well, in a minute."

A laugh. "You have news?"

"I do." Eli filled Sam in on the Ryan situation. All the while Fazil's throat tightened and goose bumps ran up his arms. He rubbed his neck and inadvertently pressed where Todd had bit him.

Shit. That was sore, and too much of a reminder.

"Well, make do with that," Sam said. "I did try to twist some arms, but he's got strong backers."

"I keep wondering what he has on them."

Sam tapped something—he must have been on speakerphone, too. "Yeah. You know how much I like blackmail." A *thud.* "How's engineering?"

Fazil coughed. "It's getting there."

A pause. "Oh?"

"There's a hitch with the whole implement-what-we-say-we-do part."

A huff that was half amused and half frustrated. "Sounds familiar."

"Sandra's going to get someone on the inside to push for change."

"Good." Something crinkled across the line. "I don't

have any word on whether they've approved you staying on for longer."

A twist in his heart. Part of him wanted this job to end, but that meant leaving Todd. "I'll assume no, then."

Eli cocked his head and frowned. Had he given something away?

Maybe. Sam's next question was laced with concern. "Is there something else going on?"

Fazil shifted in his chair and Eli gave him a pointed look. "Yeah. But it's personal."

A *click* over the line and Sam's voice was much clearer. He'd switched to the handset. "What's up?"

"One of the engineers here, I knew him in high school." Fazil's pulse had him light-headed, but Eli nodded in encouragement.

"Old friend?"

His mouth dried, but he got the words out. "Old boyfriend."

A pause. "Ah. Rekindled, I take it?"

"Yeah." That was one way to put it. "We hadn't seen each other in a while and..." He waved a hand even though Sam couldn't see. "There's still a connection."

"That's putting it mildly," Eli said, his voice all humor.

Sam coughed, though it sounded more like a laugh. "Oh?"

Eli just grinned.

"We're keeping it out of the office."

"Best plan." A very dry, amused tone. "Please don't use Eli as an example."

Most awkward phone call with the boss *ever*. "But just in case, I thought you should know."

The amusement dropped away. "I appreciate that. It's—

Well, like you said, keep it out of the office." He paused. "And enjoy."

That had his face red. "Thanks." He managed to get that out without sounding like a dope. Didn't help that he was suddenly aware of the smell of leather from his chair.

"Anything *else*?" Sam said. "No secrets from you, E?"

A deep rumble of laughter from Eli. "Sam, you already know them."

That sounded suspiciously like another coughing fit on the other end. "If that's it, you two have a nice lunch."

"Have a nice one, Sam." Eli hit the off button, then sat back in his chair. "Better?"

Not really. "I feel like I'm walking on fire."

"Perhaps." Eli tapped the track pad on his laptop to wake it up. "Only one thing to do now."

"Work?"

Eli glanced at his computer. "Lunch," he said. "With management—in a few minutes, according to this invite."

Joy. "So, work." Which was fine. That's what he was here to do, after all.

CHAPTER SEVENTEEN

Wᴴɪʟᴇ ᴛʜᴇ ғɪʀsᴛ ᴡᴇᴇᴋ ᴡɪᴛʜ Fᴀᴢɪʟ ɪɴ ᴛʜᴇ ᴏғғɪᴄᴇ had been bad for Todd's concentration, it paled in comparison to this week. They barely saw each other in person, but now there were texts and e-mails, especially once they'd left work for the night. Going out in the evening was impossible, given their schedules—they were all working late in an effort to get as much done before the weekend—and nominally Fazil and Eli's departure.

No news on whether Fazil would be staying. Given the workload, he suspected not, which didn't help his mood. Neither did the digs from Nathan about Fazil or the procedures.

The friction in development wasn't anything Fazil hadn't noticed, though that had quieted down when Erin mentioned how much running some tests on her code had saved her grief from QA. The problems QA now found were more interesting to debug, too.

But by Wednesday, Todd itched to do more than say hello to Fazil at the coffeepot. He'd love to see his smile or hear his laugh, or hold his damn hand. There were some other fantasies thrown in, but at the moment, all he wanted was a ten-minute conversation. He checked the time before picking up his cell phone.

Plans for lunch?

A moment later, the reply came. Surprisingly no. Good. Finally. Thai?

Anything. Want to see you.

That kicked up his pulse. *Want* described a great many things he'd like to do with Fazil, if only they had more time.

Meet downstairs at 11:45.

That ought to get them out of the office before coworkers noticed they'd left.

Will be there.

Todd slid his phone back onto his desk. Fifteen more minutes.

The time moved almost too fast. Sinking back into work for those few minutes got him to the front door of the office later that he'd planned, and the elevators were slow.

Behind him, the bathroom door squeaked open. "You're leaving early," Nathan said.

He nearly jumped out of his skin. "I like getting to a place before the crowd hits."

A sharp smile. Too sharp. "Your buddy just went down."

He stared blankly at Nathan, a sense of dread biting up

his spine. Thankfully the elevator dinged and he turned away, but not before he heard Nathan snort and the office door beep open.

He thumbed the ground-floor button. As the elevator doors closed, he caught a glimpse of Nathan holding open the office door, his expression calculated as he met Todd's gaze.

Shit. Had he parked on the Singularity side of the building? Todd raked his hands through his hair.

Everyone knew they'd gone to high school together. This was two friends catching up.

Except they weren't just two friends. Did Nathan know?

He composed himself before the elevator hit the ground floor. No use panicking over nothing.

When the elevator doors opened, Fazil was standing in the lobby talking to Sandra, of all people, and Todd's lungs tightened. Fazil nodded at him, and Sandra turned.

"So this is your lunch companion." No anger in her voice, thank fuck. No surprise, either.

Fazil shrugged. "Old friends, and we missed a lot of years."

She smiled at that. "Smooths over the work relationship, too, I'm sure."

Todd stepped forward. "That, and he's doing the right thing." Came out more forcefully than he'd intended.

Sandra's smile fell away. "So I've heard. I've heard the opposite, too."

Todd met Fazil's worried glance.

"But the board wants Anderson to succeed, so I'm glad there's someone Mr. Kurt can work with." The elevator opened. This time it was Sandra who turned. Todd followed her glance.

Shit. Stephen and Nathan. The *look* on Nathan's face—like he'd won a freaking prize.

"Have a nice lunch, gentlemen."

There was a perfect exit cue. Seemed Fazil had the same thought, because they both headed to the door. Fazil didn't say a thing and Todd's throat was way too tight.

"Well, shit," Fazil said, once they were safely in Todd's car. "Not that going to lunch is a crime, but..."

"I know." He turned the car over and headed out. "Nathan's not a happy camper about you or the changes or..."

"...Anything," Fazil finished. "And he dislikes you."

Todd studied the road as he drove. "Thing is, he's a really good engineer. They can't afford to lose him, because he's designed too much of the software. He knows it, too."

Fazil rolled his head back against the car seat. "So he gets away with a lot."

"Pretty much."

A sigh, then Fazil looked over. "I wish you lived closer to the office. We could skip lunch, and no one would be the wiser."

Well, how about that? "What would you rather be doing?"

"You." His voice was soft. "Well, you doing me."

Damn if that didn't make Todd shift in his seat. "The chairs in the conference room getting to you?"

A grunt. "More like your damn texts from last night. Couldn't do a thing with Eli in the room."

Which had been the point of describing how he'd have laid Fazil out and fucked him on his couch, had he been there. A hot and bothered Fazil with no outlet? Made his balls ache. "I'll remember that tonight."

Fazil slid his hand onto Todd's thigh, the sudden

warmth and pressure playing along every nerve. "I'm sure you will."

When Fazil moved his hand upward, it took all Todd's concentration not to career off the road. He turned into a strip mall, pulled into a space—out front this time—and cut the engine. "You know, if it weren't daytime and we weren't in public"—he pulled Fazil's hand onto his hard shaft—"I'd have you suck me off right here."

That brilliant smile. "Just like old times."

Him, Fazil, his car, and endless summer days. He held Fazil's hand a little longer. "I miss that sometimes."

The smile fell away. "So do I, sometimes."

Was that wistfulness, regret, or something else entirely? Todd couldn't tell. Another shiver up his spine, but this was cold and icy. *Sometimes*. They'd both said the word, but it sounded more *true* with Fazil. He let go. "Let's get some food."

They both climbed out and headed into the restaurant. While it was a basic storefront place, the owners had taken the care to make it pretty. The ochre-colored walls had wood accents and pictures of Thailand. Red cloths on the table. Soft lighting.

You're not over him leaving, a voice in his mind whispered. *And you know he's going to do it again.*

By the time they'd ordered, a thinner version of Fazil's smile returned. "Look, we'll get some time together even if they don't extend the contract. I'll stay the weekend. Fly home on Monday."

"That sounds good." He fiddled with the paper from his straw. "Well, you going doesn't sound good, but..."

Fazil traced a finger over the bamboo place mat. "How are we going to do this? My track record with long distance isn't good and..." He lowered his voice. "What are we doing? Dating? Fucking?"

Both? "I'd like to keep this going."

Sad lines around Fazil's eyes. "If the distance weren't there, this would be perfect."

Time to place that card on the table. "Well, maybe at some point, the distance doesn't need to be there."

Fazil sat up straighter. "You mean me moving here?"

"There's a decent amount of high tech, and you like the city and the mountains." Todd set the wrapper aside. "It's a thought."

Fazil seemed to chew on it. "This is... fast." He rubbed his elbow, then met Todd's gaze. "I mean, it's been just over a week since I showed up."

"Maybe?" It was, on some level. "But you can't deny the connection."

That brought out a laugh. "God, no. I can't." The grin was back. "I'll think about it. Won't stop me from going home soon, though."

Home. There it was again.

A moment later, the waitress brought their food. After they dug in, the door to the restaurant opened and a group of five engineers from Singularity walked in. They noticed Todd right away and then the back of Fazil's head, judging from the frowns.

Damn. "We've got company."

Fazil fiddled with his chopsticks. "Got it."

No more personal talk. Not when the host seated the group at the table behind Fazil. Todd picked up his own sticks. "Have you been back home at all?"

A look of understanding passed across Fazil's face. "Yeah. Last year. They tore down the high school a couple of years back."

Same conversation from before, this time entertainment for his coworkers. They discussed school for a while, then slid into work topics—mostly about Fazil's experiences rather than on the current situation at Singularity.

He'd worked a lot of interesting jobs. The way his eyes lit up when he spoke of the coding he'd done or the solutions the Anderson team had implemented took Todd's breath away.

So did Fazil's leg brushing his halfway through the meal. A wicked little smile after that, too.

The contact, soft as it was, poured heat into his body.

"Hey." One of the guys from the other table—Eric—leaned over. "You ever fail at one of those jobs?"

Fazil frowned, but he rotated to address the other table. "Yeah. It's not pleasant, and no one is happy about it, because we know what it means."

"Layoffs." Eric wore a grim expression.

"We succeed most of the time," Fazil said. "But if the goalposts are moved, or the company is in worse shape than we first realized, it's harder."

"Which are we?"

That pulled a chuckle from Fazil. "You guys are pretty normal."

That eased some of the tension at the table. "Thanks." Eric turned back to his food.

When Fazil met his gaze, there were lines around his eyes, and the smile that curved his lips was fake.

Good thing their server brought the check. They escaped back to Todd's car. Fazil closed his eyes and released a breath.

After they were back on the road, Todd spoke. "Did you mean that? We're normal?"

"Yeah." Fazil waved a hand. "The pushback, resistance

to change, and suspicion are common. That's part of the reason we come to sites. Once you work with people face-to-face, that tends to go away."

Except here it hadn't. "If it doesn't?"

"I don't know." Quiet words. "I guess we'll see."

That didn't bode well. Todd chewed on his tongue. Time to switch subjects. "Since you're here for the weekend, how does seeing Mount Rainier sound?"

Fazil's whole body relaxed. "I'd love that."

Then that would be the plan. One day at a time, with both work and play.

WHEN ELI'S CELL PHONE RANG AT NINE FIFTEEN THE next morning, Fazil nearly jumped out of his skin. Judging by Eli's wide eyes, he was also surprised. He snatched up the phone on the second ring.

"Hello?"

Fazil hefted his coffee and practically inhaled it. It wouldn't touch his rapid heart rate, but it would help him parse the e-mail in his inbox. Maybe.

"Sam?" Eli said. "Let me call you back on the speakerphone."

A bolt of shock ran through Fazil and he rolled over closer as Eli punched Sam's number into the Polycom.

"Good morning!" Sam sounded chipper, but then it was just past noon there. Fazil took another swig of coffee and hoped the caffeine hit soon. "I have news."

"Oh?" Eli's voice lifted. "I'm going to take a stab and guess you're not calling to make *my* day."

Sam huffed a laugh. "No, Ryan still stays."

He shrugged. "Worth a shot."

Fazil's breath caught and he set down his cup. "They said yes to an extension."

"For you," Sam said. Fazil could picture him smiling from the timbre of his voice. "One week extra, which is less than you wanted—"

"It's fine." Two would have been better. "I'll get what I need in place. I can manage the rest remotely." If he took a day off on the far end, he'd have two more weekends with Todd.

Eli's chuckle was so soft, Fazil doubted it carried over the speakerphone.

"Good," Sam said. "E, you're flying back on Saturday, as planned."

"It'll be good to come home," Eli said. "This has been... trying."

"I know. You've both done great work."

Fazil didn't hear much of the rest of the conversation—confirming Eli's travel arrangements for the weekend and detailing what was left on his side. His fingers itched to text Todd the news.

Another week. He missed Pittsburgh, the team, and his own space, but the extra time would give them a chance to figure out how to keep this relationship going.

"No, I think that's it. Fazil? You have anything more" Eli's words broke through Fazil's thoughts.

"No. I'm good. I'll lay out the plan for the next week and get back to you."

"Good, good. Have a nice one, guys." And with that, Sam was gone.

A sly smile from Eli. "Go on. Tell him."

Fazil rolled his eyes, but he did pick up his phone. Maybe his fingers shook a little texting the news to Todd.

Fantastic! Came the reply. We'll talk tonight.

Good. Every nerve sang, even though every night without Todd was frustrating as all hell. For now, he had work to do. The extension didn't change his job, just gave him more breathing room.

After lunch, which they ordered in for a change, they had yet another meeting with management to fill them in on the changes in the plan. Sandra wasn't there due to a conference call with the board, but her e-mail made it clear Eli and Fazil could easily fill in the rest of the team. They had her utmost support, and she'd prepped her staff.

Hopefully that would be enough.

Eli took only himself and a notepad, while Fazil grabbed his laptop. He had a game plan for the next week, and if things went well, they'd nail everything they needed. He'd clean up loose ends remotely.

The other conference room was stuffed with more than the senior management. Eli straightened to his full height and the hairs on Fazil's neck rose.

Ryan was there, along with Stephen. So were Nathan and Todd and two of the folks from QA. Todd didn't look apprehensive. Fazil focused on that and calmed his pulse down. Nathan was an asshole but still a team lead.

They both settled into their seats. Eli's smile was professional, even with the edge to it. "I suppose you've all heard about Fazil's extension. He has a plan for the rest of the week."

Nice of Eli to throw him to the wolves first. He cleared his throat, faced Stephen and the other engineering staff, and dove right in.

Stephen had a few questions, but the plan seemed to make sense to him, judging from his nods. The QA folk were on board.

"Shouldn't be a problem," Todd said.

A snort from Nathan. "Of course not. It's your old chum."

Todd shrugged.

Before Fazil could mouth off a reply, Eli spoke. "All finished?"

"Yup, that's it from me." Shutting up was a better plan than taking badly laid bait.

Eli launched into a recap of his own work and what was left, which were a few outstanding pieces. "The financial paperwork is about in order," Eli said. "I hope going forward you'll keep more... regular... records. There are some corners that can't be cut."

Ryan glowered at that, his face both pale and red. "I saved the company money."

"You nearly sank any chance Singularity has of being acquired." Eli leaned forward, one hand on the table. "And where, exactly, did the money you saved go?"

"You little fuck, are you—"

"Ryan." Stephen's voice was sharp. "Enough."

"I believe I'm done here." Eli rose from his chair, his hand wrapped around the shaft of his cane. He tucked the notepad under his arm. "It's your bottom line, Mr. Kendall. You might not be interested in that, but your investors are." He headed for the conference room door.

"It's all penny-pinching to you, isn't it?" Ryan said. "Typical. Just what I'd expect from a Jew."

The room fell silent on an intake of breath from more than one person. Eli's shaking hand hovered over the doorknob. He'd gone pale—almost gray.

Fazil's heart rammed against his ribs, his body frozen in that ticking of time.

Eli curled his hand into a fist before letting it fall to his side, and when he turned, his expression was almost neutral.

Almost. Fury peeked out from under the impassive stare. Fazil had never seen Eli so angry or so calm. Both were terrifying. He couldn't catch a breath.

"Thank you," Eli said in a quiet, controlled voice. "You've made my job much easier." He turned, opened the door, and strode from the room.

Fazil glanced at Todd. His face was bloodless as well, mouth open and eyes wide and focused on the spot where Eli had stood.

Nathan glared at Fazil, his contempt obvious. Then he turned that same sneer on Todd.

Shit. Last thing he wanted was for Todd to be in the crosshairs. Fazil knew too well how *that* went down. "If you'll excuse me." He rose and hurried after Eli, but not before he caught the words chasing at his back.

"Didn't think the camel jockey would take a Jew's side." That from Ryan. Fazil cringed and his back felt like fire.

Todd's voice rose. "You arrogant..." Then the door closed and he was out of earshot.

Eli strode down the hall at a clip, despite his limp, and Fazil had to jog to catch up. No sign from Eli that he registered Fazil's presence, even when they entered their conference room. Eli took a few steps and stopped, his hand gripped so tight around the shaft of his cane his knuckles looked unreal. His entire frame trembled. He whipped out his arm, and the cane arched across the room, striking the far wall in a shotgun of clattering before falling to the ground.

"Fuck!"

It was a cry of pure rage and sadness, and it tore into Fazil, shredding his soul down to his bones. He *knew* that rage, felt it even now, a hurt so familiar it was a second skin. To be the other. The outsider. Not *American* enough. Not *Christian* enough.

Even in high school, he'd felt that weight, but Todd had shielded him from the worst.

Eli took a deep, shuddering breath, pulled out one of the conference table chairs, and slumped into it. The fury had abated, but the deep lines of anger were carved into his face and part of his motions. "It never stops." He raised his head. "Just when I think the world might have changed..." He gave a strangled grunt. "My own fault for being so naive."

Fazil pulled out another chair and sat down. "Racist assholes are *not* your fault." He didn't have anything to throw, though he wanted to.

Eli was right. This shit never did end.

A bitter chuckle. "I *knew* what I was getting into when I went into finance. Playing into the stereotype."

"There's nothing stereotypical about you, Eli."

That earned him an honest laugh and one that wasn't as pained. "Thank you for that." His humor drained away. "You've been in this spot."

"Not since I joined Anderson." The looks. The whispers. The jokes. "But with a name like Fazil..." He waved a hand. "Job before this one, someone left a camel figurine on my desk." Same shit, different day.

Eli looked up at the ceiling. "Camels aren't native to Turkey."

"Right?" His turn to croak a laugh. "I did thank them for the pork barbecue they left. Took the can of Bud Light back and asked for a Sam Adams instead."

That garnered a snort. "Bet that didn't go over well."

"Nope. Got me fired."

Eli met his gaze. "Not a team player? Not acting professional in the office? Causing too much derision?"

He nodded. "Plus bringing booze into the workplace. Never mind that it was left at my desk."

"Bullshit all the way down." Eli worked his jaw. "The worst thing? This was *mild*. Some of the shit people have said to me and left for me..." He shook his head. "After all, I'm Jewish, gay, *and* disabled."

Fazil's heart lurched down to his toes. *Holy shit.* "They didn't—"

The door to the conference room cracked open and Sandra slid halfway into the room. "May I come in?"

Eli sat up and nodded. "Please." Sharp voice. This was Eli prepared for war.

Sandra's face was pale and drawn. Obviously she knew what had gone down. She entered and let the door *click* behind her. "Todd informed me what happened. I must apologize to both of you for Ryan's actions." She spread her hands. "There's nothing I can say to excuse his behavior."

Eli didn't move. "You're not the one who should be apologizing."

True. She didn't look happy to be doing it, either.

When she didn't answer, Eli continued, "What happens now?" The question was soft, as if Eli expected a certain answer.

She let out a breath. "He's been reprimanded and sent home."

"Permanently I hope." Fazil crossed his arms.

Eli turned his head, and there was the tremble of rage again. Not good. Neither was his stony silence.

"Mr. Kendall's employment, or lack thereof, is contingent on board approval," Sandra said.

"They have to *approve* to fire him? After that?" Fazil's voice ticked up at the end.

Eli leaned back in his chair, his hands wrapped around the armrests. "Tell your board that they can sell this company at a profit, at a loss, or grind it down into dust. It's entirely up to whether they keep Ryan."

"It's not that simple."

"It's exactly that simple." Eli looked away. "Excuse me, I need to call my boss and make arrangements to head home."

"Mr. Ovadia..."

Eli shook his head.

"What is it with that guy?"

Both of the executives turned and looked at Fazil. "There has to be some reason you're not canning him on the spot. If he were anyone else, he'd be standing outside with a box full of his shit right now."

There was the crack. Sandra rubbed her forehead. "He's related to the chairman."

Eli let out a long exhale.

She continued. "Apparently he's a 'good guy who just gets in over his head.'"

"He's over his head because he's sinking the company." Eli stood and hobbled over to the far wall to retrieve his cane. "He's also anti-Semitic, and I can't believe I'm the only Jewish person in your office." He folded his hands overtop the silver handle. Armor, Fazil realized. "You have an HR situation on your hands."

She twisted her face. "Believe me, I know. If I could, I'd fire him," she said. "But my hands are tied."

"Maybe Sam can help untie them." Eli's voice held less hostility. "I'm being truthful. No company will touch this one if Ryan stays and puts on that kind of act for them." He waved his hand at the door.

"They say Sam's a miracle worker." Bitterness in her voice.

Eli almost looked sympathetic. "I have one request."

"Anything."

"Keep that fucking piece of shit away from me."

She blanched but nodded. "I'll do what I can." She glanced at Fazil. "For both of you."

When the door clicked shut after her departure, Eli took his seat again. "That fucking jagoff say something to you, too?"

Anger tended to bring out the Pittsburgh in Eli. "Remember I mentioned the camel incident at my former employer? Similar quip. Wondered why I was defending you."

He rubbed the bridge of his nose. "Maybe because you're a decent human being?" Eli reached over and pulled the Polycom toward them. "We need to call Sam and tell him what's going on." He paused. "Did she say Todd was the one who told her?"

Yeah, she had. Trust Eli to catch that. He nodded.

"That may not turn out well for him."

"I know." Especially if anyone caught on about their relationship. "I'll talk to him off the clock. Tell him to lie low."

Eli nodded. "Smart move." He studied the Polycom and swallowed. "I hate to suggest this, but perhaps you two should cool things for a while."

Easier said than done. "I know that, too." He met Eli's gaze. "I don't want to fuck this up."

"It's already fucked," Eli said. "We're supposed to be here to *un*fuck it."

Point taken. He and Todd would have to be a hell of a lot more discreet. Eli punched in the numbers for Sam's office, and Fazil waited, heart in his throat, while the phone rang.

The usual greeting from Sam, then Eli spoke. "We have a problem."

Silence. Then an exhale and Sam's worried voice. "What happened?"

Eli filled him in, with Fazil including what had happened in the moment after Eli had left. Together they recounted the conversation with Sandra.

"Well, shit," Sam said. "No one should be subjected to that."

"But you're going to ask us to keep working," Eli said.

Fazil could almost *see* Sam's cringe. "Yes." A pause. "Let me talk to the board again."

Eli's shoulders drooped. "Think you can make them deep-six the asshole?"

"I can't promise anything, but I *am* the man who withstood a deposition on a fraud case. I believe I can get them to see my view... unless they want to be in that hot seat, too."

Eli chuckled, but there was no mirth in it. "Good luck with that."

"Can you stomach another day there, E?"

Eli's hardened expression slipped away into something that twisted Fazil's gut. Too open and too wounded. "To be honest, no."

There was silence on the other end.

"I can work from the hotel."

"Eli..." Deep concern in Sam's voice.

He clicked his tongue. "I'll be fine, Sam. I've been through worse. I'm just tired."

"Okay," Sam said. "What about you, Fazil? I know you have personal reasons for wanting to stay, but can you work in that environment?"

He didn't know—not yet. "I need to see how things are tomorrow before I decide."

A grunt from Sam. "If we need to fly you back this weekend…"

He'd need to know now to get him a Saturday flight. "Before the extension, I'd been planning to ask Justin to shift the ticket to Monday and take a day of PTO."

"That would work," Sam said. "But let Justin know as soon as you're sure."

"Understood."

"Anything more?"

There wasn't, so they said their good-byes and hung up.

"Sam's been brought up for fraud?" He'd never seen anything in his research to indicate *that*.

Eli waved the question away. "No, of course not. He uncovered shady dealings at Four Rivers while grooming it for Sundra's acquisition. Took the case a while to grind through the legal process, and eventually Sam was called to give his statement."

"And get grilled?"

"Depositions aren't fun."

He wouldn't know. Hoped he never had to know. "That has to be fairly recent."

Eli nodded. "This past winter. Right before the company party."

The cruise. God, that had been a day and a half worth of fun packed into a couple of hours. No wonder Sam had let loose harder than he normally did. "That explains a few things."

This time there was warmth to Eli's laugh, and his

humor was slower to drain away. "We still have a few hours left. Let's see what we can get done." He leaned his cane up against a neighboring chair and opened his laptop.

Fazil pulled his computer over and did the same. He was almost surprised not to see an e-mail from Todd. Then again, there were some things you didn't send over a corporate net, even from private accounts.

He desperately wanted to talk to Todd, but Eli was right —best to keep that cool, at least until after quitting time.

CHAPTER EIGHTEEN

TODD SPRINTED FROM THE PUBLIC PARKING GARAGE TO Fazil and Eli's hotel, blood pounding in his ears and the scene from earlier playing out in his mind.

Same horror, same shock. He'd left the meeting and gone back to his cube. But his gut had burned with fire and anger, so he'd gotten up and walked into Sandra's office while she was still on her call with the board.

He must have had every emotion on his face, because her hand hit the mute button and the next words out of her mouth were "Close the door and sit." He'd sat there while she finished. Then, as she grew paler with his every word, he'd told her what had happened at the meeting she'd ditched.

Once back in his cube, the rest of the day had been excruciating. He hadn't dared venture to Fazil's and Eli's conference room. It might have been his imagination, but every time he got up—for water or tea or even to take a piss —Nathan was there. That sent a bolt of ice into his heart.

He'd called Fazil as soon as he'd gotten into his car.

"We're at the hotel," Fazil said. "Getting drunk."

Todd found them in the bar. Neither man smiled when he approached their booth, though Fazil's shoulders dropped and his face softened.

"Thanks for coming." He slid over to give Todd room.

Todd sat, and Fazil's hand was in his, warm and real. "Are you all right? Are you both..." The answer was obvious from Fazil's death grip on his hand.

They weren't.

There were dark circles under Eli's eyes, and he shifted in his seat. A half-empty martini glass sat in front of him. "I'm feeling better now." Soft words.

This wasn't good. "What can I do to help?"

"Take good care of Fazil next week. Keep the assholes away from him." Eli lifted his drink and there was a shaking in his hand.

"I'll be *fine*," Fazil said in a tone that meant he'd said it several times before.

An argument in progress. Eli's words sank in. "Wait, Fazil will be here next week?"

Fazil gripped his full glass of beer. "In theory. We'll see what happens tomorrow."

"You'll stay." When Eli looked over, his eyes were rimmed with red. "In the same situation, I would, despite my better judgment." He tipped his drink to Todd.

Because of him. Todd squeezed Fazil's hand.

"Well, there's also the job. I don't want to let Sam down." Color touched Fazil's cheeks.

That drew a smile out of Eli, but it clashed with every other line on his face. "That makes two of us." Choked words. Eli cleared his throat and took a sip. "Don't you dare tell me it wasn't my fault again. I know that."

"I don't work with Ryan. He's not going to come after

me." He lifted his beer. "Besides, I'm not your typical Muslim."

Todd's blood ran cold. That didn't matter to someone like Nathan, who *did* work with Fazil.

"Fazil, my beer-drinking, bacon-eating, queer compatriot, you can't change your blood to these people. That's all they see. Believe me. I *know*." Eli threw back the remainder of his drink. "It's not just Ryan."

"That was three, by the way."

Eli set down the glass. "I'm not so drunk I can't count." He frowned at the glass. "I'm also not so drunk that I don't regret saying I'd stop at three."

There was a tiny smile from Fazil. "I won't tell."

"Yes, you will."

Todd shrugged. "I won't. Looks like you only had one from here." He raised his hand to flag the waiter. "And I wouldn't mind having a beer."

In the end, Eli didn't order another. Todd chose the second beer the waiter rattled off—a local IPA. Didn't matter to him. All the local beers were good.

When the waiter left, Eli gave Todd a long look, one with a furrowed brow and near-unblinking eyes. "You should watch your back."

"I already do." Todd ran a thumb over Fazil's hand. "Managed so far."

"Will you do what I've asked?"

Keep the assholes away from Fazil. "I'll do my best." Even if he had to take their ire.

"I don't need a protector." There was a clip to Fazil's voice, the one he got when he was fucking annoyed.

"Everyone needs a protector."

"*Really?* Who's yours, then?"

Yup, a pissed-off Z. Didn't seem to faze Eli one bit. His smile was honest and warm. "Justin."

Fazil sucked in a breath. That name knocked the wind right out of him and he thudded against the booth, practically slumping into Todd's arms.

A satisfied grunt. "And I ought to call him before it gets much later." Eli reached for his cane and stood, wobbled, and steadied himself. "Do take care of yourself, Todd."

"I will. Thanks."

With that, Eli headed out.

When he was out of earshot, Todd spoke. "So how is he, really?"

"Eli? He's tough as nails." Fazil turned his beer glass so the logo faced him. "Always has been. I used to think..." He shook his head and took a sip.

"What?"

"I used to think he was a cold bastard. He was fair but fucking exacting. Sam liked him, though, and could get the stick out of his ass sometimes, you know?"

Todd didn't, but he nodded anyway.

"Turns out he's a nice guy under that." Another sip. "He's hurting, more than he's letting on, but if there's anyone who can get through, well, anything—it's Eli."

There was a story there, but it seemed impolite to pry. "Justin?"

"Eli's husband."

Right. Sam's assistant.

"He's—wait. I may have photos from the winter cruise." He pulled out his phone and flipped through images. "Here." He handed it to Todd.

There was Eli with his arm around a drop-dead-gorgeous man. Justin looked somewhat goth even in a suit, given the blacker-than-black hair. But those blue eyes and that shit-eating grin... no wonder Eli looked utterly smitten. The two of them defined *stunning*. "That's completely unfair."

"Isn't it? They're practically opposites, and yet..." He waved his hand at his phone. "Perfect couple."

Eli's protector. Todd took a swallow of his beer before wrapping his arm around Fazil. "So next week?"

"It's supposed to be me finishing up enough that remote work will suffice." Fazil leaned into Todd. "Eli's right. Unless things are hideous tomorrow, I'll stay."

With the office the way it was right now, Todd understood the caution. "I want you here for as long as possible, but if things aren't good, don't stay because of me." He wouldn't put Fazil in danger.

"Let's see tomorrow." Fazil rested his hand on Todd's thigh. "You didn't catch any flack, did you?"

"Not that I know of." He took a longer drink. "Certainly not from Sandra. I suppose Nathan will realize who ratted Ryan out, but I don't care."

"Why are people so shitty?" All the depth of anguish there.

"God, Z, if I knew that, I'd solve the world's problems." He pulled Fazil closer. "Do you want me to stay? I can get a room."

"I'm not good for anything but sleep." He sat up and finished the last of his beer. "But I can't think of anything I want more than to wake up next to you."

The thump of his heart made his chest ache. "Me neither."

Fazil charged the drinks to the room he shared with Eli. "Normally we'd pay, but Eli says Sam owes us this round."

Made sense. And it seemed Eli was fine with the idea of spending the night alone. Fazil stopped briefly to grab a few things before they headed to the room Todd had checked into. When they finally slipped under the cool sheets, Fazil pulled Todd close and shivered against him. "Truth is I'm not okay."

"I know." Todd kissed Fazil's brow. "I'm here." And he would keep those fuckers away. He drew Fazil into his arms and held him until they both slipped into sleep.

WHEN TODD GOT TO THE OFFICE, SEPARATELY FROM Fazil, it was as if nothing had happened the day before. The usual folks stood in the kitchen around the coffeepot, and no one seemed to have the haunted feeling he did. Even when Fazil came in, there were no looks, no comments.

Which was odd, considering Eli wasn't with Fazil. He'd have thought someone would've remarked upon his absence.

The only hint anything had gone down was Nathan's wolfish grin. Despite the hairs raised on the back of Todd's neck, he ignored it and got to work.

Halfway through the day, he realized there *had* been a change. People were working with Fazil. More procedures rolled in. Information about the open source code they'd used was found. Stand-ups weren't the long monstrosities they'd been, and Stephen even decided they'd skip the afternoon meeting. No Ryan, either, thank God. Only Nathan, being as annoying as ever.

Around noon, he hazarded a text to Fazil. Lunch?

Going with Sandra and Stephen.

He should have expected that. Gotcha. All well?

Yeah. It's good.

And that eased his gut. It looked more likely that Anderson might help them turn over. More likely that Fazil would stay another week, too.

He'd take more time with Z any day.

Around three, Todd's phone buzzed with one word: Staying.

Relief dripped through Todd.

Another text came after five: Leaving now. Meet at the hotel?

Yes. Will leave around 5:30. He had no idea what the plan was, but he guessed it involved Fazil staying at his place for the weekend. He ached for the man more now than he ever had in high school—for his presence and laughter and touch.

The last minutes of the day seemed to crawl, but by some miracle, traffic wasn't utter shit. He parked and tried not to jog into the hotel.

He tapped out a message on his phone. I'm here.

A moment later, it beeped. 508. Come on up.

In short order, he was at the door, but paused when he heard the murmur of two voices. Right. Eli.

He knocked.

It was Eli rather than Fazil who opened the door. He looked a hell of a lot more relaxed today. Might have been the jeans and t-shirt, but Todd didn't think so.

Then again, the man was going home to his handsome husband. That was bound to improve his disposition.

Inside the room, Fazil stood by one of the two beds. "I'm packed; I just need a hand hauling this stuff downstairs."

"Oh, so I'm unpaid labor?" Todd grinned at Fazil.

Eli snorted and shoved a sock into his suitcase.

Fazil rolled his eyes. "I don't even want to know."

"I'm restraining myself." Laughter in Eli's words.

"Hey." The amusement fell from Fazil's voice. "Tell everyone at home I said hi."

Home. That fucking word again. The longing in Fazil's voice. Home was there... and not *here.*

Eli straightened. "Of course." He rounded the bed and clapped Fazil on the shoulder. "Take care of yourself, Fazil." He glanced over at Todd. "Enjoy staying at the Airbnb you found." A wicked grin there.

Was that how it was going to be explained? "Does your boss know you approve of such..." He searched for a word. "Shenanigans?"

Eli laughed. "Sam knows me far too well and is more tolerant of me than he ought to be."

"I think he's more tolerant of all of us than he should be, to be honest." Fazil hoisted his laptop bag onto his shoulder. "At least on the social side. Woe if you screw up the work."

A grunt from Eli. "Fair assessment." Eli held out his hand to Todd. "It was nice meeting you."

They shook hands. Eli's grip was warm and solid. "Likewise. I hope everything works out." He let go. "And I'm sorry for the way things went down."

Eli turned. "As am I." He grabbed something off the dresser and held it out between two fingers. "If you ever have need to contact me."

A business card. Todd took it, glanced at it, and slipped it into his back pocket. "Thanks." A kind gesture. And having Eli as a connection if things didn't work might prove useful.

Fazil handed him the duffel before taking hold of his wheeled bag. "We should get going."

"Enjoy." Eli went back to his packing.

"I'll be in touch." Fazil headed for the door.

"Todd?" Eli's voice was soft.

He glanced back. Eli stood, one hand on a chair by the bed. For stability, he guessed. "Yeah?"

"I was serious last night."

"So was I."

"Good." His nod seemed like a dismissal, so he followed Fazil from the room.

As they stood by the elevator, Fazil lifted an eyebrow. "Dinner?"

"Figured we'd grab something near the apartment. If we're going to Rainier tomorrow, we'll want to get an early start."

"So no debauched night on the town?" The elevator opened and Fazil flashed a wicked smile.

Todd laughed. "We can pencil that in for Sunday." They entered the car. "Like to dance?"

"Actually, yeah. I look like an idiot, but I love to dance." He pressed the button for the lobby.

"Then dancing and debauchery on Sunday. Mountain tomorrow. Relaxing tonight."

"Sounds ideal."

It did. For a while, they could forget that Monday came after Sunday. They'd have to figure out how to not look like they were staying together, but they could cross that bridge later.

CHAPTER NINETEEN

Todd hadn't been kidding when he'd said they'd get an early start. The alarm went off at seven thirty and Fazil buried his head under the pillow.

Todd chuckled. "That's not going to work."

Damn straight it would, at least for a while. "Too early."

A feather touch of fingers on his back sent shivers through Fazil. "Come on, sleepyhead. Up."

He burrowed deeper.

Todd sighed, and suddenly Fazil's body was sans sheet. A moment later, Todd kissed the small of his back, and Fazil jerked off the mattress, caught between a gasp and a moan. Todd stole the pillow, but pressed Fazil down onto the bed. "If you want to stay there, we can do that." His warm hands slid down Fazil's back and over his ass. "I wouldn't mind fucking you awake."

God, from sleepy to hard and panting in three-point-five seconds. "Yes, please?"

A deep laugh from Todd and he kissed the nape of Fazil's neck. Lingered there. Dragged his fingers up Fazil's sides.

He shuddered and a moan slipped out. If he had to wake before nine on a Saturday, this was the absolute best way to get his blood moving.

Todd's weight on the bed shifted, and there was the distinctive sound of a condom wrapper ripping opened and the lube bottle snapping. "You better be ready for this."

"Always," Fazil murmured. "With you."

Todd pressed against him and slipped inside, thick and deep. Todd grunted. "Good."

Fazil relaxed against the bed as Todd moved inside him. Slow, deep strokes, until he settled his weight down and entwined his fingers in Fazil's.

"You love this, don't you? Me holding you down." Todd shifted the tempo and picked up speed.

So, so much. Fazil bit his lip. "Yeah. It's..." *Hot. Perfect. Demanding.* He squirmed and bucked, but couldn't escape. Didn't want to. "I need..." *To be controlled and held and fucked and...* "Please don't stop." Every nerve lit inside him. Todd, his breath, his heat, his scent, filled all the empty parts of his life.

Todd kissed his neck. "As you wish."

Like the first night, Todd stopped being gentle and became relentless, pounding into Fazil. Each time, he drew out both pain and pleasure until Fazil didn't know if he wanted to moan or cry. He did both, hiccuping into the mattress. He was hard and desperate for release, but couldn't reach down to stroke himself, not with his hands locked in Todd's grip. The way he was pinned had him rocking with the bed, not against it.

Torment. Bliss.

He screwed his eyes shut. "Can't... come. Need to." He was fire and light, and something had to break.

"Not yet." Todd scraped teeth over his shoulder. "You can come when I let you."

Those words rippled through him, and he was so damn close it hurt. "Please."

God, those teeth! Not the biting that bruised, but Todd nipped and pinched and licked against his skin until Fazil couldn't breathe.

"Time to get up." Todd released Fazil's hands and pulled him away from the mattress until he was on his hands and knees. Fazil could barely brace himself, especially when Todd wrapped a hand around his shaft and jackhammered into him over and over.

White-and-gold light blinded Fazil, every nerve fired, and he pumped out over Todd's hand, a cry ripping from his throat.

Todd cursed, shuddered, and buried himself into Fazil as if he could make their bodies one. In an instant of bliss and heat, Fazil thought they had.

But all things had to end. Todd pulled out and lowered him down to the mattress. While Todd's breathing was rough, his touch when he pulled Fazil close and kissed him was gentle. They must have been facing, because Todd's fingers stroked his face.

"Z? You okay?"

He forced his eyes open and blinked away the haze. "Yeah." A million miles away, but so good. Buzzing. "That was amazing." His voice crackled.

Todd stroked his forehead. "I'm going to get you some water."

That was fine. He was content to lie there until he could move again, though by the time Todd handed him a glass of water, he'd managed to sit up.

"Better?"

He looked down into the tumbler. "Well, now I'm awake."

Todd laughed. "You're such a little shit sometimes."

"You love it."

Todd's smile shifted to something less innocent. "I'd be more than happy to wake you up like that every single day."

He couldn't help the shudder. "Don't know if I could *take* every single day." *Might be fun to try, though.*

Todd leaned down and stole a kiss. "I'm going to grab a shower. I'll let you finish coming back down."

"Down from where?"

"You tell me, Z. You were completely gone for a while." Another peck, and he headed into the bathroom.

Fazil leaned back against the headboard and sipped the water. He'd been higher than a kite. No one made him feel like Todd did.

———

After they'd cleaned up and gotten dressed, they headed out to Todd's car. "We'll pick up McDonald's on the way," Todd said. They'd spent too much time in bed to justify stopping at a sit-down place for breakfast.

"No mountainous hot chocolate?" Fazil stuck out his bottom lip.

"Not for horny little twinks who want cock in their ass first thing in the morning." He smiled over at Fazil and unlocked the car.

A tiny blush touched Fazil's cheeks. "I am *not* a twink."

"Oh, you are." Todd climbed into the car. Fazil followed suit on the other side. "I notice you didn't say anything about not being horny."

"Guilty." A shrug and a devilish smile.

Todd swallowed a laugh, started the car, and they hit the road.

It was sunny and warm, and the mountain was out in full glory. Fazil craned his neck to follow it as they turned corners. "How long is this trip, anyway?"

"About two hours, if the traffic isn't bad." Todd headed toward the freeway. True to his word, he swung by a McDonald's and ordered them breakfast sandwiches and coffee.

"Just like old times." He handed Fazil the food.

Fazil looked into the bag. "I haven't thought about those trips in *years*."

Neither had he. Another memory he'd tucked away. Between their junior and senior years, they'd day-tripped to the Jersey shore just about every weekend Todd could get away from the garage. They'd leave before light so they could spend as much time on the beach as possible. Mickey D's had been their poison of choice back then.

"Different destination, though," Fazil said.

True enough. "Ever get back to the shore?"

Fazil shook his head and dug out one of the sandwiches. "Too far away. I kept meaning to take some PTO and take Kris to Cape May, but..."

"...never any time?" He knew that from his own life. *We should do that* too often fell to the wayside. Todd gripped the wheel. He wouldn't let that happen with Fazil.

"It was hard to coordinate schedules." Paper crinkled as Fazil unwrapped Todd's sandwich. "Sometimes I think I was a shit boyfriend to all my exes."

"None of us are perfect. I bet you weren't shit at all." He gave Fazil a quick glance. "You weren't *that* horrible to me."

Fazil grunted and fingered the paper wrapper. Once

they were safely on I-5, he handed the sandwich to Todd. "Sounds like you fared better in the relationship department, what with your doctor friend."

That wasn't entirely true. "Martin was unique. I had a lot more shut-up-and-fuck-me boyfriends than I-love-you ones, so I'm not one to talk about good and bad relationships." The fuckbuddies had been easier to see come and go.

Fazil unwrapped his breakfast and set to eating it, his gaze lost out the window.

Todd ate his own sandwich and washed bites down with coffee. Fazil was unlike any of his exes, even Martin. He didn't know how to tell him that. The love there was long and abiding and had such deep roots. He adored the older, sexy, adventuresome version of Fazil that had landed on his doorstep.

The games they played were something else.

Fazil was everything.

The silence stretched on, but it wasn't uncomfortable. He turned on the radio, though, and set the volume high enough to give him the background noise he needed. Once in a while, Fazil sang along to a song, and that was familiar, too.

The scenery flew past and the mountain grew larger. They'd turn off the freeway soon. He should explain that.

"We're not actually going to go to Rainier," Todd said. "It's hard to see the thing when you're standing on it, so we're going to a ski resort nearby. The views of Rainier are stunning, especially once you get to the top of the gondola."

"Gondola?" Fazil's voice pitched higher. "*What* gondola?"

Oh shit. Fazil's fear of heights... falling... whatever the hell it was. "Um. The one that takes us up the side of the mountain to where the hiking paths are?"

Fazil pressed back into the seat and flinched. "I'm—not sure I can do that."

Panic slithered up his spine, and he gripped the wheel. "Shit, Z, I didn't think." How could he salvage the trip? He couldn't take Fazil up there. "This was supposed to be fun for you." He'd completely fucked up. "We can go to Rainier. I think we can find some views in the park and—"

Fazil gripped his knee. "Hey, it's okay. Let's do what you planned. I'll be fine."

He shot a glance over and took as long a look as he could get away with. "You *sure?*"

Fazil's voice was strong and firm, though his expression didn't quite match. "Yup. I'll do the gondola."

Todd's back unknotted. "If it's any help, the view is unbeatable." Hopefully that would be enough to keep Fazil from freaking out. Or him freaking out about Fazil.

Fazil patted Todd's leg. "Trust me."

He held to on that. He took the exit toward the resort and hope he hadn't royally screwed up Fazil's day.

CHAPTER TWENTY

Fazil stared at the gondola cars and the long, long, *long* cable that led up the side of the mountain. Usually it was his legs that itched and tingled unpleasantly when his phobia kicked in, but the needles crept up his back. *Shit.* He exhaled and tried not to look as terrified as his body wanted him to be.

Must not have worked, because Todd rubbed his shoulder. "This going to be all right?"

Stuck in a little moving box hanging from a wire for twelve minutes? "Yeah. Piece of cake."

"You're such a shitty liar." Humor there, but it fled Todd immediately. "There are trail rides down here. We could always book one of those. They're fun and you can still see Rainier from below, too. I think."

He'd never been on a horse. Never been in a gondola, either. He tore his gaze away from the little boxes of hanging death. "Eli had a good time riding. I could compare notes when I get back."

Todd nodded, but the skin between his brow furrowed

deep. Still kicking himself for not thinking about the whole heights issue, no doubt.

Not Todd's fault—it was Fazil's damn phobia.

Another gondola car slid out of the station and headed up the mountain. Inside, Fazil spotted a young girl, faced pressed to the glass. *Why can't I do that?* Obviously the system was safe. They wouldn't run it otherwise. There were kids here with more courage than him.

"Should we do the trail ride, then?" Todd shuffled his feet against the walkway.

Fazil swallowed. "I want to try the gondola."

"Z, you don't have to."

He curled his hands into fists. "I *want* to." He took in Todd, his concern, his apprehension, and his love. Todd *loved* him. He didn't know what to *do* with that. He'd leave him again because his life was elsewhere. The *least* he could do was enjoy the day Todd had planned. "It's twelve minutes. Kids manage. I need to get over this shit." He straightened his back and headed toward the station. "Let's go."

Todd caught up with him and took his hand. "It's worth the view. I promise."

He spent the entire time in line shifting from one foot to the other in an effort to calm the pain in his legs. Todd gave him a questioning look, but Fazil ignored it.

When they loaded into the car, there was a boy, maybe eight or nine, who balked at the door, his face pale and eyes wide. Everything Fazil felt was carved into that child.

"Kev, it'll be fine. It's safe," his mom said, but the boy just shook his head and walked alongside the slowly moving car.

Fazil crouched down. "Hey. You scared?"

Kev nodded.

"Me too." He looked up at the car. "Really scared." When he looked back at Kev, the fear had been replaced with confusion. *Yeah, kid, adults can be afraid, too.* "But I'm gonna ride this thing. Wanna help me be brave?"

He took one step, then another, then walked inside the car before it cleared the platform. Fazil rose, and Kev plopped himself down next to Fazil on the bench.

Todd chuckled and put his arm around Fazil. "You've made a friend."

"So it seems."

Kev beamed up at him.

From the other side of the gondola, relief covered Kev's mom like a blanket, her eyes almost as wide as her son's. "Thank you *so* much."

An older girl, the daughter he guessed, rolled her eyes.

The car lurched, swung out into the air, and Fazil's heart fell beneath the seat. "Don't mention it." His voice was thin. "I know how he feels."

The view from the window *was* pretty, if you ignored the vast quantity of air between the car and the ground. But the pinpricks subsided. Sitting helped, and the ride was surprisingly smooth. The car did rock each time they transitioned over a tower, and Kev flinched. So did Fazil, for that matter.

But after a few minutes, his tension melted. They were in this box, and it hadn't fallen. While the view was nice, it was missing *one* thing. "I thought you said we'd see the mountain?"

Todd grinned like a cat. "Wait for it."

Kev kicked his feet. "Hey! There's a person down there!"

Beneath them was a paved path—and indeed, there was someone walking along it.

"That's cool!" Kev pressed his face close to the window. It was. "You having fun?"

"Yeah!" Kev looked up. "Are you?"

Fazil nodded. "This isn't so bad after all."

He pulled out his phone and took several shots of the countryside, including back at the base station, far away down the mountain. Ripples of other mountains and pines all around. The dark green of the trees contrasted against the emerald of the grass and the bright blue sky. A few clouds dotted the sky.

"We're almost there," Todd said.

Fazil faced forward again. As the station neared, they crested and Fazil's breath caught. "Oh my God."

Mount Rainier stood, a rainbow of grays and blues, snowcapped and wearing clouds as if it pierced the heavens.

"Wow." Kev drew out the soft sound.

"Well, that's certainly worth the ride." Fazil stared at the mountain.

"Told you." Todd nudged him. "But you're going to have to get off if you want to see it for more than a minute."

They exited the car and the station, and made their way up the ridge. Fazil pulled Todd to a stop. "Let me just..." Words left him.

Be. Exist. Drink in the expanse and the sky and the enormous sight before him. The laughter from other people. The constant breeze.

Hiking the previous weekend had been fun and the views stunning. This blew that away. He was a small thing on top of the world, and everything—the shit at Singularity, the looming deadlines, his home thousands of miles away—vanished. He took Todd's hand in his and tried to hang on to the immense welling of his heart.

After a while, he shook himself. "That's something else."

"Makes you think, huh?"

Sure did. The world crept back in. Thoughts of home, his family, work, friends... and Todd. They jumbled and fought for the happiness he'd collected and pulled his heart every which way. Fazil took out his phone and took some pictures, but they would never compare to the memories.

"Hungry?" Todd nodded to a building up the ridge. "There's a restaurant. Or we could hike along the ridge for a while."

"Let's hike. I want to cram as much of this into my brain as I can." He followed after Todd. "It's amazing."

They walked along the ridge, past where a ski lift came up from below. More incredible views and beautiful vistas. Fazil would have been happy to keep walking forever, but his stomach protested loudly enough that Todd snorted.

"I'm guessing you'd like to go to the restaurant?"

Fazil patted his stomach. "Yeah. I've been overruled on the hiking."

After lunch, they hiked in the other direction and headed back to the gondola station. While Fazil wanted more of the incredible beauty, he was overwhelmed. Like fantastic sex, too much for too long drained him.

This time, they had the gondola car to themselves. When the doors closed and the car swung into the air, Fazil pulled Todd close and kissed him. Todd cupped his face and deepened the kiss until the same enormity of the mountain stirred Fazil's head.

When Todd relented, Fazil whispered, "Thank you," against Todd's lips.

Warm fingers stroked the back of Fazil's neck, right at his hairline. "You're welcome." Todd opened some space between them and his smile was as beautiful as the scenery. Fazil wanted a picture, but that would have meant letting Todd go. So they kissed and touched and made out like the teens they'd once been.

When they reached the bottom, they dutifully separated and got off the gondola car. "It's still pretty early," Todd said. "Want to see if there are any trail rides available?"

That would be a nice way to spend the rest of the day. "Sure."

After overcoming the whole heights issue, getting on a horse was easy enough, though nervousness fluttered through Fazil. Still, he understood why Eli had found the experience so moving. There was something powerful and freeing about sitting up here.

Todd had taken to his horse easily—too easily. "You've done this before," Fazil said.

A grin and Todd fake tipped his riding helmet toward Fazil. "I've taken lessons. Done some riding. Been about a year, though." He walked his horse closer to Fazil's. "When I had the income, I decided to try a bunch of different outdoor activities. Loved hiking and camping the best. Riding is great, but I don't have the time I'd need to properly maintain a horse."

Todd looked as natural on a horse as he did in a car, and that made Fazil wonder what Todd looked like astride a motorcycle.

Todd in leather. Fazil shivered. *Well, shit.* Maybe he was developing a kink. He looked Todd over. Maybe Todd *was* his kink.

Just then, the guide gathered them together, and they started out on the ride. It was different being down in the terrain they'd viewed from the gondola, but Todd had been right, there were several spots where you could see Mount Rainier. He snapped more photos, including several of Todd on his horse with the mountain behind him. By the time they returned, muscles ached that Fazil never knew he had.

No wonder Eli had looked so worn after his weekend.

When they were on their own legs again, they headed back to the main part of the resort. "Please tell me there's wine or a beer or something at the end of this day, because my legs are killing me."

Todd wrapped an arm around his waist. "You just need to ride more." His fingers brushed the top of Fazil's ass. "Or find something else to loosen your hips."

That touch and those words nearly took Fazil's legs from under him. Images, deviously delicious ones, flashed through his head. Straddling Todd and riding his cock. Or his legs stretched wide with rope while Todd plowed into him. It was a wonder he wasn't completely hard, though he was well on the way. "I *really* need a drink."

Todd chuckled and led him down toward the inn.

By the end of dinner, Fazil was beat. They made a quick stroll through the gift shop, and he bought a small carving of an eagle created by a native artist and some chocolate. "I should have some souvenirs, right?"

Todd kissed him on the forehead. "I doubt you'll forget this trip."

No, not very likely, that.

He couldn't stop yawning as they walked back to the parking lot. One glass of wine, and Todd practically had to pour him back into the car. Between Todd's wake-up sex, the majesty of the mountain, the walking, and the trail ride, he felt every single muscle in his body.

The creases around Todd's eyes were full of joy. "Lightweight."

"Am not. You wore me out."

A chuckle. "Glad to be of service." Todd shut the car door on Fazil's side and slid into the driver's seat.

"Not going to be much fun when we get back." Fazil buckled in and leaned back against the seat. "I'll make it up to you somehow."

Todd curled his fingers around Fazil's neck and drew him close. "I have some ideas," he said before devouring Fazil's mouth.

God, if only he had the energy for a night of rough and tumble sex. He whimpered and Todd relented. "Ideas?" Fazil spoke against Todd's mouth.

Another quick kiss and Todd sat back. "Ever been picked up at a club?"

"No. Never." He'd gone to bars, but he'd never attracted that much attention. "Not the type to turn heads."

"Yes, you are." Todd headed back out onto the highway. "I can show you." His grin was wide. "Assuming you *want* to be picked up at a club."

By Todd? Any day of the week. "Is this a little game for us?"

"Mmm-hmm. Sexy little twink gets far more man than he bargained for at the hot gay bar."

Fazil squirmed against his seat. "I'm in."

"Good." Todd flashed a smile.

"But I'm *not* a twink."

"Oh Z, keep telling yourself that." Todd patted his leg. "I'll prove you wrong."

If he did, that would be okay. So far on this trip, being wrong for Todd had been so *very* right.

IN THE HEAT OF SUNDAY EVENING, FAZIL WALKED down the sidewalk to the club where Todd had taken him last Friday when he'd shoved forty dollars in his pocket. Definitely a hookup place, full of beautiful men. He was here to flirt and dance, see and be seen.

"I'm not cut out for that kind of place," he'd told Todd before he'd left.

Todd had him stand in front of a full-length mirror, in the tightest pair of jeans he had in his suitcase and a red silk button-down they'd bought that day.

"No?" Todd had breathed that one word into his ear and set his blood dancing.

He'd had to admit, the man staring back was pretty decent-looking, especially with Todd standing behind him.

So here he was, outside of one of Todd's favorite places to prove a point. He could turn heads, and male heads at that. He entered and one of the bouncers, a broad man who had the short cut of someone in the military, stepped forward. "You've got ID?" A clip to his speech from an accent of some kind.

"Yeah." Fazil dug out his wallet and handed over his driver's license. "You're carding me?"

The bouncer looked at the license, took a long look at Fazil—one more thorough than to check his *face* against his photo—and handed the card back. "You look younger than you are."

The bouncer's smile sent a little shiver up Fazil's spine. "Good genes."

"Very." Another grin. The door opened again, and the bouncer turned away.

Well. Appraisal number one. That left him a bit shaky,

but a drink was a good place to start. He pressed his way
through the crowd, with some murmurs of "Excuse me" and
more than a few returned smiles. Eyes brushed over him.

Okay, maybe Todd was right about the whole *entirely
fuckable* thing.

Tonight's bartender had dark hair, a smirk, and a raised
eyebrow. "What can I get for you?" In his formal shirt, bow
tie, and perfect black pants, he looked like someone's best
man—or groom.

Fazil's mind went blank. He hadn't thought about *what*
he wanted. "How about your choice?"

The bartender grinned. "Need something strong to get
you through the night?"

"That obvious?"

"A little. Means you fit right in with the rest of the
crowd." He held up a finger. "I have just the thing." He
vanished to a spot a little farther down the bar and began
concocting... something. Fazil couldn't quite see all the
ingredients, but yeah. It would be *strong*.

When the bartender returned he handed over
something vaguely... purple... and Fazil sipped. Fruit and
almond... and the vodka went straight to his head. "Dude."
If this didn't mellow him out, nothing would.

A laugh from the bartender.

He settled up, left a sizable tip, and found a spot to
stand where he could watch the dancing. Despite the
amount of alcohol that must have been poured into his glass,
the cocktail went down smoothly. And fast. Before he knew
it, the glass was empty, his head was spinning, and a man
with blond hair and a thin gold chain around his neck was
leading him out to the dance floor.

Fazil didn't know his name—didn't know anyone's name
—but he ended up in the middle of the dancing, twisting

and turning and moving his body to the music. It wasn't innocent, but the blond—while flirty and touchy and interested—didn't bump and grind against him like some of the guys on the floor. After a few songs, Fazil was winded enough that he nodded at the edge of the dance floor. "Need to catch my breath!" And get his pulse under control.

The blond kissed him on the cheek. "Thanks for the dances." Then he was gone. The guy was cute. If Fazil had been free, he might have followed. But he was happily not free. Besides, beautiful blonds were not what he had in mind tonight.

When Fazil stepped off the dance floor, he found a man watching him. Tall. Brown hair. Blue eyes.

Dark, tight jeans, and a t-shirt that was probably three sizes too small, given the way it showed every muscle of his chest and arms, especially with the way they were crossed in front of him.

Looked like he could be one of the bouncers—except for the devilish smile.

Todd. Good God, he was large. And stunning. He shivered when Todd raked his gaze up and down his body.

He cocked a finger and beckoned Fazil over. "Need a drink?"

"Could use one." And some water, or he'd be in a world of hurt tomorrow.

Todd smiled, slid a hand around Fazil's waist, and pulled him toward the bar.

Same bartender. "Looks like the drink worked." He winked. "Another?"

Fazil nodded. "And some water, too."

The bartender gave Todd a questioning look.

"I'll take whatever you've been pouring down his

throat." He glanced at Fazil. "Seems quite good."

A flash of a smile, then the bartender was gone.

Todd gripped Fazil's waist tighter and pulled him closer, until their hips met, then he slipped his hand into Fazil's back pocket and kneaded his ass.

A game. Todd, the stranger who was not, and Fazil, the guy looking for a one-night stand in a club. "You're a little forward."

"With guys like you? No such thing." His smile was lecherous.

How many times had Todd played this role before? There was a stab of jealousy, then one of regret. No right to judge Todd for that, not when he'd left and had a life of his own, too.

He pulled Todd's head down for a kiss and whispered in his ear. "If you think I'm going to bend over for you because you bought me a drink..."

An amused grunt, then Todd took his mouth, and holy hell, the kiss. Hot, demanding, intimate. It spun Fazil's head and tightened his balls.

Someone coughed. "Your drinks?"

God, the bartender, but he didn't seem fazed at all.

Todd skimmed fingers over Fazil's face. "We'll see about that, won't we?" He took the drinks from the bartender, handed Fazil his drink and water, then paid. Like before, the concoction went down too quickly and the water didn't help the spinning of his head. But that might have been from the way Todd stared at him, as if he'd strip him right then and there.

Several other men watched them, with envy directed at Todd.

Okay. Point taken. He wasn't such a bad catch. "Interested in dancing?"

Todd finished his drink and set the glass on a table. "Thought we already were." He closed a hand around Fazil's neck and pulled him close. "But I'm fine with taking you out on the floor." He kissed Fazil's neck.

Great time for his legs to stop working. "Okay." Breathless already.

Todd's chuckle sank into his bones. They found space on the dance floor and moved to the beat of the music. Hands on skin, lips on flesh, bodies entwined in each other, like so many other couples.

Todd was rock hard and wasn't shy about letting Fazil know how much he wanted him. Fazil pressed the palm of his hand against Todd's package.

Todd grunted and swung him around. "I thought you wanted to dance."

Dance. Make out. Whatever. He ground himself against Todd, their hard lengths pressed together. "Don't like my kind of dancing?"

"I think," Todd said, in between biting Fazil's lips, "we need to take your kind of dancing somewhere more private." He rotated Fazil and put a hand at the base of his neck. "Shall we?" He pushed Fazil off the dance floor and toward the hallway with the sign for the restrooms.

Good thing the music was loud, because Fazil was pretty sure he whimpered. Being fucked in a stall? They'd talked about that. Wasn't sure he was ready for it.

On the other hand, his cock throbbed at the thought.

But rather than stopping at the door to the men's room, Todd directed him to a door with an EXIT sign. After a quick glance back, he opened the door and shoved Fazil out into an alley.

The door clicked closed and Todd had him up against the rough brick wall. "You're a little fucking cocktease."

"Got a problem with that?" He massaged Todd's length through his jeans. "Seems like you don't."

"I've got a problem with twinks who don't follow through." Todd closed a hand around Fazil's throat with enough pressure to send Fazil's pulse skyrocketing.

"What do you expect me to do out here?" The night was warm and damp. Nearby the sounds of traffic and people floated into the alley. They were alone—but not.

Todd stroked his jaw, a tender moment that belied the game they were playing, but his voice was grit and gravel. "Get on your knees."

Suddenly the alley was too hot and too cold, but he lowered himself down to the wet pavement. When he looked up, the same shock he felt coursing through his veins was etched in Todd's face.

They were going to do this. *Oh my God.*

Didn't take long for Todd to undo his belt and jeans and get his dick out. Fazil gripped Todd's legs and swallowed as much cock as he could, milking Todd's shaft with tongue and mouth.

Yup. They were doing this.

Fingers tightened in Fazil's hair and Todd gasped. "Shit. So good." After a few minutes, he took control, thrusting forward. "Now, that's what your mouth is good for."

He would have replied, but the grip Todd had on his head didn't give him any room to pull back. He looked up as best he could.

Todd grinned down at him, his lust wicked and undeniable. This was hotter than hell, and he still couldn't believe he was kneeling in an alley being face-fucked by Todd. He pressed the heel of one hand into his aching cock.

"I should come on your face so all the guys in there

know your tight little ass is mine."

That warmed his blood right to the back of his head and he moaned around Todd. He wasn't an exhibitionist, but the thought of others knowing pulsed through his veins like a drug.

The door to the club crashed open like a gunshot, and they both startled. Todd's cock slipped out of Fazil's mouth, and he turned his head, horror freezing the lust in his blood.

Their bartender stepped out with a bag of trash and halted. "Oh fuck! Didn't mean to interrupt." He tossed the bag into the Dumpster. "Um, you guys might want to take it farther down." He waved deeper into the alley. "'Cause you're right under a light, and sometimes the cops swing by." He grinned. "Ask me how I know."

They didn't because the bartender stepped back into the club and closed the door.

Todd made a sound that might have been a laugh or a croak. He pulled at Fazil's shoulder. "Come on, let's..." He hiccupped, then snorted. "Holy fuck, did that just happen?"

Fazil scrambled to his feet, laughter bubbling in his chest. They shifted down the alley, past another Dumpster and away from the light. Their little role-play scenario was shot to hell, but damn, this was almost better. "That really happened."

Todd grasped the back of his neck and kissed him hard, tongue opening his mouth, lips mashing his—and in an instant he wanted to be back on his knees. When Todd broke the kiss, Fazil whispered against his lips, "Should I keep going?"

"If you want. Or we could take it home."

He dropped to the pavement. "I want to finish what I started." He licked the head of Todd's cock and took it into his mouth.

Once more, fingers in his hair, tugging at the roots while he sucked and licked Todd's shaft before letting Todd settle into a rhythm of thrusting.

"Shit, Z. If you're going to be this filthy, maybe I *will* come on your face."

Fazil flicked his eyes up and Todd's openmouthed smile was barely visible in the shadows. He pulled off. "You think I'm going to let you?" He fisted Todd's cock.

Todd's palm slid against his cheek. "Let's find out." He took his shaft and pressed the head of his dick against Fazil's lips.

Soft, slick. He opened and let Todd slide into his mouth, rolling his tongue over the head and along the sides with each thrust.

Todd's muted gasps and moans were like music. He never imagined this would be so good. No game—they were themselves. Ex-boyfriends. Current lovers. Old friends. Coworkers. He slipped his hand inside his jeans and stroked himself as best he could.

The pounding became more urgent, and Todd's cock tightened against his tongue. "Oh fuck." A strangled cry from Todd.

The first bits of salt hit Fazil's tongue, and he pulled off, letting the rest hit him on his nose and cheek and forehead.

Todd's gasp was loud and even in the dark, Fazil caught the look of pure bliss and surprise as the orgasm rolled through him.

Hot, slick jizz dripped down his skin, and his balls ached for release. He worked his cock harder.

Todd practically dragged him up and into his arms, lips mashing against his. He smoothed some of the semen over Fazil's cheek, the wetness cooling fast even in the warm night air. "You're so fucking hot.

I can't believe you let me..." Todd laughed and leaned against the brick wall. "Where were you when I was ten years younger?"

"Boston," Fazil murmured, the past regret pricking up his spine.

Todd kissed him. "I wish I had more energy, that's all."

Fazil raised a brow. "What, tired already? You're going to leave me here, all hot and bothered?"

"No." Todd swung him around and pressed him up against the bricks. "I'm going to jack you off until you come, then take you back into dance with stains on your jeans and my jizz in your hair—and you're going to love every minute of it."

Fazil moaned when Todd unzipped his pants, wrapped his hand around his shaft and worked him to the rhythm that always boiled his blood. Didn't take long until he was panting, moaning, and squirming against Todd.

He came fast, helped along by Todd biting him hard on the shoulder. Spine liquid, Fazil lolled against the rough wall and watched Todd lick his fingers clean. "Talk about dirty."

He shrugged. "You taste good. Always have."

When he could breathe normally, he tucked himself back into his jeans and scrubbed his face. Hopefully it wasn't *too* obvious he'd been sucking cock.

Then again, who cared?

They snuck back into the club via the alley door. He probably did have a few stains on his jeans, and maybe there was some of Todd in his hair, but he didn't care. He smiled back when the bartender who'd interrupted them gave him two thumbs up and a big grin.

Shit, he really needed more Sunday nights like *this*.

CHAPTER TWENTY-ONE

Monday morning, Fazil took a cab from Todd's apartment to Singularity while Todd drove in. Overkill, yes. He could always say Todd offered to give him a lift, but this seemed safer.

Separate business from pleasure.

It was strange walking into the building without Eli, and his heart skipped a beat in the elevator. While he'd been alone on Friday, Eli had been in Seattle. Now Fazil was truly on his own at a company that proved less than friendly at times.

He spied Erin at the coffeepot, and she gave him a smile and a wave. Good portent, that. Hopefully this week would go well, they'd wrap everything up, and he'd be *done* with this job. He didn't relish leaving Todd—but he missed his own things. His space. Living out of a suitcase made his teeth hurt because he had a limited amount of *everything* and all his favorite items were at home.

He walked down the hall to the conference room—he should ask for an empty cube now that Eli wasn't here—opened the door, and strode in.

A smell hit as the door banged closed—not overwhelming but *wrong*. Smoky.

Every hair on Fazil's arms stood up and his flesh pricked from his legs to his skull. Pages of something were scattered on the conference room table, the papers charred and burned at the edges. Some had holes in the middle. Even though he couldn't read the language, he recognized the text, the patterns. Arabic was *distinctive*.

Oh my God. Icy tendrils spread out across his skull and edged forward. He needed to be sure he was seeing what was before his eyes, what sank into his flesh and heart and clenched his gut into a stone.

Hot fear melted his spine, and the sharpness of anger reforged it.

He spied the Basmala—that much Arabic he knew. *In the Name of God, the Merciful, the Compassionate.* Blackened paper had obliterated some letters.

He closed his eyes, swallowed bile and fire, and backed into the door. The strap of his laptop case slipped from his shoulder, and the bag thudded hard on the carpeted floor before falling to its side.

They'd burned a Quran. Blood pounded in his ears, a Klaxon of *no, no, no* repeating itself in his head. He wasn't religious. Barely believed in God. But this... *this...* was *evil*.

Turning, he wrenched open the door and gasped in the clean, cool air of the hall.

That's when he heard the laugh.

Nathan. The little fuck stood down the hall, teeth full of the most malicious smile Fazil had ever seen. The buzzing in Fazil's head stole his thought, and the world tunneled down to Nathan's grin, his laugh, and the heat and fire burning up through Fazil's bones.

He lunged forward, wrapped a hand around Nathan's

throat, and threw him up against the wall. "You think that's funny?"

Nathan's smile was gone, replaced with a blank stare of shock that slipped into a look of fear.

Nathan clawed at Fazil's arm. "Get off. Get off!"

"You—why? Why?" He shook Nathan, slamming him against the wall. "How could you?" His broken voice echoed in the hall, blending with the pounding in his ears.

Then there were hands on his shoulders, pulling him away. "Z! What are you doing?" Todd's voice shattered the haze.

"He fucking tried to kill me!" Nathan shouted, red-faced. He rubbed his throat. "Fucking crazy asshole!"

White-hot rage ripped through Fazil, and he threw himself at Nathan again—but Todd held him fast. "Z! *Stop!*"

"*I'm* an asshole?" He struggled against Todd, digging fingers into flesh. "I'm not the one who burned a Quran! I haven't done *anything* to you."

Todd cursed but didn't let go. His voice was soft now, close, and warm in his ear. "Z, you need to calm down. He wants you angry."

Why shouldn't he be angry? Why did *he* have to be the one to take the high road? Not react? Be *nice?* But the rage and heat dripped away and slid from him like the strength in his legs. What remained was cold, dark, and empty.

See? it whispered. *You'll never be normal. American. Real.* "I was born here," he said.

"I know." Todd loosened his grip. "It's going to be okay."

But it wasn't. Fazil stared at his own hands, then at Nathan. "Oh God." He shook his head... and didn't stop shaking. His hands, his body. Those pages, that rage and fear. His gut ate him from the inside out.

"What the hell is going on here?" A very loud, angry

Sandra marched down the hall, her heels clacking against the tile floor.

Everyone spoke at once. Nathan, Todd, even Erin, trying to slip words in between the cacophony. It was too much, too fast. Fazil fell to his knees.

"Enough!" Sandra cut through the noise, and there was blessed silence. Fazil closed his eyes. "Mr. Kurt?"

Somehow, his voice came back—the calm, rational tones he still didn't feel. "Go look in the conference room."

The *tap* of her soles, and the thunderous *click* of the door being opened. There was nothing for a time—only the sound of other people's breathing. Fazil blinked and focused on the gray spots in the white tile in front of him.

The door closed. "Who did this?" Sandra's voice was deep and twisted with anger.

No one spoke. She cleared her throat. "Well?"

"It was a joke," Nathan said. "I... did it. Just a *joke*. Then he tried to kill me."

"I wasn't trying to kill him." He'd been angry—he was still angry—but it was rage born from shock and lack of comprehension. He looked up. "I'd have squeezed a hell of a lot tighter if I had been."

"Z." A whisper from Todd.

"Don't you even try to defend him, Douglas. Not when you've been fucking him."

How? How did Nathan know? Fazil scrubbed his face. He felt rather than heard Todd step back.

Sandra's scowled. "*None* of this is a joke." She straightened. "I want all of you in the executive conference room. There will be no talking." She met Fazil's gaze. "Mr. Kurt... If you please?" She gestured down the hall.

Fazil climbed to his feet, his throat tight. No, not a joke

at all. Ice settled into his spine. What the *fuck* had just happened to their contract with Singularity?

Only one way to find out. He followed Sandra down the hall.

FAZIL PACED THE LONG LENGTH OF A DIFFERENT conference room, one without windows, leather chairs, and the charred remains of his faith. His cell phone burned in his hand. Soon, Sam would call. Sandra and Stephen had already spoken to Fazil, gotten his side of the debacle, and expressed their dismay at how he had reacted. Unlike his encounter with Nathan, he'd expressed his anger calmly and coldly, putting on his own honorific and experience.

Might have been fine to terrorize Mr. Kurt, but Dr. Kurt was having none of that shit anymore. He wasn't a cog in their corporate wheel. Fazil turned his phone over in his hand. He was Sam's employee, not theirs.

He should have never gone off on Nathan, and certainly, he shouldn't have choked the little shit, no matter how angry he'd been.

Fazil stopped pacing. He couldn't get the stench of burned paper out of his nose.

Singularity should have laid down the law after the whole incident with Ryan and Eli. Bunch of cowards.

Fazil pinched the bridge of his nose. Eli had been graceful in the face of anti-Semitism, not an idiot like Fazil had been. Sam wouldn't be happy. He'd be pulled off the job and on the next flight home to Pittsburgh. He wanted to go, too. Get away from these *people*.

Except for Todd, working at this company had become a *nightmare*. He rubbed his face and started pacing again.

There'd be blowback for Todd. Especially after Nathan's quip about them fucking.

Eli had warned him on that. Encouraged, but also warned.

His phone went off and he nearly dropped the damn thing. A quick glance told him the number was Sam's. He steeled himself and answered. "Hi."

"Fazil." Sam's voice was quiet and clear.

"I'm not sorry. Not for any of it." People like Nathan needed to be reminded there were limits. If that meant choking the asshole a bit, well, good.

"I didn't think you would be, if I've read correctly between the lines of what Sandra said." His voice was calm. "But you should tell me your side."

He did, starting with the way Nathan had nagged him for his ethnicity, then the prodding about his sexuality, and finishing with what he'd found in the conference room.

There was silence on the other end, then an intake of breath. "Why didn't you tell me about the other things?" Sam sounded incredulous and Fazil could almost see him on his feet, leaning over his desk. "Especially after the incident with Eli? Good God, Fazil!"

"That stuff is normal." He gritted his teeth. "It's the same shit I've put up with my entire life. Not everywhere, but enough places..."

"Fuck." Something thudded in the background behind Sam's voice. "Eli said something similar. He'd dealt with it all before, it wasn't a big deal, and he overreacted."

"He hardly reacted at all. I'm the one who turned into a screaming shithead." He chewed on his tongue. "I shouldn't have touched him."

"No, you shouldn't have." There was pain in Sam's voice. "But the whole thing should never have happened."

Sam. Always the idealist. "You know the world isn't like that." Sam had hidden in the closet for years out of fear.

"I know. I do." Sam paused, his breath rasping into a sigh. "There's also the issue of your relationship with Todd Douglas."

Fazil cringed. "Eli said—"

"Eli isn't your boss." Sam's voice was forceful, loud, and meticulously clear.

He caught himself on the conference room table and lowered himself into the nearest chair.

"Fazil, you're the best engineer I've ever known, but this kind of indiscretion—"

"Don't go there, Sam." His fingers tightened on the arm of the chair.

Utter silence at the other end.

Fazil's heart slammed against his chest. He knew how Sam had met his partner, Michael—everyone did. He wet his lips. "I know I should have managed things better with my personal life. Been more careful. But don't you dare get on my case about *indiscretions*." Maybe he'd end up out of *two* jobs after this. Probably shouldn't be reaming out Sam. But he'd had enough with everyone.

A cough or growl or something came over the line. "Does he mean that much to you?"

"Yes!" He practically shouted the word into his phone. "He's the first guy I ever loved, and I..." *Loved*. He loved Todd. "Look, we were careful at work. Kept our heads down. Did our jobs. I've sent you status reports. Copied you on e-mails. You *know* I'm doing my job. Todd has nothing to do with this."

"Fazil."

"And if you're going to fire me for falling in love on the job, you're going to have to let go of half the office, Sam."

"I know." Those two words ripped out of the phone. "Believe me, *I know*. I'm not *trying* to fire you, Fazil. For fuck's sake, *I am not the enemy*. Calm your shit down."

His heart and lungs ached. "I didn't realize how—" The words caught on a sob, and he coughed to cover it. "This was supposed to be a simple job," he whispered.

"It was. In and out. An easy task." There was a great deal of sympathy in his voice. "If I had known…"

Fazil wouldn't have been here. They wouldn't have taken the job. He would have never seen Todd again. "*Contains racist assholes* isn't usually on the tin."

A pained laugh. "No." That was followed by a deep breath. "I'm pulling you out. Justin's booking you on a flight tomorrow. Get your stuff, call a cab, and get the hell out of that office."

Tomorrow? *Shit.* "Wait, all my stuff's at Todd's." He couldn't drag Todd out of the office with him. That would cause even more problems. He looked at his watch. "It's only a little before eleven."

"Actions have consequences, Fazil." Sam sounded exhausted. "Theirs and yours. Believe me, I'm on your side, but that means removing you from a bad situation, effective immediately."

"Okay. I'll figure it out." It made sense to leave. "I'm sorry, Sam."

"I'm not thrilled with you *yelling* at me—but I understand. We'll talk more when you get back. None of this was your fault."

That was good to hear. "Thanks."

"Be on the lookout for mail from Justin, and come see me as soon as you're back in the office."

That put a damper on his relief. "Will do." They both hung up.

Shit. *Shit.* He stared at his phone and rose on unsteady legs to grab his laptop, charger, and all the paperwork Erin had collected from the other conference room for him. He shoved it into his laptop bag.

His phone vibrated once. A text, from Eli of all people.

Are you okay?

Yes and no. Tell me the truth. Do I still have a job?

Yes. Of course.

I yelled at Sam.

So I heard. He's fine. He's forgiving in that respect. And he does understand.

I need to call a cab.

Yes. Get out of there.

He needed to, because the adrenaline was wearing off. He pulled up a taxi app, punched in his info, and got his confirmation. Ten minutes.

Only thing left to do was text Todd.

I'm done here. Getting a cab to the Marriott. Call me later.

Fazil slung the strap of his bag over his shoulder. If he were lucky, they'd leave him alone and just let him walk out. But no, on the other side of the door, Sandra and a security guard waited.

Really? He handed Sandra his access card. "Do you need to search me, too?"

"No." She was drawn and pale. "This is for your protection, not ours."

Well, shit. He headed for the exit. "I've already called a cab. I'll wait in the building lobby."

Even after they'd passed the office door, they stuck with him, riding down the elevator and standing in the lobby while he waited. His protection. *Sure.*

"Dr. Kurt, I wish things hadn't turned out this way."

He tightened his grip on his bag and his phone vibrated in his jeans pocket. "As am I."

"For what it's worth, your work was exemplary. I told Mr. Anderson that."

"Thank you." He paused. "You have a serious problem. You know that, right?"

Her lips thinned out as she pressed them together. No words, though.

"I think you know who their next target will be." He certainly did. Another buzz from his phone. Probably a text from the very man he was speaking about now.

She met his gaze. "There are issues there." She cocked her head. "Some of which *you* caused, Dr. Kurt."

True. And false. "I think you'll find there were quite a few *issues* before I ever stepped foot in Seattle."

She shifted but said nothing.

Outside, his cab pulled up. "Men like Nathan and Ryan... I'd watch your own back, Dr. Jackson." He didn't even wait to hear her response, but pushed through the door and climbed into the cab.

"You said the Marriott, right? Town Center?" Accented. A foreigner. *Like him.*

"Yes."

The driver eyed him in the rearview mirror. "Where are you from?"

Fazil snorted. "To be honest, I'm not sure I know anymore."

That wasn't the answer the cabbie had expected, he was sure, but it meant he left Fazil alone. He kept his cell phone tucked into his pocket, even when it buzzed again. The moment he read Todd's texts, he knew he'd lose it, so he sat and stared out the window. The sky was gray and misty and there were no mountains in sight.

Tomorrow he'd be on his way home and away from this mess. Something loosened in his chest. Home, where he belonged. He looked at the back of the driver's head. "I'm from Pittsburgh."

A flash of eyes. "Is it a good town?"

"The best." There was only one thing he regretted leaving behind. For a fourth time, his phone vibrated.

Todd. Fazil closed his eyes. *Fuck.*

Todd kept his phone on his desk for the rest of the day, but there were no responses from Fazil. *Don't you do this to me. Don't up and leave.* His fingers shook as he tried to code and his gut twisted into a million knots.

He'd seen what Nathan had left in the conference room. The blaze of fury in Fazil. How his hands had been wrapped around Nathan's throat. No, Fazil wouldn't have killed Nathan, but he had managed to make the man shit his pants.

While it had been satisfying to see, it had been the wrong thing for Fazil to do.

Fazil couldn't stay, but why was he heading to a hotel?

Come get the keys from me, he'd texted.

No answer.

They'd all told Sandra what they'd seen. Except Nathan had also ratted him out as Fazil's lover, and he *knew* there would be questions about that. The whole office was pin-drop quiet. The only sounds were that of the HVAC system and the clatter of fingers on keyboards.

He stared at his screen. This wasn't happening. But it had. It was. Fazil's text was proof enough of that. His computer dinged and there was the mail he'd been both dreading and expecting from Sandra.

Please come to my office, ASAP.

Todd exhaled and pushed back from his desk. No use in stalling.

The looks he got on the way—because everyone heard his shoes on the linoleum floor—were harrowing. Some were sympathetic, some curious, but two or three were angry. He made a note of who and shoved that into the back of his mind.

At her office, he rapped gently on the doorframe. She turned in her chair. "Come in and close the door."

No helping the wince—it was instinctual. Todd lowered himself into her guest chair.

She took a long look at him. "Anderson has pulled Dr. Kurt off this job, and we concurred with his decision."

He nodded.

"We also spoke to Nathan about his prank."

"Harassment," Todd said softly.

Her eyes narrowed. "He's been put on probation."

"Just like Ryan after his little incident with Eli?" Word was that Ryan was still CFO, just on an extended vacation.

He bet it was even a paid one. "Do you realize what you're doing?"

A sigh. "I'm working very hard to make sure we survive." She eyed him. "There's another issue."

Here it came. "Oh?"

"Were you and Dr. Kurt involved in a relationship?"

Todd settled back into his chair. "Yes."

She rubbed her forehead. "What the hell did you think you were doing?"

He chuckled, but it came out bitter. "Catching up with my high school boyfriend."

"Boy..." She flattened her hand against the desk. "He wasn't just a *friend* from high school."

He shook his head.

"God, Todd. I wish you had said something to me. Apparently Anderson knew."

He looked down at his hands. "I knew you'd..." *Flip your shit.* Todd bit back the words. "You'd discourage me from pursuing any romantic ties with a consultant." He looked up. "I figured if we got our jobs done, by the time it became relevant, he wouldn't be here anymore."

She didn't look impressed. "Well, your assumption was incorrect. Apparently Nathan saw you at a club together."

At a club? He furrowed his brow. "But the only place we went to was..." That little *shit.* He had to have been on Capitol Hill Sunday night. He swallowed. "We kept things quiet. Did our jobs. Did you have any clue before Nathan blurted out information about our *private lives*?"

Oh, that had been the wrong question. She folded her hands. "That's immaterial."

It wasn't. But he gave up. "Yes, I had a romantic relationship with Fazil Kurt. It didn't change how I worked, my performance, or *anything*."

"You can't be the judge of that, Todd."

"I'm gathering that this is a greater problem than harassment?"

There was that paleness again. "Certainly not. But you bent—and broke—rules. As did Dr. Kurt."

"Is that what Sam Anderson said?"

Her turn to furrow her brow. "I'm not discussing my conversations with Mr. Anderson." She rose. "Before this, your work has received high marks and your performance reviews have been satisfactory or above. We've taken that into consideration."

We've. Uh-oh. Stephen must be in on this. Or maybe the BoD had found out somehow. *Shit.* He straightened in his seat.

She grunted at that. "You're also on probation, Mr. Douglas. Subject to review in two months."

Cold washed over him. "What does that mean, exactly?"

She stared down at him. "You're next stop is HR to find out." She looked up and away, and for a moment, extraordinarily tired. "This was the best I could do."

Double shit. "We can't keep going like this."

She met his stare, grit in her voice. "I know." She opened her mouth but then shook her head. "Go to HR, please."

Todd rose, and on shaky legs, did just that.

An hour later, he left with a stack of papers and a rock the size of Mount Rainier in his belly. Holy fuck, they were serious. An action plan. Performance goals he had to meet. Reviews by Stephen. Hours he must be in the office during. Everything spelled out. One slipup, and he was out of a job.

The cynical part of him wondered if Nathan had gotten

the same plan... or if he'd just been slapped on the wrist and handed some vacation time.

Nathan, who either hung out on Capitol Hill to bash gays, or was there to hook up because he *was* gay.

Typical. So very typical with his type. Family values, rah rah, but some cock on the side, please. He pulled out his phone. Still no texts from Fazil.

Todd set the phone down and eyed his stack of paperwork. Probably a good thing Fazil hadn't texted. They'd be watching him.

So no texts, no e-mail, no anything that wasn't work-related. He'd follow their rules, dot their *I* s, cross their *T* s. He wasn't about to become the scapegoat for Singularity.

Todd eyed his phone again. Just... don't leave before I can say good-bye.

He had all of Fazil's things, but that didn't mean he couldn't fly home and ask Todd to ship everything.

More than anything, he wanted one last chance to convince Fazil to *stay*.

CHAPTER TWENTY-TWO

At five thirty, Fazil's phone rang. He pried himself off of the hotel pillow and looked at the screen before answering.

"Hey."

"Z? Are you okay?"

"Why does everyone keep asking me that?" He hiccupped a laugh that was more of a sob. "You, Sam, Eli..."

"Jesus. Are you drunk?"

"God, no. I wish I were, but Justin has me on a flight at six fucking thirty tomorrow morning. If I drink, I'll miss the plane." Not that he hadn't thought about losing himself in a bottle. "Please come over."

"I'm on my way."

"Room three-twenty-six."

"Same hotel?"

"Yep."

The sound of an engine starting. "Hang on. I'll be there soon."

"Good." He slid the phone back onto the nightstand.

He wasn't religious. He knew how to pray and had

memorized enough Arabic to do so, but he'd never learned to read Arabic. He'd read the Quran in both Turkish and English and even prayed in the Sultan Ahmed Mosque in Istanbul. But even more so than his parents, he lived, happily, in the secular world.

Seeing those pages had embedded fear into his bones. He could ignore the stupid camel and pig jokes. Not this. All his life, there'd been twinges and reminders that he wasn't Christian and not *quite* white, but he'd never felt more alien in the country of his birth until that moment.

He also felt a kinship to Eli's rage and sadness, and marveled at the man's restraint. Stubble scratched at his hand when he scrubbed his face.

Should have left Seattle with Eli. He'd been too wrapped up in Todd to even consider it.

Fuck. Drinking was sounding more like a good idea. He could stay up until he had to leave for the airport, right? Fazil shut his eyes.

He started when someone knocked on his door moments later, except a glance at his phone told him it had been forty-five minutes. He stumbled to the door, opened it, and there was Todd.

"Shit, Z." Todd took him into his arms, which was good because the shaking had returned. "Come on, let's sit down."

"Sure. I just woke up. I think."

Todd sat him down on the edge of the bed and peered at him, concern etched in every line on his face. "You're sure you haven't been..." The line between his brow deepened. "Have you had dinner?"

He hadn't had breakfast. "I haven't eaten."

"At all?" Todd glanced at his watch. "Jesus, dude. Do

you do this often? Not eat?" Todd picked up the in-room dining menu, scanned it, and tossed it back on the desk.

He had to think about that. "Maybe? When I'm stressed." The last thing he wanted when his stomach churned was food.

Todd picked up the keycard to the room. "Come on. Let's get some food that doesn't cost way the hell too much and get your things from my place."

"Fine." Except he didn't want to leave the room, didn't want to do anything. He sat, staring at the floor while the world rotated.

Todd knelt before him and took his hands. "Fazil."

He met Todd's eyes, and his moistened. "No, I'm *not* okay."

"I gathered that." Todd massaged the backs of his hands. "You don't have to be. I'm not fine with any of this, either."

When Todd's words penetrated, it was as if the fog lifted from his brain. "They didn't punish you, did they?"

Todd sighed. "I'm on probation for fooling around with a contractor."

Well, shit. Fazil cringed.

"It's so stupid. And..." Todd stood and pulled Fazil up off the bed. "I'll tell you the rest over dinner. You *need* to eat, Z. Especially now."

Damn Todd and his ability to be right about everything. But it was getting later and later and he still hadn't packed, so he let Todd pull him from the room and take him to the car.

The evening was full of mist, not enough for an umbrella, but the cool touch on Fazil's face woke him up. He *was* hungry. And tired and numb. He entwined his fingers with Todd's. "Thanks for coming."

"Always," Todd said.

They climbed into Todd's car and drove. The streets, the lights, and the building smeared into a giant blur through Fazil's wet window until they pulled into the drive-thru of a burger joint.

"It's far from foodie cuisine, but you haven't experienced Seattle until you've had a sourdough Jack."

"I think I've had enough of Seattle for a lifetime." He wanted to be back where he belonged. That's what home was, right?

Todd ordered, paid for, and collected their food. The scent of burgers and fries filled the car and Fazil's stomach grumbled.

Before they got back on the road, Todd squeezed his knee. "Don't let those assholes ruin this place for you. That kind of shit happens everywhere. Like I said, not *entirely* a liberal paradise."

"No place is." Fazil placed his hand on top of Todd's. "I had the best time of my life here with you. I'm— I need some time." And Pittsburgh.

Todd nodded. It took them a while to navigate the roads and the traffic, but they made it back to Todd's before the burgers got cold. As fast food went, they were damn fine burgers, and eating gave Fazil the clarity of thought to breathe and function.

Anger still simmered in his sinew, but he wouldn't burst into flame any time soon. When Fazil looked around Todd's apartment, an ache rose for his own place, *his* things, the coolness and comfort of *his* bed.

He set about packing his clothes and toiletries. The art and chocolate he'd bought at Mount Rainier. The coffee beans he'd grabbed after one of the company dinners.

Everything that was his, except what he most wanted to have back in Pittsburgh.

He took his bags to the door. "You'll have to come visit. I can repay you with touristy things."

"Maybe once this shit is done at Singularity. I'm not allowed to take vacation right now." Todd leaned against the couch, where they'd watched movies, necked, and fucked.

The need, the desire for Todd flooded back. His touch, the sound of this voice. "I don't want to lose you."

"You're not going to lose me. Promise." Todd pushed off the couch. "Maybe when things aren't so painful, you can come back."

"There's a lot more I'd like to see." Fazil tamped down the lump in his throat.

"There's so much more to show you." Reluctantly Todd hefted one of Fazil's bags. "We should get you back to the hotel."

He picked up the rest of his luggage. "Morning is going to come too early."

Todd held the door open. "Yeah." Once they'd both exited, he locked the door. "I can drive you to Sea-Tac. No sense in paying for a cab, especially when I need to be in the office early anyway."

Todd planned to spend the night. A different ache chased away the remnants of cold fear nipping at him all day. "Good thing I got a king bed."

"Very." Todd's voice was full of gravel.

Fazil managed not to trip down the stairs. The distance would be hard to manage, so he'd take all he could get of Todd tonight.

THE HOTEL DOOR CLICKED CLOSED, FAZIL ROLLED HIS luggage next to his laptop and faced Todd. "Guess that's that."

Todd handed over Fazil's overnight bag. "Not yet, it's not."

God, that voice. Fazil set the bag down next to the others and reached for Todd. All thought disappeared when Todd's lips met his. He expected desperation and rough desire—wanted and needed that.

Instead Todd met him with a languid kiss and gentleness. He brushed his fingers over Fazil's cheeks and throat. "I don't want to fuck you tonight." A whisper of words.

The hardness of Todd's dick against Fazil's said otherwise. "No?" He pulled Todd closer, grinding against him. "You sure?"

The sweetest smile. "Absolutely." Todd cupped the back of Fazil's head. "I'm going to make love to you tonight. For a very, *very* long time."

He didn't know whether ice or flames lapped up his body. Didn't matter, because Todd had his mouth again and his hands were in Todd's hair. Not sure how it happened, but Todd picked him up and he wrapped legs and arms around Todd's torso. They moved to the bed. Damn, Todd was strong to carry him like that.

When they bumped into the mattress, Todd set him down, but didn't let him go. "Might not get much sleep." He pulled Fazil's shirt from his jeans and up to expose flesh, then he was on his knees gliding his lips over Fazil's abs.

Fazil couldn't breathe. "Don't—care. Can sleep on— plane." He didn't know whether to nudge Todd down to his aching dick and balls or pull him up and kiss him forever. "God, please."

"You like that?" Todd unbuttoned Fazil's shirt, kissing and licking his way upward until Fazil was out of breath and nearly levitating off the bed.

Words became impossible. He moaned something he hoped was yes, gripped Todd's shirt, and tugged because he needed skin against his hands and lips, too.

Todd sat back, straddling Fazil, and pulled off his shirt to expose his expansive chest. Broad and muscular and dusted with hair that ran down under Todd's belt. A feast for eyes, fingers, and tongue.

"Were you always so beautiful?"

"No." Todd pressed his denim-covered ass against Fazil's straining dick and his pulse skyrocketed. Todd finished unbuttoning Fazil's shirt and pushed it open. "You were, though."

"Bullshi—" Todd leaned down and found both his nipples, one with his mouth, the other rolled between fingertips. Heat and light ran through his veins.

Todd touched and nipped every part of his torso. He wouldn't make the flight tomorrow because Todd was going to kill him with pleasure. "Oh, fuck."

"Later," Todd whispered against his chest. "When you're good and ready."

"I'm ready."

That laugh had him arching up against Todd. "You're not even close."

Yeah, he was. Aching and throbbing. If he got enough purchase, he might be able to find the bliss he sought.

Todd sat up again, and this time he didn't settle his weight on Fazil. "Let's get this shirt off you." They did and Todd laid Fazil back down, their chests sliding together and mouths working in a sweet dance that only pushed Fazil higher. When Todd rocked against Fazil's cock, he gasped for air. "Please, please fuck me." He cupped Todd's ass and thrust up against him. Why were they still wearing pants?

"Getting there," Todd said.

"So am I." He wanted Todd inside him when he came. Wanted him *now*.

Todd pried one of Fazil's hands away from his body and stretched his arm up to the headboard. "You know if you do come before I'm done with you, I'll keep this up until you're ready to come again." He repeated with Fazil's other hand. "Hold the headboard for me."

Fazil bit his lip and did as told. "Please?"

"You're *adorable* when you beg." Todd slid his hands down Fazil's arms, lingering at the pits, touching and tickling until Fazil couldn't breathe. He twisted and bucked with every touch. God, Todd *was* trying to kill him! "Yellow! Todd! Wait!"

Todd stilled.

"Oh God."

"Forgot how ticklish you were." He leaned down and kissed the tip of Fazil's nose. "I'm impressed you didn't let go."

He hadn't. The solidity of the wood under his fingers and in the stretch of his arms was comforting. Calming. "I like this."

A deep rumble in Todd's chest. "So do I." He trailed kisses down Fazil's torso.

Fine, maybe he was kinky. Or maybe he felt safe with Todd. Even when they were on the outs as teens, sex had always been shelter and bliss and *home*.

He needed Todd, like air and water and food. Todd near him, against him, driving heat into his brain. Fazil squirmed against the scratch of Todd's chin, the velvet caress of his tongue.

Todd kissed his stomach and slid his fingers under the waistband of Fazil's jeans. Fazil's whole body shook when Todd worked the button free.

Lips. Fingers. The *click* of the zipper. The heat of breath. Fazil moaned.

A huff of warmth against his underwear. "I think you will come before I'm done."

"Probably." He managed a whisper.

"Even better." Todd pulled at Fazil's remaining clothes and slid them down to his feet. He let out a frustrated groan. "I always forget the damn shoes."

Laughter made Fazil even more light-headed. Todd pulled off Fazil's sneakers, then everything else, and he was naked and hard, his arms and legs stretched out.

Todd stood. "That's a nice sight."

"Care to join me?"

In answer, Todd peeled off everything below the waist and crawled onto the bed. His hands found every sensitive piece of Fazil's skin along the way.

That whole breathing thing was overrated. Fazil twisted on the sheets, every nerve electric. When Todd kissed the inside of Fazil's right thigh, he bucked hard and his groans filled the room. The heat of a laugh. "You always were so sensitive."

"Well you're—"

Todd mouthed Fazil's balls and closed his hand around Fazil's shaft and he couldn't see through the heat and the sparks dancing in his vision.

He stroked Fazil tight and slow, and swept his tongue over his sac and around his root before closing over his crown.

Heat and friction and Todd sucking him hard. Too much. Fazil let go of the headboard and tangled his hands in

Todd's hair. "Please, please!" Fire in his spine, heat everywhere. He was so damn close, there were tears in his eyes.

Todd licked Fazil's shaft and jerked him off faster. "That's it, Z. Let go."

Bliss rose until it shattered like glass, jagged edges of pleasure cutting into his veins. His cry scraped his throat, and he tightened his fingers in Todd's hair. Hot semen spilled over Todd's hand and splattered against Fazil's chest, and then he couldn't see through the blinding haze.

When he finally came down, he relaxed his hold on Todd's head and looked at the most perfect smile he'd ever seen. Blue eyes. Stubbled jaw. Lines of happiness from here to eternity.

"There's my Fazil." Todd crawled into Fazil's arms, his mouth finding Fazil's and their bodies molding together.

A slick hand traced Fazil's jaw and lip, all musk and salt. "I love watching you come."

He didn't know what to say, so he kissed Todd and let his hands and body make up for his inability to form words. *I love you. I want you. I need you.* His heart ached. Why did they have to live so far apart?

Todd broke the kiss. "You won't forget me this time, will you?"

Fazil swallowed past the lump in his throat. "I didn't forget you last time."

A flash of panic in Todd took away that sweet smile. "Please don't shut me out. I need..." His jaw worked. "I need to know you're there."

"I am." Soft hair under his fingers. "I will be."

Todd's gaze held his for a long time, as if Todd were peering into his mind. Then his lips quirked up.

Lips against lips. Flesh against flesh. Todd's hard dick

rocking against his thigh. Fazil moaned, reached up, and took hold of the headboard.

Todd broke the kiss. "Very nice."

True to his words, Todd started again, working his way from Fazil's neck, kissing down his chest, and lower, nipping and biting, tracing over every inch of Fazil's skin.

Every touch was more intense. Fazil squirmed and whimpered, wanting more, but not sure if he could take another instant.

He wasn't hard, but that didn't matter. Everywhere burned with the need to be stroked again. Kissed. Touched.

"You're gonna kill me." His words were slurred.

"Nah. Just gonna give you the night of your life."

His last one with Todd for who knew how long.

Todd's weight shifted, rocking the bed. "Be right back."

Condom and lube. "Want you inside me."

"I'm glad." Todd sank down. "Because I want that, too."

"Good to be on the same page." Too bad they couldn't *stay* here. He wanted Todd, but he wanted *home*, too. That would come tomorrow. Tonight—he had Todd tonight.

When Todd pressed a finger against his hole, Fazil groaned. "Don't need prep, just—fuck me."

"Told you I wasn't gonna do that." Still he stopped fingering him. The bed rocked and Todd pressed his cock into him, stretching him wide.

Fire burned into his brain and he arched his back, gripped the headboard tighter. "God, yes!"

A chuckle. Todd hooked both of Fazil's legs and lifted them. But rather than the pounding Fazil expected, Todd slid in slowly and deeply.

Sparks of heat flared across Fazil's head and he whimpered.

"Love that sound." He drew back and moved forward again. And again. Deep, languid, strong strokes.

Fazil moaned and whimpered and pleaded. It was too much and not enough. Each entry drove him crazy with the need to meet Todd, but the depth, the way he pressed against his sweet spot, left Fazil breathless with pleasure. His arms shook, both from the stretch of gripping the headboard and from the desire Todd drove into him with each lazy stroke.

Todd let go of his legs and leaned down. His mouth took Fazil's and swallowed every groan and cry. Fazil fought those lips, even as he surrendered to them, their bodies moving as one, slow, hard, as if each movement might be the last.

Todd was air and life and there was no one else in the world. He'd die if he didn't have more.

How long they made love, he didn't know, only that each thrust, kiss, and bite was exactly that—Todd pouring his love into him. Fazil's dick pressed against Todd's belly, until Todd opened up space and took it in his hand.

Same slow movements, even more of an effect. Light and heat raced through Fazil, coiling tight inside him. His balls ached and tears pricked at the corners of his eyes. He didn't want this to end—even as he knew it must.

Once more, he broke his hold on the headboard and buried his fingers in Todd's hair. This time, Fazil pulled Todd into a kiss and swallowed *his* moans. He thrust his tongue into Todd's hot mouth, sucking and biting until Todd responded, picking up speed and strength until he was fucking Fazil hard.

Fazil broke the kiss and arched against Todd. "Oh, fuck!"

"God, Z." Todd's breathless voice scraped words out. "Can't get enough."

Neither could Fazil—though he tried, pushing back as Todd rammed forward, until he couldn't tell their bodies or moans or breaths apart. Fire poured over Fazil until everything was bright and hot.

"Gonna..." He was gone, lost in pleasure and light that shattered and rained down into his body until he was trembling, coming, and biting Todd's shoulder.

Todd's rhythm broke. He gasped for air and buried himself in Fazil, pulling him closer as if they could merge into one being.

Nothing compared to this. Nothing. Fazil held on to every second, hoping it never ended.

But slowly, slowly, it did, resolving into breaths and weight and heavy lethargy.

Two heartbeats. Two bodies. Todd nuzzled the side of his neck. "Love you so much."

The words were lightning, and he shuddered against them. "I know. I know. Todd, I..." But nothing came out from behind the rock wedged in his throat, the fear that gripped his heart.

"It's okay, Z. When you're ready."

He'd never felt like this before, but he couldn't get the words out. He *couldn't*. So he folded his arms around Todd, let silent tears shake him to his core, and hoped beyond hope that Todd understood.

CHAPTER TWENTY-THREE

Fazil barely remembered the two flights, the layover, or the taxi ride back to his apartment in Squirrel Hill. He'd slept on and off in the air but was bone tired by the time he unlocked the door to his place. The luggage stayed in the living room and all his clothes hit the floor on the way to his bedroom. Cool sheets and soft pillows enveloped him, and he fell asleep immediately, despite the never-ending ache in his heart and head.

No Todd. His first thought when he woke up. He was home and Todd wasn't here. Fazil scrubbed his face and stumbled to the bathroom. Work. He had to go to work. Had to face Sam.

He caught himself on the bathroom counter as memories flooded back. The burned pages. His hands gripping Nathan's shirt and ramming him up against the wall. Todd prying him away.

Fazil's stomach flipped, and he fought to keep the bile down. *Shit.* The man on the other side of the mirror looked like he'd been through hell. Red-eyed, haunted, and so pale he looked gray.

Shower and coffee. Maybe that would help.

By the time he left the apartment, he'd managed to put some color back into his skin and he no longer looked like he'd been run over by a truck repeatedly. It was after ten according to his phone, but his body refused to believe that, still stuck in a time zone somewhere out west.

Grounds N'at wasn't busy, which was good, because it meant Brian started in on Fazil's drink before he even hit the counter. "Hey, you're back!"

Fazil nodded. "Mostly. I think half my brain is still in Seattle." And all of his heart. The sudden pain in his chest had him placing a hand on the counter.

"Dude, you okay?"

"Yeah. Jet lag."

Brian handed him his coffee. "On the house."

He didn't argue. He'd tried that once and Brian had turned from relaxed coffee dude to someone as stubborn as Eli. He did throw two bucks in the tip jar when Brian's back was turned.

"I saw that!"

"Did not." He headed toward the door and climbed the stairs to the office.

Once upstairs, he paused in the reception area. He wasn't ready for Sam yet, but he doubted he could sneak past both Sam and Eli's offices, even under the guise of wanting to dock his laptop. He squared his shoulders and headed in.

Justin was at his desk in the office outside Sam's. Today his hair was spiked up and purple at the ends, but he'd done away with the guyliner. Probably because of the June heat. His nail polish matched his hair.

Still hard to believe he was Eli's *husband*. "Hey."

"Welcome home." Justin's grin was infectious, but his joy twisted against Fazil. "We've missed you."

He'd missed them, too. Pittsburgh. The office. The people. "Ditto." Except there was no *Todd*. He nodded at the inner office. "Sam told me to stop by."

A softer smile. "Yeah. He's been expecting you."

The wince came, and it didn't go unnoticed.

"It's fine," Justin said. "We've been worried, that's all."

A cough from inside. "Should I come out there, or are you going to come in here?"

Fazil swallowed, entered Sam's office, and shut the door. He slumped into the guest chair. "Hi."

Sam's brows furrowed. "Do you need to take the day off?"

The coffee turned sour in his stomach and he set the cup down on the edge of Sam's desk. "No. I'm fine."

There was the raised eyebrow that every executive in the company was so damn good at. "Did you get that from Eli or did he get that from you? Because that's totally an Eli look."

Sam blinked, then leaned back. "I got it from Michael." The grin was Sam's own, though. "You'll have to ask one of them who had it first. I'm not sure *they* know at this point."

Fazil studied his coffee cup. "I feel like shit, Sam. I really fucked up out there."

"Your relationship with Todd aside, you did fine considering the environment you and Eli ended up in."

"But you can't set my relationship with Todd aside."

Sam tented his hands like he did when he was in professional mode, but his features were soft. "I can't chide you for that. You know I can't."

Too much of Sam's own history at play. The photograph

of Michael next to Sam's monitor was a reminder of that. Still. "You should. It was the wrong thing to do."

"Was it?" There was sadness in his smile. "You did have some encouragement, too." He nodded at the wall in the direction of Eli's office.

Was it wrong? He still didn't know the answer to that. All of the moments he'd spent with Todd had been heaven, even the hellish ones. The world had vanished and he'd found peace. "I don't..." He ran both of his hands through his hair. "It got so fucked up."

"From what you said, that had little to do with you or Todd."

Maybe. "So, now what?"

"Well, you get back on the horse that threw you, and we finish this job so we never have to work with these fucking assholes again." Vehemence in his voice. "I don't take kindly to my people being abused."

Abused. Hope stirred in Fazil and he met Sam's gaze. "You're not mad at me."

All professionalism fell away and Sam rolled his eyes. "For God's sake, Fazil, no. Worried sick, yes. Angry? Yes—but not at *you*."

Muscles unknotted in his shoulders and he picked up his coffee and his laptop. "I guess I should head to my desk, then."

"Stop in and let Eli see you first. He's been worse than you at the self-blame game."

Breath caught. "What? Why?"

"He thinks he should have pulled you out with him. Had an inkling something might happen."

But he hadn't because of Todd. "I'll talk to him. Not his fault, either."

"Oh, good luck with *that*." Sam picked up a pen and clicked the end.

Great. He rose and headed out, leaving Sam's door open.

"Ping-Pong later?" Justin asked.

"Yeah. But you'll wipe the floor with me."

That got him a big grin. A *normal* grin. Good. He walked across the hall and rapped on Eli's doorframe.

Eli swiveled around and his shoulders dropped. "Fazil. I'm—"

"It's fine."

Eli did that thing with his eyebrow and his foot tapped out a staccato rhythm.

The tapping foot was over-the-top, but it made Fazil cringe anyway. "All right, I'm not exactly fine, but it's not your fault I stayed."

"So Sam keeps saying." He leaned back in his chair. "I'm not convinced."

"If the blame lies with anyone—it's me."

Eli sat forward, but before he could speak, Fazil held up his hand. "See? We're both tall, dark, and cranky."

That stopped Eli, and he chuckled but quickly sobered. "How's Todd?"

"I don't know." He needed to text him. "I'm still waking up."

"Then go." Eli shooed him away. "Finish your coffee, text your boyfriend, and get back to work."

Fazil saluted Eli with his cup. His *boyfriend*. Guess he and Todd were going to try the long-distance thing. Relief washed through him as he sat down and docked his laptop. He was back where he belonged.

All he had to do was overlook the agony of being two thousand–plus miles from the man he loved.

THE WORST PART FOR TODD WAS KNOWING THE TIME on the East Coast but not knowing if Fazil was awake yet. Alive, he knew—Fazil had texted him from the cab on the way to his apartment, exhausted as all hell. The message had been full of weird autocorrect substitutions, but he'd figured out what I'm cabinet. Heading home. Will boxtop laser. meant.

Around eight fifteen, as he was pulling into the office, his phone buzzed.

Hey. I'm up and moving. Hope you understood the weird text last night.

He parked and replied. Yeah, I did. Figured you were pretty out of it.

Yeah. Feeling better now. How are you?

Worried about his job. Tired. Stressed. But above all? I miss you.

I miss you, too. It's weird not having you here.

Todd studied the words. *Weird not having you here*— not *weird not being there*. Fazil was glad to be home.

It shouldn't have bothered him... but it did. He tapped out a reply. I wish you were here. Pressed send.

Nothing for a while, so he got out and headed into the office. Dread sank into his stomach, though Fazil had every reason to be happy to be back in Pittsburgh. Once at his cube, he dragged his attention to his e-mail and started in on answering what needed to be dealt with.

First up was studying the daily plan Stephen had laid out for him, like some kind of errant child. He'd slept with a contractor, yes, but he hadn't screwed up his job. He didn't need a fucking *babysitter*.

His phone buzzed. Finally. Videochat tonight? Want to see you.

Todd bit his lip. He shouldn't answer at work, lest anyone catch him taking a second for *himself*. He grabbed his phone anyway. Yeah. Sounds perfect.

Hit me up when you get in.

I will. He didn't hit send, his hand hovering over the screen. Should he or shouldn't he? He'd said it already, so he typed the words. I love you. Hit send.

No reply. *Damn it, Z. It's not that hard.*

He turned back to his inbox and the day ahead. First, knock out what Stephen wanted him to do, then settle in on the rest of the documents he owed Fazil and Anderson.

He tried not to worry about his silent phone.

FAZIL WAS HALF-ASLEEP ON THE COUCH WHEN HIS computer dinged. Thank goodness he'd cranked the volume up as high as it would go, or he might have missed it. He leaned forward and hit accept on Todd's videochat invite.

There he was, hair slightly askew, but looking good. "Hey. You're a sight for sore eyes."

Todd smiled. "You look like you're about ready to fall over."

Couldn't help the laugh. "Yeah. That jet lag is something else. I'd forgotten how bad it is from the West Coast."

"Almost as bad as going to Europe."

"Almost." He studied Todd on the screen. "God, I miss you." Todd's touch, the press of his lips, and the beat of his heart when Fazil leaned against him. Everything.

That earned him a smile. "Ditto. It's too quiet here."

He liked quiet, though. Wished he could have *here* and Todd at the same time. "You're not getting too much flack at work?"

Todd leaned back against the black leather couch, which Fazil could almost smell. "Nah. Stephen is babysitting my ass, but Nathan's been out of the office. No sign of Ryan whatsoever."

"Well, that's good, except for the being-babysat part." He chewed on his cheek.

"I have no regrets." He leaned forward. "None, Z. About anything."

Including their past. He still had issues with that, but those were his. "Good. I'm glad you were there and we met again. Glad we're together now." They were together, right?

Guess they were, because Todd had the biggest damn grin. "I didn't know if you wanted to keep this"—he gestured between the two of them—"going."

"Oh hell yeah. We'll figure the distance out at some point."

"Well, you do like Seattle."

He did, despite the shit that went down. But he liked Pittsburgh, too, and didn't want to leave the job with Sam. "Yeah. It's a fine town." There was another option open to them. "So's this one. You should come visit. See if you like it."

Todd's brows furrowed for a moment. "You know I want to see you, but with this whole probation thing and whatever happens with Singularity, coming out there's not going to happen any time soon."

Yeah, they'd talked about it before. He hoped it really was Singularity and not Todd fixated on a *plan*. "Well, someday." Then a yawn caught him. "Oh fuck. It's not the company, I swear!"

Todd laughed. "Jeez, Z. Go get some sleep." He glanced down, probably at the computer clock. "It's nearly midnight there."

It was. "Yeah, but..." If he could only reach through the Internet and touch Todd. "I like this."

"So do I. Like it more if you were here, but I'll take what I can get." A broad smile. "I don't want you falling asleep at your laptop, though. The top of your head isn't interesting."

"Depends on the head." He grinned at the screen.

Todd rolled his eyes. "You taking lessons from Eli?"

Fazil laughed. "No. Maybe his banter is wearing off on me."

"Nice." Todd leaned back. "But you should sleep."

"Yeah." He needed to. "Talk tomorrow?"

"Of course." Todd leaned forward. "You know what I want you to do between now and then?"

Little shocks ran up Fazil's back and he scooted closer to the laptop. "What?"

"Think of how you can make our next call *interesting* for the both of us." Oh, that grin. "Use your head."

Oh. *Oh*. Fazil squirmed. "I'm sure I can come up with something. So to speak."

Todd laughed. "Good night, Z."

"Night, Todd."

They both hung up and Fazil let out a breath. He was tired. But now he was hard. *Damn it, Todd.* Undoubtedly, that was exactly how Todd wanted him.

Well, jacking off was a good way to get some sleep. He shut the laptop and headed for his bed.

CHAPTER TWENTY-FOUR

A MEETING REMINDER ON FAZIL'S LAPTOP CHIMED, pulling him out of his work. Two minutes until he and Eli piled into Sam's office and talked to Dr. Sandra about the Singularity Storage job. There'd been a shift over the past couple of days. A sense of urgency and fear, the sudden need to get everything done.

He pushed back from his desk and grabbed a can of Coke on the way. Up way too late chatting with Todd last night. They'd touched on the rumors swirling around Singularity and the shit-ton of work Stephen kept dropping on Todd as part of his probationary period. They'd slid into gaming—and Todd had brought out his bag of dice.

Fazil shivered. That had led to some fun games—none of which he was going to focus on now. Both Eli and Sam were too observant for him to chance walking in with a dopey smile and a hard-on. He cracked open the soda and took a sip outside the door to Justin and Sam's offices.

Justin nodded at the inner door. "They're already in. When you're done, we're all hiking up the hill to the PGH Taco Truck."

If that wasn't incentive to keep the meeting short, nothing was. He shut Sam's door after entering and joined Eli, who was sitting in one of Sam's guest chair. He stifled a yawn on the way down.

"Long night?" A hint of amusement in Sam.

He shrugged and tried not to grin. "The whole three-hour time difference isn't fun."

"I don't doubt it." Sam's humor melted into seriousness. "You wouldn't happen to have any intel on what we're walking into?"

"My bet is someone approached the board." Eli tapped a finger on the armrest of his chair. "That would explain many of the requests I've gotten."

Fazil set the can down on Sam's desk. "That's one of the rumors—that they're being bought. The other is that they're going bankrupt because a customer pulled out."

Sam pursed his lips. "I haven't heard of any customer disengagement. Rumblings about missed deadlines, yes, but that's normal in tech."

Fazil leaned back in his chair. "Guess we'll find out."

A nod from Sam. He leaned over his speakerphone, typed in a number, and pressed call. "Here we go."

A couple of rings and Sandra answered. After the normal hellos were exchanged, silence ruled over the line. Eli sat forward. Sam picked up a pen and clicked the end. "So, we take it there's news."

She cleared her throat. "The rumor mill has reached that far already?"

Fazil put an arm on the desk and leaned closer to the phone. "Doesn't take much to read between the lines of suddenly frantic e-mails."

Sandra sighed. "I'll give you that. The board received an offer from BinBox Group."

Eli clicked his tongue. "Reasonable company." He peered at the phone. "A good offer?"

A ridge grew between Sam's brows. "E—"

"It's a fair question," Sandra said. "There are some on the board who believe it's the best we can get, considering. There are others who believe we're worth more."

"What do *you* think?" Sam asked.

A breath. "I think they're lowballing. We have issues with meeting deadlines, but that's getting better. Our finances are solid."

"Of *course* they are." Eli practically bristled. Sam threw him a look.

"We owe you, Mr. Ovadia." She paused. "For more than just that."

Eli said nothing, though he looked very unhappy to be holding his tongue. Sam mouthed a thank-you in his direction and Eli's shoulders relaxed.

"We do need to finish putting engineering together, though."

Fazil's domain. "We're nearly there," he said. "There are a few key procedures to document, and I still need access to your source code repository to finish cataloguing the open source code."

"There's an issue there." A rattle of paper on the other end. "Stephen would rather you not have access."

Sam sat back. Fazil couldn't because there wasn't any breath in his lungs.

It was Eli who spoke, in a tone that could have frozen the Allegheny River. "Why the hell not?"

Todd. It had something to do with Todd. *Shit.*

"There's been concern with Todd Douglas, and given Dr. Kurt's relationship..."

"Then give me access," Sam snapped. "I'll do the fucking audit myself."

Fazil held his breath. Eli peered at Sam and there was almost a smile touching his lips.

"Excuse me?" Sandra's voice was breathless.

"Give me access to the code base." Sam spoke slowly and calmly, but with the same amount of venom. "And I'll do the fucking audit."

Silence from the other line.

"You'll pay for my time, of course."

"Mr. Anderson—"

"No," Sam said. "I trust my employees. He signed your NDA. He was abused by your engineer—"

"All the more reason—"

"For us to end this call and cancel the project?"

Fazil covered his mouth and his stomach heaved. No. Not because of him. Eli caught his eye and patted the air. *Don't panic*, he mouthed and pointed at the Coke can. *Drink.*

He did and his stomach settled. Sam eyed the phone.

"I can get you access to the system," Sandra said at last.

"Good," Sam ground out the word. "Because I'm sure you'd like to show yourself in the best light for BinBox."

There was a threat in Sam's voice, given the way Eli thumped back in his chair. Fazil didn't know what it was, though. He gulped another mouthful of soda.

"I— Yes. We'd certainly prefer to work *with* you, Mr. Anderson."

"As would I." Sam laid his pen down. "Is there anything else?"

"Nothing that can't be handled over e-mail."

"Then have a pleasant afternoon," Sam said, right

before he stabbed the off button. He took a deep breath. "Tell me why we're working with these people again?"

Eli snorted. "Because the tech is damn good and most of the staff aren't unmitigated assholes."

Sam rubbed his forehead. "Right. I said that, didn't I?"

"Yes, you did."

Fazil fiddled with his Coke can. "Sam—"

Sam's face softened. "You're as bad as Eli. These things happen." He flopped back against his chair. "Besides, I've read their HR policies—I had them sent over—and there's nothing that prohibits fraternization between employees and contractors—only between management and employees."

"That's not what they told Todd."

Eli shifted. "If they let him go, he gets unemployment and any unused vacation. Cheaper to make him leave."

Fazil closed his eyes for a second. "Have I mentioned how much I enjoy working here lately?"

Sam chuckled. "Good to hear, especially after..." He waved at the Polycom.

"I'm so glad to be home."

"As am I," Eli said. He rose and grabbed his cane. "Now, wasn't there a lunch plan that included tacos?"

A few minutes later, the whole office was out the door and heading up Murray. Fazil hung back and walked with Eli and Justin. "How do I help Todd?"

Eli watched the ground as he walked, then looked ahead. "You don't."

"That's not helpful."

"I know. But if they have it out for him, there's nothing you can do. Make sure every work e-mail is professional and he's only one of many recipients."

Justin glanced over. "If I understand the situation, the most you can do is warn him."

Well, great. Not exactly the conversation he wanted to have tonight, but he owed it to Todd to say *something*. "This whole thing is shit."

Eli patted him on the back. "Well, at least you can drown your sorrows in Taco Truck tacos."

He could. Especially with Sam paying.

They ended up tromping back down to Grounds N'at and bribing Brian with three tacos so they could camp out and pay him even more money for coffee.

"You don't have to feed me," Brian said. "You guys practically pay my rent."

Sam grinned. "I know who butters my bread. Or rather, brews my coffee. Besides, we're neighbors."

"To the neighborhood." His coworker Adam raised a cappuccino.

Fazil raised his cup, as did everyone else. *This is my home.* He didn't want to be anywhere else.

By the time Todd got back to his apartment, it was nearly eight o'clock. He wolfed down a pile of salad topped with some chicken in a desperate attempt to counteract all the exercise he wasn't getting stuck behind his desk fifty-plus hours a week.

At least when Fazil had been here, they'd been able to hike, walk, and fuck. This whole web-based relationship put a damper on all of that, though rolling dice and telling Fazil exactly how to pleasure himself had certainly kept him hard *and* entertained. He'd always liked porn, but watching Fazil over videochat was something else entirely.

Damn, he missed Z. Needed him here. Wanted to hold him, touch him. Breathe the same air. Exist in the same space. It wasn't the sex—it was *Fazil*. He sank down on his couch and flipped open his laptop. Fazil was online, waiting for him, looking tired around the edges. "Hey, long day?"

Fazil's smile was warm. "Kind of. Pinball league tonight. I just got home."

"Hitting flippers works up a sweat?" He tried to grin through the rolling in his gut. Yes, Fazil had a social life. That was *fine*.

He laughed. "No, but joking around and egging each other on does." He leaned back. "It's a good group. Nice to see them again."

Todd ran his tongue over his teeth. Fazil was settling back into his life. "How are things with your ex?"

"Kris?" Fazil's brows furrowed for a moment. "She's good. Her and Lance have hit it off really well. We didn't talk much, though. I think she's worried I took the breakup hard."

"Did you?"

Those lines on his forehead became deeper. "Are you getting jealous on me?"

Was he? Todd fidgeted. "Yeah, maybe."

Fazil crossed his arms. "I told you Kris and I didn't work out."

"Not about her." Todd tapped at the casing of his laptop. "You're there, having fun, and not *here*... having fun."

Fazil's face softened. "The whole getting-out-and-spending-time-with-people thing? Keeps me from getting depressed that we aren't together." Fazil scooted forward. "I miss you like hell every day. You can't take PTO. Even if I came out there, you'd still be stuck at your desk. They're watching you too closely."

"True. I know. Looking for any reason to fire me." The whole probation thing was getting weirder, too. He'd been doing everything Stephen asked, but the hairs on the back of his neck stood up whenever he got another e-mail. "Hey, what's Sam doing in the system, anyway? I saw someone created him an account."

Fazil's expression twisted into a snarl. "He's doing the open source audit."

Todd's pulse doubled. "Why?" Even as he asked the question, the answer flew into his head. "They locked you out because of me?"

Fazil snapped his mouth shut, his face as dark as his expression. He nodded.

"Oh fuck, Z." He rubbed his chin. "I hope that didn't cause you any issues with Sam."

The anger melted away. "No, if anything it made me realize how much he goes to bat for us. He threatened to pull the whole project when your CEO balked at giving him access."

"Dude." He suppressed a shudder. The chaos *that* would have caused, for both of them.

"Right? Never had anyone do that for me. Didn't expect Sam to, after how everything went down."

"Sam seems like a great guy to work for." Though it hurt to say it. "You're damn lucky."

"I know." He looked at his hands. "If only we could slice out the middle of the country, then I could work for Sam *and* be near you."

Todd stared at his screen as pinpricks ran down his back. "Wait, what if you could?" That was the perfect answer. "Most of the stuff you do is remote, right? What if you could live here *and* work for Sam?"

"Yeah, it's mostly contracting." Fazil's shoulders dropped and he bit his lip, his gaze faraway. Thinking. "But I'm not sure Sam would go for it."

"Wouldn't hurt to ask." Todd watched Fazil's expression, the deepening lines. "We could be together then."

Fazil focused on the camera, his expression neutral. "You want me to move out there."

"You like it out here, and there are plenty of jobs, if Sam says no." They'd talked about this before. Of course he wanted Fazil here.

Fazil nodded, though the lines between his brow were back. "I'll think about it. Seattle *is* nice."

Good. Todd released a breath he hadn't realized he was holding. "It is. I can't wait to see you again."

Fazil's next words were cut off by a huge yawn. He clapped his hand over his mouth.

Todd glanced at the time. Getting closer to nine, which meant midnight in Pittsburgh. "This time zone thing sucks."

"It does." Fazil blew out a breath and grinned. "Well, at least it isn't Europe or something." The smile vanished. "Long distances are hard."

Todd's chest ached. If only he could reach through the screen and smooth out the lines on Fazil's face. "It's worth it, right?"

Fazil focused on the keyboard. "I'm not sure I can drop everything in my life and move across the country."

That was a punch to the gut, but Todd tamped the panic down. "See what Sam says?"

Fazil sat back. "One thing at a time, right?"

"Yeah." Todd spoke softly and glanced at the clock

again. "I'm going to guess you're not up for a repeat of last night."

That drew a smile and a shudder from Fazil. "I want a repeat, but I don't think I can take being up that late again, not with a meeting at nine."

"True." They had played a long time, but it had been so much fun making Fazil touch and stroke himself, but not letting him jack off to completion—not until Fazil begged. "Maybe I can sneak out earlier tomorrow."

Red crept up Fazil's neck and he squirmed. "Yeah?"

"Yeah." Especially if he went to work early. "Why don't we meet back here at nine your time?"

"Sounds good." Fazil leaned forward, all smiles again. "Can't wait."

Didn't look like Fazil could, the way he fidgeted in his chair. "Neither can I."

They said their good-byes and signed off. Todd leaned back against the leather couch, caught between horny and worried. He closed his eyes. Life would be so much better for the both of them when Fazil moved here.

CHAPTER TWENTY-FIVE

FAZIL STARED UP AT HIS BEDROOM CEILING AND watched shadows and light undulate across the textured plaster as cars passed below on Murray Avenue. Even with his blinds and shades, he'd never been able to get this room completely dark. Most nights, he didn't mind.

Tonight? He wanted to blot away the entire world.

He doubted total darkness would chase away the conversation that kept replaying in his head.

Over the past week, he'd been ignoring Todd's hints to talk to Sam. Dropping his own that maybe he wasn't entirely comfortable with leaving his life in Pittsburgh. Yes, he wanted to be with Todd, was desperate at times for his touch and his voice, but moving in with him completely across the country? Too much, too fast.

They'd been together barely two weeks in person after fifteen years apart.

Fazil rolled toward the windows. He'd run from Todd back then, unable to deal with the future Todd had mapped out for them. This was familiar, the panic in his soul, the lump in his throat.

He loved Todd, but he'd made his life *here*. Why couldn't Todd see that?

The whole question of moving had come to a head earlier.

"Have you asked Sam yet?"

Todd had gotten in late and Fazil had nodded off waiting for him to come online.

Maybe that's why he'd been snippy. "No, I haven't. I'll let you know when I do." He'd set his water glass down hard after that.

"God, Z. What's your problem? How hard is it to ask?"

"My problem?" He pushed back from the table. "There hasn't been a good time. We're trying to get this job done for your fucking company and..." He bit back everything else.

"Yeah, I'm busy, too. But, Jesus, you need to make up your mind. I can't sit here forever like I did last time."

The knife stabbed deep with those words. It wrenched and hurt as much now, hours later, as it had when he'd stared back at Todd. "I'll ask him tomorrow."

"Fazil, I didn't mean..." Todd's face had been pale and horrified and nervous.

"I know. We're both beat—let's talk again tomorrow, when we're not so cranky."

Todd had nodded and they'd signed off and Fazil had spent the better part of the night tossing and turning in bed.

He needed some sleep, or he'd be shit tomorrow. Today. Whatever. He closed his eyes.

And opened them to the faint sounds of traffic, people, and birds. *Fuck.*

Fazil rubbed his eyes and forced himself out of bed. A shower and shave later, he wasn't any more awake. Still looked like hell, too, judging from the mirror.

Fazil pushed away from his sink and went to find

clothes.

Even if Sam said yes, Fazil wasn't sure he wanted to go. Every time he thought of moving to Seattle, his stomach sank down to the street below, rolled down the hill, and probably got run over by a dozen cars.

How much of a shit did that make him? You were supposed to do anything for the person you loved, right?

Coffee. He needed coffee. Fazil found his keys and his wallet, and headed down the street to Grounds N'at and work.

Pretty sure he knew Sam's answer. The pit in his stomach yawned wider. Yes, there were jobs in Seattle, but not like the one he had here. He'd go back to being a ground-down cog in a corporate wheel, and he couldn't endure another set of *issues* like he had at Singularity.

Fazil clenched his teeth and opened the door to the coffee shop.

Brian stood behind the counter and he had a look of panic when the bell on the door rang. "Hey, Fazil. Gonna be a wait."

"No problem." He got in line and squinted around the shop. Crowded today and only Brian working. No wonder he looked frazzled. When he got to the front, Brian nodded at him. "The usual?"

A shower of warmth, followed by ice. "Yeah." Brian *knew* him, knew his order. Skinny double-shot mocha with a hint of peppermint. This was *home*. "What happened to Becky?" She'd been the other morning barista, but thinking about it, he hadn't seen her since he'd gotten back.

Brian blew out a breath of air and set the espresso machine brewing. "She found a job in Shadyside, closer to her apartment." He pressed his arm to his brow. "So it's just me in the mornings until I find someone else."

"That sucks, man."

Brian shrugged. "It's what it is."

Still, Brian sounded tired. Fazil paid and stuck a little extra in the tip jar. Least he could do for the guy who fortified his day.

The coffee was good, but did nothing to close the hole inside his soul. He climbed the steps to the office and carded himself into the lobby. He knew Sam's answer. Worse—he knew his own. He'd still ask, because he owed Todd that much. Owed Sam the respect, too.

In the office outside Sam's, Justin was chewing absently on a pen while examining some kind of spreadsheet.

"Hey, the boss man in?"

"I am," Sam said from the inner office.

Justin laughed. "There's your answer." He put the pen down. "Rough night?"

He must *really* look like shit. "Insomnia." He hefted his coffee. "And a tonic."

After a sympathetic grunt from Justin, Fazil entered Sam's office and closed the door. He dropped into one of his guest chairs. "I—need to ask you something."

Sam glanced at the closed door and folded his hands on top of his desk. "All right."

No sense stalling. "Could I work from a remote location —full-time—and still work for you?"

Sam tilted his head. "Like from Seattle, for instance?"

A rush of warmth to his face. He nodded and took a sip of coffee. His throat had grown tight.

Sam leaned back in his chair, and so many emotions played along those features, he couldn't name them all. "No."

Fazil felt the fissure in his soul split wider. He'd known,

but the reality of that single word *hurt*. He tried to say something, but failed.

Sam's voice was soft. "I need my team to be able to work with each other seamlessly. Much can be accomplished remotely, but there's an element of collaboration and trust no amount of phone or video calls can ever replicate."

Loyalty. Creativity. Bouncing ideas off one another. Understanding how all the bits slotted together. "I know." He managed to push those words out. "I had to ask."

A nod. "I know you're in a rough spot. If I can do anything to make it easier..."

He looked down at his shaking hands. "I love this job. I love this city." He loved Todd, but that wasn't enough, even when it should have been. He'd never enjoyed the nine-to-five before he'd met Sam. Never understood how work could be fulfilling until he'd set foot in this quirky little office.

"You should know you were my absolute first choice for engineering." Sam's chair squeaked. "And I don't want to lose you."

That didn't help. He furrowed his brow and stared at the white plastic lid of his coffee like it might solve the unsolvable.

"I've also been waiting for you to ask this."

Fazil looked up. "Oh?"

A smile, but one tinged with sadness. "It's one of the solutions. You go there to be with him." He shook his head. "I did consider it, too. I want to say yes, believe me, but every time I hashed it out..."

"Didn't make business sense."

"It's *not* the bottom line," Sam said. "Replacing you will cost. I won't find another you, so I'll have to hire two engineers to do the work you do."

Sam was serious. Fazil stared back. "Wait, I'm—"

"Irreplaceable."

Well, shit. "I—suppose this is not the time to ask for a raise?"

Sam's eyebrows arched and he let out an amused huff. "I'd offer you a raise if I thought it would make a difference, but I doubt money will make you stay if you feel you have to go."

There was the proof of how well Sam knew him. "It wouldn't." He coughed and took another drink of his coffee. Breathing came more easily. "You pay me pretty well, especially considering the mess I made out of Singularity."

Sam rolled his eyes and slumped in his chair. "God, that account. It came shit-covered to start with." He looked a Fazil. "You've made up your mind."

He'd made the decision days ago, when he'd balked at talking to Sam. Still hurt because he was a shit of a friend and lover for his choice. He blinked back the moisture. "I'm staying."

Sam's brows creased, but he nodded. "I'm glad to have you, Fazil."

"I'm happy to be here." He rose slowly on shaky legs. "I should get to work on the shit show."

There was a heap of concern written onto Sam's forehead, but he nodded.

On the way out, Fazil tipped his cup to Justin.

At his desk, he sank into his seat and tried to get his pulse back under control. He was staying in Pittsburgh.

Which meant he wasn't going to Seattle to be with Todd.

That said *everything* about the kind of person was. A complete asshole.

But better *that* than becoming a bitter, resentful shit of a human. If he took some corporate job, he'd cycle into the anxiety, fear, and frustration he'd felt at Singularity. Being with Todd had been a bright spot, but Todd couldn't be his *only* reason for living. Wasn't fair to either of them.

He knew in the end, he'd blame Todd for the move, for upending his life, for making him leave Sam's company.

He'd rather be a jerk than *that*.

Coffee warmed his throat. Todd would find someone better for him. He wished he could be that man—but he couldn't give up his life.

Fazil swirled the remainder of his coffee, then set the cup down. Time to go to work and get Singularity sold off to BinBox Group. That at least would make Todd's life better.

He was a half hour into work when his message app flashed. Eli, of all people.

How are you doing?

God. He typed out a reply. Why does everyone keep asking me that question?

Because lately you look like you're about to shatter into a billion pieces.

He stared at Eli's words. I'm staying in Pittsburgh.

That's the other reason I asked.

Of course Eli would know. Fazil started and deleted several messages because there was too much to say. Finally he typed out five words: He's going to hate me.

He won't. Trust me, he won't.

Fazil drew his teeth over his lips. Except Todd would. It was high school all over. He couldn't let Todd control his life so he'd run away.

This time, he knew exactly what he'd be missing.

I'll be fine, Eli.

No message after that. Fazil declined Adam's invitation to go to lunch. Not terribly hungry. Horribly tired.

Completely shattered, as Eli had said.

But there was work, and even though reading those names in the e-mails—Nathan, Stephen, Todd—made him tremble, he managed to get through and sign off a hefty stack of procedures. A good day's worth of work.

The office was pretty silent when Fazil locked his screen to go home. It was after six, which meant three in Seattle.

Todd. He'd have to talk to him tonight. Tell him. *Shit.* He rose from his seat and then caught himself on the desk's edge when the room tunneled.

Whoa.

Todd's words came back to him. *Do you do this often? Not eat?* Guess he did. Time to go home and figure out food. As he made his way to the front of the office, he was surprised to see Eli, but no Justin. He rapped on Eli's doorframe. "Working late?"

Eli swung his chair around. "No. Checking up on you."

Oh. "That's a little creepy, Eli."

He snorted. "I'd like to think I know you well enough to be concerned."

"I'm..." But he wasn't fine. "Okay. But I can take care..."

Eli raised an eyebrow. "When the hell did you become the office mom?"

Eli shrugged. "I have no idea, and I'm the worst person for the job, I admit. But here I am."

Fazil struggled against his impulse to be angry and the desire to laugh. He plodded into Eli's office and flopped into a chair by the guest table in the center of the room. "I'm really fucked up, Eli."

"Aren't we all?"

"I'm not kidding."

Eli's smile was small but heartening. "Neither am I." He waved his hand to encompass the office. "We're not the normal crowd of people."

No, they weren't. "That's why I love it here." Open, accepting, creative. "I don't want to work anywhere else."

"Even if it means losing Todd?"

He stared at Eli. There was no judgment there, no anger or sorrow, only curiosity.

He swallowed. "If I go there and leave this, I'll resent him. I know I will. There's nothing like this job in Seattle. There's nothing like anywhere else." Moisture pricked at his eyes. "Either way, I lose him. It's better to stay here and let him be free." He clamped his mouth shut, because he was not about to turn into a sobbing mess in front of Eli.

Eli looked down at the carpet, his own face lined with grief. "I'm sorry to hear that."

"Don't say it."

Eli met his gaze. "That you two are good together?"

Fucking bastard. "Yes." He pushed the word out through gritted teeth.

"You are." Eli rose and collected his cane. "It's the truth."

Fazil rose as well, to the same tunneling effect as before. Eli was there in a flash, lowering him into the chair. "Fuck," Fazil whispered. "Light-headed."

"Goddamned men. Why are we so impossible?" Eli thudded his cane on the carpet. "Stay here. I'll be right back." With that, he was out the door and heading to the back of the office.

Fazil blinked a few times. Sitting might not be such a bad idea.

Eli reappeared and handed him a bottle of orange juice. "Drink this."

He wouldn't argue with Eli, not when he was wearing his you-so-do-not-want-to-challenge-me expression. Fazil took the bottle, cracked it open, and drank.

"Tomorrow," Eli said, "you're going to lunch with us."

"Eli..."

"Fazil." He softened. "I know this game. I play it myself. Don't torture yourself because you feel like shit."

"I'm not..." The words died in his mouth. The orange juice was the first thing besides coffee and water he'd had all day. "Maybe you're right." He did feel better after drinking it.

Too much sadness in Eli's expression. "Think you can make it home in one piece?"

"Yeah." He lifted the juice bottle. "Thank you for this." When he stood, the world stayed still, and his stomach whined. "I promise. Lunch tomorrow."

"Good." Eli gestured to the door. "Shall we?"

They did. Eli shut off the lights and set the alarm as they left.

They parted ways on Murray Avenue when Fazil reached his apartment. Halfway up the stairs, it struck Fazil how much Eli must have cared to stay and wait and worry. Eli and Sam and Justin. Adam and Jen and Sertab. Shit, he owed them all for the past few weeks.

Inside his place, Fazil tossed his keys on the side table

and headed to the kitchen. First food, then he'd figure out how to break Todd's heart.

It was already past seven thirty when Todd got home and tromped up the steps to his apartment and computer. *Please still be on.* Fazil usually was, but it was later than he liked. On nights like this, their conversations ended too soon due to Fazil living three hours in the future.

Fazil was there. Todd opened a chat window.

> Hey, I'm here. Traffic sucked and work was hellish. Left late. Took forever.

Little flashing dots, then a reply. It's okay. I worked late, too. Haven't been sleeping.

Their chats weren't helping. Want to go to video?

Yeah.

He clicked over to that, Fazil accepted, and Todd's heart leapt into his throat. The Fazil on the other end was pale and drawn. The only color in his face was in the red rimming his eyes and the dark circles under them. "Hi." Fazil's voice was soft. Contrite.

Shit, shit, shit. "Hey." He swallowed. "What's up?"

Fazil looked away. "I... talked to Sam." He looked back.

There was the answer, written all over his expression. "He said no."

Fazil nodded. "He wants his team with him, interacting with each other. I don't blame him. There's a camaraderie that builds."

"But you get sent out to other places all the time."

"Sure." Fazil rubbed his brow. "Alone, or as a group. Sometimes we're all working on the same project. The point is we can all work with one another at the drop of a hat, because we *do* work with one another, every day."

We. Fazil was still part of that. "Are you staying?" Was he being dumped over videochat?

Fazil looked down at his hands, his face a mass of emotion.

Oh no. Don't do this to me, Z. Not again.

Fazil exhaled. "Yeah. I'm staying. I can't leave this job."

"But you can leave me?" Todd's hands shook. "Over a stupid fucking *job*?"

"I'm not— It's not a stupid—" Fazil rose. "Fuck it. You wouldn't get it in a million years, would you?" He paced in front of his computer.

"No, I wouldn't. I thought we *had* something here, after all those years apart. And you're going to toss that away for *work*?"

Fazil leaned down, his face filling the screen. "It's my life! It's my goddamned life, Todd! You want me to leave my job and everything I've built so I can be... what? Your mindless fuck toy?"

What the hell? "No, Z!" He rubbed his hands over his face and stared back at Fazil. "What?"

Slowly Fazil sat down. "You had this planned, all along. Like before. I'd quit my job, move to Seattle, and get a job close to you—whatever's available. We'd move in together and live happily ever after with me in your bed. That's what you want, right?"

"I thought... that's what you wanted, too." To be with him and loved by him. They'd spend their time *together*.

"I was supposed to go to UPenn and become a teacher

and we'd live in Warminster together for the rest of our lives."

He had wanted that, too. A high school pipe dream, one that shattered when Fazil left for California. "Well, you killed that idea."

"Because I didn't *want* it," Fazil said. "I adored you, but I had no desire to be a teacher and didn't want to spend the rest of my life in fucking Warminster."

"You never said—"

"You never let me say otherwise! Just assumed."

Little fucking bastard. "I guess that makes two of us. At least I didn't *cheat* because of it."

Fazil's color rose. "Don't you throw that at me. I apologized and you fucked the crap out of me in vengeance and—"

"You liked that!" Moaned and squirmed and begged for it. Cried in his arms. Todd's stomach churned.

Fazil stared back. "Yeah. I did." Quiet words. He leaned against his chair and his face fell into shadows. "I never should have left you like I did then."

"And now?" Because Fazil was doing it *again*.

Fazil searched the air for words. "I told you. I don't want to be a cog. Work for Microsoft or Amazon or Boeing or whoever—that would *kill* me." He shifted in his chair. "Working for Sam is my dream job, Todd. Don't..." He swallowed. "Don't assume that I'm going to leave everything just because I made a mistake fifteen years ago. I don't owe you my life."

Todd stared at his screen. He *was* being dumped for a fucking job. "You said you'd move."

"No." Anger returned to Fazil's voice, sharpening it to points. "I said I'd *think* about moving. I'd ask Sam if I could work from Seattle." His face came closer to the camera.

"What happens when I get there? We have some fucking awesome sex and... what?"

Todd thumped against his chair. "We... do stuff. Together, as a couple. Build a life."

Tears glittered at the corner of Fazil's eyes. "I have a life, Todd."

"What life? Alone in Pittsburgh? You have a *job*, Fazil. You can get one out here. Everything you have there, you can have here, *with* me."

Silence, and the coldest look he'd ever seen from Fazil. "I have a *career*. I worked fucking hard to get where I am. I have friends and..." He deflated. "It doesn't matter. I'm not moving to Seattle."

Todd gripped his desk because the floor was spinning away from under him. "So that's it? We're done?"

Fazil opened his mouth and a croak came out. "I don't *want* to be done."

"But you damn well don't care enough to be with me." Anguish bubbled up from his soul. Work was something you did to afford the other parts of your life. It was the pain necessary for the pleasure of living. "Jesus, Z! Over a fucking stupid contracting job?"

Fazil blinked a few times, as if Todd had slapped him. "Wow. You're not listening to me, are you?" His voice was shaky and quiet.

"I'm listening, but I'm not hearing anything worthwhile." Fazil wasn't making any *sense*.

There were tears running down Fazil's face. "I guess we *are* done, then." He reached a trembling finger out...

"Wait, don't—" The computer chimed and the screen went dark. Todd raced to open a message window, but the dot by Fazil's name was hideously gray.

Todd's heart lodged in his throat and he rubbed his face.

Dumped for a *job*. He tried clinging to the anger and fury, but that slipped away and his own tears started.

Fazil's name was there in his window, but he had no way to reach across two thousand five hundred miles. "Z, I thought you loved me. I really thought this time…"

Shit. Todd stumbled into his bedroom and there was too much *Fazil* in the room. He'd not bothered to put Mr. Dragon back into the toy box. He stared at the dildo and a hole widened in his heart. *Fuck toy.* Fazil had never been that. Sure, they'd had mind-numbing sex. Played out some kink, but Fazil had *wanted* that.

He sank down onto the bed. He'd missed *something* because none of this made sense. If Fazil were here they could figure it out, but they were done.

The end. Good night.

Todd lay back and stared at the ceiling. The little voice was back, the one from ages ago. The one Martin had helped him put to rest. *Go out. Get some. You know where, and this time, you won't be the one with your hands up against the wall and a cock in your ass.*

Drown his sorrow in alcohol and orgasms. And obliterate himself again? No, thank you. Besides, it was Thursday, and he had to be at work in the morning if he wanted to keep *his* fucking job. He sucked in a breath and then another. His heart felt like it was gnawing his way up his throat.

Fuck it all. Curling up around his pillow didn't make the pain go away, but it muffled his sobs and absorbed his tears.

He wanted Fazil. *His* Fazil… who wasn't his at all and would never be again.

CHAPTER TWENTY-SIX

Two weeks. Todd sat on his couch after work and eyed his phone. Two weeks and *nothing* from Fazil. Not a call, not an e-mail. No texts.

Silence. As if he'd fallen off the face of the planet. Again.

Except work e-mails came to the engineering team bearing his name. Todd heard his voice on the weekly conference call with Sam Anderson as they tried to wrap this project up before BinBox Group came for a closer look. Those meetings were excruciating, especially when Fazil chuckled at some joke or palled around with Erin.

It was Sam who Todd interacted with now. All very professional.

Fazil was alive—just dead to Todd.

E-mails and texts had gone unanswered. Even the one he'd sent two days after their blowup. Hey. I'm sorry. Can we talk?

Obviously Fazil's answer was no.

He slid his phone onto the coffee table. He wanted to be

angry, not hurt and lost and fucking *confused*. His body ached inside and out.

Everything had been perfect. Then it wasn't. He went over the events in his head again and again. The rough sex hadn't been an issue—Fazil had wanted that. The games they'd played had been Fazil's fantasies, his desires. The only conclusion he could draw was that Fazil didn't love him.

Had *never* loved him.

How do you choose a job over a person? Easy. *Fun in bed, but not someone to take home to Mom.*

Never mind that Fazil's mom already knew him. Hell, they'd spent half of high school in her finished basement.

Everything was so fucking tied up in Fazil. The past, his memories, this job. Probably should go find some hot body to drown in or a beer to take the edge off. He stared at his television. The last thing he wanted was sex or alcohol. Or anyone to see him.

He missed his *friend*. More than anything else—he wanted their friendship back. He'd give up everything if he could just have that.

Todd eyed his phone. Fazil wouldn't even accept an apology, so what hope was there for anything else?

FAZIL STARED AT TOO MANY WINDOWS ON HIS computer. One had a procedure and Todd's suggestions for improvement. Another had his own notes about how Singularity's engineering team worked. In yet another window, there were e-mails from Nathan and Stephen.

His head hurt, because all of the procedures conflicted too much. Unit testing was a simple thing that all the engineers should be doing. Why were they making this so damn hard?

He opened a Word doc and streamlined the procedure down to something that made sense. It was close to Todd's original, with some additions.

Stephen and Nathan wouldn't like it, but they weren't paying Anderson to play nice, just fair. When he talked to Todd tonight he'd have to—

The sudden rush of pain left him gasping for air.

"Fazil?" Sertab, their network engineer extraordinaire, poked her head around the cube. "Are you okay? What happened?" She spoke in Turkish.

There'd be no calls to Todd. No messages. No nothing. "Banged my knee, I'm fine." It was easier to lie in English for some reason.

She furrowed her brow and switched languages. "You sure?"

Harder and harder to answer that question. "Yeah, thanks."

"İnşhallah." She vanished back to her cube.

God willing. God. Allah. Whoever. He should take her up on the offer to have dinner with the Turkish group she and her husband belonged to.

He dropped his face into his hands. Or not. All he wanted to do was hole up in bed for about three years. His gut—his body—shouldn't hurt this much, not after two weeks. Not when he'd done the right thing. He and Todd were done. Done and *done.* He looked up at his screen. Except he still had to work on the Singularity project, and Todd was a contact.

Only one thing to do. Finish the project so he wouldn't have to think about Todd anymore.

Close to noon, his IM flashed. This time, it was Adam.

Sam's got a hankering for Mineo's, so we're all going.
Eli said to drag you with us. Kicking and screaming, if
necessary.

Sounds like Eli, he replied.

He didn't want to go. Didn't want to socialize. Wasn't
hungry. Except he'd promised Eli he'd keep going with the
crew to lunch. He just hadn't expected the lunches to be
every other day. Wonder whose idea *that* had been?

I'll be right up.

He tromped to the front of the office and found the rest
of the crew there.

"How's your knee?" Sertab asked.

"Oh... it's fine." Heat crept up his neck at the lie. Still,
*My heart is cracking and I can't breathe because I love him
and I can't be with him because he'd never want me as a
neurotic, bitter mess* seemed far too long an explanation.

"Onward," Sam said, and headed to the office door.

He found himself walking next to Jen. "How're you
doing?" she asked.

He must have a fucking *sign* on him. "Eh, tired. I'd
blame it on the jet lag, but..."

"Well, that wipes me out forever, too." She paused.
"Hey, my girlfriend and I have an extra ticket to the hockey
game on Sunday. You interested? Pens versus the Flyers."

Up ahead, Sam was laughing with Adam and Sertab
about something. "You know, I *like* the Flyers." So did
Todd, but he wasn't there, so fuck him.

She laughed. "Dude, why do you think I asked you?"

"Well, that and you won't have to break up the
lovebirds." He pointed over his shoulder at Eli and Justin.

She snorted and pushed her hands into the pockets of her shorts. "Have you ever hung out with those two after work?"

He shook his head.

"They're somewhere between too adorable and too porntastic."

"So like at work, but dialed to thirteen?"

"More like twenty, but yes."

No, he couldn't handle that right now. Could barely manage work. But the thought of spending a weekend alone was horrifying.

Last weekend, he'd spent the days combing around Squirrel Hill and Oakland. Museum-hopping. Shopping. Eating. He'd sat on Flagstaff Hill and tried not to scream at the clouds.

He'd typed Todd's number on his cell a half dozen times. Despite deleting it from his contacts and blocking it, he'd managed to memorize it anyway.

No, he wasn't about to spend the weekend at home. There was pinball on Friday, then Sertab's dinner on Saturday, and now this. A full weekend.

"Yeah. I'll take the ticket."

It wouldn't get his mind off Todd, but getting out would dull the pain and longing lodged in his bones.

CHAPTER TWENTY-SEVEN

TODD SHOULD HAVE KNOWN SOMETHING WAS UP WHEN people stopped talking to him at the coffeepot. Still, when he read the e-mail from Stephen, his hands went numb. Hell, his whole body alternated between cold and burning.

What the fuck was this shit? Couldn't say it out loud. Wanted to scream it, though.

He cursed under his breath and scrolled back through all the babysitting e-mails from Stephen. He'd done *everything* that had been asked of him. He'd also been following the new procedures, the ones Stephen had signed off on. He'd been careful to toe the line and keep his head down.

And now there was a meeting invite to discuss his lack of progress during his probationary period in his inbox.

Nathan was already off probation, which galled Todd to no end. As far as he could tell Nathan's "probationary period" had been a week of paid vacation. Nice reward for being a racist asshole.

Todd pounded the mouse button when he clicked accept and bit his tongue to keep the string of profanity inside. He had a half hour to prepare, but the cards were stacked against him. He couldn't win against the bank.

All this because Nathan had seen him with Fazil at the club.

There had been no issues with his sexuality before, not from Stephen or anyone else. Why was being gay such a big deal now?

He blew out his breath and dug up the documents he needed to prove his progress. A half hour later, he entered Stephen's office and closed the door.

"Todd. Please have a seat." Stephen's frown seemed etched into his face.

Great. He lowered himself into the guest chair and folded his hands over the printouts he'd brought.

After fiddling with a stack of paper of his own and moving a pen around, Stephen finally looked up, his face pinched. "This isn't personal."

Todd shifted in his seat. "It's not professional, either."

Stephen's brows jumped into his hairline. "Excuse me?"

He dropped half the stack of papers onto Stephen's desk. "I've done everything you've asked." He plopped down the other half. "And then some. So why am I here?"

Maybe it was the wrong tactic, but he didn't care anymore. No job would go well with no Fazil. Life was *shit*.

Stephen focused on the stacks. "It's not your work that's an issue. It's *never* been your work." Vehemence in those words. "The problem is this." He waved his hands at the papers. "Your attitude."

His attitude? "You're saying I should be a racist homophobe like Nathan?"

Stephen sat back, his mouth a thin line and his body tense as stone. "This isn't about Nathan. It's about you."

Anger nearly had him on his feet, but screaming at his

boss wouldn't help. He let out a breath. "I don't know what you want from me." He gestured at the papers again. "I've performed. I've kept quiet. I've worked long hours."

"You've shown no remorse."

Todd stared at Stephen. "What?"

"Your relationship with the contractor. You've shown no remorse. What's going to stop you from..." Stephen trailed off. "We bring people in here all the time. We can't have you going after them."

"You think I... ?" Well, he *had* gone after Fazil, but it had been mutual and they had a long history. "He was my best friend, my boyfriend in high school. This wasn't some random guy." He looked at the papers. "No one said anything when Eric started dating that temp receptionist last year."

Stephen's huff was ugly and derisive. "You're making my point for me. All excuses. No remorse."

He didn't regret falling into bed with Fazil, not even now that it was over. He missed and ached for the man, but felt no guilt for hooking up. "I'm trying to figure out why it's a big deal."

Stephen rubbed his forehead. "The thing with Eric and Becky... She was *just* a receptionist. Didn't understand our tech. Wasn't going to do anything with it."

That was one big-ass assumption. He'd known plenty of women in tech who'd taken temp work to pay the bills. "I thought the Anderson team signed nondisclosures."

"They did."

"Then I'm still not getting the problem. I screwed up. I know that. I'm willing to take my lumps for it." He gestured at the stacks. "And I *have*. Why am I still getting shit when Nathan desecrates a holy book, Ryan slings anti-Semitic slurs, they get vacation, and everything is fine?"

"You really want to know why?" Stephen leaned forward and spoke through his teeth. "This is what you get when you fuck the help, Todd. You're not supposed to stick your dick into the competition." Stephen's lips curled at the end of that.

The words hit like a punch to the gut, hard enough that he couldn't breathe.

"What's to stop you from fucking the next guy we bring in?"

"I don't... I'm not..." He grasped at words and none of them helped. Yeah, he was gay, but he wasn't some kind of lecherous man-whore. "What makes you think I would? I've been here for years. We've had plenty of contractors through here." He hadn't touched a one. Never wanted to. He hated mixing work and relationships—but Fazil had been both from day one.

Stephen looked decidedly uncomfortable. "Nathan told me what he saw at that club."

The hollow in Todd's chest clashed with the rising tide of red in his vision. He gripped the armrests of the chair. Nathan again. Who knew what he'd seen or what he'd told Stephen. Pretty sure no one had been in the alley, but their dancing had been pretty hot and heavy—both before and after. Especially after.

That was all moot now, since Fazil wouldn't talk to him. Todd let out a breath. "Well, if it's any consolation, I'm no longer on speaking terms with Fazil. If you want remorse..." He shrugged.

Stephen shifted in his seat and looked pleased, the *asshole*. He cleared his throat. "Your attitude still leaves much to be desired."

"Apparently yes."

Stephen handed him a piece of paper. "Here's an

outline of what we expect from you for the next month. If you can show a change in work habits and more respect for your coworkers and contractors, we can discuss your continued employment."

Holy shit. They really were looking to fire him with cause. He glanced at the paper. "I see. Thank you."

Stephen nodded in dismissal.

Todd pried himself out of the chair, collected his papers, and headed back to his cube.

He had no idea what to do next. None.

FOR THE REST OF THE DAY TODD POKED AT THE overwhelming number of tickets Stephen had assigned to him and picked out the easiest to deal with first. His heart wasn't in work, though. It was buried under a mound of pain and anger and embarrassment.

He should have known they'd set him up for a fall, especially once his relationship with Fazil had been uncovered. Racism and homophobia were one thing— disloyalty was quite another.

He would've gone to Sandra, but she was away at the Singularity Storage board meeting, hopefully to help sell the company. There was no one to talk to about his predicament.

Chances were Stephen would let Todd go for having a relationship with Fazil. Having *had* a relationship. Ex-boyfriend. Ex-friend.

He didn't dare switch to personal e-mail—who knew what nannyware might have been installed on his machine —so he plunked away at work until the clock ticked into the evening hours and he'd made sure he'd put in a nice, solid nine hours.

The office was empty when he left. Like his car, his inbox, and his apartment. He ached to talk to Fazil. Hear his voice. Spill out his frustrations and annoyances. He'd tried calling out of desperation a few nights back, but the number went to voice mail and Fazil hadn't returned the call.

"Fuck." Todd turned his car over. He dreaded going home, but couldn't mope in the parking lot all night. Everything in his apartment reminded him of those few perfect days. He should move, but he might not have a job in a few weeks.

When he parked his car in his apartment's lot, his stomach growled. Given the way he hadn't been eating, he wasn't surprised. He'd hardly had the desire for anything other than coffee and beer with a sandwich here and there.

Beer it was. He locked the car and headed for a close, sedate bar. Last thing he needed was a meat market—too much temptation there for his destructive side. This place had decent food, quiet music, and nice staff. He ended up taking a seat at the bar because a table for one would have been too demoralizing.

"What'll you have?" The bartender was young and blond. His type, normally, but he wasn't in the mood to flirt at all, not with *Fazil, Fazil, Fazil* ringing in his heart and soul.

"Whatever beer is good and on tap." He picked up the dinner menu.

"That describes all but three of our beers. You want an ale or a lager? Hoppy? Sweet?"

Todd snorted. "How about dark and bitter?"

The bartender chuckled. "That kind of a day?"

"Been that kind of a month." He flipped the menu card over. "Started out great, then nosedived into hell."

"Been there, man. If it's not too cliché to say, it does get better." He slid down the bar and pulled a glass of beer. A very dark beer.

It wouldn't get better, though. Not without Z. "Can I get a bacon chicken sandwich, too?"

The bartender deposited the beer. "Sure. Fries?"

He nodded and the guy headed for the server's station. The bar wasn't crowded and he recognized the other patrons from around the neighborhood, but didn't know any of them personally.

He took a sip of the beer, swallowed, and scowled at the thing.

"Too dark?" There was a friendly but amused edge to the bartender's voice.

"No." He'd gotten exactly what he'd asked for. "I didn't know they could bottle my mood." He took another sip and leaned on the counter.

For a moment, the pain in his chest was overwhelming. More than anything, he wanted to share this with Fazil. Describe the place and make plans to come here. Fazil wasn't moving to Seattle. He was *gone*, like before.

"God-fucking-damn it." He set the beer down and tried to keep the tears from forming in his eyes. He really wanted to punch Stephen, too.

This is what you get when you fuck the help, Todd. You're not supposed to stick your dick into the competition.

He hadn't tacked the words *you fag* onto that, but Todd had tasted it in the air, seen it in the curl of Stephen's lips. He pushed the beer away.

"Hey," the bartender said. "You all right?"

"No," Todd said. "But it's a long story."

"It's a quiet night," he said. "And it looks like you could use an ear."

Spilling your guts to a bartender was one of those Hollywood clichés, wasn't it? Todd felt the knot in his chest loosen. He looked up. "I dated this guy in high school..."

He had no idea how long it took to tell the whole thing, but by the time he'd finished he'd downed two of those bitter dark beers and eaten his sandwich.

"So that's the story, more or less."

The bartender cleared away the dishes. "He chose his job over moving out here to be with you? What an ass."

Todd flinched. "Yeah." He looked down at the remnants of his dark beer. "But I kind of understand why." Especially after today at work.

"Why he dumped you rather than moving?"

"He would've moved if he could've had the job he has there out here. It was his dream job. Giving that up..." Something shifted in Todd and the room seemed too hot.

If Todd had a job with someone as open and accepting as Sam Anderson, with a coworker like Eli, and doing the variety of projects Fazil talked about—he'd struggle to let go of it, too. Especially when all Seattle could offer Fazil was the shit Todd dealt with every day. That would *kill* Fazil. Hell, what Nathan put Z through had wrung him out completely.

The night of the videochat rushed through his head. *It's my goddamned life, Todd!* Fazil had tried to get Todd to understand, but he'd been so insistent that Fazil move here.

You're not listening to me, are you? Fazil's words rang in his skull.

No, Todd hadn't been. The film in his head of them happy in Seattle had played over and over until he couldn't consider any other option. He'd rammed that vision down

Fazil's throat, planned out his life, just like he had in high school with his harebrained idea of Fazil becoming a *teacher*.

Todd rubbed his chin and neck. "Fuck." No wonder Fazil wouldn't talk to him.

The bartender lifted both eyebrows.

"He said no because he'd be miserable. I'd be miserable. We'd..." They'd be at each other's throats. Once the glow of being together wore off, hell would set in. "He was protecting himself. And protecting me." God, that was such a Z thing to do.

"I don't follow."

"Ever been unhappy in your job?"

The bartender got a haunted look. He nodded slowly.

"Me too. Right now, in fact. My job fucking sucks. It colors everything, doesn't it?" Even if Z were here, Todd's job would still be hell, Singularity would still be spiraling out of control and he'd be exactly where he was, on the verge of quitting or being fired. They'd both be depressed and moody.

The bartender nodded again.

"It seeps into your bones, that unhappiness. Changes how you look and think and interact with others. Your relationships. *Everything*."

"Yeah, it does. Bleak days. No way out." He gave a little shudder.

The more he spoke, the worse his heart twisted. "If you gave up the dream job you loved to become a cog in a corporate wheel?"

"Sounds like the definition of hell."

It did. "I was trying to make him live *my* life. He knew he couldn't, and that he'd hate me if he tried. We'd hate each other."

"I see where you're going." The bartender took Todd's empty glass. "Or maybe where you *should* be going."

So did Todd. The answer was blindingly clear. Fazil had even suggested it, though subtly.

Pittsburgh.

If he wanted to be with Fazil, he needed to quit his shitty job and move.

Fifteen years ago, if he'd had the money, he'd have followed Fazil across the country. Now that he could, what was holding him back?

Only his pride and the need for Fazil to repent for what he'd done as a teen. Except he'd told Fazil that the past was the past and Fazil didn't have to apologize for that anymore.

So just who was the asshole in this equation?

Shit. "I need the check."

The bartender slid it over. "Thought you might."

He left a sizable tip. On the short walk back to his apartment, he couldn't help recall the first night he'd taken Fazil home, how they'd kissed and how he'd fucked Z. The harshness, the need, the pain in both of them. The love.

Fazil had almost left then because of how much Todd had hurt. The separation now was killing them both. He'd seen that in Fazil the last time they'd talked.

He'd never thought those stories where a lover abandoned their own happiness for someone else rang true. How could love be one person cracking themselves into a pile of miserable pieces for someone else? He couldn't ask that of Fazil.

Except he had. He *had*.

If their roles had been reversed, Todd would've resented the hell out of Fazil for assuming he'd up and leave Seattle. But there'd never been any talk of *Todd* moving.

He staggered up the stairs to his apartment, not due to

the beer but from the hollow in his chest. He'd fucked up and lost Fazil.

Tomorrow he'd figure out if he could fix that.

Tonight? He'd crawl into his bed and let out all the tears he'd been holding back since Fazil had left.

He stripped his clothes off, leaving them where they fell, and flopped onto his very empty bed. Despite the summer heat, under the sheets he was bitter cold.

I'm sorry, Z. I'm trying to catch up. Please wait for me.

CHAPTER TWENTY-EIGHT

Work the next day was the same hell for Todd that it had been for a while. Nathan stalked the halls and chatted up everyone rather than working. They were back to meetings about meetings, and his work still was picked to pieces even though he'd hit every deadline and fixed bugs in other people's code.

Sandra wasn't back from the board meeting and his e-mails to her hadn't been answered.

Stephen wanted him gone. Perhaps this place would crash and burn, then. They'd sell off the intellectual property to some other company. Sam Anderson wouldn't like it, but they ought to have contingencies for failed projects. They'd already been paid for Fazil and Eli's work.

He stared at the little rainbow flag he'd purposefully left in his cube. He'd been taking everything else home one piece at a time. He should quit, but doing so before he had another job lined up made him twitchy due to the whole rent-and-eating thing. He *hated* job hunting. He'd been lucky to see the listing for Singularity Storage back when he had.

He had no contacts in Pittsburgh except for Fazil, and there'd be no help from him. Todd scratched at his arm and his gaze fell on the pile of business cards he'd collected. A few from former coworkers, some from tech gatherings, and one from Eli, sitting right on top. He lifted it from the stack and slipped it into his back pocket. Sending mail would have to wait until later.

The day wore on, but with Eli in his pocket—so to speak—irritations bounced off him. Maybe he didn't care anymore. He even left at five thirty after putting in plenty of hours. They couldn't fire him for that.

When he got home, he sat down at his laptop and turned Eli's business card over in his hands. Why the hell not? It was a risk reaching out if Fazil had spoken to Eli, but he had nothing to lose. And quite a bit to gain.

He kept the message professional. An inquiry stating that he was interested in jobs in the Pittsburgh area, did Eli know of any recruiters, and would he act as a reference? Once he was sure there weren't any typos, he hit send, lest he chicken out.

He didn't expect a reply two minutes later, given that it was past midnight on the East Coast.

Oh, thank God. Yes, I can help. Will send info
tomorrow.—E

Todd studied the response, his stomach churning. A bubble of hope desperately tried to form. Did Fazil miss him?

That was crushed in the next moment. Was Fazil okay? Todd rubbed his chin and let out a breath. Well, he'd set the ball in motion. All he could do now was wait to see what fortune, and Eli, brought him.

THE NEXT MORNING, THERE WAS A MESSAGE FROM ELI waiting in Todd's inbox.

> First, I haven't spoken to Fazil about this. I assume you're starting your job search and haven't reached out to him—or can't—since you've contacted me. I do know some of what happened between you two.
>
> Second, I believe your presence here would do him a world of good, which would do us all a world of good.
>
> Third, I took the liberty of copying your résumé off of a job-hunting site. I sent it to a few colleagues I believe could benefit from an engineer of your caliber. I've listed the companies and their information below. You may want to follow up with an e-mail of your own. It wouldn't be unwelcome as they'll be expecting the contact.—E

Todd stared at the e-mail, then skimmed the list. Three companies, all of which he recognized, paired with three names. All had *VP* in their titles.

An engineer of your caliber.

If he could have reached through the Internet and hugged the tall, terse, prim man, he would have. This was beyond what he'd anticipated. He'd thought he'd get some links to headhunters... not Eli hand-delivering his résumé to executives. He ran through the list again. Google had an office in Pittsburgh? When had *that* happened?

With shaking hands, he typed a reply.

> This is more than I ever expected. Thank you so much.

A moment later, Eli's reply came back.

Just get your ass to Pittsburgh, please.

Getting there was a hell of a lot more possible now. Goose bumps rose on his skin. Life would get better. Even if he couldn't repair the damage with Fazil, a new job and a new city might do him some good.

This time, he should have listened to Z. Last time, too. A glimmer of hope lay between Eli's words. He thought Todd could make a difference.

He glanced at the clock and pushed back from the desk.

Don't give up on me yet, Z. Let's try it your way for a change.

TODD'S RESIGNATION LETTER WAS SHORT AND SWEET, and nothing in the world felt better than handing it over to Stephen and watching the emotions play across his face.

He had given them two weeks' notice, as required. But when Stephen met his gaze, he knew he'd be walked out with a box of his personal belongings soon. He'd taken everything home days ago and said good-bye to Erin and a few others that morning.

Stephen folded his hands over the letter. "We'll be sad to see you go."

"Bullshit," Todd said. "But I appreciate the sentiment. I'd say I'll miss working here, but we both know that's a pile of lies, too."

Stephen winced. "Look, I feel bad about the way things happened."

"Not enough to deal with Nathan."

"He's a good engineer."

So am I. But he didn't say that. "Well, I do hope that BinBox feels that way and no one *there* ends up on his shit list."

"Where are you off to?"

"CirroBot." Top-notch robotics firm. Nothing close to Singularity Storage's business. They couldn't nail him with the noncompete clause.

Such satisfaction from seeing Stephen pale. "Oh." His brows furrowed. "They're in Pittsburgh."

Yes, they were. "Are we finished?"

Stephen startled but recovered quickly. "For now. Please stay close to your cube for the rest of the day."

Todd nodded and headed out. Before he was even two steps down the hall, he heard Stephen phone IT and order them to cut his account.

What an asshole. Not like he'd do anything to the systems. Had he wanted to, he would have by now.

A half hour later, he had an exit interview with HR, and was so *done* with all of Singularity's shit. He was brutally honest about what he saw happen to Eli and Fazil, and what had been done to him in the aftermath.

There'd be a guard waiting at his cube to see him out of the office. Fine. He had only one stop to make before he left this shithole.

He leaned up against the wall of Nathan's cube, creaking the metal frame.

Anger flashed over Nathan's chiseled features. "What the hell do you want?"

"To say good-bye." He kept his voice even, but loud enough to be heard over the walls. They still had ears, those walls.

Nathan stared at him.

"You'll be pleased to know I've resigned. Effective immediately, apparently."

Still nothing. But then Nathan wasn't stupid, just an asshole. No doubt he was waiting for something, but probably not what Todd intended.

"You know, Stephen told me you saw Fazil and me together at a club on Capitol Hill. Dancing."

Nathan's face darkened. "And more. It was disgusting."

"Really?" Todd cocked his head. "See, I know which club we were at, and it's not a place a fag-hating guy would mistakenly walk into. So either you were there to bash some head—which would be insane because I've seen the bouncers there—or you were there to get some head yourself."

He paled and his lips parted and there it was: the icy-cold edge of absolute *fear*.

Todd pushed off the cube wall and placed a business card on the edge of Nathan's desk, one for an LGBTQ center. "If you ever decide to give up hating yourself." He turned and walked away. From Nathan. From Stephen. From Singularity.

He had a new life to start in a new city with a better company. He could only hope that Fazil would forgive him and take him back.

CHAPTER TWENTY-NINE

Nothing on Fazil's screen made *sense*. He pulled his hair back with both hands and stared at the words. It was a freaking procedure. Steps. All he needed to do was read the damn thing and make sure it was correct.

Todd had written this one, though, so every word sounded like him, had his inflection, his lilt. With that voice in his head, Fazil wanted to close his laptop and find somewhere to hide.

He hurt. Every day, it got harder to push himself out of bed. Nothing had helped. Not pinball, not the Turkish club, not hockey, not lunch with coworkers.

It had been worse lately because that little thread of Todd he had via group e-mails was *gone*. Todd no longer worked at Singularity Storage.

He had no idea what had happened. Couldn't ask, either.

He'd run away from his best friend, from his love. Again. Because he couldn't give up this job. Now Todd was gone.

And Fazil couldn't do his job. Not when every word

stabbed at his heart and ached his brain. He should have been through these procedures days ago and putting the finishing touches on the project.

Sooner or later, Sam was going to call him on the carpet for not getting the Singularity work done.

Maybe Todd had been right. He *should* tell Sam he was going to Seattle, call Todd, and beg him to take him back.

But the thought of stepping back into the corporate environment turned his stomach as much as all of this did. He hadn't lied to Todd—this *was* his life. His career.

Fazil pressed the heel of his hand against his forehead. At least everyone had given him space while continuing to coax him out of his. He was grateful for that. Yesterday at lunch, Sertab's stories of her son's antics with robots had teased laughter from him, and for an hour, he'd managed to forget about Todd.

But he'd come back to Todd in every sentence and every step of his tasks. Fazil muffled a sob, his gut burning with shame.

He couldn't do it. Couldn't finish this job. Sam was going to have his head.

When his IM indicator flashed and beeped, he glanced at the corner of his screen and bile rose to his throat. It was Eli.

Fazil, please come to my office ASAP.

Oh *fuck*. Fazil swallowed, his throat full of acid. That wasn't good at all.

They didn't have an HR department. Those duties were spread among Eli, Sam, and Justin. If he had to pick which would be the disciplinarian, that hat would fall on

Eli. He also knew *exactly* what Fazil's issue was and how much he'd screwed up in Seattle.

Eli had been sympathetic. He'd even had his own issues on the job, but even during the height of Eli's difficulties with Justin, Eli had managed to *get his job done*.

With shaking fingers, Fazil typed a reply.

On my way.

Might as well get this over with. He stood and looked over the space he shared with Jen, Adam, and Sertab. The Ping-Pong table. The velociraptor sign. Might be the last time he'd see them as part of this team. Despite what Sam had said... two engineers who worked were better than one fucked-up one who couldn't.

The trip down the hall to Eli seemed extra long today. Or maybe that was his lead feet. Before he took that last step that would bring him to the door, he paused and tried to get his fucking pulse under control.

Then he entered Eli's office and *stopped*.

Eli stood, hands folded over his cane, wearing the biggest shit-eating grin Fazil had ever seen. That made no sense, not if Fazil was about to be fired.

At Eli's tiny conference table sat Todd. Dark hair. Blue eyes. His smile wasn't as large as Eli's, but he was also wearing a suit.

Todd. He was *here*.

Fazil grabbed the doorframe and croaked. Despite knowing two languages, he couldn't figure out how to speak in either one. There weren't enough words to put his racing thoughts into sound.

A deep chuckle from Eli. "Get your ass in here, Fazil." Something about the way Eli spoke made Fazil move.

Todd still sat in Eli's guest chair, his eyes wide and his hands in his lap. "Hi."

Oh God, it really was Todd. This wasn't some kind of insane nightmare. "What..." The words stuck in Fazil's aching throat. *What are you doing here? How? Why?*

Eli, shit-eating grin and all, strolled forward. "I'll let you two have some privacy. Remember what I said, Todd." With that, he shut the door behind him.

"What—did he say?" Fazil managed to push those words out.

Todd blushed. "He said not to stain the carpet. Or the chairs. Or anything else." He stood and stepped away from the table.

Fazil couldn't move. This could all still be a dream and he'd wake up any second. "What are you *doing* here?"

"Here in the office or here in Pittsburgh?"

"Both." It came out as an undignified squeak.

Todd moved closer. "I'm here in the office to see you. I'm in Pittsburgh to accept a job at CirroBot and finish all the damn paperwork."

Job. Fazil's blood burned, but his bones might have been carved from ice. He shivered. *Pittsburgh.* "What?" Todd couldn't be here for a job. He wavered on his feet.

Todd caught his elbow. "Hey. Why don't you sit?"

He didn't want to sit, not this close to Todd. He wanted to wrap his body around him and never, ever let go again. He resisted Todd's pull. "Todd, why are you here?" He met Todd's gaze.

"I'm taking a job in Pittsburgh. I'm moving here." Todd let go. "I stopped by to see if you still wanted to be friends." He backed away. "I'm sorry, Z. I'll go."

No, no. He was fucking this up. "Wait!" He reached out for Todd, but missed and headed for the floor instead.

Todd caught him. "Z?" This time, he didn't have much choice but to sit. Todd poured him into one of the guest chairs.

"I haven't been doing all that well."

Todd brushed fingers across his forehead. "You're not running a fever."

"I'm not sick." Fazil gripped Todd's arm. "I'm..." *Exhausted. Malnourished. Stressed out beyond belief.* He looked up into those blue eyes. "You're *here*."

"Yeah, I am." His brows were furrowed.

"You're *staying*?"

"Yup." His features smoothed out.

Fazil swallowed, his heart thudding against his chest. Todd was moving here. "For *me*?"

"Yes. If you'll still have me."

Fazil didn't know whether to laugh or cry. He rose from the chair on shaky legs and threw his arms around Todd.

Strong arms closed around him. "I didn't listen to you, and you were *right*. I was trying to make you live my dream."

The warmth from Todd's words clashed with the reality of his own actions. "I ran again. Shut you out after I said I wouldn't." He pulled back. "God, Todd. You shouldn't change your entire life for me, either!"

There was that amused smile. "I'm not doing it *entirely* for you."

Fazil blinked. "No?"

"Z." Todd huffed a laugh. "Can I kiss you?"

"Yes?"

"Good."

He did, and any doubts that this wasn't real were shattered by Todd's lips on his, Todd's tongue coaxing his mouth open, and the sweet feeling when he surrendered his body against Todd's. The moan was his, the thrumming pulse in his ears his—but the taste, the heat, all Todd.

Todd broke the kiss. "Better?"

Strangely enough, it was. "Kind of."

"That won't do." Todd kissed him harder, molding his body against Fazil's. Hot and tight, his shaft pressed against Fazil's hardening dick. Much better.

This time, Fazil broke the kiss and pressed his forehead to Todd's. "What changed?"

Todd stroked his face. "I was so upset you wouldn't move. Utterly shattered because I thought you were running away again."

"I was. I—"

Todd pressed a finger to his lips. "Please let me finish?"

He nodded. It was Todd's story to tell.

"One night, I ended up at a bar near home and I got to talking with the guy behind the counter. I'd had such a shitty day, so I poured out my whole sob story. When I was done, he came down hard on you for not quitting your job and moving here. And... I started defending your choice."

Oh. Fazil tightened his grip on Todd.

"You went *home*, Fazil. You went back to a job—a career —and a place you loved. You hadn't come to Seattle for me in the first place, and I was a total dick for thinking you'd dump your entire life because our paths happened to cross again."

"But if I loved you enough, I should have." Fazil spoke against Todd's lapel.

"That's not love. I'm not sure what it is, but you destroying yourself for me? Giving up your life? Not love."

"Kinda destroyed myself anyway. Or tried. Everyone here's kept me going."

Todd kissed his forehead. "You were always so hard on yourself. And everyone else."

He owed the entire office for the last few weeks. "I left you again."

"Except you *didn't*. After high school, you vanished, and I couldn't find you. Maybe we both needed that break back then. This time, I knew where you were. We talked. Texted. Everything. You were *there*. You didn't shut down until I became the jerk who pressured you to quit your job and move to Seattle."

Fazil pressed his face into Todd's suit jacket. "I wasn't even mad. You—broke my heart."

"I know." Todd caressed the back of Fazil's head. "I had my head up my ass and I couldn't see anything other than the plan I'd made. You were right all along."

Finally. "Can I get that etched in stone?" Because he wanted to remember that. Todd being wrong for a change.

He kissed Fazil's neck, and that warmth settled into Fazil's soul. "I was the one with a shitty job. Even if you guys work your magic, they were pushing me out the door."

Fazil flinched.

"Don't worry about it." Todd lifted Fazil's chin and his eyes were blue and just a little too moist. "I want *you*, Fazil. If this is your home, then it can be my home, too."

"But you love Seattle." He wasn't sure how fair it was to make Todd give that up.

"I did. I do. There are things I'll miss. Some friends. Capitol Hill. It's all still there, though. I can visit. *We* can visit." He stole a quick kiss. "I love you more, *much* more than a single place."

Oh God. He had Todd. There and then. Everything he wanted in one place. So much light and hope, like a bubble in his chest—only this one wasn't full of pain. "Pittsburgh isn't bad." Every year it got better. There was so much of the city he wanted to explore, and now he could do that with Todd. "I think you'll like it here."

"I'm sure I will." Todd smoothed away the hair from Fazil's eyes. "You know, you can just say it. I see it. I know."

Say the words that had been floating around in his head for more than fifteen years. He *did* love Todd. But if he *said* it, he knew he'd fuck that up somehow. "I'm a dick?"

Todd chuckled. "You're adorable."

"Am not."

"Are, too." Todd kissed him and Eli's warning finally made sense, because the more they kissed the more he wanted flesh on flesh. Mouth on skin. Nothing between them at all. He spoke against Todd's lips. "I should take the rest of the day off."

"Yeah, you should." Todd cupped his ass and ground against him. "I don't want to piss Eli off."

That made two of them. He stepped back. "You know, you look stunning in a suit."

Todd smoothed out his jacket and straightened his tie. "And you look amazing naked."

Fazil's breath caught and his body burned with joy. "Let me go talk to Sam about taking some PTO."

Todd merely smiled.

Yeah. He needed to be home. In bed. With Todd on top of him. He headed for Sam's office with Todd at his heels.

Sam sat behind his desk, as normal. Eli had folded himself into one of the guest chairs while Justin occupied the other, his fingers entwined with Eli's. All three men looked at him as soon as he stepped into the office.

"Uh..." Every one of them had their version of a knowing smile. "Have you met Todd?"

Sam nodded. "Yes, we have."

Fazil tried to jump out of his skin and melt when Todd slipped his hands around Fazil's waist and pulled him backward. "I had dinner at Eli's last night."

Oh. God, Todd was hard. And pressed into Fazil's ass. "I hate you all. Every single one of you."

Sam laughed and Eli looked immensely pleased with himself, the preening peacock.

"Liar," Todd whispered into his ear.

Justin giggled. "This sounds familiar." He glanced at Eli, who raised a brow.

Fazil cleared his throat because this was getting ridiculous. He didn't need to be standing in his boss's office with a hard-on. There were better places to be. Like flat on his back in the privacy of his bedroom. "I was going to ask for the rest of the day off."

"Absolutely," Sam said.

"Actually..." Eli tapped his good foot against Sam's desk. "Fazil has a fair amount of PTO saved up."

"Does he now?" Sam smiled at Fazil.

"Weeks and weeks," Eli said. "Enough that he could take the rest of the week off."

A very smug-ass preening peacock. He owed Eli so damn much.

"Then I guess we'll see you on Monday, Fazil."

Except... "What about Singularity?"

Sam snorted. "The way they've been recently? Those fuckers can sit on their thumbs for a few days."

Oh. "Well, if you insist..."

"Take that lovely man of yours and get the hell out of here," Sam said.

He didn't need to be told twice.

Todd followed Fazil out of the Anderson office. That hadn't quite been the reunion he'd expected, but they'd made it through, though Z looked like he needed about a hundred years of sleep.

Right after the fuck of his life.

"I live just up Murray," Fazil said. "Do you have a car or a suitcase or—anything?" Anxiety had grabbed hold of him again from the way he trembled.

"I have a rental car and a bag. They're both in Eli's driveway." He smoothed his hands down Fazil's arms. "They can wait until later. Take me home."

Fazil continued up the block. After a few steps, he took Todd's hand. "I still can't believe you're here."

Todd would fix that soon enough. "I really am." Glad for it. The job with CirroBot was top-notch, and he was itching to get started. Eli had been right about applying there. "And for the long haul."

Fazil squeezed his hand but didn't speak. Something about the set of Fazil's jaw told Todd he was barely holding it together. They crossed the street to the other side and continued up the hill.

Guilt twisted Todd's gut. Springing this on Fazil was unfair, but they'd been so angry with each other, he hadn't seen any other way to reach out. "I hurt you so much."

Fazil's laugh was half sob. "Can we pause this until we're inside?"

He nodded. The sound Fazil had made tore against Todd's ribs. They really didn't do well apart. They couldn't *talk* with distance between them, not like when they could see and hear and feel each other.

Another block or so brought them to a brick building full of storefronts and a nondescript entrance. Fazil fished out a set of keys and opened the door.

They climbed to the second floor and into a gorgeous apartment, one he hadn't expected, given the façade. Hardwood floors. Architectural accents. And so much *Fazil* —all of his things—including a few Todd recognized from the old bedroom back in Warminster. Even the vague lemon-and-tea scent he'd always associated with Fazil's parents' place.

Fazil closed the door. "Here we are." The keys jangled in those shaking hands.

Yup. Alone. "This is really nice."

"Thanks." He threw his keys onto the coffee table. "Do you want anything?"

"Yeah." Todd studied Fazil's back, shoulders, and narrow waist. "You. On your knees in front of me."

That made Fazil jump. He turned around and his eyes were huge. No reply, but his jaw worked as if he were trying to form words.

Maybe that had been too forward.

Fazil closed the distance and found his voice. "Just that?" He sank to his knees, his gaze never leaving Todd's. "Nothing more?"

God, this beautiful man. He ran his hand through Fazil's thick hair. "I wouldn't say no to you sucking my dick."

Fazil got a strange look. "But would you say yes, Todd?"

His own words from their first lunch in Seattle, thrown back at him. He deserved that. "Yes, I'd say yes to your mouth around my cock."

"Thought so." Fazil ran his hands up Todd's legs. "You ought to wear a suit more often."

He'd have made a comment about a businessman fetish, but Fazil mouthed his shaft through his pants and it was all he could do to stay standing. "You." He snaked his other hand into Fazil's hair. "God."

"Mmm-hmm." Fazil unbelted and unzipped Todd's pants. "Me." He freed Todd's cock and then those dark eyes were staring back again.

Such a beautiful sight. Even more so when Fazil closed his mouth over the tip. Todd moaned and tightened his grip in Fazil's hair. When Fazil started working on his shaft in earnest, Todd's vision blurred. That mouth was pure magic: hot and wet, and with a tongue that teased and pressed and flicked. Fazil had been good at giving head as a teen, but now? Holy hell.

Todd shifted his hands to the back of Fazil's head and stilled his bobbing. Once more, Fazil looked up, his mouth wide and full of dick.

"Do you trust me?"

Fazil groaned and lifted one hand, forming a thumbs-up.

Todd moved slowly, sliding in and out of that sweet mouth, and Fazil opened to him, allowing him to go deeper still. His tongue slid around and caressed Todd, though his hands had fallen away. He gave himself over to Todd's fucking.

Seeing his dick slide between Fazil's lips without resistance was glorious. Fazil closed his eyes, and the tension he'd been carrying was gone. A few deep strokes had Fazil shuddering and breathing hard when Todd withdrew. That curled Todd's toes, but as much as he wanted to spill himself down Fazil's throat, he had other plans. He withdrew and tucked himself back into his briefs. He didn't bother zipping up.

Fazil tipped his head back, stretching his neck. "That was so good."

"Glad you enjoyed it."

He opened his eyes, and his smile was stunning. "Why'd you stop?"

"Because you're still wearing clothes." And they weren't near his bed.

"I guess I should do something about that." Fazil rose—a little shakily, but looking a damn sight better than he had in the office. "Bedroom?"

"Yes, please." He loosened the knot in his tie and followed Fazil through the living room, past the kitchen and dining area, and into a large bedroom. More hardwood, very nice furniture, and a big sleigh bed, complete with a sturdy-looking footboard. Score.

Fazil wasted no time undressing. Shoes, jeans, shirt, underwear, socks. All dropped to the floor until there was only his glorious flesh and very hard, erect dick. Todd crooked a finger and beckoned him forward.

Fazil stepped close, but the tension was back. "How's this going to work? With you in town and me in town and—"

Todd smoothed a thumb over his lips. "However you want it to work." He took Fazil's mouth, but it was Fazil who deepened the kiss. He wrapped his body around Todd, grinding into him. There was still cloth between them, but Todd didn't mind. There was something wicked about being fully clothed while Fazil was naked and in his arms.

"Want you so bad," Fazil spoke against his lips.

That was the whole idea of standing in Fazil's bedroom. "On your bed. On your back."

Fazil slid his hands down the front of Todd's suit jacket. "Will you do something for me?" Sultry words.

Todd swallowed, heat racing through him. "Anything."

A quirk to that smile. "Leave the suit on."

Fuck Fazil like they were in some sort of businessman

porno? Todd couldn't help the groan. "Didn't realize you had a suit kink." He walked Fazil backward until they reached the bed and pushed him down onto the bedspread.

Fazil planted his feet on the edge of the bed and spread his knees wide. "Didn't have one until today."

Good. There were a few too many people in Fazil's office who wore suits, and he wasn't about to share Fazil with anyone. "Condoms and lube?"

"Nightstand."

So they were. Fazil bit his lip when Todd took himself out of his pants, rolled the condom on, and lubed up. "How much prep do you want?"

"None," he said. "Just fuck me. *Please*."

A bold of desire shot down to his toes. Todd spread Fazil's legs wider and pressed his cock against Fazil's hole. The groan from Fazil was delicious, as was the tight, sweet heat when he entered. He inched his way into Fazil until he was balls deep and withdrew as slowly.

Desire shook in every stretch of Fazil's muscles, in the way his hands curled against the bed. "Oh fuck, that's good."

His sentiments exactly. Fucking Fazil while in his suit had Todd flying high. The power he felt—and strangely—the surrender, too. Giving himself over to Fazil's needs. No games. His balls ached for release, but he held back, because Fazil hadn't taken his fill yet.

He thrust hard and Fazil arched against him, bucking back to take more of his cock. Fazil reached up. "Here. I need you *here*."

He wouldn't argue with that. He sank down, took Fazil's mouth and gave every bit of passion he had to Fazil. Deep hard strokes that rocked them both. His beautiful love, the man he'd nearly lost.

Fazil gripped Todd's jacket as if he were drowning and Todd were the only one who could save him. "Don't stop—please, please don't stop."

He rocked into Fazil harder, sliding against his damp skin. "Like me inside you, Z?"

Fazil met him, stroke for stroke. "Always."

"Whenever you want."

Fazil dragged him down into a kiss, and his hot body pressing cloth and buttons and seams into flesh. The friction of the suit moving on Todd as he took Fazil over and over was incredible, especially Fazil's hard cock ramming into Todd's chest. He grasped Fazil's shaft and stroked him in time with their fucking.

Fazil gasped. "Not fair. Gonna—come."

"I want you to come, Z. Want to feel you. See you. Want you all over my hand so you can suck every bit off my fingers."

"Fuck." Fazil screwed his eyes closed, threw back his head, and became so incredibly tight, Todd could barely move inside him. Warmth spurted over Todd's hand, coating his fingers. That incredible sight only pushed Todd into the heavens. His vision blurred to white and he fucked Fazil with short, hard strokes, as deep as possible, emptying himself with a long moan, then stilled.

They lay there, breathing against each other, the smell of sex and cloth and Fazil filling Todd's nose. How he wished he could stay inside Fazil, soften there, slip out without moving, but there were practical reasons not to. "Give me a minute."

Fazil groaned when Todd pulled out and rose.

They were a mess. Semen stained Todd's dress shirt, his pants, and his jacket. More dotted Fazil's chest. Still more over Todd's hand.

"You look so hot like that," Fazil murmured. "Like a goddamn porno come to life."

Todd chuckled, found a box of tissues, and got rid of the condom. "Don't stuff me in your sock drawer, please."

"Are you kidding? I keep my porn on display like a civilized human being." He waved at the bedroom door. "It's in the living room. Though some of it isn't your taste."

When Todd sank down on the bed, Fazil curled onto his side. Not the het stuff, certainly. It was interesting but didn't do anything for him. "Probably not. But speaking of taste." He held out his fingers.

Fazil sucked the longest in, and his tongue along the length screwed with Todd's pulse. "You could wake the dead."

Fazil chuckled and moved to the next finger, then the next, until they'd all been well licked and sucked. Todd gripped the back of Fazil's neck and kissed him, savoring the salty taste.

"So could you." Fazil spoke against Todd's lips.

They kissed and touched until Fazil's eyes fluttered shut. "This is the best I've felt since Seattle."

"Glad I could make up for the hell I put you through."

"Me too. But I'm falling asleep." Fazil chuckled. "Not exactly the stunning welcome."

But it was. The perfect welcome. "How about a nap, then dinner?"

"Good idea."

"Let me undress, and I'll join you."

Fazil scooted up the bed and pushed down the covers. He eyed Todd. "Still look so hot."

"The dry cleaner is going to have a field day."

Fazil snorted. "Probably seen it before."

Todd stripped off his suit and underwear. Maybe.

Didn't mean he wouldn't blush to high heaven when he picked the suit up. He slid into bed next to Fazil and wrapped his arms around him. A good fuck, a little nap, then dinner. Something in the back of his brain poked him. Oh. *Oh.* "Shit."

"What?"

"I just ruined the only clothes I had with me." He had more in his suitcase. "Everything else is at Eli's."

Fazil pressed his face into the pillow and shook with laughter.

They couldn't exactly share clothes, either. He was taller and broader than Fazil. He rolled onto his back and tugged at his hair. "Fuck."

Fazil's grin was lopsided and wonderful. "I guess you'll have to make do with some tight sweats and a t-shirt." He licked his lips. "I won't mind."

"I bet you won't." Todd pulled him close. "And I won't mind your ass in the air later."

"You say the most romantic things." Fazil snuggled closer and kissed his chest.

Todd snorted. "Only you would conflate filthy with romantic."

Fazil cracked open an eye. "There's a difference?"

Not with them. Todd smiled and kissed Fazil's nose. "Get some rest."

It didn't take long for Fazil's breathing to slow and all the tension to seep from his body.

Good. Todd closed his eyes. He'd come home again.

Fazil knew Todd slept next to him the moment he slipped into consciousness. No confusion, no wonder. It was as if Todd had always been there in his bed and everything was exactly how it should be.

He studied Todd's face. He'd moved here to be with Fazil. Finally listened and understood. That was worth so much. More than Fazil could repay after all the years. He'd try, though, with every ounce of his being.

Todd stirred and opened his eyes. "Hey." A sleepy word.

"I love you." Wasn't what Fazil had meant to say.

Todd smiled. "Good. Because the feeling's mutual."

He knew that. Todd had said it often enough. "It's hard to say."

"Is it?" Todd propped himself up on one arm. "Why?"

There was the fucking lump in his throat again. "Because if I screw this up, I won't have you." They'd be apart again. "I'm no good with love."

A snort. "No one's good with love, Z. It's messy, horrifying, and wonderful. You leave pieces of yourself all over whenever you open your heart. It's a fight, a struggle, and so much work. It's also the best goddamn thing in the entire universe. Love is bigger than everyone and harder than anything. You…" He stopped, his eyes moist. "You have to hope and hold on."

"Where…" That wisdom had come from *someone*. "Who'd you learn that with?"

"Oh, some guy who likes a little dragon cock up his ass." He stroked Fazil's cheek.

Oh. He squirmed. "And you wonder why I mix dirty with romantic."

"Yeah, well." He pulled Fazil close. "I think we both need touch to remind us of what's real—at least between us."

"I've never really thought about that before." He'd

always needed *some* contact. Didn't have to be sex, but he craved intimacy. Kisses. Cuddles. When he didn't want those, he knew there were problems.

Todd kissed his forehead.

"For the record, there's *nothing* little about Mr. Dragon." That thing stretched him so wide. He shivered against Todd. "You didn't happen to bring him?"

Todd's laughter shook the bed. "Alas." Todd quirked an eyebrow. "They do have overnight shipping."

For a moment, Fazil considered it. Then laughter took him, too. "No, no. I can wait."

"So you're saying my dick's enough?" Todd's eyes were full of light.

He rolled on top of Todd and slid his cock against Todd's length. "More than enough."

Todd's breathing hitched, Fazil caught his mouth, and they wrapped each other in kisses, touches, and tastes. Todd kneaded Fazil's ass, fingers dancing over his hole, and they moaned into each other.

In the end, Fazil rode Todd's cock, his hands tied behind his back with Todd's tie, while Todd pounded into him relentlessly from below.

Todd was certainly enough. Everything Fazil had ever dreamed. Someone who needed *him*. In the afterglow, when he lay sprawled on Todd's chest, he spoke. "Still not sure how this is going to work."

Todd stroked his hair. "Z..."

"But I'm going to hold on and hope. Because I love you."

"I love you, too. Always have."

Fazil listened to the beating of Todd's heart, the air moving in and out of his lungs, and closed his eyes.

His heart was here and that was enough.

CHAPTER THIRTY

Eight months later

Fazil raised the door on the rental van. This was the last load from Todd's storage unit. After this, they'd have everything in their new house. He peered at the place they'd bought together while Todd pulled out the ramp.

Living in his apartment had been reasonable, but it had been full of his things. Todd had never complained, but it felt unfair that Todd didn't have his own space. Todd had moved into it—but it wasn't his, wasn't theirs.

This? This belonged to both of them. Their house, their life together.

One last load to move in, if anyone came out of the house to help them. "Where *is* everyone?"

"How much do you want to bet Eli's holding court?" Todd thudded up the ramp, grabbed a box, and passed it to Fazil.

"Not taking that bet."

Good choice, too. Through the screen door he spied Eli

perched in a chair outside the living room, all legs and arms and devious smile. "...then Michael had this brilliant idea to buy a gross of bouncing balls and dump them down the stairwell..."

"You wanted to freeze them in liquid nitrogen!" Michael said.

Oh God. More college shenanigans. Those two. Fazil stood on the porch and coughed. "If someone's not busy?"

Justin, who'd been sitting at Eli's feet, sprang up and opened the screen door. "Didn't hear you guys over the sound of Eli's past."

"Five," Eli muttered and Justin laughed.

The rest of their moving crew—all of the office, a good number of his friends from pinball and gaming, and a few folks from Todd's new job—were climbing to their feet in the living room.

"Last truckload," Todd said. "Then pizza and beer."

Everyone, except Eli, marched out to the truck to begin the fun and games of carting boxes again. Eli settled into his chair with the list that matched box contents with rooms.

After a third trip up the stairs, Fazil grabbed a box marked PLATES. Ground floor for a change. He trudged inside and nodded to Eli.

"You know where you're going?" Amusement in Eli's voice.

Fazil rolled his eyes and headed to the kitchen.

He was glad they'd figured out a way to include Eli in the process. He'd never been content to sit and watch. Giving him dominion over the whole process? That had worked like a charm and had saved Fazil a few headaches. Eli salivated over organization.

Fazil set the box down on the kitchen counter and

wiped his brow. Steps sounding from the hall had him turning. Kris carried a twin box to his, this one marked GLASSES. She gave him a smile. "Hey."

They hadn't talked much at all since their breakup. Small chats at pinball, but nothing personal. He'd been surprised when she'd come to lend a hand. "Hey. Thanks for helping out."

"Thanks for inviting me." She set the box down and leaned against the counter. "This is a great place."

"We kind of owe Eli for finding it. An older couple from his synagogue were downsizing and terrified that college students or a rental company would snatch it up."

"Be a shame to turn this into apartments." She looked around before settling her gaze on him. "It's good to see you happy, Fazil."

That caught him off guard. But he *was* happy. Astoundingly so. "Thanks." Even to his own ears, his voice sounded rough.

"I mean it," she said. "In all the years I've known you, I've never seen you like this." She pushed off the counter. "You *look* different, to be honest."

Did he? He'd have to ask Todd. Or Sam. He coughed a laugh. "Apparently love does that to people." He held up his hand and wiggled his empty left ring finger.

Kris blushed in the way that had first attracted him to her, and held up her hand. Hers sported a very nice sapphire engagement ring from Lance. "Yeah. I guess it does."

They'd be married in the summer. Yet another wedding Fazil and Todd would attend.

"So when are you and Todd tying the knot?"

Heat touched Fazil's cheeks. So many people had asked

that question recently, including his and Todd's parents. "Soon-ish. The calendar seems to be chock-full of other weddings at the moment."

"So you guys are engaged?"

"Something like that." Boy, he hated lying. He was so shitty at it. "We'll have a big old wedding one of these days, don't you worry."

"Three words, Fazil: geek cookie table."

That did sound good. "Don't tell Eli. He'll scheme a way to make twenty-sided dice from marzipan."

"Or bouncy balls." She glanced toward the hall. "I didn't peg him as a gamer."

"He nearly stole Todd's D&D books."

"Did not," Eli said. "I was going to hold them in safekeeping until you moved."

He mouthed the word *steal* to Kris and she laughed. So good to see her smile, to see her happy. "We should get back to it." He gestured out into the hall and they both headed to the truck.

It took another hour or so to unload and put all the boxes where they belonged. Most were marked, and Eli directed people to the proper rooms. But some weren't. Adam came in carrying a smaller box. "No idea where this goes."

Eli took it from him and sliced the tape open. "Let's see."

Todd pounded up the steps from the truck, horror and embarrassment carved into his face.

Uh-oh. "Eli—"

He'd already peered inside. One eyebrow went up. "Well, now." He closed the box. "Best give it to Fazil." His grin was entirely too knowing.

Adam had a crinkled forehead. "I'll get another one, then."

"There're some marked ones." Todd slipped inside the house, breathless and red.

Fazil peeked inside the box, though he was almost certain what he'd find. Still, the sight of the toys heated his blood and set goose bumps on his arms. Especially when he spied a large green dildo that looked like it might have suckers. He met Todd's gaze. "You didn't tell me Mr. Dragon had a brother."

Eli burst out laughing, loud enough that he slapped a hand over his mouth and doubled over. His cane slipped and clattered to the floor.

Justin padded down the stairs from the second floor. "Did you break my husband?"

"Sorry," Fazil said. "But yes."

"Well, good," Justin said. "Someone ought to."

"Six, Mr. White," Eli said, between gasps.

"Um." Todd took a deep breath. "Why don't we take that box upstairs, Z?"

Oh yes. Why didn't they? Despite the protest of his legs, he climbed up to the second floor and strode into the bedroom.

Todd followed and shut the door. "Do I want to know what the deal is with their counting?"

"Don't ask me," Fazil said. Though he could guess, and holy hell, he didn't need that image. He set the box down on the bed. "I know too damn much about my coworkers."

Todd embraced Fazil from behind, circling his arm around him and kissing his neck. "They're a fun crew."

"Glad it was Eli who looked in the box and not Adam." He leaned against Todd. "I thought Mr. Dragon was a gag gift?"

"He was."

"And Mr. Alien Tentacle?"

Todd kissed his neck again. "Bought him myself."

"Todd Douglas, do you enjoy fucking men with toys?"

His chuckle vibrated Fazil to his toes. Todd slid his hands down and cupped Fazil's growing erection. "Very much so. Especially fucking my husband with toys."

Good. That box? Loaded with toys. "Good thing you have a husband."

"Very good." Todd breathed the words against Fazil's skin as he massaged Fazil's cock.

"Feels so good. But we can't—" He groaned when Todd bit him on the shoulder.

After a few more seconds Todd relented. "I know. Pizza. Beer. Socialization."

"Fucking later."

"You better believe it." Todd kissed his neck once more and let go.

Fazil turned and sat against the footboard of their bed. "Kris asked me when the two of us were getting married."

"Oh." Todd scratched his head. "I guess we should plan a wedding one of these days."

They'd talked about marriage on and off, but when buying the house came up, they'd discovered how much easier it was for a married couple to deal with the loan and the deed and everything.

"Or we could just tell everyone." And he could finally wear the ring Todd had given him. A simple gold band, yes, but *his*. From Todd.

"How much of an earful would you get from your folks?"

Fazil winced. "A lot." There'd be no end to the flack when he told them he and Todd had run to the courthouse to get married by a justice of the peace in a quick, no-frills deal. "But I'm tired of lying about it."

Todd got his distant-and-thinking look. "What do you want to do?"

Less than a year ago, Todd wouldn't have even asked the question—he'd have told Fazil the plan. "Let's come clean." He gestured in the direction of the living room. "At least to our friends. We can talk to our parents tomorrow—and find a date for a renewal of vows for later this year."

"Sounds good." Todd wrapped Fazil in his arms again.

He laid his head on Todd's shoulder. Hard to believe they'd come this far. He felt like a different person. Maybe that's what Kris had seen. "Thank you," he murmured.

"For what?"

"For holding up a mirror." Todd had shown him the reality of their past—but also given him the strength not to fall into the same trap as before.

Todd stroked his hair. "And what did you see?"

"Myself." His true self—the person he really was. "I'm not perfect. But I'm not the asshole I thought I was."

Todd kissed his hair. "You *are* an ass, Z. But you're the most beautiful and perfect man I've ever known."

He couldn't help the snort. "You have a very low bar for *perfect*."

"I have an extraordinarily high bar for perfect." Todd tipped Fazil's chin up and kissed him, and Fazil wanted to dig into that box of toys on the bed.

Too soon, though, Todd broke the kiss. "We should get back downstairs."

Back to their friends and their life and their house of boxes. "I love you," Fazil said. "I didn't think I could love you enough."

Todd pulled him toward the door. "Just love me, Fazil. That's all I need."

"That, I can do." He grinned at Todd, and they headed down into the life they'd made together.

THANKS FOR READING!

Dear Reader,

Thank you for reading *Due Diligence*! I hope you enjoyed Fazil and Todd's story. I really wanted to explore how our high school years aren't always what we think they were, especially since those years are so turbulent, and also how easy it is to fall back into old habits. Both Fazil and Todd were blockheads about some things, but they finally saw the light.

Up next in the series is *Daily Grind*, where Brian, the stressed-out owner of the Grounds N'at coffee shop can't resist the charm of a customer with ginger hair and a British accent. The timing couldn't be worse, though, and he's never actually dated a guy before...

If you're enjoying the kink element of the Takeover series, you may also enjoy my *Twisted Wishes* series, or the standalone novel *Cinnamon Roll*, though most of my backlist contains consensual kink of some kind.

To find out more about my books and new releases, you can follow me on BookBub, join my facebook group or sign up for my newsletter.

Thank you so much!
  -Anna

ACKNOWLEDGMENTS

I owe many thanks to LA Witt for showing me around the Seattle area and letting me borrow bits of her city for the setting of this book. Any mistakes in my descriptions of the area or tourist sights are all on me, not her!

The M&M hot chocolate exists, though. I didn't make that up. It's a thing of beauty, too.

While I took three semesters of Turkish, I am very far from expert with that beautiful and challenging language. Any mistakes in the Turkish phrases are also mine and not the fault of my ever-patient instructor.

And once again, many thanks to Jen Udden, and to my editor, Kristine Swartz for her continued support.

ABOUT THE AUTHOR

Anna Zabo writes contemporary and paranormal romance for all colors of the rainbow. They live and work in Pittsburgh, Pennsylvania, which isn't nearly as boring as most people think.

They can be easily plied with coffee or a chance to see the Pittsburgh Penguins.

Anna has an MFA in Writing Popular Fiction from Seton Hill University, where they fell in with a roving band of romance writers and never looked back. They also have a BA in Creative Writing from Carnegie Mellon University.

Anna uses they/them pronouns and prefers Mx. Zabo as an honorific. They can be found online at annazabo.com.

 twitter.com/amergina

 instagram.com/amergina

 bookbub.com/authors/anna-zabo

 amazon.com/Anna-Zabo/e/B00A7LA6OC

www.ingramcontent.com/pod-product-compliance
Lightning Source LLC
Chambersburg PA
CBHW051942240626
47153CB00005B/1597